SCORCHED BY THE DRAGON'S BREATH

As bullets slammed into Cassie's ribs, red light lances seemed to flash from her chest to her brain, and she sat down hard. By sheer reflex, she raised her autopistol and emptied it at the legs of the man who had shot her. A bullet smashed his knee without penetrating it, throwing him on his face. By force of will, she hauled herself up and lunged at him, killing her opponent.

But Cassie was staggering, losing consciousness. The gun burst had cracked her ribs, and every breath felt as if spikes were being driven into her chest. She tried to grasp the tactical situation, taking in muzzle flashes and BattleMechs beginning to move. She felt the immediate presence of danger, but couldn't locate it.

And then the very edge of her peripheral vision caught a dark shape flying at her. Cassie spun, but not fast enough, and someone knocked her sprawling. . . .

BATTLETECH®

BLACK DRAGON

Victor Milán

A ROC BOOK

ROC
Published by the Penguin Group
Penguin Books USA Inc., 375 Hudson Street,
New York, New York 10014, U.S.A.
Penguin Books Ltd, 27 Wrights Lane,
London W8 5TZ, England
Penguin Books Australia Ltd, Ringwood,
Victoria, Australia
Penguin Books Canada Ltd, 10 Alcorn Avenue,
Toronto, Ontario, Canada M4V 3B2
Penguin Books (N.Z.) Ltd, 182–190 Wairau Road,
Auckland 10, New Zealand

Penguin Books Ltd, Registered Offices:
Harmondsworth, Middlesex, England

First published by Roc, an imprint of Dutton Signet,
a division of Penguin Books USA Inc.

First Printing, November, 1996
10 9 8 7 6 5 4 3 2 1

Series Editor: Donna Ippolito
Cover art by Peter Bollinger
Mechanical Drawings: Duane Loose and the FASA art department

 REGISTERED TRADEMARK — MARCA REGISTRADA

BATTLETECH, FASA, and the distinctive BATTLETECH and FASA logos are
trademarks of the FASA Corporation, 1100 W. Cermak, Suite B305, Chicago, IL
60608.

Printed in the United States of America

To Joseph Reichert II

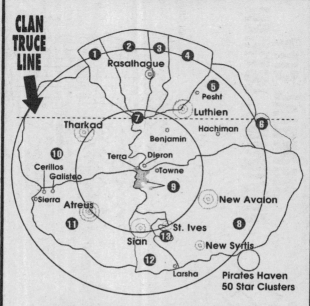

CLAN TRUCE LINE

1. Rasalhague
2.
3.
4.
5. Pesht
   Luthien
   Hachiman
6.
7. Tharkad
   Benjamin
10. Terra • Dieron
   Cerillos
   Galisteo • Towne
   Sierra
9.
   Atreus
   New Avalon
11.
   St. Ives
8.
   Sian
13.
   New Syrtis
12.
   Larsha
   Pirates Haven
   50 Star Clusters

MAP OF THE INNER SPHERE

1 • Jade Falcon/Steel Viper, 2 • Wolf Clan, 3 • Ghost Bear,
4 • Smoke Jaguars/Nova Cats, 5 • Draconis Combine,
6 • Outworlds Alliance, 7 • Free Rasalhague Republic,
8 • Federated Commonwealth, 9 • Chaos March,
10 • Lyran Alliance, 11 • Free Worlds League,
12 • Capellan Confederation, 13 • St. Ives Compact

Map Compiled by COMSTAR
From information provided by the COMSTAR EXPLORER SERVICE
and the STAR LEAGUE ARCHIVES on Terra

© 3058 COMSTAR CARTOGRAPHIC CORPS.

IMPERIAL CITY ENVIRONS, LUTHIEN

MAP KEY

 Water

 Mountains

   City

Kiyomori Mountains

Tairakana Plains

Waseda Hills

Basin Lake

Kado-Guchi River

Imperial City

Unity Palace

Takashi Kurita Memorial Spaceport

Cinema City (Eligatoshi)

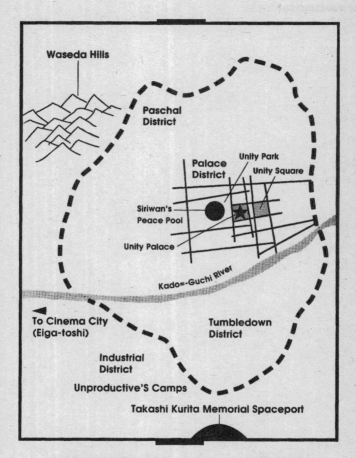

IMPERIAL CITY

Heaven and Earth are not humane.
They regard all things as straw dogs.

—Sun Tzu

This World of Shadows

Those who err on the side of strictness are few indeed!

—Confucius, Analects, 4:23

Prologue

Moons Viewing Pavilion, outside Deber City
Benjamin
Benjamin Military District, Draconis Combine
10 June 3058

"**W**e must have revenge!"

The speaker, whose fervently hissed words chased one another like rats up the square-sectioned wooden uprights and on among the exposed rafters of the great Moons Viewing Pavilion outside Deber City, was no young man. But a greater weight than years alone stooped his thin shoulders and bent his back.

His spare frame was draped in a heavy robe like an acolyte of the Order of the Five Pillars. His cowl was thrown defiantly back, revealing a long haggard face with graying hair drawn into a topknot. This was Hiraoke Toyama, powerful oyabun of the Dieron District, but none here would dare call him by name.

With burning eyes he let his gaze travel over the score of men kneeling around the long, low table. Like him they were robed, but their hoods were in place and so hid their faces.

The cowls were pure formality. These men controlled substantial resources, not least in the gathering of intelligence. Each knew who the others were. They were leaders of the Draconis Combine's still tightly regulated business community, of the Draconis Combine Mustered Soldiery, and of the yakuza crime organizations which constituted—in the yakuzas' minds at least—the Combine's shadow government. Together they formed the ruling council of

Kokuryu-kai, the ancient Black Dragon Society. The organization was an ancient one that had resurfaced in recent years to combat the social and military reforms its members regarded as a grave threat to the fabric of Combine society. The current regime outlawed the Black Dragons, and the black-clad agents of the Internal Security Force were ruthless in sniffing out and extirpating its members. Hence the masks, to serve as constant reminder that discovery was death.

Behind each man, still and silent as statues along the shadowed walls, stood a single bodyguard. By ancient usage, firearms were prohibited within the precincts of the Pavilion. Each guard was an adept at both the armed or unarmed variety of hand-fighting: karate, jujutsu, taekwon-do, ryukyu kobujutsu, savate, shorinji kempo, escrima, and ryubujutsu, the Dragon's Warrior-Techniques that were the official hand-to-hand combat form of the Draconis Combine Mustered Soldiery. Each had taken at least one life in face-to-face combat, and each was implicitly trusted to be ready at an instant's notice to lay down his own life for his lord.

Outside the stressed-cement walls, the twenty moons of the planet Benjamin marched across the sky, huge and red as bloodshot eyes. These were not actual moons, but vast reflectors placed in orbit to augment the feeble shine of the planet's type-M sun. They strewed multiple oblongs of light like fanned cards across the floor and occupants of the cathedral space, and the shadows they cast were tinted green.

Toyama stared at each of his compatriots in turn, as if to see past their cowls into the depths of their souls. Then he turned to face the head of the chamber, and gestured with a small black controller in his hand.

In a large holotank filled with color and movement, a magnificently muscled man with blond hair hanging unbound around great shoulders, clad only in the cooling shorts of a Kurita MechWarrior, knelt before the bulk of a fallen BattleMech. He stared contemplatively down at the naked *wakizashi* in his hand. Behind him stood a slender young woman holding a drawn *katana,* her hair seared short and smoking like the black garments she wore, and her face burned red by intolerable heat.

The watchers gasped in sympathetic reaction as the kneeling man plunged the steel into his washboard belly.

"The full three cuts," murmured a man the others affected not to know was a ranking officer within the Draconis Combine Mustered Soldiery. Despite Coordinator Theodore Kurita's popularity among the Combine's soldiers—he had been a distinguished MechWarrior and Gunji no Kanrei before ascending to the Dragon Throne—many in the military still objected to his liberalization of Combine society.

The young woman struck.

"*Tai-sho* Kusunoki knew how to die like a man," the DCMS officer said. The blond man's head sprang from his shoulders as blood spouted from the stump of his neck. Toyama froze the holovid display. General Jeffrey Kusunoki, a high-ranking military man and war hero of the realm, had recently led several regiments of Black Dragon and renegade Combine troops in an attempt the seize the Davion planet of Towne. The world had become ripe for the taking when the planetary governor fled for his life as the whole region of space went up for grabs during the recent Marik-Liao invasion. The Black Dragons had decided the chance to strengthen the Combine at the expense of the Davions, their ancient rivals, was too good to pass up.

But Theodore Kurita had refused to assist Kusunoki for fear of offending Prince Victor Davion, with whom he had lately allied in the war against the Clan invaders. The result was humiliating defeat for the Black Dragons and the death of one of the Combine's greatest heroes.

"Untold lives were lost in the fighting on Towne—including that of *Tai-sho* Jeffrey Kusunoki, whose death we have just witnessed in a shameful broadcast to the whole planet. Four regiments of DCMS troops were disarmed and sent back to the Combine in disgrace; two regiments of our own Black Dragon kobun were virtually wiped out. I myself lost my son, Taisuke, and my most trusted advisor, Edwin Kimura, who committed honorable seppuku after transmitting a hyperpulse message describing the catastrophic end to our heroic undertaking."

The withered old man held up his left hand. The little finger was absent. "I myself have performed *yubitsume,* offering my finger to this Council to atone for my own role in this shameful failure, and if the Black Dragon so demands, I shall give over my life as well. But blood cries out for blood. I beseech you, my brothers, permit me to live long enough to see the shedding of so many Dragon's Tears avenged!"

"Your, ah, your fervor is noted, Brother," said another man, turning his cowl nervously this way and that as if to try to gauge his comrades' reactions from their postures, "but avenged against *whom,* precisely?"

He was an important industrialist whose business was the manufacture of vital BattleMech components. Like many Combine corporate magnates, he believed Theodore Kurita's reforms were sapping the morale and productivity of Combine workers—not to mention the near-feudal prerogatives of privileged people like him.

"Against the traitor Chandrasekhar, who dishonors his noble surname, which I will not speak in the same breath as his given name," rasped another hooded figure. Like Toyama, he was a noted oyabun. "Not to mention his *gaijin* hirelings—like this one whose filthy claws besmirch the *Tai-sho's* sword." Chandrasekhar Kurita was the rich and powerful businessman who had hired the mercenary scum to defend his interests on Towne. It was those same mercenaries who had managed to defeat the Black Dragons.

" 'Besmirch' may be too strong," the DCMS officer spoke up. "She wields a blade like a warrior. She severed the neck at a stroke, which not many can do, even with a blade as fine as poor Jeffrey's. Her style's not much to speak of, but her *makoto* is impeccable." *Makoto* meant, roughly, *sincerity,* and was the artistic attribute prized above all. It signified a work, such as a painting or bit of calligraphy, that was executed directly from the heart, without self or thought interfering.

"Still, she must pay—she and her money-grubbing comrades, and their fat paymaster!" Toyama cried, his voice ringing like a temple gong.

"And why," a voice asked from the entryway, "do you not name the party ultimately responsible?"

Hooded heads snapped around. A figure stood in the open doorway, a shadow edged green in the light of the false red moons. It wore a floor-length black *hakama* and a padded gray jacket with great flared shoulders, making its exact height and build impossible to distinguish. Its head and face were concealed in a black cloth mask such as those associated in the popular consciousness with the ancient ninja. Its voice was a highly sexless baritone, obviously run through some sort of speech synthesizer.

"Who are you?" demanded the seated oyabun. "How dare you interrupt *Kokuryu-kai*?"

"As to who I am," the figure said, "you may think of me as *Kaga*, the Shadow. As to how I dare—"

It gestured with black-gloved hands. Two figures slipped inside to stand flanking the Shadowed One. They were clothed in form-fitting black, and from behind the left shoulder of each protruded the hilt of a *ninjato*, the straight-bladed ninja sword with the square *tsuba*, or hand-guard. Each wore a helmet of some black synthetic, and their faces were obscured by red visors. The uniform was unmistakably that of the dreaded commandos of DEST, the Draconis Elite Strike Teams.

"ISF!" somebody shouted. "We're betrayed!"

Laughing, the Shadow held up its hand. "Do not be disturbed. Had I wished you dead, none of you would still be breathing. Not all within the Internal Security Force are under the sway of its leader, the archtraitor Subhash Indrahar."

The council members settled back to the floor, exchanging hooded looks. The intruder had just given definite corroboration of his—or her—sincerity. For an internal security agent to refer to the Smiling One, head of the ISF and possibly the most feared man in the Inner Sphere, in such a way would mean death if Indrahar ever learned about it.

"What do you want?" Toyama asked.

"The same thing you want. To return the steel to the

Combine's spine and to remove the traitors who weaken the Dragon. You know who they are as well as I—the Smiling One, his red-headed whelp Ninyu Kerai, and the real author of your miseries—the Coordinator himself, Theodore Kurita."

The men gathered around the table gasped, and not just the council members. The nervous manufacturerer of BattleMech components shot to his feet.

"I won't hear such treason!" he shouted.

The Shadowed One turned its hidden face to him and nodded. "*So ka,* Durkovich-*san*?"

The hooded Black Dragon sagged at use of his real name.

"Yes, I know you," the Shadowed One said. "I know much about you. Perhaps more than you know yourself. For example, Park, your bodyguard there."

The intruder nodded again at the square-bodied and square-jawed man who stood behind Durkovich. "He is a member of Tosei-*kai,* the Voice of the East Syndicate." The Voice of the East was the confederation of Korean gangs operating in the Draconis Combine. They kept neutral in the gang wars, but on a day-to-day basis they often served the yazuka as mercenaries.

Durkovich's hooded head turned briefly back toward his guard, then toward the Shadowed One. "What of it? Lots of industrialists and oyabun use the Koreans for security. They're known for loyalty and impartiality."

"Impartiality in the petty struggles among gang leaders, yes," the Shadowed One said. "But the Korean dogs believe they owe their greatest loyalty to the Coordinator, who has given them much of what he stripped away from the Dragon's true servants. Your man there is a pipeline to ISF. You are lucky indeed to have a friend in position to divert the flow from the eyes of Indrahar and Ninyu Kerai."

Park glared, dropped into fighting stance, blocky fists raised. The Kaga laughed again and whipped out his right hand. A seven-pointed *shuriken* leapt from his fingers and spun toward the Tosei-*kai* bodyguard. The Korean leapt back with a litheness belying his bulk, leaving the throwing-star to rebound from the wall with a musical clang.

But the bodyguard's leap took him in front of a window,

and at once his chest exploded in a geyser of blood, wine-dark in the light of Benjamin's moons.

"I have honored the prohibition against bringing weapons into the Pavilion," the Shadowed One said as Park collapsed to the ferrocrete floor. The delayed report of a Zeus Long Rifle shot rolled like thunder through the window. "But my sniper, located a kilometer from the grounds, is under no such judicature."

Durkovich jumped away from the sprawled corpse of his guard. His hood fell away, revealing a jowly, panic-stricken face.

Once again the Shadowed One turned to him. "You are careless, Durkovich-*san,*" it said in its neutered voice. "That makes you an unacceptable liability."

A black-clothed figure dropped to the floor behind Durkovich. Before the magnate could move, it had encircled his throat with the curved blade of a *kyotetsu-shogi,* the traditional ninja weapon resembling a knife crossed with a sickle and attached to a rope.

The figure in black stepped back. Two more descended from above, holding the ring on the end of the rope attached to the *kyotetsu-shogi,* which had been looped over a rafter. Their combined body weights jerked Durkovich's body into the air. His blood showered his comrades as the blade bit into his thick throat.

The Shadowed One gazed up until the blood-spray and kicking had subsided. The figure nodded to its operatives who released the rope. The corpse fell across the table with a sodden thump. The operatives retrieved the weapon and stepped back against the wall.

"Now that we have winnowed weakness from our midst," the Shadowed One said, "permit me to tell you a tale—rather, a truth. The story was put about that the old Coordinator, Takashi Kurita, Theodore's father, died in his sleep of heart failure. This was a lie.

"There is a conspiracy, coiled like a serpent around the Dragon's heart. Its members presume to call themselves the Sons of the Dragon. In truth, they are no more than servants to the will of the demonic spymaster Subhash Indrahar.

"Among their sworn number is Theodore Kurita, Coordinator of the Draconis Combine."

The Black Dragons stirred uneasily, their cloaks rustling like autumn leaves. "I have heard rumors to this effect," the DCMS officer said in half-grudging tones.

"Those rumors are true. Look at what has befallen the Combine during the rise of Theodore Kurita, and you will see the hand of the conspirator on every side. A conspiracy to gnaw the Dragon's heart out from within!

"Takashi Kurita was a *bushi*. More than a mere warrior, he was also a samurai who devoted his whole being to selfless service of the Dragon, and the Dragon is greater than any individual—greater, indeed, than the Coordinator. Takashi-*sama* stood for the traditional virtues of the Dragon. He grew sickened by the way his son was drawing the spine out of the Draconis Combine with his so-called reforms. He intended to put a stop to them once and for all. But before he could act, the Smiling One, Subhash Indrahar, and his devil-pup Ninyu murdered him—with the connivance of Theodore Kurita."

Deadly silence filled the Moons Viewing Pavilion. "How can we know you're telling the truth?" the hooded DCMS officer asked in a subdued voice.

"You answer your own question," the Shadowed One said. "If you truly doubted my words, you would leap to slay me, despite knowing that my operatives wait all around and in the rafters above your heads. For you are true sons of the Dragon, who would not hesitate to sacrifice your lives to bring down one who dared falsely accuse the Coordinator.

"But you do nothing. And that is because in your *hara*, in the center of you, you know the truth of what I say. You've known it for a long time, though you would not face it."

Hiraoke Toyama dropped to his knees. "He's right," the oyabun of Dieron said. "For too long we've hidden behind the myth that Th—that the Coordinator was being misled by evil advisors. We can hide no longer. The evil lies at the very core."

Toyama looked at the Shadowed One, tear tracks gleaming down his grief-ravaged cheeks. "What can we *do*?"

"Theodore and his reforms are a cancer, eating away at

the Combine from within," the figure said. "You must act quickly and decisively to expunge that cancer before it is too late. Opportunity awaits us in the forthcoming Celebration of the Coordinator's Birth.

"And I will help."

PART 1

Origami

The world is a vast temple dedicated to Discord.

—Voltaire

1

DropShip **Uyeshiba,** *Approach Vector*
Luthien System
Pesht Military District, Draconis Combine
18 June 3058

With a stuttering crash like God's own jackhammer the short-range missile volley slammed into the T-IT-N1M *Grand Titan*.

The mammoth 'Mech had left a trail of shattered and blazing enemy machines behind it. Yet already it was nearing the end of its savage run. Its awesome Durallex Heavy armor had been penetrated in a dozen places, burned through by energy weapons or peeled back from explosive hits. Its left arm was gone, its shoulder actuator a gaping wound bleeding smoke and sparks. The *Titan*'s expendables were long since expended, but somehow it had kept driving single-mindedly toward its destination, as if held upright solely by its pilot's determination.

The SRM salvo was just too much. Three missiles struck its right hip and blew off its leg. Like a felled forest giant, the *Titan* toppled forward in slow-motion.

But its pilot was not to be turned aside. With a final thrust by the 'Mech's remaining leg he hurled the machine forward. Its massive armored head smashed through the yellow stone façade of the sinister Dragon's Claw Palace.

Inside the palace, guards in ninja black, faces hidden behind the unmistakable red visors of the Draconis Combine Elite Strike Teams, scattered away from the avalanche of masonry and metal. Before they could recover, a hatch popped open beside the anti-missile system mounted in the

BattleMech's head. A curled-up figure shot out like a cannonball, bowling over a pair of guards.

The figure uncoiled to its feet. It was a young man dressed in a short, sleeveless black bodysuit, with black slippers on his feet. Dark hair hung in a face that was a striking mixture of Chinese and Western. Black-almond eyes flashed.

A DEST guard struck at the young man overhand with a *ninjato*. The young man danced back; the blade hissed down, missing him by millimeters. The commando advanced, slashing diagonally downward, left to right, right to left. The young man retreated, ducked to the side, then seized the swordsman's right wrist as the second cut missed. He snapped a backfist into the visored face and as the DEST man's head whipped back, the young man yanked hard on the trapped wrist, locking out the elbow, which he broke with a left forearm smash. Then he plucked the sword from the man's hand and hacked him down with it.

Not a moment too soon. A half-dozen guards were closing on him from all directions, swords naked in gloved hands. He passed among them like a steel-edged whirlwind, striking them down without slowing.

From an upper gallery, a flashing of laser fire. The young man hurled himself into a forward roll to avoid the cracking beams that pitted the marble floor at his slippered feet. He somersaulted through a high-arched doorway.

A door slammed behind him with titanic finality. He turned, took in the fact that he was trapped, spun back, *ninjato* held ready.

He was in a domed chamber rising four stories overhead, pillars and galleries of yellow stone. Across the room, on a dais before a mirrored wall, sat an old man in a wheelchair. His shrunken body was swaddled in blankets. His head, shaven to a snow-white topknot, slumped listlessly to one side. He stirred, raised his head to peer at the intruder through round-lensed spectacles.

"And so you have come," he said in a quavering voice. "I knew my guards would not be able to stop you. You have what you want now: No one will interrupt us. It is just you and a crippled old man."

"So you are the Dragon's Claw." The young man looked from the invalid to the sword in his hand. He cast the weapon away.

"I don't need this," he said. "I don't like the idea of doing harm to an invalid, but justice must be served. Your time has come, spymaster."

Withered lips smiled. "Your scruples do you honor, David Lung. But you need shed no tears on my account. While it is true that age and sickness have robbed my limbs of their power—"

He threw back the blankets. Body, arms, and legs were encased in a powered exoskeleton of gleaming alloy. He flung forth his arms and rose three meters in the air on roaring jets.

"—the Dragon's technology has given me back all that I've lost, and more." He too wore a black bodysuit, but with a yellow claw glowing on the breast.

"Technology you have no right to!" David Lung returned defiantly. "You're a traitor to your own people as well as an enemy of mine!"

The spymaster's laughter rang. "My people are fools. They have grown weak, and their backbones have atrophied." He settled on to the marble floor to stand facing his opponent with legs braced wide. "The Dragon will return to the path of conquest. I shall lay all the Inner Sphere as a tribute at His clawed feet. The weakling Coordinator will fall, and after him the Federated Commonwealth. Prepare to die, interloper!"

David dropped into a wary fighting stance. The Dragon's Claw stood, apparently relaxed, metal-reinforced arms hanging flexed by his sides. He seemingly invited attack, yet was prepared to defend himself—if his powered exoskeleton lent him sufficient quickness.

Cautiously the young man advanced counterclockwise, bringing him to the Dragon Claw's left side. The aged spymaster did not move, only stood watching him with a bemused half-smile on his still-bespectacled face. When the young avenger was at the very verge of his peripheral vision, about to move behind him, he moved with blurring speed, sidestepping and driving a side kick into David's ribcage right below his guard.

David flew back and struck a carven wooden pillar. As he fought to pull air back into his lungs, the Dragon's Claw advanced with measured steps, unhurried, smiling benignly.

The young man lashed out with his black-slippered right foot. The spymaster pivoted slightly and shifted stance to bring one of the flat curved braces that upheld his ribcage into the front kick's way. David struck immediately with his right fist, jabbing his opponent twice in the face, snapping his head back so that his scalplock whipped like a pennon in the breeze.

The older man stepped back, touched his nose, scowled as he saw blood scarlet on his fingers. David danced toward him, feinted another jab for the face, then wheeled to launch a spinning back kick for the solar plexus.

The Dragon's Claw stepped back with his right foot, pivoting his body out of range of the kick. His left hand flashed down and seized the younger man's ankle. With a caw of triumph he flung David Lung across the chamber to slam into a wall.

David picked himself up to a crouch, shaking his head as if to clear it. The spymaster launched himself in a jet-assisted jump, then came down with steel-shod feet aimed for the young man's skull.

But David was not as badly stunned as he seemed. He rolled away at the last instant. The metal soles of his enemy's powered skeleton struck sparks from the flagstone.

David started to come to his feet, then hurled himself forward as the spymaster turned, sweeping the metal man's legs out from under him with the backs of his young calves. The Dragon's Claw fell with a mighty clang. David sprang to his feet, kicked the Dragon's Claw in the face as the spymaster fought to rise.

With a roar the Dragon's Claw's leg-jets ignited, sending him skittering across the floor in a shower of sparks. David stared, then came somersaulting toward him.

Using jets mounted in the shoulders of his exoskeleton, the Dragon's Claw thrust himself upright as David landed confronting him. He had lost his spectacles. David slammed

a storm of punches, left and right chained in blinding succession, into the spymaster's face.

The spymaster roared, stepped back. David struck for his
face again. The Dragon's Claw caught the fist in his left
hand, twisted. David groaned as his elbow joint locked out.
The spymaster kept applying torque, so that it seemed
David must drop to the floor or suffer damage to his right elbow or shoulder. Instead he brought his left foot up and
around in a sweeping crescent kick that knocked the spymaster's hand away.

He followed with a spinning straight-legged kick that
slammed the sword of his right foot against the side of the
spymaster's jaw. The Dragon's Claw's head snapped
around, but his exoskeleton's gyros kept him from falling.
He roared in anger and pain and brought his right forearm
slamming down toward the top of David's head.

The younger man managed to jerk his head aside and take
the blow on the shoulder. Its force drove him to his knees,
blinking at the pain. The Dragon's Claw aimed a straight
punch at his face, but David weaved his head to the side,
evading it.

With a sinister snick, three long steel claws snapped from
the armor at the back of the spymaster's fist. He swiped
bearlike at the younger man's head. David rolled to the side,
but when he came up to his feet three bloody grooves had
been gashed in his handsome face.

The Dragon's Claw advanced on him, slashing with his
artificial claw. David tried backing away, but the older man,
aided by his powered exoskeleton, moved with unnatural
quickness, laying open the skin of David's belly.

Desperately David closed into the next stroke, seized
the spymaster by the arm and threw him over his shoulder. Away the older man went skidding across the floor
again. As David sprang for him, his jets once again righted
him. He gathered his augmented legs beneath him and
jumped straight up.

David took a deep breath, summoned his *ch'i,* and
jumped with the old man—straight up, far higher than a normal man could leap, all the while trading blows and blocks
with the Dragon's Claw. They landed. David leapt once

again, straight up, knocked the spymaster's shaven head with a looping outward kick, then a flying crescent kick.

The Dragon's Claw bellowed, charged at David, lashing out furiously. David gave ground, trying to guide the other man's attacks past him with slap-blocks, not daring to block him directly for fear the exoskeleton would snap the bones of his forearm. His back fetched up against an ornamental wooden pillar. The spymaster cried out triumphantly and thrust his claw straight for the young man's throat.

David dodged sideways. The claw struck deep into the carved and painted wood and stuck fast.

Crying out in anger, the Dragon's Claw tugged on his trapped arm. All the power of his metal skeleton was not enough to free it. David slipped behind him and began jack-hammering punches into the Claw's kidneys, between the curving armor plates.

The Dragon's Claw smashed his left arm across his body, snapping off the deeply-bedded spike. Then he spun, catching David in the face with a savage backhand that sent the young man flying through the air.

David struck on his tailbone, skidded, reeled to his feet. The spymaster was on him, burying the steel-capped point of his toe in the younger man's belly. David doubled. The spymaster punched him in the face, straightening him up for a side kick to the gut that bent him over again, then performed a spinning back kick that caught him in the side of the face and launched him away once more, tendrils of blood trailing from his mouth.

"Your kung-fu is good," the Dragon's Claw said, stalking towards the bloodied young man for the kill, "but you have no chance against me. The Dragon shall reign triumphant! The Inner Sphere shall be mine."

David Lung lay propped on his elbow. He shook blood droplets from his eyes, spat out blood. He felt as if a thousand workmen had been pounding him with sledgehammers.

He fought to control his breath, breathing from the diaphragm, drawing air in through the nose, expelling air through the mouth. And from all around him, it seemed, he felt fresh energy flowing into him: his *ch'i.*

Step by clanking step, his nemesis came closer. David

felt the energy accrete within him as if each molecule of air were made of fire, until it achieved critical mass at the pit of his belly, until it burst like a bomb—

The Dragon's Claw was standing over him like a colossus, legs braced wide. "Prepare yourself, David Lung," he said, raising both hands above his head, interlocked for the killing blow.

David came off the floor as if he were the one propelled by rockets. He uttered a cry that shook the Palace to its foundation as he drove his fist with all the nova fury within him against the spymaster's sternum.

Such a blow might normally collapse the ribcage and drive broken ends of bone through the heart beneath—were it not for the Dragon Claw's armor plate. But this was not a normal blow. It was a special, focused blow. Its energy— David's *ch'i*—was transmitted through the metal, through bone and meat to deep within.

Eyes starting from his head, saliva and gobbling sounds spilling from his mouth, the Dragon's Claw staggered back. His limbs trembled uncontrollably. And then, as if his heart had been replaced by a fusion bottle, and David's mystic blow had breached it, yellow light vomited from the spymaster's mouth and shot from his eyeholes.

As David hurled himself backwards, the Dragon's Claw exploded in flame and sundered flesh.

Shortly thereafter David found himself lurching down the broad steps of Claw Palace. Behind him, flame and black smoke began to lick from the haughty yellow edifice.

And before the battered but victorious young man sprang up the white letters:

EXIT THE DRAGON
A RUN RUN SHAW XLIX PRODUCTION

Cheers, wolf-cries, and wild clapping filled the holotheater. The lights came up in the terraced compartment deep in the guts of the *Overlord* Class DropShip *Uyeshiba,* two days from the Combine capital of Luthien, washing out "David Lung" and the doomed palace in the FedCom holovid the audience had been watching so avidly.

Lieutenant Senior Grade Cassie Suthorn unhooked the bungee that held her floating in place, clasped her hands, arched her back, and stretched like a cat. Around her, several dozen of Camacho's Caballeros—men and women of the mercenary Seventeenth Recon Regiment—began doing likewise. The regiment was on its way to Luthien for the Coordinator's Birthday, a three-day celebration held every year. They'd been invited in honor of their successful defeat of renegade Combine military units and the outlawed Black Dragon Society on Towne, saving face for Theodore Kurita, who did not want to endanger his non-aggression pact with the Davions now that everyone needed to unite in order to stand fast against the Clans. Riding high and proud in their 'Mechs, they would pass in review for Teddy the K himself in a great military show of might organized just for the occasion.

"What about that Johnny Tchang?" Misty Saavedra asked. She was a diminutive MechWarrior from Kali Mac-Dougall's old Bronco Company. She was just beginning to get back some of the ebullience she'd lost after her best friend Mariposa Esposito was killed by a terrorist truck bomb on Towne, which they had gratefully left behind them several weeks before. She was doing her best to keep off the weight she'd dropped at the same time, and was succeeding so far. "*Hijo la,* he's a dream!"

"They say he's going to be on Luthien for the celebration," said Captain Angela Torres breathily. The captain, who amply lived up to her callsign "Vanity," was not known as an aficionada of action flicks. "I can't wait to meet him."

"You and every other female on the planet," remarked Kali MacDougall.

Vanity favored the tall blonde with a look of bland incomprehension. "So?"

"He's not so tough," said Cowboy Payson, extending to his full rangy length in a vertical stretch. "I could take him."

"You and what 'Mech battalion?" Raven O'Connor—ash-blond and acerbic—asked.

"No battalion," Cowboy said with a smirk. "Just me and

my little ol' Yellowjacket." The *Wasp* he was referring to was his 'Mech.

"Don't be too sure, *cuate*," Jesse James Leyva said, slapping him on the shoulder and setting him spinning. "He might turn out to be like our little Cassie here, and take you out anyway."

Cassie's mouth tightened. The thought that a mere actor—even one who was a credible martial artist—could take down BattleMechs afoot the way she could was ludicrous enough to annoy her. Slightly.

"And what does Lieutenant Suthorn think?" Vanity asked ingenuously. "She's our little expert on all this bare-handed rolling-around, after all."

Controlling the urge to flip her off—Vanity behaved poisonously to every reasonably attractive female who came within eyeshot—Cassie said, "He's very pretty—his style, I mean. But it's not realistic. You couldn't really do most of that stuff. Not and expect to survive, anyway."

Cowboy clamped both hands on his chest in a shot-through-the-heart gesture. "I don't want to hear about it! Cassie, ain't you got any romance in your soul?"

"Not where you're concerned, Cowboy."

From across the half-lit compartment Kali caught Cassie's eye, winked and mouthed the words good job. Cassie's mouth tightened involuntarily. She was glad to see her friend show a flash of the easy humor that once was as much a part of her as her long-legged showgirl looks—not to mention a lot more indicative of who she really was. But it reminded her of how different Kali had become since her terrible experiences on Towne. The Seventeenth may have won the war, but Kali had been abused and raped, and that would take a long time healing.

From the back of the compartment, near what was perforce the ceiling since the anchor points arrayed along the terraces constituted a de facto floor, the new commander of Scout Platoon took a pull from his bulb of beer and remarked, "Anybody ever see marble spark like that?"

"Where's your suspension of disbelief, Rooster?" asked Cowboy's inseparable pal Buck Evans, an older man with straw-blond hair cut fairly short except for a long skinny braid hanging down his back, and a face he described as being like forty klicks of bad road. "It's only a holovid."

Rooster, or Lieutenant Senior Grade Daniel Patrick Morgan, a vest-pocket hell-raiser with untamable red hair who was even wirier and uglier than Buck, just laughed. As she made her way toward the exit, Cassie tossed him a glance. He caught her eye, hoisted his bulb, and grinned. She smiled back.

She was still grateful to the little man, and not for the way he had come out of nowhere in the Towne Popular Militia movement to prove himself a skilled and deadly jack-of-all-military-trades, and master of more than a few. Without his quiet competence and skill at managing his often temperamental compatriots in the local resistance movement, the Seventeenth Recon Regiment would have had an even harder time spoiling the Black Dragons' plans to make Towne a possession of the Draconis Combine whether the Dragon wanted it or not. And she did appreciate the fact.

But what she really felt she owed him for was taking over command of Scout Platoon, whose old boss, Captain James "Badlands" Powell, had found a warrior's death in the final assault on Towne's capital city, Port Howard. Had the Rooster not turned up, with a gift for leadership as great as his gift for unconventional warfare, and an unpretentious follow-me style that made the cantankerous Caballeros take to him like flies to honey, there would have been no graceful way for Colonel Carlos Camacho, the regiment's commander, to avoid making Cassie Boss Scout. And Cassie knew she was nowhere near fit for command.

She slipped out into the corridor. She was still rolling her shoulders, trying to work out kinks; she disliked inactivity. Time to go practice some *pentjak-silat,* she thought. The idea warmed her. Her friend Kali MacDougall claimed Cassie used her martial arts and other lethal exercises as a drug, and over the months she had come to see that was true.

As she began to pull herself along the passageway by handholds set into the bulkhead, she felt a touch on her ankle. She looked back into the face of Kali MacDougall.

"You've been frettin' yourself about me again, haven't you?" Kali asked.

Cassie stopped and let her friend draw up alongside her. Kali was moving gingerly, favoring her right shoulder, which was still immobilized by a sort of lightweight synthetic housing. The explosion of a stray SRM had broken it during the assault on the Black Dragons' headquarters in Port Howard.

Cassie could not meet her friend's eyes. "It's just that, since you got out of the hospital, you've just been so . . . so different."

"Hon, I don't recall ever promising you I'd never ever change," Kali said softly.

"But—" Cassie raised a hand, moistened her lips, and then looked away in an agony of doubt and frustration. Now that she had committed herself—at what point she could never quite say—to the path of becoming a human being and not just a killing machine, Kali MacDougall was her lode star, her guiding light. For her to change seemed akin to betrayal. But Cassie—who had destroyed more Battle-Mechs than anybody the Caballeros had ever heard of, who had almost been burned to death in Kali MacDougall's *Atlas* trying to keep *Tai-sho* Jeffrey Kusunoki from escaping from Towne—did not dare open herself enough to articulate that fact. Though a high-ranking member of the Combine military, Kusunoki had been an even more loyal member of the Black Dragon Society, and over time had filled his command with those who shared his renegade views.

And Kali had changed so much since Towne. To start with, she was no longer Lady K. Instead, she'd taken to calling herself Dark Lady, the name she had given to her *Atlas,* now lost forever. And she lived up to the name. Her face was still beautifully sculpted, but where it had once held a kind of prettiness, her beauty was now stark-haunted and haunting. When she looked at you, her green eyes seemed to blaze like emerald lasers. Kali had never carried much excess body fat, but now she was spare to the edge of gauntness. The radiant golden-blonde hair that had once spilled to her shoulders was cut short.

And now she made a point of always dressing entirely in black, and wore her laser pistol in a fast-draw thigh-holster at all times.

"Look, Cass," she said, "I know it's hard to get a handle on. But I've told you before, and I meant it, something happened to me and now you've got to let me get through it. I can't promise I'll go all the way back to where I was before—mainly 'cause you never can go back, much as you always think you can. But at least I'll be headed in a good direction."

Cassie turned her face sharply away so her friend couldn't see her gray-blue eyes fill with tears. After all this time, there was still a part of her which said, *See, stupid? This is what you get for trusting, for letting someone get inside you. She's going to change and leave you. Just like everybody does.*

Cassie felt a hand on her shoulder. "I'm not going to forsake you," Kali said quietly. "There's not much life lets us promise, but I can give you that. No matter how I may change, I'm in with you for the long haul. Satisfied?"

Cassie dabbed tears from her eyes with a thumb. "Yes," she said.

It wasn't wholly a lie.

2

Kneeling in the moonlit garden, his blood-splashed kimono pooled about his waist, Takashi Kurita thrust the *wakizashi* into his abdomen. Very deliberately, he made the three ritual cuts of seppuku.

Waiting behind him, *katana* upraised in his hands, Theodore struck. The head of the aging Coordinator of the Draconis Combine flew free of its thick neck on a column of blood, black in the light of Luthien's moon. It rolled against a weathered basalt rock carefully picked out of the wastelands by some long-dead gardener, and came to a stop. The blood-tide ebbed with the heart's last beats. The decapitated body slumped to the side.

But then the head opened its eyes. They were bright blue, Kurita blue. And they fixed on Theodore like the lightning bolts of a PPC.

"Look upon me well, my son," it said. Its gums were hideously scarlet with blood, and blood ran from its lips. "As I was, so you are. As I am, so shall you be."

Theodore tried to back away, but it was as if his feet had sunk into the soft raked sand, which had then set like cement about his ankles.

"Give me a son's last kiss," the severed head said. The blood from its mouth was now a torrent, staining the sand in a vast pool around it. Theodore saw that the blood was running up his legs through some capillary action, staining his belly, his chest, the sleeves of his tunic, and at last his hands. "It is your filial duty. A Kurita must always do his duty . . ."

Theodore Kurita's eyes came open. For a long time he lay feeling his kimono glued against his skin by cold sweat. He almost feared to move, as if *this* was dream, and if he disturbed the dream he'd be precipitated back into the reality of horror.

First of all, a warrior must not shrink from confronting that which is before him. It was almost as if Tetsuhara-*sensei* were repeating his earliest lessons from long ago. Theodore made himself stir, rolled off the tatami mat, went to the sliding panel, rice paper translucent with moonglow in a teak frame, and slid it back. Outside was a railed balcony. He knelt, letting the subtly green-hued light of Orientalis, the outermost moon of Luthien, fall on him past the tops of the mighty sequoias that screened Unity Palace against the urban sprawl of Imperial City. It was the same moonlight as in his dream, the same moon that had witnessed his father's suicide . . .

No. Not yet. Wait until your spirit is calm once more. He let the fragrant air wafting from the garden below wash his brow and cleanse his lungs and mind.

If only Shin were here, he thought, *at least I'd have someone to talk to.* But Shin Yodama, his closest friend, was on special duty on Tanh Linh, near the frontier with Smoke Jaguar/Nova Cat-occupied Combine space. He was commanding a special rapid-response force, keeping watch lest either Clan should decide to test Luthien's defenses a second time in the wake of the confusion created by the recent Jade Falcon incursion into Lyrian space. Not to mention the anti-Clan mission the Combine had recently sealed with the Northwind Highlanders. Though Shin Yodama was commander of the Izanagi Warriors, which had been permanently attached to the Otomo ever since the battle for Luthien, there were some things that Theodore could only trust to Shin.

No. Self-pity's no better than brooding. For a span he tried to make himself think about anything but his dream: of the ring of orbital-defense satellites nearing construction around Luthien to help safeguard the planet known as the Black Pearl of the Combine against Clan raiders; of the upcoming celebration of the Coordinator's Birthday, which was no festive occasion for him but an opportunity to conduct crucial state business. But the memory of the dream was stronger.

As I was, so you are . . .

His father had been nearly maddened by his fears, and it was that which eventually led to his death. Takashi Kurita's hatred of mercenaries, Colonel Jaime Wolf of Wolf's Dragoons in particular, had obsessed him for much of Theodore's life. Indeed, it had turned into a vendetta that diverted valuable military and intelligence resources enough to threaten the security of the Draconis Combine itself. And the Coordinator had no greater duty than to preserve the Dragon, the heart, soul, and spirit of the realm.

Takashi's father Hohiro had been mad too. His megalomania had provoked unprecedented general strikes, near-mutiny in the armed forces, and had even driven the ISF to remonstrate. His iron-handed harshness would probably have broken the Combine's back, had not one of his Otomo bodyguards assassinated him first.

Theodore had heard the rumors that Takashi himself had a hand in Hohiro's death, and he firmly believed that his father had at least had guilty knowledge of the assassination plot. For his part, Theodore honored his father's memory for that. *Giri,* duty, must overcome *ninjo,* or human feelings. The Combine's welfare came before even the strong ties of Kurita blood.

Sometimes it seemed that madness plagued every leader of the Inner Sphere. Sun-Tzu Liao, current ruler of the Capellan Confederation, had begun to display the sort of capriciousness that had marked the reigns of his mother Romano and his grandfather Maximilian. Sun-Tzu and Thomas Marik, his future father in law, had mounted a joint invasion of Davion space, both men winning back worlds they'd lost to the Davions years before. But to Theodore this was just more wild posturing. Did no one remember that the clock was running on the Truce of Tukayyid—assuming that the Clans would even continue to honor it?

And Thomas Marik, who most considered to be the shrewdest leader ever to take the helm of the Free Worlds League, had permitted the Word of Blake fanatics to make him into a messianic figure. Was that truly sane? And the way Victor Steiner-Davion—a man Theodore was proud to call his comrade-in-arms, and whom he could almost call a friend—and his sister, Katherine or Katrina or whatever she was calling herself these days—were tearing apart the mighty Federated Commonwealth, the greatest power the Inner Sphere had seen since the fall of the Star league, like a wishbone at a feast: was that sane?

Am I the only sane ruler left among the Great Houses? Or am I just like the rest?

Does the fate of humankind rest in the hands of mad children?

"We have received confirmation, Director," the tall red-headed man clad all in black said even before he had completed his bow. "Clan Jade Falcon has honored its acceptance of *hegira* on Coventry. All Clan forces have been withdrawn."

An uguisu sang from the branch of a plum tree. Subhash Indrahar looked upward at the stars, dimly visible through Imperial City's light-scatter. He sighed, worked the controls of his powered wheelchair to turn him to face his adopted son and second in command, Ninyu Kerai. Ninya stood to the side of a sliding *shoji* panel open to a well-lit corridor of that wing of the sprawling Unity Palace that served as the aboveground component of the ISF's headquarters on Luthien. It was as much a part of him as his red hair not to stand silhouetted against a light-source.

The other four individuals gathered in the garden remained silent, which was not altogether characteristic of them. The report might as easily have been delivered by Omi Dashani, whose Metsuke division had almost surely provided the information, as by Ninyu Kerai Indrahar. But Omi, head of the Internal Security Force's intelligence-gathering division, was not a forward person; she was small and plain, and preferred to remain as inconspicuous as her spies. Subhash appreciated her reticence, although certain of her peers within the ISF leadership took it as a sign of weakness.

The long domed head, bald but for a snow-white scalplock on top, nodded deliberately. "It would appear the Crusader faction still accepts some constraints upon its conquest-lust," Subhash said, laying aside the ancient scroll he had been perusing. "For the present."

"The Clanners are warriors," said *Tai-sho* Hohira Kugiri, commander of the Draconis Elite Strike Teams, or DEST. The one-eyed commando was a shadow monolith looming against the overhanging plum-tree limbs and the stars. "They abide by their code of honor."

"And we of all people should know how far warriors are willing to stretch their honor, when it suits their interests— or their egos," Constance Jojira said, and drew on a cigarette in a long ebony holder with an ivory mouthpiece. The Covert Operations head was as languildy elegant as Dashani was dumpy and unassuming. She seemed to take up the slack of the ambition the smaller woman lacked.

"Is there new intelligence from our Clan-occupied worlds?" the Director asked.

"No changes of consequence have been noted," Dashani said quietly, almost apologetically. "And of course the Jaguars aren't going to appreciate the surprise visit from the Highlanders out in the Periphery. Just the same, we must be on our guard. The Coordinator's Birthday celebration will provide a tempting target."

"I must concur," said Daniel Ramaka, who led the Internal Security division of the ISF with rather more relish than the Director was comfortable with. He affected a sinister hiss through the prominent incisors that had done so much to earn him his departmental soubriquet of "the Rat." "The Clans recognize our Coordinator as their most determined foe. To neutralize him would provide any Clan great honor."

Subhash suppressed a sigh. For a moment he let his head hang forward, and tasted again the bitterness of being a warrior trapped in an increasingly useless husk of a body. He felt fatigue all the time now. Yet he slept little, for it seemed to do him little good.

He knew the kind of rest he needed. Yet he could not surrender himself to death until the no-longer-young Ninyu Kerai, who stood apart from and slightly before the others, acknowledged that he was ready to become his successor.

"There is further news that might conceivably be of interest," Ramaka said. "The JumpShip carrying Franklin Sakamoto has just entered the system. He will set foot on the soil of Luthien eight days from now."

"It's a mistake to permit him to come," said Kuguri.

Jojiri blew out smoke. "We could always let Ninyu wrap up the business he left unfinished so many years ago."

The Smiling One's eyes were old, but they still saw more than others' did. Few would have noted the way his adoptive son stiffened at the words. In 3033 Ninyu Kerai had assassinated a boy he believed to be Theodore Kurita's bastard son, in an attempt to clear up a potential cloud over the succession—without the then-Heir's knowledge. But Kathleen Palmer, herself an ISF operative, had smuggled her real son by Theodore off-planet; the murdered boy was a ringer. The real son grew up under the name Franklin Sakamoto.

Normally it was Daniel Ramaka who reveled in reminding others of failures past, but Ramaka feared Ninyu Kerai. Constance Jojira had a knack for putting the needle in, and she feared no one. She hated Ninyu for putting paid to her dreams of becoming the first woman Director of the ISF.

You dance along the edge, Constance-san, Subhash thought. She was bringing more than just Ninyu Kerai's failure back to mind. A rebel faction had gotten to Sakamoto in 3050 while he was fighting the Jade Falcons on Somerset alongside FedCom forces, revealed the truth of his ancestry to him, and attempted to enlist him in a plot to usurp the Dragon Throne from his grandfather Takashi. That rebel faction was Kokuryu-*kai*, the Black Dragon Society.

I underestimated the Black Dragons then, as I did before Towne. If I do so again, it shall be time to join my ancestors, regardless of what my adoptive son believes.

"I failed," Ninyu Kerai said bluntly. "I make no excuse. But it was a failure that did the Combine no harm.

Sakamoto served bravely against the Clans. And perhaps it has slipped your mind that he renounced all claim to the throne."

"The Coordinator has seen fit to invite his son to attend his birthday celebration," Subhash said. "He wishes, it would appear, to come to terms with the past. It is not the part of ISF to make policy." Which was thin, and he well knew it. When the Smiling One found Takashi Kurita's policies—in this case, his obsessive feud with Jaime Wolf—insupportable, he had tried to assassinate the Coordinator. But the point remained that it was ISF's function to dispose, not propose, except under the most extreme circumstances.

"I still don't like it," Kiguri said. "The Black Dragons tried to use him once. Who's to say they won't again? And Sakamoto worked for years as a smuggler for one of the shipping companies owned by Chandrasekhar Kurita, a man much too clever to be trusted. He's about to make planetfall himself—along with his pet regiment of *gaijin* mercenaries that Migaki insists on making heroes out of—"

"And speak of the devil," Ramaka said, as Takura Migaki himself strolled into the garden with his hands thrust into the pockets of his garish *happi*-coat. *Zaki*—gangster kitsch—was the rage among Luthien's smart set this season. The head of the Voice of the Dragon was always fashionable, if not always punctual.

"Apologies," Migaki said. "There were problems with the day's shoot. I had to take charge myself."

"And here I thought you were in charge of making propaganda for the Draconis Combine," Jojira said, "instead of for its long-time enemies."

Migaki looked at her. A corner of his mouth quirked up. He was a handsome man who appeared much younger than he was; as usual he wore his long black hair gathered in a topknot so large that it hung down over his left shoulder.

"*Dragon Phoenix* is propaganda for the Combine, and very effective it will be," he said. "It is also, incidentally, propaganda on behalf of our current allies in the fight against the Clans. And it will earn the Dragon good-will among the billions in the Capellan Confederation who still idolize Johnny Tchang despite his defection to the

Federated Commonwealth. In the meantime, our allies are also proving generous enough to pay some eighty percent of production costs, thereby freeing vital ISF resources for operations against the Clans. I'd say that's worthwhile, Constance, wouldn't you?"

"Such transactions reek of the purely mercantile," Kiguri said.

Migaki laughed. "Ah, Hohiro-*sama*, and can an assemblage of spies, torturers, terrorists, and professional liars really look down upon even the merchant class? We're closer to *eta* than *samurai*, and even you know it."

The General's one eye flashed in the starlight. His hatred and contempt for the propaganda boss were among the ISF's less closely guarded secrets. And his pride was stung by the comparison to the lowest class of Unproductives, whose very name meant filth. But Migaki was right. The ISF was descended from the ancient ninja as truly as the Combine's nekogami clans, and the ninja were *eta* themselves.

"What Takura-*san* is doing, he does with my approval," Subhash Indrahar said. "If he feels his duties are more pressing than arriving at meetings on time, that lies within his discretion." The Director thought Migaki had too wide a frivolous streak, too, and he hated a lack of punctuality. But if Subhash hadn't been willing to overlook character flaws in favor of sheer ability, Migaki's matinee-idol face was not the only one that would be missing from this gathering. And the Smiling One hadn't thought the gathering necessary to begin with. He felt doing things was more useful than talking about doing them.

"Since you've chosen to grace us with your presence, then," General Kiguri said, "perhaps you can answer a question for us: is all this puffing-up of these *gaijin* money-soldiers necessary?"

"Yes." The propaganda boss spoke the single word and then stood there, face composed, smiling faintly in the moonlight, as if that answer was a sufficiency. In spite, or perhaps because, of his mastery of words, he used bluntness well.

The one-eyed DEST chieftain wasn't going to be deflected so simply. "Why?" Kiguri demanded, as if unwilling to let this glib fop outdo a soldier in terseness.

"First, they have done the Combine a service. The key factor there is that it's a service that might have some controversial components among certain sectors of our society."

"Controversial," murmured Jojira. "Your talent for understatement outshines the moons tonight, Takura-*kun*. They killed Combine soldiers on Towne."

Migaki ignored the sarcastic use of the honorific, which was one a teacher might employ to a favored male student. He shrugged. "Theodore himself did as much during the first Ronin War," he said. "Still, it has the potential to stir ill feelings, so we have chosen to promote the heroism—the rightness—of their actions aggressively. At the same time, of course, the Coordinator retains his usual distance, and can be dissociated from the affair on Towne if that for some reason becomes necessary."

In "his usual distance" the propaganda expert was alluding to a cultural paradox inherited from the Japanese: Combine culture admired a man of action, and a strong leader; yet the proper leader, be he the head of a family or the empire as a whole, was expected to actually do very little. His job was to serve as center, a rock of calm dignity, while others served him. The use of the word *oyabun,* or father figure, for the head of a yakuza gang was not originally facetious, but descriptive. A leader who did too much was liable to be regarded as rambunctious, and while no one was likely to criticize him openly, even to themselves, such demeanor made people uncomfortable and promoted disharmony. That had been one of the late Takashi Kurita's more signal failings, from the viewpoint of the Voice of the Dragon as well as ISF as a whole: he wouldn't behave.

"As a secondary consideration, the Clan invasion made it necessary for us to rely more and more on mercenaries, and the policy directives we have received indicate no change. Indeed, as the rulers of the other Successor States become increasingly distracted by their own ambitions, it seems likely that the Dragon will have to recruit huge numbers of mercenaries to effectively oppose the Clans once the Truce expires—in the ever-more-unlikely event the Clans honor the Truce to its expiration. We have a long legacy of disdain for *doitsujin yohei* to overcome, and the late Coordinator's obsessive hatred for Wolf's Dragoons didn't help."

He grinned. "Finally, it's good drama. An exciting adventure story. People enjoy that. And any glory we shine upon these mercenaries can only reflect upon our Coordinator."

"Is it wise to glorify the killing of the Dragon's servants?" Daniel Ramaka asked.

"The *gaijin* killed rebels, in the Coordinator's service," Kiguri said gruffly. "And they killed many of them, I'll give them that."

"If there is no more business, then," Subhash Indrahar said, in tones which indicated there had better be no more, "let me remind you all that rest serves action better than talk does. And I for one need rest."

The Division heads withdrew. Ninyu Kerai remained behind. "Adoptive father, we have received a communication from Chandrasekhar Kurita's DropShip," he said. "Abdulsattah, his head of security, inquires as to whether we have fresh intelligence concerning possible Black Dragon plans to take advantage of the Coordinator's birthday."

Subhash rubbed the side of his face. "Ah, the fat fool Chandrasekhar," he said. "Who turned out not to be such a fool after all. He's proven himself wise enough to engage that looming skeleton the Mirza Abdulsattah—and that formidable young mercenary woman who got the better of you when they were assigned to Hachiman."

His adoptive son stiffened. Subhash waved it off. "He got the better of all of us on Hachiman, as it turned out. And proved us wrong about the Black Dragons on Towne."

"I have been guilty of underestimating the Coordinator's cousin," Ninyu said, hanging his head.

"As have we all. And I bid you remember that the missteps that have been called to mind tonight constitute most of the mistakes you've made throughout your long service to the Dragon: hardly a disgraceful record."

He folded his hands in his lap. "I only hope misreading this gross fat hedonist doesn't prove the single worst mistake of my tenure as ISF Director. Fortunate indeed that all we can learn of his actions indicates that, if he does have a potential for subversion, it lies in excessive devotion to the person of Theodore, rather than to the Dragon."

"How should I respond to Abdulsattah's query?" Ever since concluding their truce on Hachiman, the ISF and Uncle Chandy, as he was known among the *gaijin,* had been cooperating to a limited extent. Even Ninyu Kerai, who would never be an admirer of the Coordinator's obese and self-indulgent "uncle," had to acknowledge it went further than indulging the whims of a member of the Imperial family—the ISF had derived useful information from Uncle Chandy's huge organization.

More, in fact, than it had made proper use of—as the recent Towne fiasco showed.

"What's your assessment of the situation?"

"*Kokuryu-kai* showed much greater resources than we suspected they possessed in the Towne invasion," Ninyu Kerai said. "They also lost every man, machine, and cartridge they committed to that operation. Not even a Great House could absorb such a catastrophe without feeling ill effects. The Coordinator is enormously popular among all levels of Combine society. I believe that the Black Dragons have shot their bolt."

Subhash gave him a level gaze. "Are you sure?"

"*Hai,*" Ninyu affirmed without hesitation.

"Be wary of certainty, adoptive son," Subhash said, raising an admonitory finger. "The decisiveness that enabled you to render the Dragon such service as a field operative is not always optimal in an administrator—although mind, I'm not counseling you to indecision. But except in the most pressing emergency it is good to think twice before deciding—even though, as Confucius tells us, thinking three times is unnecessary luxury."

"I thank you for your instruction, Subhash-*sama.*"

"It is probably unnecessary itself; you really have learned all you need to know. As I grow older, I grow fonder of hearing myself talk. A peculiarly unattractive vice."

"I agree with Ninyu Kerai," Kiguri said. "Surely the yakuza dogs will never dare trouble the Coordinator."

The Smiling One raised a thin brow at him. "Not yakuza

alone, by any means, General. *Kokuryu-kai* also enjoys support among the Middle classes, business executives, and even the DCMS. It's risky to dismiss them too readily. Ah, well, Ramaka also concurs, and Dashani's *metsuke* report that the Black Dragons have become almost completely dormant since their surrender on Towne."

He sat a moment, then picked up his scroll again. Then he looked up at Ninyu. "Was there something further, adoptive son?"

"As you say, it is not our duty to make policy, nor to question it. Still: the Way of the Dragon has always been the way of the sword. Might *Kokuryu-kai* not have a point, that in making common cause with our enemies we risk straying too far from the path of our ancestors?"

"*Hakko-ichi-u,*" the Smiling One said. "The Eight Corners of the World Under One Roof. The motto of the Black Dragon Society. I believe that the Dragon's destiny is to rule over all the Inner Sphere, and one day the whole galaxy, as that slogan suggests. Yet, as our friend Chandrasekhar Kurita perceives, there are many paths by which that end might be attained. I believe our Coordinator goes too far in accommodating the Davions, yet all things considered, his feet are on the proper path."

Ninyu stiffened. "I had no intention of criticizing the Coordinator's conduct in this matter."

"Of course not. And I am pleased to see you practicing reflection."

Ninyu looked puzzled. "The way of the warrior is to act, not reflect."

The Smiling One sighed. "The final and most difficult part of your education," he said, "consists in convincing you that you are not a warrior. You are a sneak-thief, an assassin, and a spy, just as Migaki-san reminded us. More to the point, you are a commander and director of same. Our honor lies in service to the Dragon, not adherence to the nineteenth-century counterfeit called *bushido.*"

Ninyu stiffened at his adoptive father's unwonted vehemence. Subhash waved his fingers at him again. "It's late. Even though sleep holds little virtue for me, you still require yours. Go to bed."

Ninyu Kerai bowed and withdrew. Subhash fumbled with his scroll, steeling himself against the agony the incompetence of what had once been a master swordsman's hands caused him.

You must find your own rest, a voice inside his shaven skull said. Soon.

3

"**R**egard the vastness of outer space, granddaughter," said Chandrasekhar Kurita, waving a chubby hand at the huge transpex viewport set into the bulkhead of his stateroom aboard the DropShip *Uyeshiba,* now on approach vector for the planet Luthien. "Is it not splendid?"

"It's very pretty, Chandrasekhar-*sama,*" Cassie replied.

He swiveled his great shaven Buddha head on its chins and gazed at her with soft reproach. "I understand how you might feel a desire to resist the constraints Combine society places upon feminine demeanor," he said. "But you should make at least the occasional concession to softness and beauty. A warrior without due regard for yin is like a broken wheel."

"Did Confucius say that?"

"No, child; I did, just now. And it's not really the sort of thing the esteemed sage *would* have said, in between those bouts of moaning about not being able to get a government job that make up the bulk of his *Analects.* It's more of a medieval Japanese sentiment, something he probably took for granted. The warlord Oda Nobunaga used to astound and delight his troops with the delicacy of the ritual dances he performed before going into battle, and, truth to tell, I'm afraid he was pretty much of a frightful thug. On the other hand, if *he* could express his *yin* side, I daresay you can make a go of it."

Cassie looked out the viewport. Certainly the stars splashed across it were impressive in their number and brilliance.

"I'm sorry, grandfather," she said, shaking her head. Chandrasekhar Kurita was not her literal grandfather, of course; it was a term of affectionate respect in Japanese, and delighted Chandy when she used it to him. Actually, he was no more old enough to be her grandfather than he was actually Theodore Kurita's uncle—he was in fact the Coordinator's cousin, his senior by no more than a year or so. While Chandrasekhar Kurita could be a supreme realist—and sometimes hard enough to truly live up to the name Kurita, hard enough to startle Cassie, Drac-born and Capellan-raised though she was—he was a man who tended to make up reality to his own satisfaction as he went along. And he had the force of personality to pull it off.

At least so far. But then, Cassie knew, that was the most you could say about being alive, too: at least so far.

"When I look at the stars," she admitted, "all I see are a lot of little lights."

"And I suppose, when you beheld the legendary grandeur of the Eiglophian Mountains on storm-haunted Towne, all you saw was potential battleground?"

The words caught at her heart. For a moment she was back in the rear seat of a propeller-driven *Ruedel* attack plane, banking above a great mountain bowl filled with clouds, and over the headset Tim Moon saying, "Welcome to the Vale of Shamballah." She'd been in love with Tim Moon, and he'd died defending his world from the cockpit of that aircraft.

She raised a forefinger to the corner of one eye to remove a drop of moisture that had somehow gotten there, and smiled a slender smile. "Not altogether, grandfather."

He beamed. "Excellent! There's hope for you yet. Have some grapes?" He gestured toward a cluster of fruit floating in a red plastic net anchored to a bracket on the bulkhead.

"No, thank you, grandfather, I just ate. I was mainly wondering why you asked to see me." You could no more hurry Uncle Chandy than you could a glacier, but it was Cassie's nature to try. As was the minor impertinence involved.

She could speak frankly to him. Magnate of the Draconis Combine though he was, and a full-blood Kurita into the bargain, Uncle Chandy took no offense at the barbarian brusqueness and crudity of his *doitsujin yohei,* his foreign mercenaries. In fact the Caballeros' Southwestern manners—which would have shocked most upstanding residents of the Inner Sphere, truth to tell—tickled him immensely. And he found none more delightful than this strange little tiger-girl he had all but adopted.

Also, he found that what she had to say was usually well worth hearing. "Mere woman" or not, she was the best he had ever seen at what she did. Chandrasekhar Kurita was a man to use talent as it came to him, whether in noble's silks or Unproductive rags. That trait, far more than his last name, accounted for him being the richest man in the Combine, if not the whole Inner Sphere.

He chuckled. "I see that I can hide little from you, even though I mask it with the grandeur of the stars."

"It's Luthien, isn't it? There's trouble."

"So I expect."

She sagged, though she had known it when she received her summons. Had known it since the invitation—wangled somehow by Uncle Chandy himself, she never doubted—had arrived, inviting the Seventeenth Recon Regiment to attend the Coordinator's Birthday celebration on Luthien, where they would be honored for their service to the Draconis Combine. It was the greatest holiday of the year, spreading out over three full days.

"Who?" she asked half-despairing. Then:

"The Black Dragons."

Uncle Chandy beamed. "Precisely. You are percipient as ever, granddaughter."

Slumping in zero-g wasn't very gratifying. She felt herself drifting, kicked, then floated close enough to the wall to snag a silk streamer provided for the purpose.

"I thought we'd finished them on Towne," she said.

The events on Towne were still fresh in Cassie's mind and heart. The final thrust by the Caballeros and the Popular Militia against *Tai-sho* Jeffrey Kusunoki in Port Howard, coordinated with resistance-force risings all across Towne, had hurt the renegade DCMS/Black Dragon troops under Kusunoki's command. But he still had five regiments of ground forces, including two BattleMech formations—one consisting of Black Dragon MechWarriors—and an aerospace regiment to throw at them. Dispersed and battered though they were, they had still outweighed, outnumbered, and outgunned the Caballeros by an uncomfortable margin even after taking a savage beating at Port Howard.

The bottom line was, as always, that a planet is a big place. Kusunoki's six regiments were not enough to pacify Towne by force, especially after the battle for Port Howard. The only thing that could have saved him would have been help from Theodore Kurita. Which created a brutal dilemma: the Coordinator must either betray his Davion ally or plunge the Draconis Combine into civil war.

To prevent Uncle Chandy's cousin Theodore from having to make that awful choice was what the Seventeenth Recon Regiment had been sent to Towne to do. And they would have failed, despite the victory bought with so much Caballero blood, had Jeffrey Kusunoki escaped to rally his scattered forces. But Cassie had blocked his way at the controls of Kali MacDougall's *Atlas*.

His disgraceful defeat in 'Mech-to-'Mech combat by someone who wasn't even a MechWarrior—and a mere woman at that—had been broadcast all over the planet by Mariska Savage and ISF propaganda man Enrico Katsuyama. So was Jeffrey Kusunoki's ensuing *seppuku* with Cassie acting as his second.

The broadcast demoralized the remaining Black Dragon force. And though Teddy could not be seen to involve himself openly in the Towne mess, the Combine had managed to slip the Caballeros a measure of covert help. When Ernie Katsuyama was smuggled onto Towne, he brought two prerecorded holomessages. One, by none other than Theodore Kurita, called upon the invaders to lay down their arms, and granted full amnesty to all those who did so. This was broadcast to all Black Dragon forces. A second message had been recorded by the Smiling One explaining in graphic detail what would happen to anybody who tried to hold out, not to mention their families and associates back in the

Combine. It was delivered to the renegade DCMS and Black Dragon commanders by various covert means.

All told it added up to a devastating double left-right combination: shocking defeat followed by the disgrace and death of the commander, Teddy's carrot and Subhash's stick. The Black Dragons folded.

Uncle Chandy was smiling at her. "You finished two regiments of the troops *Kokuryu-kai* had somehow managed to recruit and train," he said in his serene way, "and in doing so you richly earned the honor my cousin has seen fit to bestow upon you." *With plenty of prompting from you, I'm sure,* Cassie thought.

"But you are aware of what the yakuza call their soldiers?"

Cassie nodded. The usual term was *kobun*—literally "child figures," as the word for "boss," *oyabun,* meant "father figure." She knew that wasn't what Chandy meant.

"Teppodama." Bullets.

"Just so. Expendables, meant to be used, used up, without thought. No, along with these 'bullets' you and your comrades also accounted for destroying a whole regiment of BattleMechs. In this you struck a mighty blow at the Black Dragons' purse, which for all their pretense of patriotic selflessness, is their most cherished organ. However . . ."

He spread pudgy palms. Floating there in mid-air, crossed legs concealed by his rich scarlet kimono, he looked more like an absurd jovial Buddha than ever.

"The Black Dragons' roots run very deep. You did not destroy the *Kokuryu-kai* on Towne. You only injured it, and so aroused its fury."

She stared at him.

"So what now?"

Then she sucked in a breath and squeezed her eyes tight shut. When she opened them again, she answered her own question.

"So that's why you sweet-talked your cousin into inviting us to his birthday celebration! I've been trying to figure that angle. I mean, you're a good employer, you give us the kind of reward that means something: cash. You don't waste a whole lot of energy stroking your own ego, though, so I couldn't make out why you'd be so concerned with ours."

"Do not underestimate the effect of honors—empty though they be—on your fellow humans, Cassiopeia. Your adopted family puts nearly as much store in such things as those among whom you and I alike were born."

"You're sticking us right back on the bull's eye, aren't you?" she said, ignoring his interjection. "You think the Black Dragons are going to make a move against Theodore at his own birthday party."

"Of course," Chandrasekhar Kurita said. "I promised you lucrative employment, and have, as you were gracious enough to acknowledge, delivered. I never said anything about *easy* employment. Besides, these Southwesterners are never so happy as when they're faced with some desperate challenge—and you so much more than they." Galisteo, Cerillos, and Sierra, the so-called Trinity or Southwestern Worlds, in the Free Worlds League, were the planets from which most of the regiment hailed.

"Don't you ever do *anything* without ulterior motives?"

"Granddaughter, you dishonor me. No man in the Combine has motives more exterior than mine: to serve the Dragon, in the person of my cousin Theodore, as best I humanly can. With the corollary motives of turning a handy profit and gaining such amusement as I may along the way. Can you name a single occasion on which I have concealed those motivations—or acted in the least way counter to them?"

She couldn't, and the fat, smug old fart knew it. "Don't you do anything—" She floundered for a moment like a newbie in zero-g. "—*simple?* Don't you ever take an action that has just a single purpose?"

"My child, I am but one man. The Draconis Combine is vast, and so is the Inner Sphere, and so are the menaces that confront them. I can do only so much, especially if I am to allow myself to steal the occasional moment to savor the pleasures life offers us. I am a rich man, and stint myself nothing, but the one luxury I cannot afford is to do things *simply*."

Cassie turned to stare out the wide viewport. The stars

didn't comfort her. They really were just so many little lights, still and cold.

Her head whirled. *What else did you expect?*

"What else did you expect?" he asked gently, displaying his unsettling gift for saying aloud what she was thinking. "You know my methods."

She gave him a narrow gaze. "What does that mean?"

He sighed like a mountain that had just shrugged off a couple climbers. "A quotation from classical literature, my dear. Really, we must see to your education one of these days. You have a fine mind, but it remains largely unformed."

"Let's worry about forming my mind another time. What are we getting into on Luthien? What did the Mirza tell you?" The Mirza was Uncle Chandy's head of security, and his efforts rivalled the best intelligence agencies in the Inner Sphere.

Uncle Chandy shrugged. "We have little specific information to go on. Shall we say we have two of the classic elements of a crime on hand: motive and opportunity?" Cassie knew Chandy had been on a binge of reading detective novels of late. She wondered if that had given rise to his earlier quote, too.

"The Black Dragons have long wanted to rid Theodore of the 'evil advisors' whom they blame for his reforms. Now they're burning for revenge. Don't you think it's likely they'll find the Coordinator's Birthday too ripe an opportunity to pass up? I should also mention that it may occur to them to seek some means of avenging themselves upon your regiment, the author of their recent misfortunes, since you happen to be conveniently at hand."

"Which means we're bait."

"Once again, your acuity does you credit. But consider, granddaughter: I do not do this lightly. It is a very dangerous tiger I'm hoping to draw out by staking a lamb. And, if I may say so—also a highly dangerous lamb?"

She frowned. Yes, the Seventeenth were mercenaries, and danger really was their business. But they were her family, and neither they nor she had had the chance to heal from the wounds incurred on Towne—as if wounds like that ever healed, as if she didn't still wake at night sweat-soaked and weeping from dreams of Patsy Camacho, who had died five years ago on other missions, other battles, on Jeronimo. Even though it was what Uncle Chandy paid them for, she felt a white-hot plasma-jet of anger at the high-handed way he'd hung them up for the Black Dragons to take a swing at like a piñata at Teddy's birthday party.

Then she clamped her mouth shut on her complaints. Because it occurred to her who was the *other* author of the Black Dragons' disaster on Towne. Someone who would inevitably strike the ultra-conservative *Kokuryu-kai* was an abomination, a disgrace to the name he bore, a festering symbol of all that was wrong with the Draconis Combine.

If Uncle Chandy was setting Camacho Caballeros out for bait, he was plopping his own broad butt down right beside theirs.

"How about Theodore?" she asked quietly. "What if the Black Dragons decide to simply forget about all this 'wicked advisor' crap and go right to the source?"

The fat man laughed uproariously. "Ah, no, my child. There you are allowing your fine imagination to get the better of you. Not even in its arrogance and folly would *Kokuryu-kai* act directly against the person of the Coordinator. Especially when that Coordinator is Theodore Kurita."

"Strike at me," the one-eyed man commanded.

General Hohiro Kiguri was a tall man, and not only by the standards of the Draconis Combine, whose populace ran to the diminutive. Commander of the Draconis Elite Strike Teams, he won obedience as much by stature and sheer presence as by voice. His booming baritone rolled off the dark, oily-looking boles of the trees as the wind made the black and green leaves click like tiny hyper castanets. He alone among the two dozen men and women gathered in the clearing left his iron-gray buzz-cut hair bare to the chilly air of the Kiyomori Mountains to the northwest of Luthien's Imperial City.

He was otherwise clad the same as his audience: black from the base of his muscle-thick neck to the split toes of his flexible boots. All he lacked was the helmet-hood of black ballistic cloth with the one-way red visor obscuring the face, and the straight-bladed, single-edged sword with a square, outsized *tsuba*—a handguard—that the others wore strapped across their backs.

A man only slightly shorter, though considerably younger by his lighter build and the way he moved, faced the one-eyed man in a tentative crouch. His black-gauntleted hand made no move toward the cord-wrapped hilt of his own sword.

"Strike at me!" Kiguri roared. His face, which could never have been called handsome, bore the marks of long and grueling service to the Dragon, of which the black patch covering his right eye-socket was only the most immediately obvious. He was large in the belly, but that was not considered a deficiency in the strongly Japanese-influenced Combine; the fat was backed by thick, domed muscle, so that he possessed what was considered a well-developed *hara,* or center. Whatever extra weight he bore, he carried lightly.

The DEST trooper still hesitated. The trademark red visor hid his features. But his body language, what was called in Japanese *haragei,* "belly talk," was that of someone feeling trapped and indecisive. The usual reward that might be expected for striking, much less striking down, the commander of a branch of the Internal Security Force was death. Immediate, if one were very lucky, followed by the massacre of one's entire family, plus a sizable percentage of everyone the offender had talked to within the last twenty-four hours, to encourage the survivors to pick their friends better.

"Strike me right here," the General insisted, tapping himself between the eyes with a blunt-instrument forefinger. "If you can, then I don't deserve to command the Draconis Elite Strike Teams."

The DEST trooper jittered his weight from the ball of one foot to the other. *"Strike!"* the General roared, face going purple, "or by the Dragon's jade pillar none of your clan shall live to see another rising of their homeworld's primary! The Dragon has no use for bloodlines that breed cowards."

It was an insult and a threat worthy of a Clanner, and like a Clanner the reluctant operative was deep-stung by it. With rattlesnake quickness he seized his sword hilt and thrust it toward the General's scar-crossed face, bringing the blade free of the sheath with a singing sigh and whipping it around with his strong wrist for a pivot. It was a stroke designed to generate more speed than power—but speed was sufficient for the special DEST blades, crafted by hand according to the dictates of an art that was ancient before humankind left Terra, to sever a limb or split a skull.

Glittering like rain in a sun-shower, the *ninjato* arced toward the General's face.

Kiguri clapped his hands together on the blade, stopping it with the biting edge no more than a centimeter from his forehead.

For an instant they held the tableau. Even the wind seemed to hold its breath in shock. Then with a flick of his powerful wrists Kiguri snapped the weapon from his subordinate's grip and flipped it spinning into the air.

As it came down he snatched its hilt. With a two-handed crosswise stroke he severed the young operative's head. The ballistic-cloth armor at the neck gave no more resistance than cheesecloth.

The General turned to face his congregation. Behind him the torso stood fountaining blood from its neck stump for two surging beats of the heat. Then it collapsed, as the blood spray dwindled, became erratic, stopped. The General cleaned the blade with another wrist-flick. A DEST blade shed water like a duck's wing.

"The Dragon has no use for those who hesitate to follow orders, either," the General rasped in a voice as rough from comprehensive abuse as his face was. "No matter what the order may be. *Wakarimasu-ka?*"

He was taking a big risk here, riding the edge. He knew it, relished it—reveled in it. Despite the weak-livered reforms instituted by Theodore—over his father Takashi's strenuous objections, as Kiguri well knew—superiors in the DCMS pretty well treated inferiors as they chose; corporal punishment for minor infractions was commonplace. But these were no mere conscripts. These were the cream, the best of the best. Predators, every one.

For all the lore of *bushido*, *gekokujo*—"those below rising against those above"—was a fact of life for samurai no less than commoners. Obedience was absolute, to be sure—but when it snapped, it snapped clean. And while the penalty for *failed* disobedience was ignominious and generally painful death, a successful piece of usurpation was met with acceptance. Like the Japanese before them, the people of the Dragon had a keen eye for the bottom line, and a respect for evolution in action.

Indeed, one day he himself would be pulled down by one of these fine young wolves—even as it was among real Terran wolves, some of which prowled these very woods, descendants of beasts introduced by a symbolically minded Coordinator. He relished that eventual fate as well. It was the proper nature of things.

Indeed, that should have happened within the ISF, long since, he thought. *Just as Theodore Kurita proved his own weakness by allowing his father to hang on so long.*

But today was not to be the day upon which the General's throat would be torn out. *"Hai!"* his listeners shouted, signifying their comprehension—and submission—by throwing their hands in the air.

He nodded. "Good. Very good. Now, what do you learn from this demonstration, other than the need for instant and absolute obedience?"

One of them left a hand raised. *A mere woman,* he noted with a flicker of dissatisfaction. It was another sign of the creeping decadence that was overtaking the Combine, that more and more women were being allowed to serve as full-scale operatives, instead of mere *kunoichi,* seductresses and spies. Still, he was no blind fool like the departed *Tai-sho* Jeffrey Kusunoki who denied that women could serve the Dragon as warriors. No one who was not fully qualified could ever hope to become one of the feared commandos of DEST.

And no one who was not entirely loyal, body and soul, to DEST commander Hohiro Kiguri joined the exclusive cohort to which the men and women gathered in the clearing belonged. It was anomalous that out of so many highly qualified operatives, no DEST agents had ever been invited to join the Sons of the Dragon, the Smiling One's own super-elite within ISF. None but General Kiguri himself.

Anomalous, but not inexplicable. Kiguri smiled. Warrior though he was to the core, he was also a spy. He understood the value of information. And while he had less use for the womanish fop Migaki who ran the Voice of the Dragon—not to mention Katsuyama, the degenerate toad to whom he was delegating so much authority these days—than he did for that self-inflated prig Ninyu Kerai, he knew as well as Migaki that one's eyes saw the world through the information they received. Whether or not that information bore more than a passing resemblance to *truth*.

As far as their dossiers indicated, none of these men and women quite measured up to Subhash's exacting standards. At least, the dossiers to which the Director had access.

There were many things going on in ISF these days that the Director didn't know.

The confounded woman still held her hand in the air, resolute as a sequoia in Unity Park. *So be it,* Kiguri thought. If even those great trees could bend with the wind, so could he. Besides, he was the one who had selected her for his meta-elite.

"So then, Hajima," he said, "what lesson do we learn?"

She turned her hand into a fist. "That even though his hands are empty, the warrior is never unarmed."

Kiguri's single eye stared balefully at her a long moment. Her own dark eyes never wavered, and her hand stayed raised.

He nodded. "Correct. You have been paying attention." The woman lowered her hand.

"And now," the General declared, "to drive home that lesson we will practice close combat, unarmed against weapons. Then we shall run thirty kilometers to the top of Mount Baldy. May the Dragon reign ten thousand years!"

The little group threw hands in the air again. *"Ryu heika banzai!"* they echoed.

And may the fools in Kokuryu-kai serve their function well before I dispose of them, the General thought.

4

After weeks of travel time, the Seventeenth had finally reached Luthien, and the unloading of their DropShip at the Takashi Kurita Memorial Spaceport just outside Imperial City was proceeding apace. Cassie and two other members of the Caballeros stood waiting for the chopper that would take them directly to Imperial City as a kind of advance party. Standing there with her in the hundred-meter-wide blast pit next to the DropShip's landing-jack were Dolores Gallegos and Father Roberto García, watching intently as the first 'Mechs descended the *Overlord* Class DropShip's offload ramp. The plump Jesuit was the Seventeenth's new Chief Intelligence Officer, and Red Gallegos's role was to finalize transportation and billeting arrangements. Cassie, of course, was to scout the ground in advance.

"Cassie-*san.*"

She spun, her hand reaching instinctively for the hilt of her *kris,* Blood-drinker, which she wore openly on her right thigh today. Public display of firearms was forbidden in the Combine to all but DCMS and the Friendly Persuaders, Luthien's planetary police, but edged weapons conferred status. Cassie was unused to being addressed in that particular way. Chandrasekhar Kurita customarily spoke Japanese to her, but didn't use that form. And while the landing zone walls were ringed with tens of thousands of Imperial Citizens, no doubt gathered here to greet the *gaijin* mercenaries for the purposes of propaganda, Cassie didn't think any of them knew her.

The person addressing her was Captain Sharon Omizuki, commander of the Seventeenth Recon Regiment's spanking-new aerospace lance. The taller woman was walking toward her with swinging strides of long legs encased in trousers of form-fitting black trichloropoly-ester. A stiff, cool, early-spring breeze, still smelling of pavement heated by the Dropship's drive jets, ruffled her curly chestnut hair. She was armored against the wind in a bulky aerojock's jacket made from the hide of some large and surly land creature on some unknown Drac planet. Her not-quite-pretty face was wrapped around a look of dismay.

"Maybe it's a bit late to be thinking about this," the fighter jock went on in Japanese, "but I'm worried. You're a Drac too. Maybe you can help."

"I was born in the Draconis Combine," Cassie said guardedly. She was wearing her own leather jacket today, looking even more dwarfed by it than Omizuki did. Slung over one shoulder she carried a light rucksack of the kind Caballeros called a *possibles* bag. "But I was raised in Liao space. I'm a Capellan as much as anything."

Omizuki laughed, shrugged, and shook her head. "Still, I suspect you'll understand better than most of these crazy Cowboys and Indians I've gone and hooked myself up with."

"Probably."

"I'm concerned about, you know, the terms of my separation from service in the DCMS," Omizuki said.

Cassie nodded. It *had* been pretty informal. Omizuki's *Shilone* aerofighter had been shot out from under her during the final fight on Towne. She'd been splashed by a puny atmospheric fighter, propeller-driven, no less, piloted by Tim Moon of the Towne Air Rangers, one of the local militia groups. Though Omizuki was a company commander and double ace, General Jeffrey Kusunoki had decreed that any of his pilots who suffered such disgraceful defeat should be stripped of flight certification and demoted to the ranks of the infantry. Her belly already full of the man's misogynistic antics, Omizuki had been happy to surrender—despite her training in the Drac warrior tradition—to the first Caballero she came across. And that happened to be Cowboy Payson. She had resigned her commission on the spot, and asked to join the Seventeenth Recon.

At the time she'd fully expected to be recaptured and sent to the wall just as soon as the invasion force overwhelmed the impertinent Towne rebels and their offworld allies. She was prepared to face the firing party. Not only was she disgusted with Kusunoki and his Black Dragon sympathies and allies, she had come to suspect the truth, that the whole invasion was taking place in defiance of the wishes of Theodore Kurita. And though she had served the Dragon her whole adult life with courage, skill, and passion, she owed the Combine little: her family secretly practiced Judaism, which was punishable by death under Kurita law.

But she hadn't died. The invasion had folded like a cheap fan after Kusunoki's globally 'cast seppuku. After a brief, tempestuous affair with her captor (which was pretty much the only kind Cowboy had), Sharon Omizuki found herself in command of the Caballeros' new aerospace lance—and bound for the capital of the Draconis Combine.

"Don't forget that Uncle Chandy got his cousin to issue a decree allowing any DCMS personnel from the Towne invasion to resign," Cassie said. "Made it retroactive, too. Chandrasekhar-*sama* takes care of his people."

Omizuki looked around nervously, fingering the little silver Star of David she now wore openly around her neck. "I just hope the Internal Security Force didn't overlook that piece of paper."

Cassie laughed. "I don't think you've got much worry there. Unlikely as it seems, we Caballeros and the Dragon's Breath have history. After what happened on Hachiman and Towne, the Smiling One either had to kill us off or work with us. We've proven too darned useful to the Dragon to kill."

"So far."

"So far." Cassie agreed with a fatalistic nod. "You know, if you're concerned about that, you didn't pick a real great place to talk about it. The ISF's got its Metsuke operatives up there in the mob with long-range holocams trained on us right this instant, you can bet, and they have lip-readers who can reconstruct every syllable we've let out of our heads."

Omizuki jumped like a startled cat. "I didn't think about that. See? You've got a better head for this kind of thing than I do."

And that's the difference between a pilot and a scout, Cassie thought. *MechWarrior or fighter jock, you fight all swaddled up in your nice, spotless metal cocoon while we're down in the dirt.* She didn't vocalize the thought; the newly recruited flygirl seemed a decent enough sort. And while empathy was not Cassie's strong suit, she knew in her gut the kind of culture-shock abrupt immersion in the Southwesterners' bizarre world was laying on Omizuki.

"Try growing up in the Capellan Confederation," she said. "The ISF is brutal as a matter of policy. The Mask is brutal just for fun."

"Yow," Omizuki said. "You make it sound so attractive. Say—is it a good idea for you to talk about ISF like that?"

Cassie laughed. "Subhash Indrahar knows what the ISF is, and what he is."

"You almost talk like you know him."

Well, I am sort of a friend of the family, Cassie thought with unwonted impishness.

"Maybe I should go ahead and change my name," Omizuki said, "just to be on the safe side. I've been thinking about it anyway. 'Omizuki' was never anything but camouflage, and I'm none too attached to it."

"Go for it," Cassie advised. "Here in the Caballeros, people change their names the way they do their pants."

The pilot made a face. "Well, come to that, I'm not too enamored of my traditional family name, either. 'Goldblatt' just doesn't have much of a ring to it."

"Why don't you talk to the Maccabee?"

"Who?"

"Force Commander Bar-Kochba. He's Second Battalion CO and the regiment's chief rabbi. He's got a lot on the ball. He can give you better advice on that than I can."

"I don't know," Omizuki said, shaking her head. "*Kya*, I hate this—uncertainty. But—the Southwestern Jews are so, so *defiant*. What'll he think of the fact that my family's hidden its Judaism all these years?"

"The Jewboys' ancestors moved to the Trinity to keep from getting assimilated into the Catholic church," Cassie said. "Your bunch has kept the faith for generations in spite of ISF and everything. I think you'll be just his kind of girl." Jewboys was the group's own name for themselves.

A roar went up from the crowd. The Luthien mob was a lot more ruly than crowds on Hachiman. But then again rioting wasn't the most popular outdoor sport here under the very eye of the Coordinator—and his Internal Security Force.

Still, the inhabitants of Luthien loved a spectacle just as much as the Hachimanites did. And now the show was beginning.

A BattleMech stalked down the DropShip's ramp. It was an NG-C3A *Naginata*, 95 tons of malice, one of the newest and most formidable 'Mechs in the Dragon's arsenal—so new that an audience less sophisticated than Luthienites, who got to see the best and the brightest of the Combine's BattleMechs on a regular basis, would likely not have recognized it. As it was, the onlookers gasped to see such a valuable piece of equipment in *gaijin* hands.

But the twelve-meter-tall machine was spectacular enough in its own right. From the tips of the fin-like heat-sink radiator flanges mounted just inside the shoulder housings to the ends of its broad, blunt feet, the *Naginata* was painted blood red. On the front plate of its right-hand Coventry Star Fire LRM launcher was painted the insignia of the Seventeenth Recon Regiment: a coyote *couchant*, raising its head in a defiant howl against a full moon. On its left was the gaunt figure of a lone knight on horseback against a red ground, the personal arms of the BattleMech's pilot. And on the broad plate of Durallex Heavy Special armor that curved smoothly from its right shin to its foot was a beautifully airbrushed painting of an angel with his steel-shod foot on the neck of a vanquished dragon and a fiery sword upraised: *San Miguel Vengador,* St. Michael the Avenger, namesake of the 'Mech itself.

The crowd applauded. They wanted barbarian flash, and *here it was.*

After the *Naginata* stalked a *Shadow Hawk.* The audience *oohed* at the red-tailed hawk, wings and talons outspread, beak open, painted in gorgeous detail across its chest and belly.

And then the onlookers fell silent, because the third machine to stalk into view was the most feared shape in the Inner Spere: the bullet-nosed form of a Clan *Mad Cat.* The Clans had bigger, meaner, more powerful BattleMechs, but somehow the *Cat* had come to symbolize the invaders' implacable might.

This 'Mech was enameled glossy black all over. Angry red eyes glared from behind the cockpit, and a mouthful of sharp white teeth was painted on its snout. On the outside of each of the extended-range PPCs that tipped its arms was painted a sword of curious design, with a flaring pommel and knuckle-duster hilt, whose broad, straight blade split at the end into two single-edged tips.

It struck the crowd at the same time that the Clans would scarcely have given this magnificent and terrifying mechanism to these *doitsujin yohei.* The crowd went crazy—by Luthienite standards.

"Nobody's even hitting each other," Cassie observed. "These folks are pretty uptight." On Hachiman, the onlookers' response would have signified the mildest form of approval.

"Sir Boxer did a hell of a job repainting Kali's 'Mech," Omizuki said. "Gives me goosebumps just to look at it."

It gave Cassie a clammy feeling in her stomach pit. Not because of the design, impressive though it was. But for what the scene implied for her *familia.*

Ever since the Clan invasion and the retreat from Jeronimo, Colonel Carlos Camacho had piloted that *Mad Cat.* He had killed its pilot in single combat, after the Clanner killed his daughter Patricia, known as *la Capitana.* The 'Mech had symbolized the Seventeenth's loss and perseverance alike.

But *Tai-sho* Jeffrey Kusunoki's *Naginata* had been captured intact on Towne. And since the machine was the most advanced command 'Mech deployed in the Inner Sphere, complete with an excellent C3 computer, sheer practicality dictated that it become the ride of the Caballero commander.

So Don Carlos Camacho, not without regret, had passed his former "Great White" on to the new commander of First Battalion, Kali MacDougall, promoted to that position when Camacho's son Gavilán got boosted upstairs to Lieutenant Colonel and regimental operations officer. Kali herself had lost her BattleMech on Towne, so the change made sense.

Cassie knew about that, all too well: it was she who'd ridden Kali's *Atlas* to the death, bringing down Kusunoki.

Cassie felt only a little remorse at burning up her best friend's 'Mech. She had a pathological hatred of Battle-Mechs, and none more so than the *Atlas,* one of which had destroyed her childhood home and killed her father before her eyes when she was a mere child. And while Kali Mac-Dougall, convalescing from her injuries, had had little chance to practice piloting her new machine before embarking for Luthien, the skill that had enabled her to handle the ponderous *Atlas* as if it were a medium 'Mech should by rights make her a demon at the controls of a fast and shifty *Gato Loco.*

But the only thing that unsettled Cassie more than the changes that had come over her friend in the last few weeks were changes to *la familia.* The two machines in their splendid new jobs symbolized both all too vividly.

"Whoa," Sharon Omizuki said, breaking in on the darkness of Cassie's thoughts. "Even in this overcast, that thing hurts my eyes."

The blood-red *Naginata* had marched most of the way to the roadway cut into the blast-wall, with the rest of the regiment following like baby ducks. Cassie looked up to see the 'Mech belonging to Frontera Company's commander lumber down the ramp. It was a solid-gold *BattleMaster* that dazzled even in the heavily filtered sunlight.

During the fight for Towne somebody had finally pointed out to Cassie's none-too-friendly rival Captain Vanity

Torres that, if her *BattleMaster* really was "Vanity's Mirror," as the name had it, it meant Vanity weighed 85 metric tons and had thunder thighs and a huge ass. Vanity—who lived up to her call sign religiously—promptly rechristened her ride "Golden Vanity," and had the damned thing anodized a mirror-finish gold.

For a few moments Cassie stood beside the pilot and watched the parade. It was an impressive show, even she had to admit. But for her it was mainly an exercise in controlling the visceral, nape-hair-raising dread that came with seeing so many of the metallic monsters at once—and the frustrated itch, situated somewhere between her belly and her sex, at not being able to *kill* any of them.

And here was another sign of change: there were more 'Mechs than the Seventeenth had ever boasted before, lots of them. According to the surrender terms, the four DCMS regular units involved in the Towne invasion—the 15th Dieron Regulars: Devotion Through Combat; the 5th Galedon AeroSpace wing: Desolation Angels; the 227th Armored Regiment: Hard Targets; and the 503rd Mechanized Infantry Regiment: A Better Tomorrow—had received the honors of war, getting to keep such of their equipment as had not already been destroyed or otherwise fallen into the planetary defenders' hands. The Black Dragon units, however—the 1st Spirit of the Dragon BattleMech Regiment, known as The Eight Corners of the World Under One Roof, and the 1st Dragon's Joy Infantry Regiment: The Drawn Sword—had been permitted to carry away from Towne only their personal effects, their uniforms, and their lives. Their 'Mechs and other arms had fallen as booty to the victors.

The resulting windfall had gifted the 'lleros with 141 functional 'Mechs and a handful of aerospace fighters. Manning the plundered machines was little problem, as there were always Dispossessed MechWarriors among the ranks. Volunteers kept trickling in from back in the FWL, mostly fellow Southwesterners unable to put up any longer with Thomas Marik's dictatorial ways or his attempts to impose the Word of Blake as the League's official religion, or simply avid to seek glory among the Trinity Worlds' favorite sons and daughters. Finally, no few Townians had stuck to the Seventeenth when it lifted offworld, including the Rooster, once-and-again FedComb MechWarriors such as Pik Vosloo and Ganz Harter, late of the Towne Popular Militia, and even some disenchanted Dracs like Mouse Omizuki and her fellow Desolation Angel Johnny "Smoke" Herlihy.

The Caballeros wound up with enough machines and pilots to create not only Omizuki's aerospace lance and a dedicated artillery-support lance—sadly without long-time chief artillerist Diana Vásquez who had been executed by Howard Blaylock's quisling regime on Towne—but an entire Fourth Battalion.

Cassie didn't feel altogether easy with that, and she wasn't the only one. Fourth Batt was led by fresh-minted Force Commander Robert Begay, callsign Navajo Wolf. Bobby the Wolf was a devilishly handsome man with a mane of straight blue-black hair and eyes that flashed like obsidian mirrors in his leather-dark face. The long-time boss of Cochise Company, he was in line for the new command. And too successful as a combat leader and *Griffin* pilot to be denied the promotion.

But there were some *problems* with Bobby. For one thing, he hated Cassie. His old *Wolverine* had been the very first BattleMech Cassie downed, back on Larsha where she grew up. That wasn't enough to unfit him for command, even in Cassie's mind, but he was also crazy. The names he had chosen for himself and his machine, Navajo Wolf and Skinwalker, both signified a witch who was also a werewolf. The Navajos of the Trinity took that sort of thing very seriously: it was as if a Cowboy MechWarrior had chosen to call his ride "Baby-Sacrificing Satan Worshipper," or if a *norteño* used "Protestant" for a callsign. He had made himself an outcast from his own people; no Navajos or Apaches would consent to serve in Fourth. And aside from the tact issues his choices in nomenclature pointed up, his wild-eyed brand of courage might not translate too well to a larger command. Cochise Company hadn't been the safest unit in the regiment to be in as it was.

There had been rumblings already . . . a drumbeat throb

in the sky drew Cassie's eyes up, and her thoughts away from Begay.

"Here comes your chopper," Omizuki said. "Catch you later." She waved and strode away.

And here, here came the Rooster, with his trademark bandy-legged banty-cock strut, looking as if the whole damned Black Pearl of the Combine was his personal hen-house, and Teddy the K, his Ottomo, and all of ISF be damned. Cassie got a guarded look again. She respected his skills as scout and operator, and that respect was not lightly given. She'd go through a door or window with him at her back any hour of night or day. But trusting him as a combat comrade and trusting him as a man were beasts of two distinct genera.

He's going to pull rank, she told herself with a sinking feeling, *pull me off this and go himself.* The thought sickened her. Her *familia* needed her. And she needed . . . to be needed.

"Hey, Cass," he said as he approached.

"Senior Lieutenant."

He cocked an eyebrow at the unaccustomed formality. "Just wanted to make sure you're squared away on this, nothing else you need."

"I'm ready," she said, bracing herself.

He nodded. "All right, Lead Scout. Go do some scouting. I'll catch you when the rest of us hit that place they call Cinema City." And he went rolling off, leaving Cassie blinking.

The chopper touched down with a swirl of noise and bits of debris.

═══ 5 ═══

*Takashi Kurita Memorial Spaceport, Imperial City
Luthien
Pesht Military District, Draconis Combine
20 June 3058*

A small man in a shirt printed with a war of colors hopped
from the hatch of the VTOL and came running toward the
waiting Caballeros, bent low to clear the whirling rotor.
Once out of the circle of death he straightened to his full
height, which wasn't much.

"Hi, I'm Mishcha Kurosawa, of the Voice of the
Dragon," he said with a big smile full of bright white teeth.
"Welcome to Luthien, Black Pearl of the Combine. I'll be
your guide." Voice of the Dragon was the Internal Security
Force's propaganda division.

Standing next to Cassie, the stocky woman dressed in
businesslike skirt-suit, a dusting of freckles across her
dark, broad-cheekboned face and hair the color of red wine,
nodded. "Thank you. I'm Force Commander Dolores Gallegos. I'm the Executive Officer for the Seventeenth Recon
Regiment."

Mishcha smiled again, shook the hand she offered,
bowed over it. Cassie, the Caballeros' resident expert on
Drac culture, had briefed the contact party in advance that it
would be a big help to use titles whenever possible, even to
Draconians as evidently accustomed to dealing with *gaijin*
as Mishcha was. The XO part was a typical Caballero diver-
gence from common military usage. The actual second
in command was Gavilán Camacho; Red Gallegos was actually a combination of S-1 and S-4, handling personnel,

supply, transport, and of course accommodations for the regiment. Her own description of the job was "chief cook and bottle-washer."

Her rank of Force Commander was brand new. Although Red was doing the same job she had done since long-time XO Marisol Cabrera had been killed defending Don Carlos on Hachiman two years ago, she had been held no rank in the Caballeros; she was a civilian auxiliary. That seeming lack of standing had drawn her some static on Towne, even though the Davions were much less strung on titles than the Dracs.

So, Don Carlos swore her in and jumped her to FC. Even among all the Caballero egos, inflated and delicate as bubbles, nobody popped. Red's job was staff level, she did it very well, and frankly, no one else was any too eager to get stuck with it.

Besides, while Red was no MechWarrior, she was a combat vet. There were few noncombatants in the regiment anyway, at least not over the age of eight. Red had traded her share of shots with ill-intentioned strangers, and the fact that she didn't know how to *pilota* BattleMech didn't mean she hadn't fought in one. Having been trained by chief artillerist Diana Vásquez, she had taken over the controls of the experimental OBK-M1O *O-Bakemono*—a heavy support 'Mech and knockoff of the Clan *Naga*—lent the Seventeenth by Luthien Armor Works during the battle of Port Howard on Towne. Her big Shigunga Arrow IV missiles had smashed a key Black Dragon counterattack, saving many Caballero butts and ensuring the fall of the planetary capital.

Red Gallegos introduced her companions: Cassie and Father Doctor Roberto "Call Me Bob" García, himself recently promoted to captain. The Jesuit was getting some last-minute tips from his new assistant, Lieutenant Senior Grade Daffodil Chu, a small plump woman with short dark hair and a complexion that reminded Cassie of uncooked dough. He excused himself and joined the others in a bent-over dash beneath the feathered blades.

The VTOL leapt into the air. The big bulbous DropShip

Uyeshiba and the marching 'Mechs assumed the semblance of toys, glistening with rain.

"Even from up here," Father Doctor Bob murmured, "the Luthien mob looks orderly."

Mishcha, who was sitting on a fold-down seat in the passenger compartment with his guests, showed him a grinful of teeth. "People around here aren't wild like they are in the Federated Commonwealth," he said. "Or even on Hachiman. But we still know how to have a good time."

"I'm sure," García said heartily.

It might have struck the Voice of the Dragon guide strange had he realized the portly priest was the Seventeenth's new Chief Intelligence Officer. Or maybe not. In the Draconis Combine it was taken for granted that, on any kind of significant expedition, *somebody* was a spy. And indeed, Father Bob was there to keep his eyes open, but mainly he was going because he was the most sophisticated of the Cabelleros, and the most diplomatic.

The helicopter was flying northwest, passing over the outermost of the blastwall-ringed landing pits of the Takashi Kurita Memorial Spaceport. Ahead lay the southeastern fringe of Imperial City. Here it was mostly warehouses and transport yards, changing to grim compounds with razor-tape loops topping chain-link fences, the *buraku,* or barracks, in which masses of Unproductives were housed, run by an agency with the arch acronym ETA, which was the word—*eta*—for the pariahs of old Japanese society. These gave way in turn to the characteristic cement-slab blocks of Worker-class housing. From the center of the great urban sprawl rose a cabochon of glittering black, glass and marble and polished teak, in obsidian contrast to the predominantly drab surroundings.

"There you see the heart of Imperial City," Mishcha intoned, "which is the heart of the Draconis Combine. Truly, this is the Black Pearl."

"It's beautiful," García said.

"Wonderful," Red Gallegos said, angling in her seat for a better view out the port. "Will we fly closer to it?"

"It must be truly breathtaking at night," Father Doctor Bob added.

"Regrettably, our current course will take us south of the city center," Mishcha said, pitching his voice to penetrate the rotor chop and turbine howl, "and we have appointments we must keep. However, you are the Coordinator's guests. If you wish an aerial tour of Imperial City—by day or night, Captain García—"

"Call me Bob."

The guide grinned and bobbed his head. "Sure, Captain Bob. As I say, any questions or requests you have, come right to me and I'll take care of them. Just think of me as your *kuromaku*."

Cassie's eyes widened. *"Kuromaku?"* she echoed in Japanese. " 'Fixer?' That's *ingo*, isn't it?"

Mishcha grinned still wider. Despite his first name he had a very Japanese appearance, oval face, pronounced epicanthic folds at the corners of his dark eyes, wheat-colored skin. "That's right. Sorry. Yakuza slang is very popular on Luthien right now."

A look of appraisal came into his eyes. "You must be the scout. Lieutenant Senior Grade Suthorn. They told me about you."

"So ka? What did they tell you?"

"Mostly that you spoke flawless Japanese—which you do."

"Domo." Thanks.

"Do-itashimashite." You're welcome. "They also told me under no circumstances ever to let you out of my sight."

Cassie grinned.

She looked across the compartment to see Red watching her with a suspicious look in her eyes. The XO looked away when Cassie noticed her.

Cassie pushed her chin forward, crossed her arms and let her back slide down the padded interior of the compartment. The chopper smelled of sweat and lubricant and the eye-watering formaldehyde tang characteristic of alcohol-burning Combine internal combustion engines.

It wasn't that Red thought Cassie might be hatching some betrayal scheme with their guide; the scout had proven her devotion to the Caballeros in blood and hardship many times over. Red disapproved of Cassie on general principles, as had her predecessor Marisol Cabrera, and she also did not like the fact that Cassie was close friends with her husband Richard, a.k.a. Zuma, the Chief Aztech. Had she been a more traditional *norteña* of the Trinity worlds she might well have shot the scout for spending so much time with him. But as defiantly—sometimes pathetically—as the 'lleros tried to cling to their cultural identities, they had to accept some measure of compromise to function as Caballeros. The regiment was *la familia* for everybody, and when all was said they all were every bit as cut off from their homes as Cassie herself.

Unlike Cabrera, Red Gallegos did not allow her disdain for what she saw as Cassie's scandalous character to color her assessment of Cassie's abilities. Each woman respected what the other did for the regiment, and so they could work together smoothly.

Beneath them the city ended as if severed by the stroke of a *katana*. Below them a river valley flowed away to the west, its steep walls rising to rolling hills, green parkland and forests surrounding occasional industrial islands bounded by high cement walls. The ride smoothed as the chopper left the great urban heat sink behind.

"That's the Kado-guchi Valley down there, isn't it?" García asked. The shine in his dark brown eyes showed there was nothing pro forma about his interest now. He was a passionate student of history, and history had been made below.

"That's right," Mishcha said proudly. "It was right beneath us that our Coordinator stopped the Clans cold in 3052. Many brave deeds were performed by both sides, and many great warriors fell like cherry blossoms."

Red Gallegos's thick lips curled in an expression of disgust. *"Los atéos,"* she murmured in tones of malediction.

Mishcha looked at her with his head cocked like a curious bird's. He was either well-briefed on foreign body-language and intonational nuance or spoke Spanish, or both.

"You disdain the Clans? It was my understanding that you Southwesterners gave honor to a brave foe, as do we of the Combine."

"Men," Red said with unaccustomed shortness. "Not devils." The way she said *devils* made it clear she was not speaking metaphorically.

"The characteristic, ah, Clan means of reproduction," Father Doctor Bob said in his best pedantic mode, "is very disturbing to the Southwestern psyche. It strikes many of us as actively blasphemous. Our warriors commonly refer to the Clanners as 'mudheads'."

"Ah, yes, I have heard of them," Mishcha said. "They are supernatural beings often represented by actors in ceremonies held among your Indian peoples. They are clowns, yes? Figures of fun."

Cassie laughed. She would dearly love to see the ISF's dossiers on the peoples and cultures of the Trinity. Trying to make them intelligible to analysts deep in the heart of the Dragon would fry the mind of any self-respecting Metsuke agent.

"Clowns, yes," she said, "figures of fun, no. They're sinister beings, something mothers use to frighten bad children. They're the products of incest among the gods."

The guide goggled at her. Cassie hadn't been much closer to the worlds of the Southwestern Trinity than he likely had. But the Pueblos among the Caballeros kept up their rituals as assiduously as did the unit's Catholic majority. She had witnessed *kachina* ceremonies herself often enough, at least those open to outsiders. The secret ones were guarded as jealously from fellow 'lleros as from the rest of the universe. A Caballero foolish enough to try spying would simply disappear, and the loss would be accepted by comrades and relatives with no thought of payback, despite the fondess for the blood feud typical of most Southwestern cultures. It was part of the web of paradox and complexity that made Southwestern society so hard for outsiders to grasp, much less integrate themselves into. Which was why, after eleven years, Cassie was still referred to by her comrades in the Seventeenth by the Clan word of Abtakha—outsider.

The helicopter cut south from the river valley. It crossed a line of hills and emerged over a broad basin bordered by forests of tall conifers. A walled compound occupied the center of it. A road spooled away east over a brushy ridge. To the west tall, vaguely humanoid figures glinted in fugitive sunbeams as they lumbered toward one another.

"BattleMechs?" Red said. "It looks like they're fighting."

"Filming would be a better word, Force Commander," Mishcha said. "They're shooting a battle scene for the new Johnny Tchang holovid—the story of the Clan attack on Luthien a few years back. Welcome to Eiga-toshi—Cinema City, as you would call it." The Seventeenth would be housed on the grounds of the holovid studio, which possessed dormitory-like housing sufficient to a group the size of the Caballeros and their families. Their 'Mechs would be parked in a big prefab hangar annexed to the north side of the compound proper, just outside the wall that surrounded the Cinema City complex.

Cassie stared out the port as the pilot swung west to give them a better view. "That looks like a *Vulture* down there. And that's a *Thor,* got to be." She frowned at the guide. "The DCMS isn't letting go of captured Clan machines for a silly holovid, is it?"

Or maybe, she thought, *the gnomes at Luthien Armor Works let go of some more of their Clan-knockoff prototypes, like that* O-Bakemono *they lent us for poor Diana to try out?*

"Ah, no. Give the credit to our glorious Coordinator himself. As *Gunji no Kanrei,* during the fight at Basin Lake north of here, he thought to lure the Jaguar Guardsinto a field sown with vibrabombs to serve as mines. To do so he ordered technicians to build sheet-metal superstructures to make common *LoaderMechs* appear to be actual BattleMechs such as *Thunderbolts* and *Archers*. The Jaguars believed the trick, and the Otomo caught them in the minefield and gave them a fine beating."

Mishcha laughed. So did the Caballeros. *Too bad we*

didn't have that trick on Towne, Cassie thought. *We'll have to keep it in mind.*

"What worked for the so-clever Smoke Jaguars will surely work for holovid audiences, yes? So behold, we have all the OmniMechs we want at our disposal."

The compound itself was huge, at least a square kilometer. It encompassed vehicle parks, ranks of prefab structures, hangar-like studios, a Japanese-style garden, and an archaic village of huts with thatched-reed roofs and paper walls. The helicopter swooped low over a procession of men dressed in oddments of ancient Japanese armor, trudging back from a shoot with plastic weapons slung over their shoulders, and landed in front of a sandy-colored oblong barracks.

"They aren't in the same picture as the battling 'Mechs, are they?" Father Doctor Bob asked their escort as they dismounted, with a wave at the marching spearmen.

"Oh, no. We're also doing a historic epic. *Chushingura.* Very stirring subject for my people."

"The tale of the forty-seven *ronin*?"

Mishcha beamed. "You are familiar with the story? You are a very educated man, Captain Bob."

With Red by his side he set off toward the barracks, which would house the Caballeros during their several-week stay on Luthien. Cassie hung back, giving the black sleeve of García's cassock a discreet tug.

"Hang a moment, Captain Bob?" she suggested *sotto voce.*

He nodded. "Captain Bob. You know, Cassiopeia, I rather like the sound of that."

"I *don't* like the sound of Cassiopeia," she reminded him, not that she expected it to do any good. They began walking toward the building more slowly than the lead pair. "Just wondering if you noticed the road cutting east of here?"

"Why, yes, certainly. What of it?"

"Cut right straight toward the spaceport, didn't it?"

He blinked. "Why, so it did. You know, I wondered whether our BattleMechs were going to have to march here by way of Imperial City proper."

"I wonder why we flew that route. Could be our hosts just wanted to give us a better snap on their pretty city. *Or*—"

He nodded. "Or there might be something on the more direct flight-path they didn't want us to see. D'you think that's significant?"

"Probably not. Just something, y'know, to keep in mind."

He colored and hung his head. "I'm not suited for this job. I've said so all along. I'm not cut out to be a spy at all, must less a spy-master."

Cassie patted him on the arm—tentatively, so as not to give him ideas. He was a man of ideas, was Father Doctor Bob. "Here, now, here," she told him. "Don't take it that way."

"But I just don't know what I'm *doing*."

"None of us is trained in Intel. That's why Don Carlos hired Lieutenant Chu to be your head assistant. She *is* trained, and she worked a lot of years for Davy M1I4. Shoot, she's still a Stealthy Fox spy, only we're not supposed to know that."

"The Colonel should have made her intelligence chief, not me."

"Get real! We're not going to have an outsider for S-2." The word *outsider* kind of stuck coming out. "Besides, you've got all that shifty Jesuit training under your belt. You're a trained shrink; you know how people work. And you know all that stuff about other cultures and history and things. Unless all that doesn't really matter as much as you always told me it did—"

She gave him a look from the corner of her blue-smoke almond eyes. He liked to trap her and lecture her on history, a subject that only interested her when it impinged on her chosen craft of killing men and 'Mechs. He was big on urging her to broaden her horizons. By that he meant, her sexual horizons, with middle-aged members of the clergy. Catholic priests everywhere still took vows of celibacy, but to a Southwesterner that didn't mean quite the same thing necessarily as it did to everybody else in the Inner Sphere. Which was the way of most things. You had your Trinity, and then you had your rest of Creation.

He nodded slowly. "Those things do matter, Cassiopeia. In fact, if you'd only let me, I could help you see for yourself the wonders—"

She started walking farther away from him. He was getting a dangerous shine to his eyes.

"Not right now. For the moment, just focus on the fact that I wasn't trying to shoot you down. Just help with a bit of on-the-job-training. *¿Comprende?*"

"*Sí.*" They walked up the cement steps and into the dusty cool dim.

Off-duty cast and crewfolk all came to hang by the big main gates of *Eiga-toshi* when the Caballeros arrived. The make-believe BattleMechs had long since been put to bed. Now it was time to gape in awe at the real thing.

As Buck Evans' big *Orion* lumbered into the compound a hovercraft wove around its right leg, cutting it dangerously close. Buck let a couple of blasts from the air horn he had mounted atop the combo SRM/Narc-pod launcher on the 'Mech's right shoulder. In response, someone in the open-topped vehicle vented off a shrill rebel yell that would have done credit to any Cowboy.

The hovercar slowed, straightened, and made right for where Cassie stood in the front row of onlookers. Extras, grips, production assistants, and minor execs scattered. Cassie, Red, and Father Doctor Bob held their ground. Cassie unsnapped the buttoned breast pocket of the olive-drab FWL fatigue blouse she wore under her battered leather Aero-Space-jock jacket and reached inside.

At the last possible instant the blower jock threw his machine into a broadside skid, hurling an ocher-dust tsunami over the Caballero trio. Red and García threw arms up before their eyes. Cassie smoothly consummated the act, already begun, of slipping on a pair of wraparound shades.

With a dying whine of twin driver-fans the hovercar settled to the packed earth of the compound. A lanky familiar figure with a black topknot and a black patch over one eye popped up from the driver's seat and scrambled like a monkey over the windscreen.

"Buntaro Mayne," Cassie said. "What's up?"

The MechWarrior took skittery baby-steps down the flat sloping snout of the hovercar and jumped to the ground. He had a gold assault-rifle cartridge slung on a chain around his neck.

"Happenin', Cass?" he said. They exchanged the complicated Secret Handshake that had evolved over the Hachiman garrison months between the 17th and the 9th Ghost Regiment during the Caballeros' tenure on Hachiman, involving a forearm bash, a bump of fist-base against fist-base, and high, medium, and low fives. The two units had become fast friends back during the Seventeenth's stint on Hachiman two years before.

The Caballero BattleMechs continued to lumber by as *Heruzu Enjeruzu* piled from the hovercar like baby scorpions from Mommy's chitinous back. They mobbed the three 'lleros for a boisterous reunion with longtime friends and erstwhile—and unwilling—enemies.

Last of all, lean and mean, long and languid, a woman with wine-red hair unfolded her considerable self from the front passenger's seat and stilted forward on legs that went on forever in tight pants made of the hide of some appalling Hachimanite ocean carnivore. She gave Cassie a slow grin and a nod.

Cassie grinned back and actually let the woman hug her. *Tai-sa* Eleanor Shimazu, commander of the 9th Ghost Legion, a.k.a. *Heruzu Enjeruzu*—and, by the way, the Yakuza *oyabun* of *oyabun* for the planet Hachiman—was more of a close friend to Cassie's best buddy Kali MacDougall than to Cassie herself, but that still brought the much-taller woman closer than the scout allowed most people to get.

It was just as well that she didn't feel as close to Lainie as she still did to Kali, Cassie realized, looking up at her friend. Lainie had changed, too, in the months since the 17th left Hachiman, but Cassie couldn't put her finger on exactly what it was.

"I heard about you tearing *Bishonen* Kusunoki a new one in person," Shimazu said. "Couldn't have happened to a nicer guy."

"He more tore himself one," Cassie said. "Good to see you, Lainie."

"You, too. I could even almost feel sorry for those Black Dragons knowing you and the rest of your bunch of misfits were on their case." She smiled grimly. "*Almost.*"

A sudden roar and a shadow that blotted what light managed to make it down with the drizzle that still seeped down intermittently made even Cassie duck. A *Wasp* was rising above them on the thrust-columns of its three Rawlings 52 jump jets. As it passed overhead it tucked its little antenna-horned head and performed a flawless forward somersault. Then it landed about thirty meters into the compound, its right foot crushing a stand from which a vendor was selling teriyaki beef on a stick. The vendor bailed just in time.

"Oh, dear," Father Doctor Bob said.

"I'd give it about a nine-five," Buntaro Mayne said, "but that landing's gonna cost some points."

The former booth-operator was jumping from foot to foot, shaking his fists and screaming imprecations at the light BattleMech. Apologies cascaded from his Cowboy's own external speaker system.

"Lieutenant Junior Grade Payson's still a confirmed Sierra-for-brains, I see," Lainie said. "I'm glad certain things don't change. It fosters the comforting illusion of stability in this cherry-blossom world."

"This is Jinjiro Coleman, the concierge," Cassie told the clump of her comrades who were getting a guided tour of their new digs while Red and García negotiated the pots-and-pans aspects of the 17th's stay on lovely Luthien. "Be nice to him. He's boss of these barracks."

Jinjiro bobbed his head, beamed. "Any trouble you have, you come to me," he said. "Any trouble at all. Soon, no trouble." And he grinned wider.

In his brown jumpsuit he stood 170 centimeters or so, a bit above average for the Combine—on Hachiman he would have towered—with brown hair, faintly red in tint, brushed over a bald spot on top. His face was round, his eyes almond-shaped and brown, and the fact that his smile never quite seemed to reach them appeared to rise more from weariness, or maybe sadness, than any kind of guile. His age was impossible to determine, other than that he wasn't young; like a lot of Dracs with a healthy slug of Asian genes—like Cassie herself, for that matter—he wore his cloak of years with relative grace. He was a strongly-built man, thick in the middle and in the wrists. When he shook hands, as he punctiliously insisted on doing with all and sundry, including Lainie, Buntaro, and a handful of other Ghosts who had tagged along, his grip was dry and strong.

They walked away along the top-floor corridor. The superintendent vanished down a stairwell. The barracks were strikingly well-designed and constructed by Draconis Combine standards, comparable to those Uncle Chandy provided his favored employees, such as the 17th Recon. The corridor was wide and well-ventilated, its illumination augmented by regular skylights overhead. Floors and wall framework were of blond local timber, its natural color preserved behind clear varnish, and the walls themselves were of a white synthetic designed to mimic the translucent brightness of *shoji*, rice paper, while being more durable and easier to clean. And Jinjiro kept all spotless and smelling subtly of a native conifer.

"These're pretty spiffy digs," remarked Buck Evans. "That con-see-airge keeps 'em up right. He seemed like a nice enough fella, too."

He should *seem nice*, Cassie thought. She had taken the precaution of bribing him with a bottle of fine brandy from the Ophir region of Towne's main continent, Hyboria. In fact the building superintendent had been pleasant enough before the brandy, but such gifts were not considered bribes in the Combine. They were the way business was done, one of the lubricants which kept society's wheels turning.

But then, it was for knowing things like that Cassie was sent with the advance party, far more than to scout out any possible ambushes or booby-traps, which even Cassie, paranoid as an alley-cat, did not expect to find awaiting them on a movie lot.

"Yeah, maybe he seemed like a nice fella," Cowboy said darkly, stilting along with a musical jingle of the spurs he wore attached to his bulky insulated MechWarrior's boots, "but maybe looks can be deceivin'. Didn't anybody else see the back of his arm where it stuck out of its sleeve—all covered with them fish-scale tattoos? Now, I might know not know much—"

"You got a real talent for understatement, *carnal*," said Jesse James Leyva over his shoulder. Known as Outlaw, Leyva sported a black handlebar mustache that was the perfect complement to his dark complexion and historic name.

Cowboy ignored the gibe from his pal and rival. "—But I know me a Yak tattoo when I see it. What's that called now? Itsahootie?"

"*Irezumi*," Cassie corrected. "And if you say *gesundheit*, I'll kill you."

Cowboy produced a choking snort that made his eyes crossed. "And what's wrong with being a Yakuza?" demanded Buntaro Mayne holding up a fist to allow his sleeve to slide down and expose his own intricate and colorful skin art. Lainie just laughed.

"Well, yeah," Cowboy said, "but you guys are *good* Yaks." He looked back over his shoulder, as if expecting to see the concierge creeping along behind them in black holovid-ninja garb. "What if he's one of them Black Dragons?"

"What's a Yak doing holding down an honest job, anyway?" Buck demanded.

Buntaro gave him his own one-eyed glare, then laughed. "Well, OK. We're warriors, not Workers. I'll give you that."

"He's semi-retired after long and loyal service," Cassie said. "He got this job, which is pretty plush by local reckoning, as a reward for work well done. Notice he had all his fingers? He never screwed up in a big way."

"But why would the movie people hire somebody out of the local gang?" asked ash-blonde Raven O'Conner, who took her name from the reconnaissance 'Mech she drove. "They have to know what he is."

"A big part of what a Yak org does is labor contracting," Cassie said. "The headman of Luthien probably supplies most of the unskilled and semiskilled workers here in *Eiga-toshi*. You don't expect ISF to clean its own floors and cook its own food, do you?"

The other 'lleros stopped and stared at her. "What was that word you used there, Cass?" Raven asked.

"*Eiga-toshi*? Cinema City?"

"No, not that," Jesse James said. "That other one. Those three little initials?"

"ISF?"

"Those're the ones," Raven affirmed. "What's Drac Internal Security got to do with this place?"

A snicker escaped from Lainie's long fine nose. Buntaro squeezed his good eye shut and shook his head.

"You guys knew the Voice of the Dragon owned and operated this place, right?" Cassie asked.

"Yeah," Cowboy said. "But we reckoned that meant, like 'Voice of the Dragon Productions,' or something."

"It means that, too," Cassie said, "but what it all runs down to is still the Drac information ministry. Which is a wholly-owned subsidiary of the Internal Security Force."

Cowboy pointed a trembling accusatory finger at her. "And here I thought we were just coming for this big party, and it was gonna be the plushest gig ever! I sure shoulda known better. Nothin' with you involved is ever that durn simple!"

Lainie laughed out loud. "It's taken you how many years to figure that out?"

6

"**S**o, my pretty," a voice from behind her said with a bit of a slur, "how do you find our Black Pearl of the Combine?"

Cassie forced her face to smooth away the reflex frown, lest the man in the DCMS dress uniform who stood behind her see it reflected in the smoked-glass window through which she regarded Imperial City's nighttime heart. She had heard him approach through conversation-buzz and music that throbbed like a wound in the multi-level party pit scooped out of the upper levels of some noble's high-rise. From the falls of his boots on padded drizzle-colored floor tiles she had known he was drunk before he spoke.

Careful, girl, she reminded herself. While she was ostensibly here, on this planet and at this party, as an honored guest, her status was provisional, could vanish like a moth in a Bessemer furnace. The very fact that the man behind her—tall, athletic but going to seed—was present at this party in honor of Luthien's barbarian visitors indicated he had plenty of pull. Whereas women in the Combine were still generally regarded as a type of domestic livestock, albeit prone to unruliness. And Cassie was by far the lowest-ranked person present except for the servants.

Then there was the helpful Drac tradition that drunks, like very young children, could do no wrong. This *pendejo* could get awful free and easy with her. Sweat from more than the overamped heat in the body-crowded room ran down inside the high stiff collar of her dress tunic. The dance beat pounded behind her eyes.

With a motion that would have required keen and sober eyes to detect she slumped her shoulders and let her spine curve. She let her mouth sag and her eye-corners droop. Then she turned, trying to project unprepossessingness: *I smell bad. I have diseases. Also, I weep a lot.*

What she saw standing there was a man with unruly straw-colored hair that had a tendency to get into his mud-green eyes. The way the flesh was loosened at the edges of his big oblong face, and his nose reddened, she guessed his current condition wasn't too far off his baseline. A samurai was supposed to be a ready drinker; Dracs didn't take the puritanical view of what the Townies, say, would've termed alcohol abuse. By the looks of him, though, he was getting near a point where his performance would start to degrade, and that the Dragon *did* frown on. Still, he wore the *katakana* numeral four on his collar, along with the aerospace insignia on his shoulder-boards. A *Sho-sho,* a brigadier general, was generally a staffer, so maybe his days of pushing plasma out of the ass end of a *Sholagar* were as far behind him as unbroken nose capillaries.

"My lord?" she said, putting a nasal whine to her voice.

Subtlety was lost on this one. He smiled and patted her cheek. "If Luthien is a pearl, then surely you are a, a—a lovely tropical flower."

Now, that's *suave.* The Caballero dress uniform she wore was modified from Free Worlds League issue; she didn't want people at this party to see her in civilian garb, or associate her with same. Unfortunately, the uniform—whose stiff-necked white tunic resembled that of the official DCMS issue—did nothing to conceal the slim perfection of her figure. The jackboots rolled up the legs of her white trousers to the tops of her thighs had the unfortunate effect of accentuating the round muscularity of her rump. Silently she cursed herself for letting Raven talk her into wearing a wig done into a confection of looped braids over her real hair, which was still pretty stubbly after being seared off in Kali's *Atlas.* Though it served the intended effect of making an impact on an observer's mind, helping create a gestalt markedly different from any silhouette she'd display in the field, it also gave the impression she was a woman minded to attract masculine attention.

"My lord is too kind," she said. "Now if you will only just excuse me, General, I was on my way to powder my nose."

She turned, slipped past him and down a brief flight of stairs, making toward the nearest exit. "Wait!" he called after her. "Don't rush off, little *gaijin*. We've hardly just begun—"

She sensed him closing, reaching for her. She set her jaw. *If he grabs me*—no. There was always a way, if one kept alert to one's surroundings . . .

In the midst of a conversation-clump was a meter-high pedestal of polished teak, with the miniature figure of a Kamakura-period samurai in full armor standing on it. It was a damnfool thing to leave lying around at a party, but that wasn't her lookout. As if to avoid a large quartermaster brigadier who was trying without success to impress Kali, she swerved, passing close to the pedestal. As she went by she gave it a quick sideways bump with her knee, causing it to tilt slightly and spill the figurine onto the floor behind her.

The sotted *Sho-sho* stepped on it and pitched forward onto his face. He bounced up with considerable alacrity and a bellow of anger. "That bitch! She tripped me!"

At the exit, defiant reflex made Cassie stop and turn. She did so in time to see two giant smiling retirees from the All-Combine Sumo League materialize on either side of her pursuer. At the same time a tall figure with a long black topknot, broad-shouldered and suave in a black *happi*coat printed with crabs and bamboo latticework in pale blue, sauntered up to him with a drink in his hand, which he proffered.

"*Sho-sho* Donaldson," the tall man said in a rich baritone. "Get yourself around some of this fine plum brandy. It'll smooth out the wrinkles in your *wa*."

The general's flushed face knotted, and he made as if to knock the drink from the other man's hand. The two big *sumitori*, still grinning like weasels in a henhouse, squeezed along either side of him, catching him in a big flesh vise. They air-marched him down a set of steps and through obliviously gyrating dancers and darting witch-ball lights to a side exit. Maybe this was the Draconis Combine, and maybe drunks and children could get away with anything, but *this* was a high-level high-visibility function with many important *gaijin* to hand. Face could not be lost to embarrassing incidents.

It was little inconsistencies like this that gave the Combine its unique charm.

The man in the *happi*-coat caught Cassie's eye and nodded. She recognized him. Aside from Subhash Indrahar himself, who was at pains to maintain his benevolent Smiling One persona in public, this man was the only other member of the ISF's leadership to court publicity. She gave him a quick smile.

I've put in my appearance here, she thought, *done my duty. Not that I ever wanted to come.* The idea of an operative whose job description comprised a great deal of undercover snooping and pooping appearing in her own persona at one of *the* parties of the social season made her head hurt. But she had been invited by name. Red Gallegos, in her official capacity as liaison officer, thought it would be rude for Cassie to pull a no-show. Don Carlos backed her.

And aside from making her face potentially all too familiar, it wasn't getting her job done. The air was curdled with the smell of conspiracy, but it wasn't *that kind* of conspiracy. The glittering attendees were busy plotting how to get this one in bed, or maneuver that one into committing some gaffe at one of the court functions which, like rumors and parties, were flying thick and fast as SRM salvos in the midst of a major 'Mech battle in the run-in to the Coordinator's Birthday. There was nothing for her here. If any of these gilded pheasants were Black Dragon fellow-travelers, they were keeping the fact to themselves. Had threat been here, she would have tasted it.

She felt a longing for the streets and the night, the way a desert-stranded frog yearns for cool water. She had work to do elsewhere.

Next time I'll glue a fake mole on my bloody cheek!

She was gone.

* * *

The man who had intercepted the drunk sauntered toward the balcony. His eye had caught a hint of something most interesting outside. As he slid through the crowd, effortless as an eel, he swirled the dark purple liquid in the snifter he had offered and smiled slightly to himself. Though he cultivated the manner of a *tsu*, a rakish man-of-the-world—and the lifestyle as well, he'd be the first to admit—he deplored rudeness. Politeness was a Combine cultural tradition he was only too happy to help promulgate.

It was a very Zen door, a Gateless Gate for true, an air curtain that kept the overstuffed warmth in and the nocturnal spring chill out—*gaijin* tech, old news in Marik space and the Federated Commonwealth, but only just becoming available as something other than contraband in the Combine as the industrial sector, pumped by the huge trade expansion made possible by Theodore's reforms, began sending tentative tentacles groping out of the old milspec mass into the consumer-goods zone. Of course, they'd had these goodies on Hachiman for a decade, and, he noted with a wry smile as he stepped through the invisible barrier into the Imperial City night that hit him in the face like a splash of spring water, the ones making an appearance on Luthien were manufactured by Hachiman Taro Electronics, owned by one Chandrasekhar Kurita. He'd had one installed in his own loft apartment, located on the fringes of Imperial City's *ukiyo,* the pleasure district.

"You saved that *bakayaro*'s life," said the tall woman with the strident red hair shaved away from her temples as he came up behind her. The shaved temples revealed her instantly as a MechWarrior. "Is he really worth more to the Dragon alive than dead?"

He laughed. The air curtain had the fortunate effect of deadening the music. Their host had execrable taste.

"That's not my decision to make, thank the *bosatsu*," he said. He moved to the rail alongside, rested his forearms on polished teak and gazed out over the heart of the city. The uniform blackness of the Palace District buildings made them eerie by night. Sometimes the rows and cluster of dim-lit windows seemed to float in emptiness, as if they were unusually orderly constellations in the sky itself. Other nights—such as this one—the tall teak and glass buildings were great blots of shadow against darkness, like mountains flecked with campfires, or orbital battle stations.

"Is she really so formidable, then?" he asked. "She seemed mainly interested in avoiding confrontation. Wise, under the circumstances."

"Lieutenant Senior Grade Suthorn would do nothing before witnesses that might shame her colonel," the redhead said. "But, never fear, if that fool had succeeded in manhandling her, he'd have been found come morning floating face-down in some canal, neatly folded." "Folding" was one of the numberless yak euphemisms for murder.

He nodded his narrow head. "*So ka?* Our brigadier was really in danger of reenacting the climax of *Inherit the Shadow*?"

She gave him a quizzical look.

"A twenty-ninth century Davion adventure holovid. You're not a fan of classic movies?" The redhead shook. He shrugged and asked, "She's really that good?"

"You should be well aware of that already, Deputy Director Migaki."

Takura Migaki gave her a world-weary smile. "I'm a propagandist, not a secret policeman. I don't have endless access to intelligence dossiers—'need to know' and all that. I did get to read the condensed version of her file, I will admit, as I did for all our more important *gaijin* guests. The better to spin tales of their deeds to the greater glory of the Dragon and our illustrious Coordinator. May I offer you this fine brandy? Spurning it was not the least of *Sho-sho* Donaldson's unwisdoms this night."

"I'd be honored to drink the Coordinator's health in your brandy, Migaki-*sama*." She accepted the glass, raised it, drank. All the while her eyes held his. Her eyes were maroon, with highlights of flame within.

"I read enough of her file to suspect I was doing the man a favor, even though my Helping Hands won't coddle him," he said. The redhead was several centimeters taller than he. *Truly magnificent,* he thought.

She laughed low in her throat. "*Sewanuki,*" she echoed. "That's good." "Helping Hands"—*sewanuki*—was yak-speak for a strong-arm man, but its main, arch sense was "drunk-roller."

"You use our thieves' talk with panache, Migaki-*sama*."

"Takura, please. And considering its source, I cherish that compliment, *Tai-sa* Shimazu."

She arched a narrow brow. "You know who I am?"

"Your file also happened across my desk, since your Heruzu Enjeruzu were invited here to be honored too. Fascinating reading. And I'm enchanted and honored to make your acquaintance at last, *Tai-sa*."

"So ka?" The eyebrow stayed arched.

"Indeed." He took her hand, raised it to his lips, and kissed it.

She made a low sound in her throat and smiled, an expression half-ironic, half-predatory. "Such a very Occidental gesture," she murmured, "from the man charged with preserving our Combine traditions."

He held her hand an extra heartbeat before releasing it. Then he shrugged. "Our culture's evolving, thanks to the Coordinator's reforms. For the better, I think—and not just because it's my duty to say so. And it's always been the Dragon's way to assimilate the best from other cultures, *iie*?"

She laughed. "You're a glib scoundrel, Takura Migaki."

It was his turn to laugh. "That's my job description, Colonel."

He looked up and down her considerable length, and noted the way she stiffened. He finished his scan, then looked back into her eyes. His relaxed posture and slight self-mocking smile said that while his appraisal was predatory, it was not demanding. Seeing that, she unbent— slightly.

"Lainie," she said. "Aren't you afraid of losing face by being seen with me, Migaki? A yakuza, the next thing to *eta*?"

He didn't blink at the use of the forbidden word. "Not at all. At worst it can only enhance my *iki,* my rakehell affect. I more expect my reputation to be enhanced, consorting with a war hero of your stature."

She made a non-committal noise and leaned her back

against the railing, studying the crowd through the invisible barrier with a hunting-cat's eye. "You don't flatter easily, then," he said matter-of-factly. "So it goes, although I meant what I said. Do you like movies?"

She gave that a moment's thought. *"Chambara,"* she said, referring to hack-and-slash sword operas, usually but not invariably historical. "And vids where things blow up."

"You're not a three-handkerchief woman, then?" Vids that induced weeping—their effectiveness measured in handkerchiefs—were just as popular among Combine men as women.

She shrugged. "What about *mujo*?" It was a Buddhist term for the transience of life, and colloquial for the cinema of cruelty.

"Too pretentious."

He pulled a mouth. He was a *mujo* fan himself, although even under Theodore's more permissive rule the making of such films was a fairly subterranean enterprise.

He was about to say more when he saw the color fall out from behind her freckles, giving her face a greenish tint. He turned.

A broad-shouldered, square-headed specimen had made an entrance. He wore a dark Occidental-style business suit and a blue silk cravat with a knot the size of a baby's head tied around what passed for his neck. A pair of taller and even broader specimens had winged out either side and were scoping the crowd with big, dark, round-lensed shades and an air of menace so transparently stagy he would have ranked out any director who allowed any such thing to appear in one of his Eigatoshi holovids. Migaki recognized the man immediately, of course. It was Benjamin Inagawa, yazuka boss of the Benjamin District.

The host, a wispy man with a goatee and samurai top-knot, tarted up in voluminous seventeenth-century ceremonial garb as if to make up for the fact that he was a blue-eyed blond, rushed up with effusive greetings. Which, for the dance mix and air curtain, Migaki could hear none of.

He felt a grip on his arm, firm as a strong man's. "Let's go," Lainie Shimazu said hoarsely.

"Go?"

"To your flat."

Migaki raised an eyebrow. The broad-jawed man and his own *sewanuki* were moving through the crowd, which was doing a new approach/avoidance dance: some of the partiers, the elegant *buke* and their escorts in particular, seemed to want to rush up and patronize the newcomers. The military types, for the most part, veered away from them as if similarly charged.

Migaki was startled to see this newcomer. This spitfire Laine Shimazu was one thing, a warrior who had shed much blood—hers and others'—on the Dragon's behalf. And he'd have had no objection to seeing Hiroo "the Cat" Yamaguchi, head oyabun of Luthien's own yakuza, for the old man was an unswerving supporter of Theodore's. Yet neither Yamaguchi nor any of his more-prominent *sabu* were anywhere in evidence. And there was something about seeing the cream of Imperial City nobility suck up to some off-world gang lord that turned Migaki's stomach.

Now, that's not proper iki, he chided himself semifacetiously. Aloud he said, "Your sudden migratory impulse wouldn't have anything to do with the no-neck who just honored us with our presence, would it?"

"No questions."

The maroon eyes that met his were more hunted than passionate. "If you want me, we'll go to your place now," she said. "Otherwise, forget you ever saw me, Propaganda Man."

"That wouldn't be easy."

Migaki's mind boiled over with questions. The whole scene seemed straight out of a holovid, which in most circumstance would mean it fulfilled most of his most cherished fantasies. But his air of hard-won experience wasn't counterfeit, even though it most definitely was for show. And the experience he'd won so hard suggested that when something seemed too good to be true, it was.

Nonetheless, the true *tsu* courted risky romance, and knew when to shut up and go.

So he extended his arm to the tall woman, and, guiding her by a path that scrupulously avoided the newly arrived oyabun and his pet legbreakers, he shut up and went.

7

Cinema City, Outside Imperial City
Luthien
Pesht Military District, Draconis Combine
22 June 3058

"Look! There he is!" The gaggle of Caballero kiddos broke and streamed toward Johnny Tchang like Wasedian geese heading for a pond at the end of a hard day's migration. Their escorts followed across the hard-packed lot, no less eager but too proud to show it. Mostly.

The golden boy himself was performing wonderful evolutions atop wooden pilings randomly sunk into the ground and sawed off to various heights. He seemed to flow from one to the other like fog along the ground. The children surrounded the pilings and stood staring up adoringly. Without interrupting his fluid movements, the star flashed them a quick greeting grin.

Cassie followed at a more deliberate pace, along with twenty or so adult 'lleros, mostly but not all women. She and Raven were pulling childcare detail this morning. The rest were, like the kids, avid for a first glimpse at the Inner Sphere's favorite martial arts star in the flesh.

Much as she hated distractions when she was on the job, Cassie didn't mind babysitting. Children were her one weakness—at least the one she'd acknowledge to herself—and they loved her. Besides, it wasn't as if she was turning up anything yet.

Or maybe she was turning up too much. She was playing street games, operating in several of her stock personas, trying to draw a look from the yaks. Normally they would have been all over her; they didn't take kindly to competition. But with most of the yak orgs in the whole Draconis Combine attending Teddy's birthday party in force, the street was one big seethe of outlaws. The gangs were too busy sniffing around each other to pay mind to one little stray. She felt urgency darting around like a loose rat in her rib cage, but she could rationalize this break for the children's sake.

Aside from her customary aplomb, Cassie's lack of haste was dictated by the short legs of Marcos Vásquez, aged four, who toddled by her side clutching a lop-eared stuffed rabbit with one chubby hand and Cassie's hand with the other. Once a voluble talker, he had not spoken a word since his mother had been executed by Howard Blaylock's firing squad on Towne.

He would come out of it in time. For a Caballero child to lose a parent was nothing new—although for one so young to have his mother murdered literally before his eyes was rare. If the former Lady K had not been raped by Blaylock, and thus gone straight to the head of the score-settling list, the other 'lleros would have been seriously torqued at her for flash-boiling his brains with her sidearm laser during the intaking of his stronghold.

But now little Marc had several hundred mommies; the support mechanism of *la familia* had kicked in. And four or not, Marc was still a Southwesterner. That meant he was a survivor. Not for nothing was the Cerillos coyote the mascot of the Trinity worlds in general and the Seventeenth Recon in particular.

The adult Caballeros were nosier than the children as they caught up. The dazzling bravura of Johnny Tchang's performance shut them up.

And then there was the man himself. Up close and personal he was no disappointment. Bare-chested, in loose white silk pants and black Chinese slippers, he was tall, 180 centimeters or so, and one of those seamless blends of Chinese and *gweilu* genes: smooth tanned skin, unruly crow-black bangs hanging almost in almond eyes, long features redeemed from near-effeminate beauty by a squarish jaw. He had the greyhound musculature of an acrobat, broad in chest and shoulders, flat in the gut and narrow in the hips, but rather than bulky wads of fiber, his muscles were tight as the wire windings of a magneto.

He leapt panther-like from one piling to another one half a meter higher, landed on his right foot, with his left thrusting out behind him in a back kick while he bent forward into a right-hand punch. Then, holding his pose, he pivoted slowly through 180 degrees, as smoothly as if he were mounted on a turntable.

The pattern went on, kicking, punching, lightly leaping. Cassie was not a fan of the martial arts *per se,* but since her speciality was close-quarters combat—against anything from alley-bashers to *Atlases*—she had at least a rude acquaintance with most of the Inner Sphere's major systems, there being far too many subsystems, variants, and one-off special arts in human space for any one individual to keep the names of all of them in her mind, much less know anything about them. What they were seeing here was Chinese *wushu* of a high order, she knew that much. While *wushu,* like many arts, had its lexicon of set patterns or forms, practitioners also made up their own forms, including their own original moves. She guessed that was what Johnny Tchang was performing here.

"Ooh," cooed Misty Saavedra, who had an expression on her face that *norteños* usually reserved for apparitions of the Virgin. "Isn't he *beautiful.*"

Cassie caught herself thinking the same thing. He was quick and smooth, and his balance was almost as finely tuned as hers—and *pentjak-silat* practitioners made a religion of balance, almost, or at least her guru, Johann, had. And yes, the man himself was pretty, almost achingly so . . .

She shut her eyes and shook herself. When she opened them little Marc was looking up at her with concern in his wide brown eyes, and Tchang's set was ending.

The crowd broke into wild applause and wolf-howls of approval—yipping *gritos* and drawn-out rebel yells. Grinning, as if he were unused to being the center of all this attention, Johnny Tchang jumped down, gave a stand-easy sign to the plainsclothes security types who were starting to get visibly nervous about the mob scene, accepted a towel from a trainer and began rubbing off the coat of sweat he'd worked up in the morning sun.

"Thanks, folks," he said. "It's good to be appreciated."

"You were *wonderful,*" Misty breathed. She was so lathered up she said it in Spanish, and Johnny did a curious take at her before she caught herself and repeated it in a language even a Davion transplant would understand.

He shrugged self-deprecatingly. "I've been doing this a long time."

"It's very pretty," Cassie heard a voice say, "but it's just dancing."

Silence fell like a knee-capped *Awesome.* Suddenly Cassie was primary to a whole solar system of staring faces. Belatedly she recognized the voice that had spoken as her own.

She was never one to back down. "I know that isn't easy," she said, "and you do it very well. But it doesn't have a lot to do with fighting."

A growl rose from the mob around her. Most *norteños* and a certain number of the Cowboys would argue that *mariachi* action star Tino Espinosa was the best, but the rest, particularly the Indians who were mad for kung-fu, hailed Johnny Tchang as supreme. And even the Tino boosters acknowledged Tchang as the number-two god of the cosmos. This was pushing the envelope even for Cassie.

Why did I have to go and open my mouth?

She was no big vidbuff, but from her vernacular knowledge of stars, what she expected Johnny to do was shoot up into the air like a rocket, trailing sparks. Instead he just shrugged and kept toweling himself.

"You're right," he said. "It doesn't. It's mostly an art form. It always has been, ever since it was invented in the twentieth century. But that doesn't mean it doesn't have applications. And I have studied other arts: White Crane, wing chun, kickboxing. Migaki-*san* has been thoughtful enough to provide some excellent *ryu*-squared instructors for me since I've been here, too."

"*Ryu*-squared" was a nickname for *ryu-bujutsu,* the Dragon's Warrior-Techniques, which could also be called *ryu-ryu,* for Dragon School. Though they sounded identical, the two words were written with different *kanji* ideograms. It was a popular kind of pun among the Dracs.

Cassie didn't know why she was feeling so flustered and fluttery, but she was for once willing to swallow her skepticism and let things lie. And then Vanity, who had been undulating through the mob of adults and children like a bad actress trying to portray a stripper in a B-holovid, said, "So you think you could take him, do you, Cassie?"

Cassie looked neurotoxins at her. "I'm not saying that—"

"Oh, but you *did*," Vanity purred. "Back on the Jump-Ship, watching *Exit the Dragon*. Remember?"

Cassie remembered no such thing. She hadn't said that and never would. She *thought* it, but it wasn't the kind of thing she advertised.

"Yeah, that's right," Misty Saavedra chipped in. "You were saying he wasn't so hot."

The other 'lleros were agreeing, damn the lot of them. Maybe they honestly didn't remember correctly, or maybe they were trying to pay her back for her apostasy. Or maybe they just had a hankering to indulge the age-old Southwestern fondness for seeing things fight.

"Don't you think this would be a good time to let us see if you're for real, or all show and no go?" Vanity asked with venomed sweetness. "Or if you're *afraid*—"

That showed what Vanity knew. Cassie could give a dead rat's ass what others thought of her motivations, even her *familia*. Just because she loved them desperately didn't necessarily mean she *liked* most of them.

And then Johnny Tchang said, "It would be hard to make it an even match," he said.

Something in Cassie broke like a trigger sear. She turned to face the actor. "Maybe you think so," she said, interrupting whatever he was going to say next. "But I'm willing to try. That is, if *you're* not afraid to risk being shown up by a mere woman."

He blinked, obviously taken aback by her hard-eyed anger. Mishcha Kurosawa had materialized on the scene, as was his wont, like a good little secret-police spy or a good fixer, whichever. He moved between the two like a teacher breaking up a schoolground fight.

"Here, now, Lieutenant, don't bother yourself," he said. "It's almost lunchtime, and Mr. Tchang has a busy shooting schedule—"

"I can wait for lunch," Cassie said.

The *kuromaku* looked to Tchang, who nodded. "It's all right, Mishcha. I've got a little slack in my schedule right now. They're having some trouble with the crew over at Sound Stage 5. Some new people who aren't quite broken in."

Mishcha turned from him to Cassie. His assignment was the Seventeenth, not Johnny Tchang, but obviously if the Liao-turned-Davion superstar who Takura Migaki had moved heaven and earth to get into one of his productions came to harm through anything Kurosawa did or didn't do, young Mishcha was going to find himself a combat grip on a crew making a you-are-there documentary about a kamikaze raid on Kanowit in the Smoke Jaguar Occupation Zone, and no mistake. For a secret-police *bancho* Migaki was remarkably human, maybe even the weakling Kiguri and Ninyu Kerai and the other *koha*—"hard school"—tough guys in the ISF made him out to be. But as a studio boss he was a screaming perfectionist.

Still . . . Cassie could almost see the little logic-gates clicking behind Kurosawa's anthracite eyes. Here was Johnny Tchang, the most famous martial artist in the known universe. And here on the other hand was a little near-*eta* scrap of fluff, who had a mean rep but couldn't mass more than 45 kilos in a wet bathrobe and was, after all, *only a girl* . . . He stepped back.

The Caballero crowd had stepped back too, leaving their scout hanging in the breeze. Little Marc Vásquez was staring worriedly up at her as if she'd got into the Jimson weed. He was small and not talking, but he wasn't stupid.

"I've never known you to let your mouth write checks your body can't cash, honey," said Raven out the corner of her mouth, as she scooped the little boy up into her arms, "but I reckon there's a first time for everything."

"You're probably right," Cassie said under her breath. She stripped off her heavy aerojock jacket and let Raven take it. Then she unfastened the web belt holding Blood-drinker in its scabbard and handed that off too. Raven faded back with Marc into the mob.

Cassie stood facing Tchang. She was dressed in a khaki Marik-issue undershirt, baggy trousers camouflaged in Ghost Bear gray-on-gray pattern, and black athletic shoes. She felt vulnerable and small as she and her opponent bowed ceremoniously to each other.

No. She told herself. *You've got nothing to fear. Combat isn't a sport. You've done it for real. He does it for show.*

But maybe the advantage wasn't hers, she realized. Because her opponent was used to sparring, to launching attacks without deadly intent. She was not.

She began to shift her weight left and right, moving her hands supple before her. Her movements were pretty dancelike themselves—like Balinese temple dances, Guru Johann told her. Johnny Tchang stood in neutral posture, watching. His eyes widened. He nodded, barely perceptibly, and dropped into a low, wide stance of his own, bringing up his hands.

So ka. Whether he was a *fighter* remained to see, but a martial artist he unquestionably was. Cassie's sinuous, soft-looking motions offered no opening, and their softness was sheer illusion. He had realized that at once.

She let her motions become broader, slower; it was the *pentjak* way to invite attack. She saw that Golden Boy was bright enough to realize that too. But he was bigger, he was male, and he had the interstellar-badass reputation to protect.

He did her the favor of making the first move, sliding in with a quick-flick Phoenix Eye strike for the face. She deflected it with a backhand flip. The hand recoiled, snake-quick, and snapped back in a jab. She ducked her head aside.

Having focused her attention on his hands, he spun around with his left leg stiffened for a sweeping heel-kick to her head.

She sat down cross-legged. The straight leg passed harmlessly over her head. She grinned up at him.

His pupils expanded the way your eyes do when they take in something hot-damn irresistible—a sumptuous banquet, a gorgeous naked woman, or an opponent who has just made an unrecoverable error. Johnny Tchang might have held the Black Pantyhose in half a dozen flavors of chop-sockey, but he didn't know *pentjak.*

He raised a straightened leg to drop on her in an axe kick—a blow that's almost as impossible to defend against as it is to get yourself into position to deliver it without setting yourself up for a testicle-crushing countershot. But Cassie was planted on her cute little fanny, her legs neutralized, the length of his leg putting her out of range to retaliate with a hand strike.

He thought. Cassie came up off the packed yellow dirt as if God had hit the Rewind button on the reality recorder. She was half turned to his right when the kick whiffed harmlessly down her back, just brushing her fanny. She sidle-stepped into him and flicked her fingernails against his cheek.

He jumped back up onto the pilings like a startled cat. Then he smiled.

"You're good," he said. "I've never seen that move before."

"I'm full of surprises."

He nodded. Then he launched himself in a forward roll right over Cassie's head.

She gaped. Too late she came out of it, started to turn. He touched down on his feet behind her, gave her a shoving back-kick in the posterior that sent her sprawling.

She didn't think the watching Caballeros should applaud *quite* so vigorously.

She came up quick enough, spun to face him in a deep stance. "You're full of surprises, too," she said. He gave her a big old grin.

They started to circle, each giving the other respectful distance. He was stronger than she was. She had no need to test that hypothesis. Men were generally stronger than women, and he was bigger.

And she lacked the weapon that had always served her best: utter all-out ruthlessness, an entire lack of hesitation. Since her training days with Guru Johann she had never gone into a fight with anything other than the intent to kill her opponent as quickly and savagely as possible, or barring that, to cause such rapid and horrific damage that not just her foe but any of his allies would lose all stomach for further confrontation.

It wasn't simply that she did not shrink from horror; when the time came, she savored it. In the popping of a joint, in the spurt of blood and bone and ruined flesh from a bullet-hit, in flesh embracing the knifelike lover's arms, a tortured child found both the promise of security and vindication. The reason she did not kill anyone who happened to cross her path was lack of motivation to do so, nothing more; and had she continued to walk the way she had until Kali took her under her wing on Hachiman, she now ruefully realized, she would in time have lost even that token inhibition.

With the help of her friend, she had become more human. But she was still unused to fighting as play.

He advanced. She sprang backward and landed on a piling, balanced on one foot with the other cocked sideways to the knee. Tchang looked her over and nodded approval. He jumped onto the pilings himself and attacked.

Jumping from stub to stub, feinting, dancing from foot to foot, they traded blocks and blows to no real effect, as much putting on a show for the onlookers as anything else. The audience had grown quiet. They were beginning to realize that, while Johnny Tchang really *was* that good . . . their little Abtakha was holding her own with him.

Making use of his greater reach Tchang drove Cassie backward. As she backed onto the last piling, he rushed her, hoping to push her off-balance.

It didn't work. Without glancing she leapt back and landed on the ground. He hopped down and walked deliberately toward her. She stood her ground.

The actor feinted a punch for Cassie's belly, then jumped straight up, aiming an inside-out crescent kick for her temple. She screwed herself to the ground again, under the attack. When he came down, she kept her spinning motion going, lashing out with a leg in a kick meant to sweep his feet from under him just as he was landing. The sweep was a specialty of hers—and coming down from his jump kick he was especially vulnerable.

Her kick cut air. He had launched himself straight up the instant he touched down. She kept the kick going, three-sixty, hoping to catch him when he came back to earth.

Instead he jumped again, millimeters ahead of her sweep. She went around again. This time when he landed, he took off in a forward leap, over her head again.

As he passed over he reached down to snag a handful of her shirt. He tucked his head and rolled as his weight carried her over backward. They landed side by side, shoulder to shoulder with feet pointing opposite directions. Cassie had clawed fingers poised right over Tchang's eyes. His free hand, stiffened, lay like a blade across her throat.

He gave her that grin again. Boyish and infuriating. "I guess it's a draw."

She moved her other hand. He went rigid, then looked slowly down to see the tip of a 100-mm hideout knife pressed against his groin.

"When it's for real," she said, "it's never a draw." And she turned the knifetip aside and drove it five millimeters into his thigh, just enough to break the skin.

"You've done some ballsy things in your time, Abtakha," Raven remarked as they walked toward their quarters. They had handed over charge of the children to their reliefs. "But I still can't believe you actually *stabbed* Johnny Tchang."

"I wanted to teach him the difference between the sound stage and the street," Cassie said darkly. She had Blood-drinker strapped back on and her jacket slung over one shoulder.

"I reckon you did that. You have to admit he took it pretty well. And it was worth every minute of it to see the look on ol' Mishcha's face when you pig-stuck the biggest holostar in the Inner Sphere."

Cassie shrugged. Raven was crowding her, though she didn't seem to realize it. She was none too sure why she'd pricked Tchang. That gave her a creepy feeling. She couldn't stand the thought of being out of control. It was one reason she'd never sought big-time solace in drugs and alcohol.

They walked up the steps and into the foyer. Someone stood up off one of the low sofas set to the left. Both women turned, hands unobtrusively slipping toward weapons, Cassie's for her *kris* and Raven's for some holdout piece. Cassie wasn't the only Caballera who never let her guard down—particularly when they were on the capital planet of the empire most of them had spent most of their adult lives fighting.

But if the movement represented a threat, it wasn't apparent. It was a skinny young woman—girl, actually, probably no older than fourteen even allowing for the common Drac ageless genes, a brown-haired waif whose face was mostly eyes and mouth and nose and freckles, and would likely be quite pretty when they all finally fit themselves together. Two smaller children, a boy and a girl, sheltered behind her, peering fearfully at the *gaijin*.

"*Chu-i* Suthorn?" the elder girl asked.

"That's me," Cassie said.

"I'm Sariko Corelli. These are Anna-ko and Tommy, my brother and sister."

Cassie smiled. "It's an honor to meet you," she said. The children were obviously acutely uncomfortable, more than mere fear of exotic foreign money-troopers could account for. That set all Cassie's nerves to jangling, but she knew better than to try to rush things. Whatever was spooking these kids, they'd tell of it in their own time.

"Jinjiro Coleman is our grandfather," Sariko said. "Our father died fighting the Clans with the Sixth Ghost Legion. Our mother was killed during the Clan attack on Imperial City. Our grandfather is all we have."

"I'm saddened to hear about your parents," Cassie said. "What may I do for you."

The girl glanced back at her siblings, then again at Cassie. "Our grandfather is missing. He never came home last night."

So that's why he wasn't around this morning. Cassie had

figured the concierge of the Seventeenth's dormitory had the day off. Even Dracs got a weekly break.

Sariko's self-control broke. Tears poured from her eyes. "He's never done that before! I'm so afraid something has happened."

8

Cinema City, Outside Imperial City
Luthien
Pesht Military District, Draconis Combine
23 June 3058

"They found your concierge," Mishcha Kurosawa said. Although it was morning Cassie had just dropped off to sleep when a knock came at the door of the room she shared with the currently absent Kali. Cassie had been working late again.

The fixer was dressed in his customary loud shirt. Cassie wore only a long tee-shirt she'd pulled on after getting out of bed. She made no move to invite him in. While making her own inquiries about the missing Coleman, she'd asked Kurosawa to check with the local authorities.

"Or rather, they found his body," he said, "floating in the canal. Natural causes, the police say."

The chamber was walled in white tiles scrubbed to blinding, and the fluorescent lights overhead made the edges of her vision vibrate. Cassie looked down at the body on the rolling slab, bluish, with little wisps of condensation drifting from the compartment, and was glad the Dragon's obsession with cleanliness meant she could smell nothing but disinfectant that stung her eyes like pepper gas. Jinjiro-*san* had not been in the water long enough to swell too much. The dark-blue ligature mark was still inescapably visible around his throat.

"Natural causes," said *Chi-i* Tzu-Chien McCartney of the

minuscule Criminal Investigations Bureau of the Imperial City Civilian Guidance Corps.

She turned to him with one eyebrow cocked in a question. She was dressed in a slate blue skirt-suit with black stockings, and shoes that matched the suit. Her wig was piled atop her head in a bun and held in place by polished teak sticks. Her dress and manner put her comfortably in the Executive echelon of the Middle Class.

He looked at her out of a sad wide Chinese face sagging around a cigarette. "See the tattoos? *Irezumi.* He's yakuza."

She nodded. McCartney was of middle height for the Inner Sphere, which put him a few centimeters above the Drac average. The weather had changed last night before Cassie bagged it, but he still wore the gray flare-shouldered Combine-style raincoat he'd had on outside, caught at the sternum by a red and white medallion displaying the insignia of the Civilian Guidance Corps. Beneath it, eschewing the customary robes of the minor functionary, he wore a baggy blue Occidental-style suit with a loosely knotted tie. Whether it was baggy because it was cheap or to fit his rather baggy physique Cassie couldn't tell. Probably both. He was what passed in the Combine for a street cop.

One of very few.

He gestured with two fingers of his right hand as if tapping the ligature marks. She noticed he didn't actually touch the chilled flesh. "Origami," he said.

"Origami?" She felt a flash of annoyance at the way he was turning her into an echo. But if he was out to score points off her—a mere woman—he didn't show any triumph. His face did not look familiar with that particular expression.

"The yaks have a lot of words for killing," he told her, taking hold of his cigarette and regarding it as if he wasn't sure what it was or how it came to be stuck to his underlip. He held it in standard Combine fashion, between thumb and index finger, ember toward palm. "One of the current favorites is *folding*. To fold someone is to kill them." He shrugged. "Origami."

"The report says natural causes."

His face showed nothing, but she expected that. People in

the Combine, like people in the Capellan Confederation, had lots of practice at showing stone faces to strangers. Millennia of practice. But he bent ever so slightly in the middle, as if taking a light shot to the gut.

Haragei. Just as the yaks had a lot of words for homicide, Japanese speakers read a lot of different meanings into this one word. It meant, literally, "belly talk." It could refer to what a Marik or Steiner would call playing one's cards close to one's chest, or to the habit of channeling one's emotions to the *hara*, the body's center, just as one did *ki*. *Haragei* also referred to the periodically fashionable practice—on the wane in Cassie's lifetime—of sketching the *kanji* characters for certain words before the stomach with the fingers as one conversed, and was used to ameliorate the confusion inherent in a language in which a single word could boast half a dozen wildly disparate meanings. Raised in an expatriate Drac community, Cassie was adept at reading *haragei* in most of its forms.

"We have a saying," he said, taking another hit off his smoke. "If you cross the *kai* and wind up floating, that *is* 'natural causes.' "

"You're serious?"

The tired eyes sized her up. The *Gestalt* of dress, manner, and word-choice told her something about what he thought about her status—or the status she was scamming for on this job, at any rate. The fact that his boss had ordered him to give her every cooperation told him even more. She was retainer to some noble; whether or not his superior had mentioned that the noble happened to have the surname "Kurita" she didn't know, but she guessed he knew anyway. One way or another, in the great totem pole that was Combine society, she was levels above him. Woman or not.

"You know we report the lowest crime rate of any Successor House," he said. "But how safe do you feel when you walk our streets? This is how we keep our face, how we keep the low crime stats the FedRats and the Mariks are so envious of. Natural causes."

"You're a brave man, McCartney-*san*."

"What? Talking like this? You think I'm afraid you might be a spy for the Eye?" He shook his head. "We're not just poor relatives to ISF. We're scarcely an afterthought. They pay more mind to the doings of the Unproductives than they do to us Friendly Persuaders. Especially the Criminal Investigations Bureau. They'd have to be pretty bored to take notice of anything I say or do."

He laid a scarred hand on the end of the drawer. "Seen enough?"

She nodded. He slid the drawer shut with an echoing final slam and started to walk away.

"Doesn't it bother you?" she called after him.

He turned. His eyes seemed to have retreated into his skull. He plucked the cigarette from his mouth, slammed it to the shiny immaculate tile floor, ground it in with his heel. For a Kurita it was a gesture akin to dropping his trousers and relieving himself on the spot.

"What do you think?" he snapped. "We're police. But they don't call us that. The vast majority of us are nothing more than glorified hall monitors, more concerned with making sure the citizens show a decorous face to Authority than whether they're cutting each other's throats in alleys. This unworthy one standing before you has the honor of being among the elite minority assigned the duty of investigating actual crimes. My specialty is murder."

He walked back and pounded a fist on Jinjiro Coleman's cold drawer—just one in a wall of such drawers. "And every day I see murders that I have to pretend are something else. Of course it bothers me!"

Cassie looked at him in genuine surprise. She had a lifetime's experience of cops. And very little of cops like this. She was used to street cops, harness bulls, like the Friendly Persuaders in their candy-striped uniforms. Drac, Davion, Steiner, Liao—it made little difference. The cops she had dealt with, as a street kid on Larsha and as scout for the Seventeenth, were mostly time-serving bullies looking to break heads and jack the straights for cumshaw. They weren't usually as bad as the Maskirovka Guardsman who had raped her when she was a child, but to her mind it was a matter of degree, not kind.

So here she was confronted with something new: a cop

who *cared*. A cop who was actually interested in catching bad guys. And his bosses wouldn't let him.

For the first time in her life she pitied a policeman.

She pressed palms together before her breastbone, bowed shallowly. "McCartney-*san,* forgive me. I phrased my question incorrectly. What I meant to ask was, don't the circumstances of this particular homicide bother you?"

And then he did look like the kind of cop she knew: he gave her that hard eye cops give civilians who presume to tell them their business. But she had status enough that he had to listen.

"How so?" he asked hoarsely.

"We can both see he's yakuza, McCartney-*san.* Why was he killed?"

Shrug. "He fouled up. Disappointed the oyabun once too often."

"You saw his hands. He had all his fingers."

"So he bugged up big."

"McCartney-*san,* I knew this man. He worked as a building superintendent in visitor housing at Eiga-toshi."

This time it was the widening of his pupils that gave him away, as it had Johnny Tchang the day before. "*So ka.* That's a good job. Plush."

"Just so. He wasn't a soldier anymore. He was retired. What could he have done to make his oyabun have him killed like this?"

The detective took out another cigarette and lit it. "Old Yamaguchi—he's top oyabun on Luthien; we call him the Cat—the old man is a beast like the rest of them, but he's got an ironbound sense of what passes for honor among the yaks. *Ninkyo* they call it."

Cassie knew that, but her game face didn't. She said nothing.

"Your man here obviously did good service. The Cat takes his obligations seriously. And this is an ugly way to check out, even if it's comparatively painless. If the deader had done something he had to die for, Yamaguchi would either have given him a more honorable exit, or a much nastier one."

He scanned her reappraisingly. "You make a good point.

You're one of these New Women, as much *gaijin* as Kurita. I don't know if I like that. But you're not stupid."

"Thank you," she said, trying to keep anger out of her voice. "Who do you think murdered him, then? Some rival?"

"Yamaguchi has no rivals."

"Not usually. But oyabun are coming from all over the Combine to honor our Coordinator on his birthday."

"There's a truce on for the occasion. And it wouldn't be an easy job to knock Old Cat Yamaguchi off his perch. He's one shrewd alley-fighter, a tough one. He has the Coordinator's favor, too. Criminal or not, he's always been a strong supporter of Theodore's, and our Coordinator isn't the type to let scum show him up in the matter of returning loyalty. Even a very large creature would think twice about poaching on Yamaguchi's turf."

"Then who did kill Jinjiro-*san*?"

All the air went out of him, like a paper bag that's been blown up and then punched. Cassie had never heard the myth of Sisyphus, and would have been rude to Father Doctor Bob if he'd tried to tell her about it. But if she had heard the story, she would just have gotten a better feel for it.

"What difference does it make?" he said. "There's nothing for me here. 'Natural causes.' "

"Would you like to catch the murderer, though? Even if it's just in this one case."

A gleam flared in his eyes, then died. "I'll go water-skiing on Orientalis long before that happens."

"Maybe not. Maybe I can help make justice happen. If you're willing to help."

"You? What could you do?"

Afterward she was never sure what impulse made her say, "I'm a scout for the Seventeenth Recon Regiment. We were invited here to attend the Coordinator's Birthday ceremonies. I have more freedom of action than you do—and you might be able to help me hang onto that."

He goggled. "What's this? You're *gaijin*?"

"I was born in the Combine, McCartney-*san*. My parents took me away when I was small. The Colonel of my regiment saved me from a bad place, and I swore loyalty to him.

But I'm what you were told I was, a retainer to Chandrasekhar Kurita. We're contracted to him. You were not lied to."

He looked at her with flat disbelief. She choked back a wild laugh. For the first time in her life she was telling a policeman the pure, unvarnished truth, and he didn't believe her.

He waved a hand. "Even if all this is true—why should you help me catch a killer?"

"Because of the children—the dead man's grandkids," she said. "And because I believe the killing may have something to do with us, my regiment. With something that threatens us." By nature as well as occupation, Cassie was as paranoid as any alley-cat herself. An unexplained violent death in such close proximity to *la familia* was cause for concern. Besides, she couldn't afford to overlook any clues to the threat Uncle Chandy had warned her to expect.

McCartney turned the cigarette around in his hand and rubbed his face. "You talk like a lunatic now, but you talked sense before. I don't know what to believe."

"Believe what you want. If I'm not what I say I am, if I can't help you—you're no worse off than before."

"That's true. But if you waste my time, I don't care who you are, or who's protecting you. I'll break you."

"Fair enough, McCartney-*san. Domo arigato.*" She bowed and started to walk away.

"But if you can catch the killer," he said as she reached the door, softly but distinctly in the echoing sterility, "if you can help solve even this single crime, unfold this origami, then I will bless you.

"For what a policeman's blessing is worth."

PART TWO

Haragei

A gentleman is not an implement.

—Confucius, *Analects*, 2:12

9

Blasts of water roared at the naked boy from nozzles set in the compartment's six bulkheads, icy as a Lyran money-lender's heart. Tethered to a bulkhead by a bungee cord, bobbing at the convergence of high-velocity streams, the youth sat in full lotus and struggled to breathe.

Near him, just clear of the streams, floated a man garbed in the scarlet robes of the Order of Five Pillars—the O5P. His belt was tied in the complex five-fold knot signifying his rank as an Illuminatus of the Order. His shaven head was bare, and he did not wear the characteristic flared Pillarine collar. His eyes were crescents in hard fat. He held a 150-centimeter staff of blond hardwood, a *jo*, in pudgy hands.

"What is the world?" he barked at the boy.

The young man was round-faced, well-muscled, and would likely have been handsome if icy water weren't blasting him every which way. "Illusion!" he shouted without hesitation.

"What is the Self?"

"Nothing!"

"And what are you?"

"Nothing!"

Whack! The staff cracked against the side of his head. The boy tumbled wildly for a moment before the converging streams forced him back into place. He managed to stay in lotus.

"You are a Kurita! You must never forget that! Now say it."

"I am a Kurita!"

The staff cracked against the young man's head again.

"And that's to help you remember!"

In another part of the ship two floating men watched the scene on monitors.

"Our young charge's Zen instruction proceeds," said one whose drab and slightly shabby robes revealed him to be an academic of no great rank. His face was long and seamed, his head a high narrow skin dome with a fringe of long, lank, neutral-colored hair surrounding it. He had, until recently, been a Professor of History and Moral Philosophy at the Sun Zhang MechWarrior Academy on New Samarkand. He smirked. "He'll find achieving the state of 'no-mind' easy enough, at any rate."

The other man wore Draconis Combine Mustered Soldiery undress uniform with the apple-green *katakana* numeral 3 of a *Tai-sa* on the collar. He was an instructor in tactics at Sun Zhang. He was also a moustached, bullet-headed thug of the sort who had been such a prominent stereotype in a millennium worth of propagandistic anti-Japanese, and subsequently anti-Combine, movies. His personality was the sort that had kept that stereotype alive for all those years. He thought humor frivolous. Mostly he just didn't get it. In the amber pilot-light glow that provided most of the small compartment's illumination, he resembled a bronze statue of a balding war god in contemporary garb.

"I still don't see why this charade is necessary," he barked. He gave the impression that, unlike the priest on the monitor, who barked for effect, he did so all the time. Which he did. "The boy is no fine intellectual. But that's good; he's a true samurai. He'll do what he's told."

"Ah, *Tai-sa* Ohta, but there exactly is the rub. He does think of himself as a samurai, and thus will follow his duty with exemplary single-mindedness. But alas, thanks to that same single-mindedness, in spite of all our efforts during the two years we've had to work with him he still conceives his duty is to his cousin the usurper." He gestured with long fingers—what the Lyrans would call *Spinnenbeine*, spider's legs. "That's why the estimable Banzuin is so invaluable to us."

"Because he squirts him with ice water and bats him in the head?"

"Classic *bushi* toughening exercises, of which I'd think you would heartily approve."

"Toughening's one thing, Professor Tomita. These confounded riddles are another. They make *my* head hurt."

The Professor briefly compressed his wide, mobile mouth, as if to hold in a sarcastic comment. The *Tai-sa* wasn't big on sarcasm, either. Especially from civilians.

"Think of it as shock treatment, Ohta-*sama*. That's the purpose of all this Zen gymkhana, after all—to knock loose preconceptions, not to mention inconveniences such as individual will."

The *Tai-sa* made a growling sound deep in his well-developed *hara*. "We'll have our work cut out for us, thanks to all the soft and decadent nonsense about individualism the Usurper has allowed in."

Professor Tomita blanched, and a line of sweat-beads demarked the retreat of his hairline as on a tac display. Nevertheless he managed a shaky smile. "Of course the *Tai-sa* remembers that the ISF undoubtedly has this chamber bugged."

Ohta blinked. Then he glared at the academic as if suspecting him of trying to pull a fast one. "Of course they do. It's their ship. Why shouldn't they have it bugged?"

"Indeed, *Tai-sa* Ohta. These limbs of the Dragon are on our side, fortunately. On Luthien it will be otherwise. Once there, it will be wise to remember that the silent dog attracts few kicks."

"Nonsense. We won't land until the traitor Theodore Kurita is dead."

The Professor winced. "An officer of your vast combat experience is surely aware," he said, "that few things go as planned. And may this unworthy one humbly request you not so blithely juxtapose words such as 'traitor' and 'kill' with the name of our young charge's cousin? While the

Smiling One remains Director, it may be unwise to assume that all ears overhearing us are friendly to our cause."

"Bah. A senescent cripple. He's being dealt with."

"I only wish I had the strength of your conviction in Subhash Indrahar's inadequacy."

"It's intolerable!" exclaimed *Tai-sho* Shigeru Yoshida to those assembled in this most private room of Unity Palace in Luthien. "The barbarian's presumption is not to be borne."

The Coordinator's informal council sat on their knees around a low table cut from a native tree whose grain was a startling purple against ivory wood. Theirs was no fixed roster; who sat with the Coordinator was determined by need, knowledge, and availability. These were the "bad advisers" Black Dragon rhetoric inveighed against. This indeed was the group's function, as much as tendering advice: to shield the Coordinator's sacrosanct person from blame. According to ISF reports, even the *Kokuryu-kai* fanatics still held back from criticizing Theodore himself, although the catastrophe on Towne had provoked them to unprecedented fury.

At the table's head sat Theodore Kurita, clad like the rest in formal kimono. He was trying not to fidget. He had vital questions of policy to answer, such as how the Draconis Combine should respond to the recent Word of Blake conquest of Terra and what the leaders of the Inner Sphere would do in the wake of the Jade Falcon attack on the Lyran Alliance world of Coventry. He had to make conscious acts of will almost from moment to moment to keep from obsessing on the Clan threat, even though Subhash Indrahar assured him the Clan setbacks in Lyran space had knocked the invaders onto their collective heels. And here he was wasting time discussing protocol for this confounded birthday party!

He looked to Marquis Fellini, who was overseeing the Coordinator's Birthday festivities. The Marquis's broad face was placid as always.

"The commander of the Seventeenth, Colonel Carlos Camacho, refuses to swear fealty to our First Lord, although he hastens to reassure us as to his profoundest respect."

"What seems to be the problem?" Theodore asked.

"*Tono*, it would appear he has already sworn his personal loyalty to Victor Davion, during the Clan War. He fears that precludes offering a similar oath to the Coordinator."

Theodore didn't actually give a burned-out *Locust* bearing whether the *gaijin* swore an oath to him or not. He had allowed Uncle Chandy to talk him into inviting his pet mercenary regiment, and to be sure, the Seventeenth had done the Dragon valuable service, however uncomfortable it might have been.

"Tradition requires that the commanders of all units granted the supreme honor of presentation to the Coordinator join in swearing an oath of eternal loyalty to the Dragon and to the Coordinator," Yoshida said.

"Might I remind the *Tai-sho* that it is rather taken for granted that such commanders are serving members of the DCMS?" the Marquis said.

Yoshida scowled darkly. He was not terribly fond of extending recognition to mercenaries. He had been a Takashi man, had risen to command of the First Sword of Light Regiment—considered by many the lead unit of the whole Draconis Combine Mustered Soldiery—under Theodore's father.

The *Tai-sho* had never been overly fond of Theodore. Before the Smoke Jaguar/Nova Cat invasion of Luthien in 3052, he had called the then-Kanrei a fool for pulling DCMS forces away from the Federated Commonwealth frontier to meet the anticipated threat. Theodore was not the man his father was, he'd said.

Theodore had agreed he was not his father. His father would have killed Yoshida on the spot, rather than waiting for the Otomo to arrest him. Yoshida had backed down and apologized. Theodore refused to acknowledge that any apology was due from a man whose sole interest was the Combine's welfare.

After Theodore acceded to the Dragon Throne, he had promoted Yoshida to full general and appointed him his Chief Military Aide—functionally the same role Theodore himself had performed as Gunji no Kanrei, Chief Deputy for Military Affairs, although Yoshida had a different title, since Kanrei was inextricably associated with Theodore throughout the Inner Sphere. The move surprised many of those closest to Theodore, not least Subhash Indrahar, not to mention the military commander of Kagoshima Prefecture, who also happened to be Theodore's wife, *Tai-sho* Tomoe Sakade. Like Japanese history before it, Combine history was full of stories of overreaching subordinates who had been set back in place by a perfect gesture from their superiors and gone on to serve with fanatical devotion. The problem was, there were almost as many occasions in which the subordinate had smiled and backed down and then gone off to plot lurid revenge.

Theodore knew it was a risk. But Yoshida had earned the position, through ability as well as long service. And Theodore, who was conscious that one of his father's main weaknesses was that he refused to hear anything he didn't like, wanted to ensure that he was not surrounded by yes-men. So far, the gamble had paid off. Yoshida had served well, and while he was not afraid to speak his mind, he had never shown the least sign of disloyalty.

"Such arrogance is an affront to the Dragon, as well as the Coordinator," Yoshida continued.

"We should not be hasty, Yoshida-*san*," said *Tai-sa* Oda Hideyoshi, commander of the Coordinator's bodyguard, the Otomo. He was stockier and gruffer than Yoshida, with thick black eyebrows. "The Dragon prizes loyalty. If this *gaijin* Colonel Camacho lightly casts aside his oath, even to an enemy, how can we trust him to honor a promise made to our *Tono*?"

Theodore nodded, not permitting himself to smile. It was what he was thinking himself. Even though he made the real decisions in the Combine, and everyone in human space knew it, he had to play the role of Coordinator as father figure, an essentially passive entity who was served, rather than who commanded. While he had a deft hand at dropping leading *haiku,* he was happy to be spared the effort. He had enough on his mind as it was.

"Thank you, *Tai-sa*. You raise a very telling point." He looked at the fat Marquis. "Could you come up with an oath that Colonel Camacho might find acceptable, without compromising the honor of the Dragon?"

The Marquis bowed. "I am confident the Dragon will see to it that my poor efforts will be crowned with success." Which was how he said *yes*.

Theodore looked at the Otomo commander. He was another who had served his father; in fact he had commanded the Coordinator's bodyguard the night Takashi went to join his ancestors. Because the old Coordinator's death came officially from natural causes, Hideyoshi had been allowed to keep his position, not to mention his life.

Theodore squeezed his eyes shut on a vision of blood spurting from his father's severed neck. *That dream.* The Order of Five Pillars, then headed by Theodore's aunt and ally Constance, had seen to disposing Takashi's body. But Hideyoshi had to know that Takashi Kurita had died by his own hand. And he almost certainly had guessed, from the chaotic events of that night, that a failed attempt had been made on the old Coordinator's life.

Does he think I was behind that? Theodore wondered, not for the first time. *Does he think my leaving him in place is a bribe to buy his silence?* He rubbed his eyes. He had not studied the *ki* disciplines of O5P in depth enough to read another man's thoughts, or even to know if it was true that the highest Illuminati possessed that ability. Then, he didn't even know whether those tales were just incense-smoke the O5P blew in order to maintain its mystique. Hideyoshi, too, had served well, and survived continued scrutiny by the Smiling One. *And that,* Theodore thought ruefully, *is as close as I'll ever come to telepathy.*

"Were there other matters for discussion?" he asked.

The Marquis cleared his throat. "Coordinator, there remains but the trifling issue of how we are to handle Franklin Sakamoto upon his arrival."

Theodore shut his eyes.

10

Ukiyo District, Imperial City
Luthien
Pesht Military District, Draconis Combine
24 June 3058

"People here are nervous," Usagi said, slurping pickles and noodles from a bowl held right under what passed for his chin.

"They don't know how to have fun," added his partner Unagi, working his own chopsticks like an eggbeater.

Cassie sat at the outdoor table with legs crossed, trying not to bob her right pump too conspicuously from impatience. The two were doing her a favor. She couldn't rush them.

The noodle shop was in the *ukiyo* quarter, far enough from the palace that everything wasn't gloomy black. The buildings ran to cheap stucco and an odd orange brick that seemed to be made of native clay. The passing pedestrian hordes gave Cassie as much eye as indirect Drac manners permitted. As usual she was worth it. She wore a dusty burgundy skirtsuit over a dove-gray blouse, something a receptionist for a forward-looking *zaibatsu* might wear in place of the dowdy traditional robes. Her abbreviated hair was done blonde with a rinse that would come out with a simple application of solvent and not strip her hair and make it stand out like straw—or so Raven had assured her. The Mech jock's true mane was perhaps not exactly the shade of ash-blonde she herself preferred to show the world. Cassie topped the ensemble off with a pair of sunglasses with red horizontal grooves across the tops—very now on Luthien, which meant they'd gone out of fashion on Hachiman before the Seventeenth ever set foot there.

But her skirt hit her well-turned thigh a little too high above the knee and was slit too high up the sides. That gave her away as a prostitute, specifically one kitted out to attract a mark with a fetish for OLs, Office Ladies. The noodle shop lay on the outskirts of the *ukiyo*—in its own subdued way, Imperial City's lowlife district—but so situated that Middle Class types who wanted to feel daring without real risk to person, purse, or face could lunch here, and did. But the short, officially prescribed lunch hour had passed. The specialty streetwalker routine was a charm to avert evil eyes, specifically the ones belonging to the Friendly Persuaders of the Civilian Guidance Corps rolling by in twos in their candystripe unis, fondling their omnipresent stun guns.

Cassie's companions launched into a disquisition on how boring the local Water Trade was in contrast to Hachiman. Too many *gei-boi-san* clubs and hostess bars, it seemed, and no good jazz. Usagi and Unagi: the Rabbit and the Eel. "Eel" meant "rope" in *ingo,* signifying a second-story man. "Rabbit" was a petty thief. The names described their civilian occupations before being welcomed into the Ninth Ghost Legion, by way of the Drac penal system; they also hinted at their roles in the regiment.

The two were scouts, so-called. What they were was recon 'Mech pilots. As far as Cassie was concerned, scouting from a BattleMech was like trying to do it from inside a hundred-story air-conditioned high-rise with double-paned transpex windows. But they considered themselves her peers if not her equals, and because they did know the streets, she was willing to go along with the gag.

Besides, they were real tattoo men, no-mistake yaks. They could pass where even she could not.

Finally she couldn't hold back any longer. "Did you *learn* anything?" she asked.

"Sure," Unagi said, sucking down his final noodle like a baby bird with a worm. "Gang war."

"Outsiders're putting the moves on old Cat Yamaguchi," Usagi said.

"You're kidding," Cassie said.

"Nope," Usagi said.

"Why should we be kidding?" Unagi asked. He pushed forward his empty bowl. "You wouldn't care to shell out for a little more?"

The two ate like starving Ghost Bears—the real thing, not the Clanners. They somehow still looked like washboards with pipestem legs. Even Cassie, who packed away a fair amount herself, wondered where they put it. She crooked a finger. The proprietor, a little wrinkly blond man, came out bowing and hissing as if they were slumming nobles—which first off they might have been. But even if they weren't, yaks and streetwalkers made up a respectable, at least in terms of volume, share of his customers.

Eel and Rabbit got rattling over nothing in particular again. Cassie drummed her fingers on the tablecloth and glared off at the busy street with its oddball Drac mixture of the high tech and the damned-near tribal: men with poles balanced across their shoulders with a chicken in a wicker basket at either end, marching past giant electronics-store display windows where naked zero-g ballerinas cavorted like dolphins in holovid. She was seriously torqued at herself. Here she was, the Perfect Scout, the ultimate long-range low-heat ass-in-grass operator, and she had missed a little detail like gang war in the house.

She had already gone through her self-rage routine—admitted it and talked it out with herself, the way Kali had helped her learn to do it. Her left forearm still bore a very fine network of ancient white cut-scars from her older mode of punishing herself for glitch-ups. That technique, with its strong negative reinforcement, had helped her learn to survive in the jungle, both metaphorical and actual. But now, by trial and error almost as painful as self-mutilation, she was learning ways and means of processing that didn't mean destroying herself by degrees.

One way she processed was to work out *why* the glitch happened. Not making excuses but trying to scan how to keep from putting her foot back in the same paint can with the nails driven inward and downward through the rim.

I've been making assumptions. For someone with her job

description that was like flying on autopilot through a high mountain pass in a thunderstorm. The more so since it had been a solid, fact-based assumption.

The yakuza of the Combine had themselves a federation, *seimeiyoshi-rengo*. That federation had rules. The most ironbound concerned truces and no-man's land. Since Teddy the K, who had brought the yakuza into Combine society as no one had ever even thought about trying to before, had become Coordinator, no safety zone was more inviolate than Luthien during his big birthday bash.

And now—during the biggest Coordinator's Birthday celebration in history, or at least living memory—she'd expected the gang armistice to be plated in ferro-fibrous armor. It was a natural assumption.

Those are the worst kind.

She had been trying to get in with the local org, Yamaguchi-*gumi*. The Old Cat was the host oyabun, so his *kai* should have held the heart-meat of anything going down. And indeed it was so, only not in the way Cassie let herself anticipate.

Therein lay the friction-point. Yakuza society was closed society. No surprise—*Drac* society was closed society. But the *irezumi* world was even more hermetic. Unlike the realm of *katagi,* the squares, you could not slide inside by faking status, which Cassie was adept at, much less by having someone with mega status extend his coverage to you, the way Uncle Chandy had gotten her the interview with McCartney the tired homicide policeman. No, you had to *know* somebody. And not just to get into the gang. Even the people who worked the usual gang hangouts, the floating-world denizens, the waitresses and dealers and showgirls and even, yes, the prostitutes, had to have references.

There were ways to get to know somebody. Cassie knew how to do that too; she'd pulled it to perfection on Hachiman. But she found the local Luthien *kai* was jammed up tight as the fusion bottle in a BattleMech's belly. They were not accepting introductions today.

Unagi and Usagi had introductions in spades. Since their boss Lainie Shimazu was known for fanatical dedication to Theodore, and had no history of a negative stripe with Yamaguchi-*gumi*, these jokers had been able to dive right in and resurface with the data Cassie needed in hours.

But the answer was almost as puzzling as the original question. "I thought the Coordinator's Birthday was hands-off time," she said.

The two scouts looked at each other and shrugged. "Supposed to be—" Usagi began.

"—But Inagawa-*san* makes his own rules," finished Unagi.

"Inagawa?" Cassie looked from one junior scout to the other.

Usagi shrugged. "He's boss oyabun for the whole Benjamin District."

"And he feels big enough to take on Yamaguchi on his home ground?"

"He's a real up-and-comer in *seimeiyoshi-rengo,* Cassie-*chan*," Usagi said.

"He's got stones, and he's got muscle," Unagi added. "Maybe not so much brains, though."

"Isn't Inagawa worried what Teddy's going to do? I thought the Old Cat Yamaguchi was thick with him."

The noodle-shop owner came bustling out with two more bowls heaped with steaming noodles. "The Old Cat's got pride," Usagi said, tucking in as if he hadn't seen food in a month.

"He'd never ask Teddy for help," Unagi said through a mouthful.

"What do the other oyabun say?"

Shrugs in stereo. "He won't take their help either," said Usagi.

"Except some from Tosei-*kai*," Unagi said.

"The Koreans were working with him anyway," Usagi said. Tosei-*kai,* The Voice of the East, was a predominantly Korean org of gangs not tied to any planet or region of the Combine.

"But isn't it a major breach of etiquette for Inagawa to be making his move right now?"

Another shrug. "If a little dog barks, he gets a kick. If a big dog barks, he gets a bone," said Usagi, quoting a common Drac proverb. Which was something outsiders didn't understand about the supposedly consensus-based culture of the Combine: if you had the status, you could be as selfish and cantankerous as you wanted, and then "consensus" would consist in everybody accommodating *you.*

"Inagawa-*san*'s a major leg-breaker," Unagi said. "And he's pals with old man Toyama."

That brought Cassie up. She lowered her outrageous sunglasses and peered over the top at them. "Hiraoke Toyama? Out of Dieron?"

They smirked at her. "That's the one," Usagi said.

"The one whose only son you bent on Towne," Unagi added with malicious glee.

"*I* didn't put Junior to sleep. It was Red Gallegos with her rockets. He's here? On the Pearl?"

"Right here in Imperial City," Unagi said.

"Why not?" Usagi asked ingenuously. "He never went against Theodore."

"In public," added Unagi.

That was key to the Combine: appearance was everything. That was also key to the recent history of the Caballeros. It was why they'd had to fight and die on Towne without the help, say, of a couple of DCMS regiments bone-loyal to Teddy, like the Ninth Ghost Legion. Because the Combine could not be seen to be warring against itself. Because neither Theodore nor the Black Dragons cared to publicly admit they were in conflict. Kusunoki and his Black Dragon allies pretended to the Universe—and assured their own soldiers—that they were acting out the Coordinator's wishes by claim-jumping his most powerful ally. Teddy pretended he was taking no action against them. So Hiraoke Toyama had done nothing wrong.

Sometimes even Cassie found the Combine seriously weird. Almost as weird as the Caballeros.

"So Inagawa is *Kokuryu-kai*?" she asked.

"He doesn't advertise," Usagi said.

"No matter how big you are, the ISF will still scatter you big-time if they learn you're a Black Dragon," said Unagi.

For that matter, Hiraoke Toyama had never publicly admitted the least connection to *Kokuryu-kai*. The army he had helped to raise—and sent into battle and ultimate destruction on Towne—did not announce to the world that it was a Black Dragon production, although its insignia did in fact sport a dragon that was black, but then, so did the Kurita state symbol. As far as *appearance* went, it was just a private army of the kind which, while discouraged inside the Combine, was not illegal to raise.

Cassie sat back and folded her arms. This gave her plenty to think about.

"Did we do good, Cassie-*chan*?" one of them asked plaintively. Cassie was so lost in her thoughts she wasn't sure which it was.

"Sure. You guys did great. I'm just trying to figure out where to take what you got for me. Anything I can do for you—?"

They looked at each other. "There's one thing, maybe, Cass . . ." Usagi said tentatively.

"Trigger it."

"Do you think you could get Johnny Tchang's autograph for us?"

She stifled a sigh. "No problem."

She started to rise. "One more thing," Usagi said. "It's about Lainie—"

"—She's been acting funny since that party the other night. Not herself."

"I heard she was posing for pillow prints with the head of Voice of the Dragon. Our host." Cassie tugged at her skirt.

"That's not unusual for Lainie," Usagi said.

"Well, Migaki must be punching some buttons she didn't know she had. He's not her usual blond bimbo with biceps bigger than his brain. Maybe it's love."

The two looked at each other and tittered. "The Red Witch in love?" Unagi said incredulously.

"Her heart's shielded like a Hermes 320 XL fusion engine," Usagi said. "That's not it. There's something *wrong*."

Cassie held up her hands. "I don't know. I'll see what I can scope out." *Like I don't have enough plates in the air.* She didn't feel any closer to IDing a threat to the regiment, although the certainty was growing heavier in her gut that a threat existed. And here she was committed to solving a murder and straightening out a crazy redheaded MechWarrior's love life. It didn't help that all the women in the Seventeenth hated her for puncturing Johnny Tchang's perfect tanned hide.

A whistling roar. The tablecloth blew off as the pedestrian flow parted and a garishly painted hovercar careened around the corner, almost caromed off a building front, then shot down the street with a turbine whine. Cassie jumped up, neglecting the way the fan-blast blew her skirt up around her waist. The vehicle's occupants were four or five young males with their hair shaved to scalplocks, dressed in what looked in a flash like yellow-trimmed black and green Jade Falcon dress uniforms. They catcalled at her as they blew by. She flipped them off before it even occurred to her that was perfectly in character.

Belatedly it occurred to her that it would do her cover no good to have to litter the Impy City streets with bleeding bodies. Before they could take umbrage at her gesture, the hovercraft had rounded another corner with a noise like an Elemental-sized mosquito and was gone.

"What the *hell* was that?" she demanded. Around her the citizens were picking themselves us, gathering their groceries back into covered baskets or whatever. Down the block people were stepping gingerly around a snowfall scatter of broken glass where the buggy's blast had taken out a display window. The owner had emerged and was losing it in buckets, jumping up and down and hollering.

"Dekigoro-zoku," Unagi said. "Sudden impulse tribe."

"Rich kids out looking for trouble," Usagi added with a sneer.

"How rich?" Cassie asked.

"Upper Middle Class," Usagi said.

"And some *buke,*" Unagi said.

"Don't remember them from Hachiman," Cassie said. "I recall the rich kids mostly riding around on crazy motor scooters."

"They don't seem to've caught on as much there yet," Usagi said.

"For once," Unagi said, "the Pearl's ahead of the fashion curve."

11

Basin Lake, Outside Imperial City
Luthien
Pesht Military District, Draconis Combine
24 June 3058

A brisk breeze stirred the stiff leaves of the capylar trees on shore into a noise like distant applause. Lainie Shimazu let her hand trail over the graphite-fiber gunwale of the sailboat into the cool green water of Basin Lake.

"I grew up rich and spoiled," she said to Takura Migaki, who lounged in the stern with his hand on the tiller. "Daddy was determined to bring me up so no one would ever guess where I came from. Of course you know how futile that is; the stain never comes out. Everybody in our whole society might as well have their station tattooed on them, not just us yakuza."

Migaki nodded judiciously. He was wearing a plug hat, a black tailcoat, a pair of sunglasses with little tiny black disks for lenses, a very arch parody of the pseudo-Western dress Draconians affected for certain formal occasions. She was wearing a maroon silk shirt and issue MechWarrior noncombat trousers, dark gray with red stripes down the legs, over calf-high black boots. He thought she looked altogether exotic, dangerous, and delicious. Then again, he had a self-acknowledged tendency to romanticize the tawdry and even the depraved. It went with being a *tsu*.

Is she the most intriguing woman I've met? he wondered. *Or is she just mad? Are they one and the same? Does it matter?* One thing was certain, she had him chasing his own intellectual tail like a freshman at university, an invigorating thing in itself. He caught himself at the brink of laughing out loud. He knew it would not be well received.

She extended a finger, watched the tiny wake spreading away from it. Servomotors made tiny whirs as they trimmed the ballistic-fabric sail to the nuances of the wind, as interpreted by the computer built into the base of the carbon-filament mast. Several boats shared the lake with them, their sails white triangles cut out of the low green line of Waseda Hills.

"I rebelled. Of course. He wanted me to be the perfect lady; I chose to be the perfect tomboy. Got thrown out of the finest private schools on half a dozen worlds—schools he spent a fortune on bribes to get me into in the first place. I wanted to learn to ride and shoot and beat people up. Well, finally he brought me home to—to the planet where we lived. He would keep me under his watchful eye. He'd even let me take lessons in the things I wanted to learn, if I promised to make an effort at being a lady. And I made an effort, even if it was half-assed."

She lifted her hand from the water. "And then—" She flicked droplets from her fingertips. They caught and split the morning sunlight, so that they glittered like fragments of shattered rainbows. "—*Gekokujo*. Those below rising against those above. A trusted lieutenant thought the old man was losing his touch. So he went for it. There's another dark secret we inherited from our Japanese ancestors: loyalty to one's lord is absolute—unless you figure you can topple him and get away with it. If you can, everyone figures you're entitled to the job."

She shrugged. "So the treacherous lieutenant became a respected and powerful oyabun. Daddy became dead. And the tomboy became a fugitive, and suddenly life wasn't a game any more."

Silence came down like premature evening. For a while they let the lake's voice have the floor, the bubble and swish of water on the hull, the hiss of wind.

"Incredible story," Migaki said, shaking his head, when it became apparent he wasn't going to have any more of it just now.

She looked at him with a lopsided grin. "Just like a movie. You like it that way, *iie?*"

He laughed. "*Hai.* I do. Real life is never so sweet as when it imitates the holovids."

"We've led different lives, honey."

"So we have. I'd love to make your story into a movie. Except—"

"Except the yak lifestyle isn't exactly an aspect of Combine life the Voice of the Dragon is supposed to be glorifying, is it?"

"It would be controversial," he admitted. "Still, if you'd be willing, Lainie-*chan,* I could—what is it?"

Something like a look of pain had flashed across her face. She waved him off. "Nothing. Just—can we talk about something that isn't me for a while?"

"To be sure." He rubbed his chin and thought furiously. Nothing for making one's mind go blank like having someone demand a topic change. "I know: I've come up with a way to solve two problems at once, and I'm very proud of myself."

She clasped hands, steepled her fingers before her mouth, and grinned. "Okay. Impress me."

He tipped his hat sardonically. "First of all, our guests— Voice of the Dragon's guests—are getting bored. They can only sit still for protocol lessons for so long and I for one can't blame them. After a year on Hachiman our Luthien society doesn't have much novelty for them, except what amusement comes from us being five years behind Hachiman trendwise. And when they get bored, they act as if they were raised to our old proverb, that one has no shame away from home."

"The Seventeenth? A bunch of total maniacs." Lainie spoke matter-of-factly. If there was inflection at all, it was a touch of admiration.

"To say the least." Most recently a water fight that had erupted in the dorm's communal baths—the Caballeros scrupulously segregated the men's bathing hours from the women's, which even a sophisticated man-of-the-Inner Sphere such as Migaki found startling—had escalated into a running battle up and down the corridors and stairwells, involving water-balloons, waste baskets filled with water, fire hoses, and eventually flying fists and furniture as noses got bumped and tempers spiked. Fortunately the *yohei* officers had restored order before too much damage was done. Then there was the incident in which the *gaijin*'s wild-woman scout poked a hole in the prodigiously insured hide of the star Migaki had moved heaven and earth—which not only regarded all things as straw dogs, but were damned heavy—to get on his lot. At least the she-demon had the decency to puncture him where it wouldn't show.

"The other problem has been realism in the new holovid I'm making with Johnny Tchang. *Dragon Phoenix*. The ruse of Theodore's that *Sho-sho* Hideyoshi pulled on the Clanners beside this very lake is looking a little too threadbare in our version of it. The Smoke Jaguars might fall for LoaderMechs tarted up like *Thunderbolt*s and *Archer*s, but our Combine viewing public is much too discerning."

"You're going to hire the Caballero 'Mechs to be in your movie?"

"With them inside, of course. From what Ernie Katsuyama tells me, they're very good."

"They are that," Lainie told him. "But watch out for that natural exuberance of theirs. Otherwise you could wind up with a *real* mess on your hands."

Migaki nodded self-assuredly. His companion watched him with lids low over those magnificent amber eyes, as if she suspected his ego was getting the better of him.

"Meanwhile," he said, "we're near completion of our shooting schedule on my other big project. Costume dramas present their own layers of complexity, but they tend to be less expensive than the ones for 'Mech operas. In my own *cinéaste* I'm more thrilled with it than with landing the Inner Sphere's biggest action star. There hasn't been a good *Chushingura* vid for better than two centuries, more if you discount the ones updated to contemporary Kurita society . . ."

His words ran like water down a storm drain. The healthy wheat-color of Lainie's skin had drained right out from behind her freckles, and her eyes looked like holes punched in a *shoji* door.

"Lainie-*chan*! What's the matter? If I've said something—" On the Observing Self level he was amazed and amused to hear himself contrite as a stripling. *Or maybe a seventeenth-century artist who feared he had offended his favorite courtesan.*

"It's . . . nothing." She gave her head a terminating shake. "Can we just not talk about that historical drama of yours?"

"Certainly," he said, blinking. Maybe that was what drew him to her, as much as her beautiful body, exotic face, and untamed samurai spirit (although she'd react to that suggestion with the same vehement contempt a real samurai would): she was capable of surprising him. Few people of any gender could make that claim. "What would you—?"

She looked him in the eye. Her amber eyes were maroon in the sunlight. They reminded Migaki of an animal's eyes. A hunted animal.

"Take me somewhere," she said from low in her throat, "and make me forget the whole damned universe."

"So what's this here say?" Cowboy Payson asked, leaning down to squint at a discreet brass plaque set into black marble next to three steps leading down from street level to a door. The writing was in *kanji,* Chinese ideograms.

"Oh," said Mishcha. "It's the entrance to a night club. Nothing to interest you here."

Cowboy hiked up an eyebrow at him. "You got that tone of voice again says you're trying to keep one of us round-eyes outta trouble, Mishcha old pal." He straightened slowly. "Maybe I should mosey in and check out the action."

Mishcha rolled his eyes up in his head. They were slightly sunken into a face that was noticeably paler than when the 'lleros first encountered him. Even the overamped colors of his shirt looked wilted. Cowboy started down the steps.

"It says, *'gei boi-san-tachi to enjoi shite kudasai,'* " said Buntaro Mayne, Cowboy's one-eyed friend from the Ninth Ghosts.

"What's that mean?"

" 'Please enjoy the Mr. Gay Boys.' "

Cowboy stopped dead, then backed up the short flight. Buck Evans slapped him on the back of his tattered chambray shirt as the other six or seven Caballeros out taking in the sights burst into laughter.

"Not so fast, *mijo*," Buck said. "State you're in now, a body can't afford to be choosy."

Cowboy batted his hand away. They moved along. A park opened up to the right. The sidewalks were lined with kiosks, selling items for the impending celebrations: strings of firecrackers and origami cranes, paper kites, banners with patriotic slogans painted on them. The 'llero party trolled along in the gutter, risking stinking buses emitting belches of formaldehyde fumes from the alcohol fuel they burned.

"What are we looking for here, anyway?" Raven asked.

"I'm hunting souvenirs, myself," Cowboy said, examining a figurine of pot-bellied Hotei, the jovial Stick-and-Sack Priest. The Caballeros were very familiar with that particular one of the Seven Fortunate Gods; the most popular brand of whiskey on Hachiman was named for him. "Always kind of hoped to loot Luthien someday. I'm sure as heck not going home empty-handed."

"Hey, these folks are big on giving presents, *cuate*," Jesse James Leyva said. "We'll get something out of this when we go meet the big guy."

"Yep. A two-bit rice bowl and a pat on the fanny. 'Good job, boys and girls. Thanks for coming. Next.' "

"I'm after diversion at any cost," Risky Savage said. She had relaxed enough about being a mother to be able to leave her son Bobbi at the nursery with the other kids and go off on her own for hours at a time. "If I spend any more time being lectured on how to behave by someone I can barely understand, I think I shall go mad."

Just then a hovercar appeared from down the block in a cloud of litter blown up by its road fans. It settled in the middle of the street with a dying whine as five youths in mock-Clan costume vaulted over the sides. They came strutting up to a rickety stand selling paper lanterns with chests thrown out, conscious of the nervous stares turned their way.

"My, my," Buck Evans said. "What have we here?"

"Nothing," Mishcha Kurosawa said nervously. "Let us be moving along now. We have to be back at *Eiga-toshi* before it gets too late. You have a shoot this afternoon."

The youths had gathered around the lantern-stand and were fondling the merchandise. The tallest of the five, a lanky fellow with a green-dyed scalplock, picked up a ribbed orange lantern on a stick and began to poke holes in it with gauntleted fingers. The kiosk woman, an elderly lady in black, came teetering out from behind the counter on stick legs, expostulating wildly. The boy sneered and pushed her down to the pavement."

Cowboy set down his idol. "Now this kind of thing just torques my nuts," he said, and strode toward the lantern stand.

"Looks like Risky's going to get her wish, *¿qué no?*" Jesse James said.

The youths were playing keepaway with a stick with seven lanterns tied to it, laughing at the market woman's efforts to snatch it back and the way she limped heavily on her right leg. Cowboy walked up behind the ringleader. "Hey, man, don't you think you're getting a little out of hand?" He grabbed the boy by a padded shoulder-piece and turned him around.

The boy wheeled into him, leaping up to deliver a stiff-legged spinning kick aimed at Cowboy's head. Cowboy bobbed his lean body out of the way and took a step back. The boy dropped into an L-stance, hands stiffened into *shuto* blades.

"Hey, man," Cowboy said, holding up his hands. "I don't want no trouble—"

The ringleader grinned like a shark. The *gaijin* was showing throat. This was going to be fun. He made ready to destroy.

About then Cowboy looped an overhand right into his face, slamming down at just the right angle to break the kid's nose. The kid squawked and went down, blood spurting between his fingers. Cowboy commenced to kick him in the ribs with the pointed, steel-reinforced toes of his lizard-skin boots.

A second kid whipped his hand, which suddenly held a gleaming half-meter of extendible brass baton. He advanced on Cowboy. Without breaking the rhythm of his stomping, Cowboy whipped open a lockback folding knife and pressed the blade up under the base of the kid's nose.

"Don't go sticking it into other people's business, Sparky," Cowboy said, "unless you're looking to get it cut off."

The other rough boys started to wing out to take Cowboy in a pincers movement. The other Caballeros suddenly sprouted an astonishing array of knives. Mishcha had discouraged them from carrying firearms, banned to private citizens in the Combine, and word had come down from the Colonel himself to respect their hosts' wishes. On the other hand, carrying edged weapons reinforced one's status as a warrior. The Caballeros loved guns. But they liked knives too.

Brandishing a Bowie with a 25cm blade in one hand, Buck Evans reached out to pull Cowboy back by the collar with the other. The hard boys scooped up their fallen warrior and fell back toward their vehicle. Just before they got there, the boy with the broken face shrugged off his pals' helping hands to point his finger at Cowboy, his blood-bearded mouth twisted in fury.

Cowboy strutted forward a couple steps. "Any time, *pinche*," he called. "I'll be waiting."

"Come. We go now. This very bad," said Mishcha, whose grasp of English was slipping like a speeding 'Mech that had suddenly found itself on a frozen lake. "Their fathers very big men. Very important."

"Well, you just tell 'em my Daddy's a tornado and my Momma's a, uh—"

"Volcano," supplied Jesse, slapping Cowboy on the shoulder. "That's why you're so full of hot air."

From an alcohol-burning sedan parked just around the corner, two men watched what was happening through dark polarized vitryl as the gang boys retreated to their hovercar, hurling Parthian insults like a pack of apes. Both men were compact and tightly muscled. Both wore dark, nondescript clothes and black wraparound sunglasses that hid most of their features.

"Fools," said the man behind the wheel. He was the broader of the two, in face and shoulders, and had the good fortune that his skin showed the wheat-colored tone popularly associated with strong Japanese ancestry. "These *gaijin* with their silly notions of chivalry. Predictable as a ball rolling down a chute."

"I wouldn't be so sure, boss," said his partner, whose skin was black. Like his superior he had thick black hair planed off in an abrupt flat-top like a slab of basalt. "Might turn out they're as predictable as pachinko balls."

"Nonsense. They were so eager to fall into our trap they scarcely waited for us to set it. Those young *chimpira* were supposed to work their way up to insulting the moneytroopers' women, remember?" *Chimpira* was yak-speak for "punk," with the usual street and jailhouse connotations. Neither man would strike any but the most naïve stranger as yakuza, however. They were cut from different cloth altogether.

"It might be so," the black man said, crossing his arms and settling himself lower in his seat. Under his breath he muttered, *komatta ya,* "this worries me."

The rough boys piled back into their vehicle and rushed away in a swirl of blown-up debris. The *gaijin* stood looking after them in postures of belligerence.

"Don't be such an old woman," the first man reproved. "The *yohei* have made enemies in public. It'll be child's play to get them to step over the line. Everything will turn out just the way Big Number One says it will. Mark my words, you'll see."

The black man grunted.

12

Cinema City, Outside Imperial City
Luthien
Pesht Military District, Draconis Combine
24 June 3058

The lobby of the dorm that was housing the Seventeenth buzzed like a cow carcass on a midsummer morning on Galisteo. Some of the 'lleros were dragging back from an afternoon as enemy extras in Migaki's epic. Others, having gotten off earlier, had showered and dressed and were headed downstairs in search of refreshment and recreation. All of them, whether they were too vain to show it or not, took note of Johnny Tchang, dressed in black turtleneck and dark gray blazer, loitering by a potted plant with a bouquet of flowers behind his back.

"My, my," Captain Vanity Torres said to her entourage, pausing at the platform where two sets of stairs converged from the mezzanine to form a broad staircase leading down to the central lobby. "Will you take a look at that?"

Her retinue, mostly younger *norteñas* not pretty enough to challenge the captain's namesake trait, made appropriately admiring noises and gestures at the sight of Migaki's expensively imported star, who was answering greetings with smiles and friendly nods. That won him points among the Southwesterners, who were a pretty informal bunch themselves most of the time, and liked a man who didn't put on airs. Everyone politely ignored the two immense shaven-headed ex-*sumitori* who flanked Tchang at a discreet remove.

"Good thing I'm dressed for the occasion," Vanity went

on. And indeed she was. She wore a form-fitting white dress that began at mid-breast and stopped at mid-thigh, with various cut-outs in between, that set off to perfection her skin, the color of cinnamon toast and smooth as a Voice of the Dragon newsreader on the Laborers-go-to-bed news vidcast. She wore white bangle earrings that would have overwhelmed a lesser woman, and white high heels. She looked like a million C-bills wrapped around a one-up in the great holovid game of life.

Leaving her retainers in the dust she accelerated without showing hurry, descending the steps and approaching the waiting superstar. As she approached he got a big smile on his long, handsome face, then pushed himself off the square pillar he was leaning against to walk toward her. He brought up the flowers—

—And cruised right on past as if she were a stand-up ashtray. "Lieutenant Suthorn," he said to the slim, dark woman who was trying to slip unnoticed past Vanity's colorful hangers-on and out the door. "You're just the person I've been waiting for."

She stopped and got a guarded look in her eye. "Yes?" she said.

"We seem to've gotten off on the wrong foot the other day," Johnny Tchang said. He held the flowers out to her. "I'm sorry, and I wanted to give you these as a sort of sign that I hope we can start over again."

She accepted the bouquet warily, as if suspecting a stinging insect was concealed within. "Thank you," she said uncertainly. "I—I'm sorry I cut you."

Vanity turned and stalked back up the stairs, plowing through her retinue like a 'Mech through a flock of sheep. One of her little hangers-on tittered behind her back. Vanity stopped, turned, reduced her to cinders with a single glare, and continued on her way. The other followers backed away from the victim as if she were radioactive.

As oblivious of the striking captain's departure as of her existence at all, Johnny shook his head at Cassie. "I understand why you did what you did. And you didn't do me any lasting harm, although hearing about the nick gave Migaki-*sama* a real shock. I was wondering if you were free for dinner tonight? I've been told you've scouted the city over pretty well. I hoped you might know of a good restaurant our hosts might not be too eager to take me to. They have a pretty exaggerated outlook on my expectations, and are knuckling themselves out trying to live up to it."

"Well, thank you, Mr. Tchang, but I've got some work to do—"

"Cassie, can I talk to you just a minute, hon?"

Cassie stifled a groan. It was the person on Luthien she least wanted to catch her right now.

"Excuse me a minute," she said to Tchang. She turned and walked over to where Kali MacDougall, dressed all in black again, was propping up a wall.

"Hi, Kali."

"You sound like a schoolgirl who got caught wiring plastic explosives under the math teacher's chair. Not feeling guilty, are you?"

"Guilty? Why guilty? You know I never feel guilty, I—"

"And the only time you run off at the mouth is when you're nervous. You aren't thinking of turning Mr. Tall, Dark, and Charismatic over there *down,* are you?"

"Well—"

"Leaving aside the fact that it'll make Vanity want to kill you, since by the looks of her she wants that already, you will turn the females of the Seventeenth Recon Regiment into a raving lynch mob. If you go out with Johnny Tchang you'll make everybody jealous. If you *don't* it'll make everybody just outright hate you. Everybody—even the guys—will get a major vicarious charge out of Johnny taking one of us on a date."

"Why don't you go out with him, then?"

"Because he didn't ask me, doll. Look, Cass, it's up to you, as always. But the boy seems to like you, he's not hard to look at, and there's at least a measurable chance he's not too stupid to live, even if he is an actor. Besides, you're just spinning your wheels on this yak-war thing right now. If it were me I'd quit pushing so hard and *live.*"

Cassie sighed. "All right." She walked to where the actor stood waiting with his hands in his pockets.

"Thank you, Mr. Tchang," she said. "I'd love to take you up on your offer. Shall we?"

She half-turned, stuck her elbow out from the side. After a momentary hesitation Johnny Tchang grinned and slipped his hand through.

The watching Caballeros applauded. The two *sewanuki* took up vee-formation behind the pair.

As they strolled arm in arm through the front door, Cassie said from the side of her mouth, "One condition."

"What's that?" Johnny asked, equally discreet.

"We lose the leg-breakers."

"You think we can?"

"If you're up for it," she said, "I know we can."

He grinned.

"Somehow I feel like I know you very well already," Johnny Tchang said, pouring red wine from a green bottle. The restaurant was small, dim, and crowded. Conversation was muted. The tablecloths were checked, red on white.

Cassie stiffened. "Why do you say that?"

"No offense, Lieutenant," he said, setting the bottle down and taking a chunk of bread from a basket. "It's just, somehow I can't see too many people taking me to dinner dead in the middle of Impy City and winding up in an Italian restaurant."

She shrugged. "Actually, there are quite a few scattered around. Italian food's popular on the Pearl." She shrugged at the mystery of it all.

He laughed in appreciation. "So. How'd I do at giving my friendly escorts the slip?"

She broke off a chunk of bread, began to gnaw at it. "You followed my lead pretty smooth. Maybe playing all those spies and secret agents, something's rubbed off."

"So would you say I'm streetwise yet?"

"Let's just say you're a hell of an actor, Mr. Tchang."

He laughed. "Johnny. Please."

"Only if you lose the 'lieutenant' stuff. My rank isn't who I am. Call me Cassie."

He nodded. Their meals arrived, his spaghetti primavera and her linguine with chunks of native pelagic arthropods in white sauce. He sampled his, smiled big, and dug in. She did likewise.

As they ate they talked. Tchang told stories of his experience making adventure vids. He was as passionate about movies as was Lainie's new boyfriend, and displayed a surprisingly broad knowledge of all phases of holovid production. His ambition, like Migaki's, was to take off one day and form his own independent company. He had a light, easy touch, good timing, and a way of keeping himself off center stage. Despite herself, Cassie found herself enjoying his company. Almost she managed to relax. Almost.

The other patrons kept shooting them discreet sideglances. Nobody's gaze lingered long enough to trip any of Cassie's internal alarms. And she could understand the scrutiny. Even if her escort wasn't recognized, he was a strikingly handsome man. And she had not dressed to hide her appearance tonight. She wore a form-fitting black top, long-sleeved, with cutouts that left both shoulders bare. Her trousers were a black synthetic that looked and felt exactly like the finest Capellan silk but resisted dirt and tearing even better than Drac trichloropolyester. The trousers were baggy in the leg and snug in the rump, and had slashes running hip-to-knee down the sides, baring flashes of smooth brown hide as she walked. She looked like a beautiful woman of Bohemian propensity out for an evening on the town. She was a sultry whisper to Vanity's shout.

What the other diners—and presumably Johnny Tchang—did not know was that the openings at shoulder and thigh could be sealed with invisible clingstrips, turning the ensemble into a serviceable nighttime snoop-and-poop rig. The outside slits on the leg were matched by slashes running down the inside, currently sealed, which provided her quick access to Blood-drinker strapped to her right thigh and to her snubby hideout revolver on her left.

As they finished their pasta, a plump Upper Middle Class type in tie, coat, and trousers, came bowing up. "Please excuse the intrusion by this unworthy one, but would you happen to be Johnny Tchang?"

Johnny flashed his grin. "You got me dead to rights," he said, evoking a brief look of consternation from the ques-

tioner. It went away soon enough when he agreed to autograph a paper napkin.

In moments they were surrounded by a crowd, jostling, shouting, thrusting forward objects for the superstar's
signature.

"You have a direct approach, Cassie," Johnny remarked
as they walked down a side street at the fringes of Imperial
City's central district, where the black teak and marble were
giving way to less somber facing materials. The street was
still dark; the only illumination came from sporadic purplish
mercury-vapor streetlights and Tsu Shima, the planet's innermost moon, bluish-white and three-quarters full. The
shops were hidden away behind armored shutters. The street
was full of smelly steam from the underground mass-transit
system. Few pedestrians were abroad in the area, shutdown
as it was, and fewer vehicles. Private car ownership was
comparatively rare in the Combine, and more so here on
tradition-minded Luthien than on Hachiman. "Triggering
the sprinkler system was a pretty abrupt way to spring us
from that mob scene back at Lo Scalo."

"I guess I'm what they call result-oriented," Cassie said.
"Goes with being a scout."

The man glanced down at her. She wore a bulky jacket
against the cool of the late-spring night. She was holding
her flowers as though they were a pet bunny somebody had
given her as a birthday gift. He thought it was a charming
counterpoint to her subdued air of tough competence.

"Sometimes it's not exactly real easy to tell when you're
joking, either," he said.

"I'm not to everybody's taste."

"You are to mine, if you don't mind my saying so."

She shrugged. For a space they walked in silence. The actor had expressed a desire to get a look at some of Luthien's
steamier night-life—from the outside, he hastened to assure
her. His Voice of the Dragon handlers had carefully steered
him away from anything that might reflect badly on the
Combine in *gaijin* eyes—which his were, despite their distinct Chinese epicanthic folds. Cassie was taking him by a
shortcut she knew.

"So tell me something, if you don't mind," he said. "Why did you agree to fight me? You didn't strike me as the sort to fight for fun then, and you don't now. I thought you were going to refuse. Not that I'd've blamed you."

"I was about to. Then you patronized me."

"Patronized you? When did I do that?"

"You said it wouldn't be a fair fight—a man against a mere woman."

"No, I never said that. Be honest."

"You did say it wouldn't be a fair fight."

"I said that and nothing else. I was *about* to say it would be hard to make up for my greater weight and reach. But somebody didn't let me."

She looked up under her brows. "So it's my fault."

"No. It was *our* misunderstanding."

"You're glib."

"I'm an actor. I've been taught to be smooth, and maybe that's not always a good thing. But 'smooth' doesn't mean 'insincere,' not always." He looked at her. "I'm sorry we had a misunderstanding."

She had her head ducked down farther inside the jacket collar. *It'd be real easy to blame Vanity,* she was telling herself. *But I'm afraid I was all ready to take offense.*

"Me too," she said softly.

"You have a different perspective on the martial arts than I do," he said. "I mean, my whole life's been devoted to them. I was the son of a famous Capellan martial artist, and I was given over to the Ducal Opera Theatre Company of Sian for training when I was four." The brand of classical Chinese opera that the Ducal Theatre Company had made famous throughout the Inner Sphere combined musical theater with martial arts and acrobatics.

"So I've done this a long time. It hasn't been exactly easy. You know what training's like with the Ducal Company, and I do all my own stunts. I've always tried to keep as much realism as possible in my fight scenes, even the really gymnastic or slapstick ones. But despite the danger and the injuries—the broken back, the plate in my skull, that's one aspect of my life the tabloids haven't exaggerated— I've actually led a very sheltered life." He spread his hands.

"Which means I haven't had call to do much actual *fighting*."

"That might be about to change," Cassie said.

She spoke so quietly that he did a double-take at her before looking down the street to see three men approaching, spreading out across the sidewalk to keep them from slipping by. A glance over his shoulder showed three more approaching from behind.

Cassie had stopped and taken a step away from the actor's side. Her hand was in the right pocket of her jacket—before setting fire to a menu right under Lo Scalo's smoke sensor, she'd palmed her snubby and slipped it unseen into the holster sewn into the pocket. She would draw the piece only in emergency. On Luthien even the yakuza used firearms only on particularly serious occasions. Strewing the sidewalks with bullet-riddled corpses might attract ISF interest, and despite her past association with the Dragon's Breath, not to mention its sinister Assistant Director Ninyu Kerai, she didn't really want the ISF looking at her.

"Evening, lady, gentleman," said the man in the middle of the street, approaching them most directly. He was about midway between Cassie's and Johnny's height, with a moon face, pronounced charcoal-smudge eyebrows over black Asian eyes, well-mashed nose, full lips, and neat beard. He wore a light gray sports jacket with pale blue pinstriping, like a mattress cover, whose padded shoulders—and the body armor possibly concealed beneath—bulked out his already sizable torso to the point of caricature. His shirt and trousers were black, his tie white silk that appeared self-luminous in the moonlight. His legs were bowed and so skinny and short he looked to've borrowed them from somebody else. His shoes were two-tone Oxfords with dagger tips. It was classic *zaki*, gangster bad taste. His companions were dressed with similar discrimination. "Do you enjoy our lovely neighborhood?"

"It's real nice," Johnny Tchang said. Cassie kept quiet.

"It is of course customary to bring gifts for your host when you visit someone's home," the barrel-bodied man said. He held out his hands. "These streets are our home."

By this time the six had come up to form a ring around

Cassie and Johnny, who stood almost back to back. "We're guests of the Coordinator," the actor said. Cassie winced.

"Then you can afford to be real generous," said one of the men who had come up behind them, a tall, thin mugger with a face like something hacked out of a log by untalented tiki-makers and eyes like slits in ping-pong balls.

"Yes," Cassie said in Japanese. "May the *kami* bring you good fortune. Now get out of our way."

Moon Boy took a slap at her. She sat down beneath the blow. Johnny Tchang hopped lightly in the air, brought his straightened right leg up and around pretty and flowing as a stroke from a calligrapher's brush, and axed the fat mugger behind the ear with the heel. The yak fell down.

Cassie sensed Tiki Face rushing her from behind. Without even looking she fell forward, caught herself on her arms, and swept his right foot out from under him. As he landed with a thump and muffled outcry, she did a forward roll into the man charging from her right, passing him to his right and gifting him with a roundhouse kick in the solar plexus as she rolled by. He folded like a cheap jackknife. She jumped up and dropped a serious elbow to his kidneys. He screamed and dropped to his knees.

She gave him a hammerfist to the nape that put him on his face, moaning, turned to see Johnny block a left-right combination from the thug who'd come up to their left, then just sort of walked a series of triphammer *wing chun* punches up the front of him, ending with a shot that squashed his nose like a tomato. The goon stumbled back squalling like a cat with a stomped-on tail.

Tiki Face had gotten up. Cassie glided forward to engage him. The remaining two behind them grabbed Johnny by the arms. Moon Boy clambered to his feet, shaking his head. Roaring with ursine wrath he slammed two punches into Johnny's gut.

Johnny kicked him in the crotch. As he clutched himself the actor planted his feet against his paunch, then ran up the front of the barrel-shaped man, culminating in a backward somersault that brought Johnny behind the men who still held his arms. He slammed their faces together and threw them at the fat man.

Tiki Face feinted two jabs for Cassie's nose. She bobbed out of the way. He front-kicked for her belly. She grabbed his foot, began to twist it to the outside. He jumped, rolled in the direction of the twist, bringing his other foot around in a scissors-kick for her temple. Cued by his shift in body weight, she leaned back out of harm's way. Momentum spun him face downward. She slid a hand up his calf and levered him face-first into the cracked blacktop.

Moon Boy bellowed and shoved his two underlings back at Johnny. As much by luck as anything else they grappled his arms again. Moon Boy's ham hand dove into his mattress-cover sports coat and came out with a big shiny black autopistol.

Unfortunately for him that move was of a nature to catch Cassie's eye if it happened anywhere in her field of view, which thanks to naturally generous peripheral vision and her guru's training, was upwards of two hundred degrees. She had her snubby out and thrust forward into an arms-locked isosceles stance before his bigger piece cleared his shoulder rig.

"Johnny—*down!*" she screamed. To his credit the actor went utterly limp without hesitation, dragging his captors down with him.

Cassie fired twice. Her vision had shifted from soft-focus to pinpoint particularity; she saw two holes appear within a handspan of each other in that vast expanse of sportscoat. The autopistol blossomed fire. She heard no sound from the gunshot, but very clearly heard the *crack* of the bullet going past her ear at better than the speed of sound. She gave the mugger the last three right in his fat moon face, her own reports thunderously loud, the distinct *slap-slap-slap* of the impacts blending with the echoes from the buildings fronting the narrow street.

There came that special silence that falls after sudden gunplay, a silence such that it seems no sound will ever be heard again—which for the big-bodied guy in the sports coat was just about the size of it. From the ground Tiki Face kicked the hideout revolver from Cassie's hand. *Big deal,* she thought, *it's empty.* He jumped up with a *tanto* in his hand. She drew Blood-drinker, began to weave it and her live hand—as Guru Johann taught her to call the hand that didn't grip a weapon—sinuously before her.

She was back in soft focus. She sensed Johnny Tchang whomping on the two he'd been playing catch with, plus the man whose nose he'd punched concave—the thug Cassie had dropped with blows to nape and kidney was showing no sign of relinquishing his grip on the street. She was concentrating her attention on her own opponent, who was making quick cobra-strike flicks of his knife at her face. She sensed that he wasn't even trying to feint so much as he was to get her hypnotized with the knife, fixated on its moon-glittering menace, so that he could score an attack with foot or empty hand.

He's good, she realized, and then he astonished her by saying, "I know you. You're the mercenary bitch. I'll teach you to interfere," in Cantonese.

The shock of having the language of her childhood streets thrown in her face froze Cassie for a microsecond. The *tanto* licked for her throat. She threw her weight back and dropped her head. The blade sliced across her chin.

Blood-drinker struck. Tiki Face screamed as the tip of its wavy blade skewered the back of his forearm, passing cleanly between radius and ulna.

But he was very good indeed. Even as his knife-arm was impaled, he flicked a spike-bladed stiletto hidden in a pen open in his left hand. He stabbed toward Cassie's belly. She pivoted into him. The triangular-sectioned spike sank into the side of her right buttock.

She yanked Blood-drinker free in a spray of gore and poked it through Tiki Face's throat. Then she put a foot in his belly and thrust him away from her.

She turned, Blood-drinker dripping in her hand, face sprayed with blood, the pen-stiletto jutting from behind the ball of her right hip-joint. Johnny had reduced the odds against him to two, and them visibly the worse for wear. When they saw Cassie stalking for them with her horrible-looking knife, they gathered up their wounded but still-breathing comrades and made it out of there.

Cassie made a beeline for the man she'd shot, who lay on his back with arms outflung and eyes staring like glass marbles out of the red ruin of his face. She tore open his jacket, began to rip at the silk shirt beneath with her *kris*. Johnny came up beside her, said, "Wait one." Then he pulled the stiletto out of her.

"Thanks," she said. "Give me a hand."

Johnny closed the stiletto, dropped it into the blazer pocket. He helped Cassie manhandle the dead man's bulk onto his side. She ripped open the clingstrips that held his vest shut, pulled the polymer armor panel away from his back. The skin beneath showed a couple of scars, but was all skin-colored.

"No *irezumi*," Cassie said. "I thought so. These aren't any yaks."

"Then who are they?"

She was going through his pockets now. "Come *on*. You grew up speaking the same language I did. Don't tell me you didn't hear that skinny puke with all the knives yell at me in Chinese."

She looked up at the actor, who looked barely disheveled for all his own exertion. "These're Maskirovka. Looks like Sun-Tzu Liao wants your skinny butt back, Johnny Tchang."

He went pale. "These jokers aren't long-term on the Pearl, either. If they were, they'd have gone ahead and got the tattoos to pass for yakuza, if I know anything at all about the Mask—and unfortunately I do."

And then Johnny startled Cassie by grabbing her by the back of the jacket and throwing her bodily away from the corpse.

13

Johnny landed on top of Cassie. She uttered a catamount-squall of outrage and rolled him off. She was just climbing onto his back with her *kris* out when the fat man's corpse exploded.

Cassie froze with Blood-drinker's point jammed in under the hinge of Johnny's jaw. "Kidney bomb," he said.

Then she became aware of something warm and wet stuck in the hair above her forehead. Inner Sphere operatives often had one kidney replaced by a bomb that would be activated when certain vital signs zeroed. Some could even be triggered at will by the operative, lending a certain spice to interrogation. Agents of the Maskirovka's Capellan Operations Branch almost always had them implanted. She tasted copper and salt, spat.

"I forgot all about that," she admitted, withdrawing the *kris* and climbing off. "Good thing you knew about it."

He rubbed under his jaw and laughed. "It's all those spies and secret agents I play," he said. "Something wore off."

He started to get up, but Cassie suddenly pushed him down and fell on top of him. Tiki Face exploded.

"Forgot about him," Johnny said. Cassie made the knife go away and extended a hand to help him up.

"I hate to cut the evening short," he said, "but we'd better get back to Eiga-toshi and get cleaned up."

"Don't you think we should buzz the ISF to the fact you've got the Maskirovka bird-dogging you?"

"No."

She recovered her snubby hideout revolver, ejected the spent casings into her palm and swapped them for fresh cartridges from her pocket. "How you doing, Johnny?" she asked, looking at him hard. "Did those bad guys blowing up tumble your gyros? You're a Capellan defector. You've got the Mask on your case. It won't be long before they're all over you like Elementals on an *Enforcer*."

He cocked his head to the side. "You seem like too much of a free spirit to feel comfortable about running to the secret police."

She opened her mouth, used it to draw in a deep breath of much needed cool spring air. It was palatable as long as she kept her sense of smell and taste suppressed by blocking her nose.

He was right. The fact that she'd fought alongside the Internal Security Force as well as against it wasn't anything she lived comfortably with. And even though at last notice ISF regarded the 'lleros as being on the side of the angels, no one with all her chips pushed down tight in their sockets wanted the Dragon's Breath looking at her if she could conceivably help it. As far as Cassie was concerned, the ISF was smarter and meaner than the Maskirovka, and while it didn't have quite the Liao service's reputation for gratuitous nastiness, this game was being played not in their home field but in their locker room.

She shrugged and snapped her cylinder shut with a sidewise flip, even though she knew it was bad practice. "As my *cuates* say, it's your funeral."

He shuddered. "You have a real way with words."

"Tact isn't my department."

"Hey—you're bleeding!"

"How can you tell?"

He pulled out a handkerchief, came to her, tipped her face up. "Hmm," he said, dabbing at her with deft strokes that cleared blood away without stinging the wound too much. "Your chin's bleeding pretty well, but facial cuts are like that. Looks like a clean slice; your friend kept his knife good and sharp. If we can find some way to slow the bleeding down before you bleed out, it should heal up without leaving much of a mark. Which is good, 'cause I'd hate to think of a mark on this pretty face."

"You sound like you know what you're talking about." She pulled something out of her pocket.

"I told you, I do all my own stunts. That includes things like swordfights with real swords. I've taken my share of nicks and scratches. What's that?"

"Pressure bandage," she said, stripping off the backing. "Dosed with coagulant and antiseptics. I'm not exactly new to this either."

"Let me do that."

She hesitated, then let him pluck the bandage from her fingers and press it to her chin.

"How are you doing?" she asked, studying him closely as he worked on her.

"Fine. Just fine. Why?" His eyes were unnaturally bright, and he spoke faster than normal, but he didn't look too far out there.

"Well, for starters, now you know what a serious fight feels like," she said, "and you saw two men die."

He laughed, a bit too brassily. "I shouldn't have given you the impression I'm a total hothouse flower. I've been in a few scrapes."

"Streetfights like this?"

He shook his head. "No. Nothing quite this serious. It's . . . it's kind of exhilarating, actually."

"Maybe you shouldn't get to liking it too much. It's not like the big leagues when you've been playing street ball. It's real, and you're not playing for points. Ask those two who got strewn all over the street—not to mention your face."

His eyes got wide, and he quickly turned away. "Don't take too long with that," she advised as he heaved in the gutter. "The Friendly Persuaders will linger over their rice balls and sushi until they're dead-certain the shooting's over, but sooner or later they'll come poking around."

"Who are you?" he demanded, straightening and wiping

his mouth with his bloody handkerchief. "The reality fairy?"

She smiled sweetly as sirens began their distant boop-bop song.

Next day the sky of Luthien was clear blue as a *Vulture* strode past the feet and lower torso of a wrecked and smoking *Grand Dragon* on the Tairakana Plains near Imperial City. The leaping feline insignia of Clan Smoke Jaguar was painted on the side of the *Vulture*'s truncated-beak head. Red and blue-green lances of light flashed from the large and medium lasers mounted at the end of either arm.

As it stomped toward a *Hatamoto-chi*, the boxy twin racks mounted to either side of its head released a ripple-fired volley of long-range missiles. Explosions threw up turf and dust to either side. The Clan monster strode on, unstoppable.

"Wait for it," muttered Pyrotechnics Director Eddie Kim, watching the mock battle for Luthien from half a kilometer away, into his headset mike. "Ready . . . *now*."

An explosion blew sparks and smoking chunks from the *Vulture*'s snout, mimicking a hit from the Otomo *Hatamoto-chi*'s Tiegart particle projection cannon. The 'Mech staggered, then plunged on, firing its lasers.

"Amazing," breathed Buntaro Mayne, who was watching the shoot from beside the F/X trailer where Kim and his crew had their command center set up. "It looks real."

"It *is* real, hoss," said Cowboy Payson. "Sorta." He had on a set of plastic two-thirds scale Elemental armor painted with the Nova Cats' heavily stylized panther-head-on-sunbursts insignia. He wasn't wearing either of the gauntlets that would mimic the small laser right arm or the machine gun and manipulator arm of the left.

Command-detonated charges blew more pieces from the *Vulture* in response to the touch of incoming lasers—low-powered like the ones mounted in the apparent Clan 'Mech's mockup arms, which wouldn't boil a pot of water for tea in a week. "You'd never imagine that's Pipiribau and his dinky little *Locust* in that thing, would you? Can't tell for diddly that big old head's nothin' but papier-mâché and baling wire."

One of the nearer F/X techs winced at the Cowboy's description. While the false *Vulture* head mounted on the head of El Pipiribau's *Locust*—from which Zuma had carefully dismounted the small-laser arms and medium-laser chin turret—was made out of many materials, neither baling wire nor papier-mâché were among them. It was a highly sophisticated model, crammed full of small smoke and explosive charges, painstakingly placed.

"O.K., everybody," Eddie Kim was saying, "here comes the money shot."

A *Hatamoto-chi* strode to meet the Clan machine. Ostensibly it was piloted by Johnny Tchang's character, but in fact was under the control of its normal jock, Lieutenant Senior Grade Elvis "Stretch" Santillanes, commander of the Caballeros' Eskiminzin Company. It fired twin salvos of short-range missiles at the *Vulture*.

Like the missiles the mock *Vulture* fired, they were nothing but big skyrockets. They carried black-powder warheads big enough to produce a flash, bang, and satisfying cloud of smoke, but not enough to scratch the paint on a real 'Mech, or even, barring bad luck, do much damage to the plastic *Vulture* appliances stuck all over the *Locust*.

The F/X wizards' luck was in. The volley struck on and around the built-up 'Mech. One of Kim's men triggered a charge that mimicked an explosion of the LRMs in the *Vulture*'s left rack. The whole left side of the "head" flew apart. Vomiting smoke from concealed pots, the BattleMech toppled over sideways.

Though it was small by BattleMech standards, a *Locust*'s twenty tons was a respectable chunk of metal. The onlookers felt the impact from some five hundred meters off. Buntaro Mayne shook his head.

"The pilot must be crazy to willingly make his machine fall over like that," he said, as the F/X crew cheered and exchanged high fives. "Unless he likes having his teeth rattled loose in their sockets."

"Nope," Cowboy said admiringly, "the Peep's just crazy."

* * *

"What I'm trying to achieve," Takura Migaki said, pouring a cup of steaming tea for his new friend during a break in shooting, "is something not only faithful to the look and feel of the period, but to the real *story*."

Father Doctor Bob García accepted the tea with a smile and thanks. They were sitting in a tent pitched near the old battlefield on which the new holovid was being recorded. They weren't discussing *Dragon Phoenix*, though, but the Voice of the Dragon chief's other project.

Migaki settled himself onto a camp stool. The ground trembled as a column of Caballero 'Mechs rumbled past outside. "According to legend, Lord Kira was an evil conniver who manipulated the young Lord Asano into drawing his sword in the Shogun's presence. That was a capital offense, and the only way for Asano to redeem his family's honor was to commit suicide. Asano's forty-seven retainers became *ronin*. For a time they lived as common laborers, utterly disgraced. But when they felt the time was right, they assaulted Kira's castle and avenged their lord by killing him. They were ordered to commit suicide in turn."

He sipped. "That's all true enough, as far as the bare events go. It glosses over certain details such as that the *bakufu,* the military government, did not in fact want to punish the forty-seven *ronin* for their act, but that the *ronin* forced the government's hand. What intrigues me is that accounts from that time suggest Lord Kira was a man of compassion and wisdom who did nothing wrong, while Asano was a hot-headed young idiot. That's almost never been brought out in any dramatic presentation of *Chushingura*. But it's how I'm presenting mine."

Migaki's cheeks got flushed when he spoke of his projects, and his eyes gleamed. Father Doctor Bob sipped tea and nodded.

"That sounds fascinating from a dramatic standpoint," he said, "but I hope you won't be upset if I admit to a certain confusion. Isn't the role of Voice of the Dragon Productions to produce films that reinforce Combine values?"

"Of course." Migaki set his teacup on the ground and leaned forward, making emphatic gestures with his hands.

"But that's just what I'm doing. We're conveying the message that *giri*—duty—is absolute. The fact that its objects may be unworthy does not obviate its force."

"Ah." The Jesuit smiled. "That's very neat. Worthy of my Company, if I might say so. So your own desire and the interests of the Dragon coincide in this matter."

Migaki grinned like a twelve-year-old. "I love it when that happens."

García held up a finger, "Ah, but how do you tell the one from the other? How do you know you're not letting your own desires color your view of what's good for the Dragon?"

Migaki sighed. "You know, I used to think that was the simplest thing in the world to do. I *knew* what was right, and that was that." He shrugged. "And maybe that's how I know I'm no longer young. It's not so easy anymore to assume automatically that what I want is the right thing."

An aide stuck his head in the flap of the tent. "Deputy Director Migaki, you have a call from the Marquis Maturro."

Migaki made a face. "Bring me a handset. If I have to talk to him, at least I don't have to look at his ugly face."

"Hai."

"Apologies, Bob-*sensei*," Migaki told his guest. "The Minister of Finance." He shrugged.

"I understand. Have no worries."

The aide brought a hand communicator and left. Migaki spoke some, listened a lot, then broke the connection.

"Mattaku!" he exclaimed as he set the hand phone on a table. "Damn. Those wild men and women of yours have gone and stepped in it this time. The Minister just left a new set of rat-shaped tooth marks on my posterior thanks to them."

"What happened?"

"They assaulted his son in an open-air market downtown. Broke the lad's nose. The Minister is flying around in the air about it." He shook his head. "We're going to have to do something to rein them in."

The Jesuit carefully set his tea cup down. "May I say something about this matter?" Migaki made a go-ahead gesture. "In my capacity as Regimental Intelligence Officer, not to mention Chief Psychologist, I try to keep abreast of incidents our people are involved in. I have some information about this one. Apparently, the young man in question is a member of what I can only call a street gang. He and his fellows were harassing a vendor—a Combine citizen. Driven by what as a native Southwesterner I have to admit is a rather quaint concept of chivalry, several of our people intervened to protect the woman. The Minister's son, I gather, assaulted a Caballero. He was injured as a result."

Father Doctor Bob picked up his cup. "I hope I'm not injuring our cause when I mention that the younger Maturro is lucky to be alive. Our people are warriors."

Migaki made a disgusted sound.

"I'll be happy to put all the information I have obtained at the Deputy Director's disposal."

Migaki waved him off. *"Dekigoro-zoku,"* he said. "I should have known. It rings too damn true. The Minister's son is known to be running with those packs of young animals, relying on their status to protect them from any consequences."

He paced left several paces, then right. With his back to García he chopped air by his head. "Even for me it's not exactly easy to put a good face on this kind of thing. All I can do is appeal to your understanding. This is a strong society, a fundamentally healthy one—I really believe it." He turned. "But it isn't perfect."

García smiled. "I wouldn't be so rash as to suggest our own society's perfect. I'm in no hurry to judge yours. In truth, our people might as easily have been responsible for this incident. But I honestly believe that not to be the case."

A smile stole over Migaki's face. Negative emotions didn't seem to hang around him long, the Jesuit noted.

"Actually, I think your barbarians have done me a favor," Migaki said. "It'll be a pleasure to rake that shaven-headed buffoon Maturro over the coals for letting his son act like a beast. I do believe I'll take you up on that offer to show me your evidence on this thing, Father. I'll need to be sure of my footing for this job."

García rose. "It will be my pleasure, Deputy Director."

Migaki took several steps toward the exit. Then he checked himself and swung around.

"One thing," he said. "It might be best to restrict your non-essential personnel to the compound until after the celebration. Just to prevent further incidents."

García laughed. "You really think that's wise?"

Migaki rubbed his face. "Maybe I'm thinking with my mouth again. They'd tear the place apart. Very well; forget about that.

"Just make sure your people know that they've made themselves a powerful enemy. Likely more than one."

══════ 14 ══════

Tumbledown District, Imperial City
Luthien
Pesht Military District, Draconis Combine
25 June 3058

When she heard the distinctive crack of lasers Cassie knew she was onto something.

She was cruising in the southeastern sector of town, out toward the spaceport. It was not the most elegant sector of Imperial City. The buildings ran to slablike apartment blocks for the lowest class of Workers, big people-boxes with raw edges and flaking cement. Between them rose warehouses, and also the makeshift shanties of the Unproductives and those who were slipping close to that status. The Friendly Persuaders tore down the shanties regularly, Cassie's informants told her, but the squatters put them back up just as regularly.

The streets were stiff with vehicles, farty alcohol-burning trucks and buses whose formaldehyde-laced exhaust fumes brought tears to the eyes and a profusion of pedal-powered carts and cabs. The interstices between vehicles were filled with people, who somehow managed not to get squashed. Apparently the trucks' horns, and the bells and fervent curses of the pedicab pushers exerted some magic repellor-field effect on pedestrians.

There was a lot of construction going on down here, and just as much destruction, much of it by the usual ravages of time—and that didn't take long, given the shabby building materials that went into low-Worker housing. But most of the deconstruction could be attributed to the standard damage caused by the wrecking-ball and bulldozer in the name of some definition of progress. Cassie wondered if it was meaningful or just government make-work. For all Theodore's reforms, the Combine was still saddled with a military economy big-time. With the Clans hanging like a guillotine blade above the Tukayyid truce line and about a hundred years' economic progress separating the Combine from its erstwhile main rivals—now doing business as the Lyran Alliance and the ramp Federated Commonwealth—that meant millions of Draconians were unemployed, and millions more hard at work in the one-gang-digs-holes-another-fills-them-in type of job.

That wasn't her problem. Her problem was finding somebody hidden in this teeming ratbox jungle whose name, description, and even gender she didn't know.

Going by way of Lainie and her people had borne fruit, although as yet Cassie had enjoyed little free time to devote to the problem of why the *Tai-sa* herself was acting so odd. Through her long-time bodyguard Moon, Lainie kept lines of communication open to Tosei-*kai,* the Voice of the East Syndicate, made up predominantly of ethnic Koreans. Tied to no territory, they tended to have contacts everywhere—in every city of every world of the Combine.

Cassie had them out looking for anything unusual. It was too broad an order to expect much to come of it, she knew, what with thousands of people flocking to Luthien for the Coordinator's Birthday, not to mention a gang war in progress. But she was trying roughly everything at once, feeling time's press. She had tried kicking the bushes to see what kind of animals she could stir up, and had roused some exotic ones indeed—and she probably owed Johnny Tchang an apology for using him as bait. But the Maskirovka leaping at her, or at Johnny anyway, was just too weird—it had to be happenstance, not connected with the still-hypothetical Black Dragon menace.

So she discounted that, and kept pumping energy into the system in a variety of ways. She had faith in chaos, especially in a society as order-obsessed as the Combine. A little turbulence could carry a great distance. Plotters would be

especially susceptible to feeling their comfort-zones en-
croached upon by spreading waves of chaos.

She didn't know if the tip from the Koreans that there
was somebody interesting hiding out in the Tumbledown
District was signal or noise. The tip was no more specific
than that: there's somebody down there who doesn't belong.
That meant somebody who was willing to balance the risks
of being an outsider who didn't know the moves, and therefore was a designated target, against the fact that down there
in the Tumbles no one who wasn't a paid informer said anything to the Man.

So she went diddy-bopping down the lane, with the sun
peeking through the clouds after a brief sprinkle, and the
moisture freshening the various organic stinks. She was
dressed as a low-Worker girl, a menial laborer who was
pushed hard to hang onto that much status, with baggy
clothes and a cap pulled low over a face artfully smeared
with grime, so that nobody would get to wondering why a
near-Unproductive girl that pretty didn't just bag it and
make a life for herself in the *ukiyo* pleasure houses.

Cassie stopped when she heard the noise, coming as if
from a street or two over, but unmistakable. It wasn't the
firecrackers beginning to be heard singly or in strings, let off
in spasms of premature celebration. Nor was it conventional
gunfire. It was lasers, not the full-throated thunderclap of
the big 'Mech variety, but the snap of hand-weapons. More
than one, by the sound.

Somebody was hunting somebody.

She started running for the sound. It made her very definitely a standout nail: everybody else on the street was
heading purposefully in the exact opposite direction, no
matter where they'd been headed a moment before.

Cassie had small faith in coincidences. She was hunting a
standout nail. If someone else was doing this much pounding in the Tumbles, how big were the chances they were
looking to drive in a different target?

She turned a corner. The street fell away in a long rutted
slope. It was empty as a politician's promise.

That flash confirmed a strong suspicion: the people doing
the hammering were official. If this were an escalation of

the turf war between the Old Cat Yamaguchi and the interloper Inagawa, people would be shifting out of the line of
fire, but at no pains to be making themselves this scarce.
The almost miraculous evaporation of traffic in the area
meant people very urgently wanted no part of what was going down here.

Besides, lasers were not common in civilian hands in the
Draconis Combine. When the yaks wanted to shoot each
other they favored pistols, SMGs, and the odd shotgun.
Lasers generated too much heat, and not of the kind Mech-
Warriors worried about.

It wasn't just any official Snakes shooting their way
closer, either. The Friendly Persuaders were not permitted
to use laser weapons. The Combine military *sometimes* got
issued hand lasers, but unless the Clans had invaded again
and Cassie just hadn't noticed, the DCMS had no reason to
be rampaging through the slums of Imperial City.

She crossed the street. Instinct made her hunker down to
peer back around the corner of a building. Two streets down
a pair came into view, paralleling her course, male and female. The woman covered around the corner, the man
crossed to the corner opposite, then covered from that side
while the woman darted a few meters to the shelter of a light
standard. They wore nondescript worker-class mufti, but
their true nature was given away by the clear wraparound
transpex face-shields they wore and the laser pistols they
carried—and by their actions.

ISF. Cassie felt her blood temperature plunge. Whether
these were DEST or the Internal Security Division, she
couldn't tell. But the way they were equipped, what they
were doing, and the way they did it indicated they could be
no one else.

From somewhere off and to her right lasers were still
blazing away. A fight was still in progress. A delaying action? No way to tell. The hunters were being cautious as
well as methodical.

Cassie dashed on the way she'd been going, looked
around the next corner. Another deserted street—deserted
except for a single feminine figure in torn spacer's coveralls
limping up the far side of the street. She paused, glanced

back fearfully the way she had come and ducked into a
three-quarters-finished apartment bloc.

Cassie raced for the entryway. The wounded woman had
to be the one she sought. And she must be important somehow. While it was not unheard-of for the ISF to shoot up
sections of Drac cities, even the capital of their whole empire, in broad daylight, they weren't going to do it the week
before Coordinator's Birthday in pursuit of somebody
who'd spray-painted a scurrilous haiku on a men's room
wall in the Yoshiwara pleasure district.

She hit the side of the doorway with her snubby in both
hands, then rolled around, extending the piece before her
like a probe. The entryway was dark and cool and full of the
smell of cement. That was one way Luthien differed from
the Capellan world of Larsha: not even the corridors of the
cheapest public housing stunk of piss and vomit.

Her quarry had left a trail of blood-droplets on the floor.
Lasers sometimes partially cauterized wounds, but it wasn't
a reliable effect. Because they flash-boiled the fluid in tis-
sue, causing bursting damage, they tended to be messy. She
followed the blood-trail quickly. Right now it was a help.

When the hounds caught up, it would be a lot less so.

To the left and right, empty doorways yawned like eyeholes in a skull. By the light that trailed down through cat-
walks overhead Cassie could see tiny cubicles as she
passed. The trail led into one on the right. She tucked her
pistol into her waistband in back, beneath her rude wind-
breaker, and walked in.

A semiauto hideout pistol appeared centimeters from her
nose. The firing-pin clicked on an empty chamber. Cassie
froze.

"Oh! You're not one of them!" The wounded woman
staggered backward into a supply-laden board propped between two sawhorses, upsetting it with a clatter that almost
made Cassie's heart—already in her throat—explode.

"I'm . . . sorry," the woman said, and let the little hand-
gun fall from her hands.

Through swirling white dust Cassie saw that the woman
was about her own age, mid to late twenties, probably plain,
but her face was too transfigured with grime and blood and

fear to tell. The right side of her jumpsuit was dyed maroon with blood, and smoldered.

Cassie couldn't judge the exact extent of the woman's injuries, but doubted the trickle of blood down her chin was from having bitten her tongue.

"I want to help you," Cassie said. Her own voice sounded distant and alien through the pulse-yammer in her ears.

"Is this a trick?" the woman asked. She came up against the far wall, slid down, leaving a broad trail of red.

"There's no time. If you don't trust me there's no hope."

"Are you a loyal daughter of the Dragon?"

"Yes."

"I—" The woman coughed violently. Blood poured from her mouth. Cassie moved to help her, but the woman waved her off. "I am *metsuke*. Do you know what that means?"

"Yes."

"My verification code is 25 Chrysanthemum 6. Can you remember that?"

"25 Chrysanthemum 6."

"Good . . . good." Her voice was weakening. "The Director must learn: there is treason—"

The room filled with ruby brilliance. A crack, a stench of ozone, and burned meat as the woman was slammed back against the wall by the jet effect of her own body fluids boiling away from a laser beam.

Cassie spun, her hand already behind her back. A blonde woman wearing a clear wraparound face-shield and a hands-free comm set stepped into the room, holding her laser pistol before her. She glanced at the fallen woman, whose chest was blown open. Then she turned toward Cassie.

What Cassie saw in her brown eyes was . . . nothing. Not even regret: sorry, citizen, you're in the wrong place at the wrong time, but the Dragon demands his sacrifices now and then. . . . Not the satisfaction of a job well done. Not anything. She was going to wipe Cassie off the face of Luthien, and she wasn't even in any hurry about it.

Cassie crossed her ankles and sat down. Her vision filled to overflowing with glare. A patch of cement exploded right over her head with a thunderclap sound, right where her sternum had been an eyeblink before, blasting fragments against the back of her head and neck.

She pulled her snubby out from behind her and thrust it to her arms' full extension, then shot the blonde woman in the stomach. Not even DEST body armor would let a person to take a hit at that range and not react; the other woman bent forward, laser slipping off line, left hand falling away from the grip. Cassie waited for her to straighten up, walked two more shots up her torso, then put the last two rounds through the woman's upper lip, just beneath the bulletproof visor. The bullets trashed the medulla and snipped the spinal cord, switching off her central nervous system. The blond operative went down like a length of rope allowed to hang from the hand and then dropped.

"You bitch!" Cassie hissed. "You God-damned bitch, you were going to kill me like a roach." Running on autopilot, she thumbed the catch on her hideout piece as she spoke, swung open the cylinder, pocketed the empties and reloaded her piece. The rage was like an explosion within her, white-hot and roiling.

She moved quickly to the body of the woman she'd followed here, and found her still breathing. Her eyes looked up at Cassie with more sorrow than pain. "Sadat," she whispered, and her head lolled to the side.

Cassie did not spend any time feeling for a pulse. The blonde operative's partner would be here within heartbeats. She looked around, saw the *metsuke*'s fortuitously empty hideout pistol lying on the floor, pressed it into the dead woman's hand, then headed out the door.

In passing she kicked Blondie in the ribs. "Bitch."

The corridor was empty. From the front of the building Cassie could hear minute rat-sounds of stealthy movement. The blonde agent had outrun her backup. There was a back way. Cassie found it and was gone.

═══ 15 ═══

DropShip Garryowen, *Takashi Kurita Memorial*
Spaceport
Imperial City, Luthien
Pesht Military District, Draconis Combine
25 June 3058

"**C**hu-sa Sakamoto?"

The tall man paused in the act of shouldering his kit bag. His black hair was cut in an unruly shock. Despite the scars that seamed his tan face, he looked younger than his age, which was late thirties. His eyes were blue and watchful.

"Hai," he said.

Like himself, the three men who had come into the Drop-Ship's debarkation area wore the simple MechWarrior uniform. The two flanking were young men with very erect carriage and holstered sidearms. The central of the trio was a chow dog of a man with thick black eyebrows. He was the one who had spoken.

"I am *Sho-sho* Oda Hideyoshi," the chow dog said. "I command the Otomo. Your father has directed me to greet you in his name."

Franklin Sakamoto bowed. "I am honored to make your acquaintance, *Sho-sho*. Your reputation is formidable."

"As is yours. Your exploits against the Clans are not widely known to the Draconis Combine, but I have enjoyed the privilege of following the reports, from your days with the Somerset Strikers onward."

"I serve the Dragon as best I can, Hideyoshi-*sama*."

"Your father sends regrets that he could not meet you in

person. However, he is sure you will understand that the press of imperial business does not permit."

"Indeed."

"Please permit my man to take your bag."

Sakamoto hesitated, then nodded. One of the armed Otomo stepped forward and shouldered the bag.

"Is it permitted to ask where we're going?" Sakamoto said.

"Of course. I've been instructed to escort you to a villa just outside the city, overlooking the Katsura River. A lovely location, quite secluded."

He gestured with a square hand covered with small white scars that attested to his long-time fondness for *kenjutsu* training with live steel. "If you please."

They started down the ramp. The sun was falling toward the hills west of the city. The light had that curious vibrancy that precedes dusk, which makes everything it touches seem to glow. A hovercar waited at the foot of the ramp.

"You will be comfortable at the villa, but you will be kept in seclusion for the next few days. Security."

Sakamoto frowned. "My father doesn't think I can take care of myself?"

Hideyoshi grinned. "There is no dishonor in being guarded, young man; otherwise my regiment would not exist. Few in the Combine would raise their hands against the Coordinator, and he is still a formidable warrior. But it has never occurred to him to disband the Otomo."

He stopped at the foot of the ramp. "You have renounced all claims of inheritance. Still you cannot change the fact of your parentage. You do not bear the name of Kurita, but you bear many of the responsibilities that attend the name. There are always malcontents, men who might seek to use you as a weapon against the Coordinator, and they are powerful. It would not be wise to expose yourself to them."

Franklin Sakamoto produced a lopsided smile. "Wisdom is among the Virtues of the Dragon. I am in your hands."

Oda Hideyoshi grinned again. "Good boy." He slapped Sakamoto on the shoulder. "Come on then. You won't regret it. We'll see you're properly entertained at the villa."

* * *

"The moons are very beautiful tonight, Theodore-*sama*," the old man said. He was short, big-bellied, bandy-legged, with a scruffy beard and a balding head. But his chest and shoulders were big and solid; there was vigor in his gravelly voice and a youthful glitter in his eyes.

"It's so, old friend," Theodore Kurita said. They stood by a boulder carved by the wind into a hunched shape that suggested a bird about to take flight. A Coordinator from long ago had personally selected it from the Kiyomori Mountains and had it transported here, to the Unity Palace garden. In the light of green Orientalis and blue Tsu Shima, it cast pink and orange shadows on the raked white sand.

The two men crossed the basalt flagstones set at calculated but irregular intervals designed to force strollers to walk deliberately and to encourage unhurried appreciation of the garden's subtle beauties.

For a time they shared the silence of friends who are comfortable with each other. An imported nightingale sang from a native trilander bush, whose thick leaves filled the air with an exotic aroma. At night, powered vehicles were banned from the vicinity of the Palace, and so the night was quiet save for wafts of music drifting up from the yellow-lighted apartments surrounding the tiered and flanged black mass of the Palace. The faraway noises blown from the streets outside were one of the few things able to penetrate the Palace's high walls, studded with both motion sensors and broken glass. From the distance came the pop of fire-crackers lit off in early celebration.

Or of small-arms fire. Theodore glanced at his companion. Hiroo Yamaguchi was the much-feared oyabun of Luthien's yakuza, and just as familiar with the sound of weapons fire in the streets.

As if sensing the trend of the Coordinator's thoughts and wishing to shift their course, the stocky man said, "I have a present for you, *Tono*."

"My birthday's not for another week, Yamaguchi-*san*."

Yamaguchi grunted. He was a man who always got great mileage from guttural sounds and rolls of his wrestler's shoulders. It wasn't that he was inarticulate, merely that he was eloquent with grunts and shrugs.

He held forth a black plastic box, small and flat. He pressed a button with a crack-nailed thumb. Minute yellow and green lights chased each other across the object. The soft sound of a clarinet flowed from it like smoke.

"Nan da yo!" Theodore exclaimed. "What the hell! It can't be."

The old man smiled and handed the player over. "What do you think it is?"

The Coordinator was turning the gift wonderingly over in his hands. "I think that's Les Hoffman and his Tragic Band, and I think they're playing 'April Morn.' "

"What's so impossible about that?"

"I didn't think any recordings existed any more. I've been looking for almost twenty years."

It was twenty-fifth century natural jazz, which had originated in the Lyran Commonwealth, although Hoffman hailed from Atreus in the Free Worlds League. Theodore had acquired the taste when a collection of the recordings fell his prize after he forced the Third Lyran Guards to retreat off Vega in December of 3028. Though he'd carried them with him—and added to the collection—for years, such treasures were not likely to survive the life of a soldier. This one was lost in a hasty withdrawal on Exeter when the Fox Hanse Davion took Theodore's bait and committed his Fourth Davion Guards to the world, thereby setting up the counterstroke called Operation Orochi during the War of 3039.

Theodore had since reconstituted the collection, and even improved on it. But he had never been able to lay hands on another copy of Hoffman's understated "April Morn," revered by cognoscenti as the crown jewel of the short-lived movement.

"Tetsuhara-*sensei* taught me never to ask questions I didn't want to know the answers to," he said, "so I won't ask where you turned this up, you old pirate."

The Old Cat produced a sound like pebbles being stirred into a cement mixer. "Your wisdom does honor to your teacher."

"I thank you, Yamaguchi-*san*. You know how I'll treasure

this gift. But why tonight? My birthday's not for almost another week." *And how glad I'll be when it's passed.*

"Mujo," the old yakuza said with a shrug, signifying the transience of life.

Theodore frowned. He knew about the gang war going on in the back alleys of his capital city. But his compact with *seimeiyoshi-rengo,* the confederation of yazuka gangs, was explicit: as long as the underworld kept its own house in order, the Coordinator did not meddle in its affairs.

But still, he thought, *this is friendship, not politics.* "He is a poor lord who neglects the interests of his subordinates," Theodore said, "or who believes that *giri* is a sword that cuts one way only."

"The way of the oyabun is hard," Yamaguchi said. "One must never be seen to favor."

"Kimochi ga tsujita." The feeling is understood. Theodore recalled all too well his father's tendency to favor toadies—and disfavor his own son. He thought, with a sense of internal impact, of the son he had had arrested today.

Not arrested, he told himself. *Detained for his own good.* At once he was ashamed and angered at himself for such a clumsy swipe at self-deceit.

"Besides," the old man went on, "while one may love one's subordinates as one's own children, in the end it is on the basis of how they serve the *uchi* that they must be judged. If one cannot bear his weight, is it not best for all that he be pruned, like a withered branch, instead of being propped up to draw nutrients from the more productive limbs?"

For answer Theodore gestured to a faldamon tree by the path, stout and gnarled, whose trunk rose half a meter from the ground before diverging into limbs thick as a man's leg that ran parallel to the soil before rising sharply upward. One branch was supported by a discreet scaffold.

Yamaguchi laughed. It was a bold, uproarious laugh. One overly concerned with punctilio might find it boisterous and vulgar, not at all *basho-gara,* appropriate to the circumstances. Theodore found his old friend's laughter elemental, like the force of wind and rain.

"If only the world beyond was as simple as our Japanese gardens, Theodore-*sama!*" the old outlaw proclaimed.

"But isn't pruning a fruitful branch the hallmark of an inept gardener?" Theodore asked, a little desperately. He felt weary, disgusted with this game, disgusted with himself, disgusted with the limitations wound like unbreakable, adamant kelp from Luthien's Silver Sea around the limbs of the man who was, all things accounted for, one of the most powerful individuals in the whole Inner Sphere. He could not help his friend unless his friend asked his aid. In his marrow he felt the need of the sleep denied him by his dead father's reproaches in dreams.

Yamaguchi smiled. His battered old face looked beatific in double moonlight. "Only the Dragon is forever, Theodore-*sama.*"

Theodore opened his mouth. Before he could speak, the old yakuza leader bowed to him, and walked calmly but purposefully away into the perfumed night.

It was the next morning and in a place very different from the fragrant gardens of the Imperial Palace that a tray hit the restaurant's floor with an emphatic plastic thump, followed in a beat by the secondary clatter of used dinnerware hitting tile. The patrons' heads turned from their rice balls and hummus. The big man in the loud jacket, whose neck was wider than his head and sat nearest the hapless pot girl, jumped as if he'd heard a gunshot. *Precisely* as if he'd heard a gunshot.

"*Chikusho!*" he bellowed, rounding on her. "Stupid beast. I don't know why the owner employes such fools. She's probably Korean."

The pot girl, who was small, skinny, and snub-nosed, abased herself, crouching on all fours and bouncing her forehead off green and white tiles. "Apologies for this poor one's inexcusable clumsiness!" she wailed in abominably accented Japanese. "It won't happen again. Please pardon this poor one, merciful sir!"

The yakuza kobun sneered and turned back to trying to impress the waitress, a pretty, vacant-eyed young woman with dark roots to her blonde hair and a way of rhythmically snapping her chewing gun that the yak evidently found irresistible.

"Like I was saying before that clubfooted *animal* interrupted, I got a big job tonight. The Top Number has a big meet tonight."

"How exciting," the waitress said through her nose.

"I can't tell you anything about it," the gangster said, not at all furtively. "It's a big secret. Let's just say there's gonna be a few *changes* around here."

"How exciting."

The proprietor Luko, a large man with an impressive expanse of apron, came out to berate the pot girl in a loud voice for her clumsiness. The pot girl babbled apologies, still on hands and knees, grabbing at plastic bowls and trays. These eluded her grasp as if alive, skittering like small animals across the smooth glazed surface of the floor.

And all the while she listened to the yak footsoldier running his face to impress his little waitress, missing nothing. Cassie Suthorn was adept at tuning out noise. She was, after all, the Perfect Scout.

She had thought about calling Ninyu Kerai about yesterday's encounter with the ISF. They had history, after all. She wasn't foolish enough to believe that her brief liaison with him back on Hachiman would gain her anything now. But she knew he had learned to respect her, as opponent and ally. He would be likely to take her seriously, not dismiss her as a hysterical *gaijin* woman, or yet an *agente provocateuse*. She could not expect that from anyone else in the Internal Security Force, especially not Ninyu Kerai's adoptive father, the enigmatic Smiling One.

And there was the problem of reaching Ninyu directly. She had no direct line to him. She could hear the conversation with the ISF receptionist in her mind: "Hello, I'm a foreign mercenary woman in town for Theodore's birthday party, and I'd like to talk to the Assistant Director. Yeah, he and I go way back. We did it on Hachiman. . . ."

Resorting to authority figures usually bugged her. Even friendly ones. But with the Coordinator's Birthday bearing down like a *Texas* Class battleship plummeting from orbit, she had no time for niceties. As soon as she was sure her tail was clean of pursuit the day before, she'd hustled it out to Eiga-toshi for a talk with the Mirza Peter Abdulsattah, Uncle Chandy's head of security.

"You want me to try to set up a meeting for you with Ninyu Kerai," the tall man asked. "And you can't tell me why."

"Right," Cassie said.

"But this concerns your assignment."

"I don't know." Cassie was never sure why she felt such an urge to speak frankly to the Mirza. Perhaps because, like his employer, he had never yet abused it when she did. "I believe it does. And that's all I can tell you."

He sat and looked at her a moment with his heavy-lidded gaze, his eyes the kind a Kurita would have called Arkab, that being their linguistic corruption of the word "Arab." She felt that chill in her bowels that she often did with him, the conviction he was seeing more than eyes should, more than she wanted anyone to see.

"Very well," he said. "I'll see what I can do."

For a moment she just stood there before the desk in the modest office Migaki had assigned the Mirza for his stay on Luthien. Perhaps because of her long association with Lieutenant Colonel Gordon Baird, the Seventeenth's late S-2, she wasn't used to a security chief acting more like a security agent—one who understood that he only needed to know what he needed to know—than a boss. Nor was it the sort of demeanor generally expected from a Drac boss, but then, Cassie and her companions had long since learned not to expect much orthodoxy from their rotund employer, or anyone connected with him.

"Thank you," she said, and left.

As far as she was concerned the matter was out of her hands. She knew the Mirza would do what he could, and she respected his ability. So she went back to trying to find a handle whereby she could pry loose information on the Black Dragons—and whether Benjamin District Inagawa's power play on Luthien was connected to some bigger Black Dragon scheme, or purely personal.

The Voice of the East Syndicate—Lainie's friends the

Tosei-*kai*—had come through again. She learned that Inagawa had brought a battalion-sized entourage with him to Luthien, as had his pal Hiraoke Toyama from Dieron. And all those hungry yaks needed a place to feed, not to mention places to stay and to hang out. For obvious reasons these would *not* be the same hangouts frequented by, say, the Old Cat's bully boys. Cassie's Tosei-*kai* informers had identified this part of Luthien's Pascal District, on the fringes of the Yoshiwara *ukiyo,* as a favored rookery for the Inagawa-*kai* bachelor males.

Because the Tosei-*kai* served much the same function for the Combine's Water Trade, and for the yaks themselves, as the yaks did for government and what passed for the private sector in Drac industry—providing cheap grunt labor—they had little trouble sliding Cassie into her current employment as junior pot girl at Luko's Rice Ball Palace, Home of the Hummus Burger. Despite their traditional neutrality in the intramural squabbling among the predominantly Japanese yakuza orgs, the Tosei-*kai* were devoted to Theodore Kurita—and hostile to *Kokuryu-kai,* which regarded ethnic Koreans as dogs, whether straw or otherwise, and thought they should be treated accordingly. Should Inagawa's power struggle with Yamaguchi be nothing more, the Koreans would maintain their neutrality. Should it be connected with the Black Dragons, however, they would be only too happy to help Cassie shaft Inagawa six ways from Sunday.

In any event, getting Cassie a job at the Rice Ball Palace wasn't prejudicial to Inagawa's interests, as far as Voice of the East was concerned, since if Inagawa wasn't involved in any Black Dragon conspiracies against Teddy or the Seventeenth she had no interest in him. She had not mentioned her purely private undertaking to avenge the murder of concierge Jinjiro Coleman. But unless Inagawa had throttled the old man with his own hands, that matter didn't concern him either.

"I really shouldn't be telling you this," the foot soldier was saying to the gum-chewing waitress, "but you look to me like the sort of woman who knows how to keep her lips sealed. It's at a mansion in Paschal—"

Luko's abuse against his employee reached a crescendo of vilification. The yak soldier's ears turned red and he twisted in his seat. *"Bakayaro!"* he thundered. "The Korean bitch only made noise a little while. Will you *shut up*?"

The shop-owner dissolved into near-tearful apologies. The pot girl gathered up the last of the errant dishes and scuttled for the safety of the rear.

Imperial City, Luthien
Pesht Military District, Draconis Combine
26 June 3058

The villa where the Big Meet was taking place was an imitation Japanese castle of black teak, rising five stories among lofty capylar trees in the northwestern Upper Middle Class suburb of Paschal. It had been built by an ambitious courtier to Coordinator Martin McAllister after McAllister ended the previous regime with a coup and the usual atrocities more than five hundred years before. The neighborhood had since declined, in terms of standing within the hierarchy of Combine society, if not in terms of wealth. It was still a favored locale for high-level executive types angling to win a patent of nobility and, barring that, hoping a bit of the district's *buke* legacy might rub off. As was standard for the district, a three-meter-high stone wall surrounded the grounds, which sprawled down the side of a low ridge. The wall was topped with the usual array of broken bottles, motion sensors, and photo cells.

Flanking the traditional-style horned-lintel gate stood two large men with necks wider than their heads. Their suits were dark, as opposed to garish, as was appropriate to the circumstances. That notwithstanding, and despite the fact that the button-down collars of their white shirts thoroughly concealed their *irezumi*, few observers of Combine origin would have trouble pegging them instantly as yakuza. They were, like the similarly clad—and sized—foot-patrol men walking leisurely around the perimeter, armed only with *wakizashi,* shortswords, sheathed discreetly beneath their coats. It was assumed that their presence would suffice to warn off all but the most determined ill-wishers. For those there were heavy machine guns and portable short-range missile launchers tucked away in hardpoints within the pagodalike structure.

Through the eye of an ambient-light enhancing scope mounted on a Zeus heavy sniper's rifle, the gate guards looked vaguely green. The DEST operative, dressed in the classic black infiltration suit, who lay on her belly on a wooded ridgetop seven hundred meters from the gate, looked them over without interest. Then she continued tracking her heavy bipod-mounted weapon along the front of the compound.

Cassie was sixty meters from the junkyard entrance when she sensed something wrong.

As guests of Teddy the K, the mercenaries of the Seventeenth Recon Regiment were ostensibly free to come and go as they pleased. Not having any investment in them to speak of, Takura Migaki didn't see any reason to paste grunt-tech security types to them the way he had to Johnny Tchang. But the ISF was likely to bird-dog the foreign money-troopers at random, just on principle. Now was not the time Cassie wanted an audience.

Dressed as a low-level cinetech in baggy jumpsuit and carrying a gym bag, she'd taken the new tubeway spur that had recently been run out to Eiga-toshi. There was a lot more turnover at Cinema City than at most Drac workplaces, what with new projects always starting or being wrapped up, and crews going on location. She fit in perfectly with a crowd of Workers headed for home.

The first stop in from Eiga-toshi was Kossovo Street, on Imperial City's western outskirts. Cassie got off there. In an alley behind a closed shop that by day sold incense and images for home shrines devoted to the state-brand Shinto the Workers were allowed to practice, she shucked the jumpsuit, stuffed it into the bag, and stashed both out of sight. Then she set off north, dressed in tight black burglar's togs and a dark jacket that concealed various tools of her trade.

It was three klicks to Buraku Pete's junkyard where she had stashed a motorbike. That gave her time to warm up and work the kinks out of her limbs, and also to keep her antennae out for signs of unwanted attention—which was any attention more committal than an alley cat's wary swiveling surveillance as she passed. She'd gotten some tingles already. Nothing concrete, no bodies following hers through muddy half-paved lanes that ran between the fenced lots and the blank blocky buildings. Just feather kisses on her consciousness. But she had learned to trust the totality of her sensory suite, from the guru and from her life as a scout. There could come those nudges—the glint of starlight off a lens from somewhere behind even the sweep of her soft-focused peripheral vision, a shift of shadow in distant shadow—too faint or fugitive for even her paranoid and practiced cerebral cortex to process, but which might nonetheless bear witness to danger.

Twice she felt the nudge, and so twice she became one with shadow, to freeze and watch and listen and smell and *feel,* and then to take off on tangents, over fences, along rooflines, making no more noise than one of those alley cats in pursuit of a big surly alley rat, or vice versa. Neither time did she sense anything more overt; neither time did she sense pursuit. She kept onward, then, still making good time. She allowed for such diversions when she drew mental schedules for her nocturnal prowls.

Buraku Pete wasn't just Unproductive, he was actually *eta,* as his defiant nickname attested. Despite that, he was quite affluent by the somewhat shabby standards of the Draconis Combine. In fact, Cassie suspected he was well-off by even Steiner or Davion measurements, despite the fact that, with his perpetual squint and limp, his greasy well-holed jumpsuit, and the bone-white bristle that stuck out all over his massive jaw, he resembled nothing so much as a slightly larger and bipedal member of the noisy, aggressive, and astonishingly variegated pack of dogs that overran the place.

The key lay in the word *eta* itself. It meant, literally, "filth," and while an old-line Japanese might tell you—if you could somehow get him to discuss the subject at all—that it was usual Japanese shorthand for "gatherers of filth," the shorter definition summed up how the overculture regarded the people hung with the name. But it was the latter definition that described the *eta*'s role: in ancient Japan good Buddhists could have no contact with items like human corpses or slaughtered animals, and to be honest, good Shintos weren't wild about it either, so to the outcast caste fell such jobs as undertaker, butcher, and garbage-man. Not glamorous jobs, but very necessary. So while they didn't enjoy any rights even the lowest peasant was obliged to respect, *eta* could in fact prosper. They also learned even better than the citizenry at large how to hide their prosperity, which accounted for Buraku Pete's defiant scruffiness.

Of course no ritual impurity was attached to the "corpses" Buraku Pete handled—the hulks of wrecked or clapped-out vehicles, industrial machinery too worn or outmoded for even Drac factories, metal casualties of industrial society. But traditions died hard, especially in a nation-state that devoted so much of its resources to keeping them alive. *Eta* ran junkyards, and that was that.

More to the point, old Pete was not the sort to strongly feel the citizen's duty to report any nails he might happen to notice standing out to the attention of the Friendly Persuaders. He might, given proper inducement, share the code to the big and exceedingly modern electronic lock on his junkyard's gate with a *gaijin*. He might even introduce a foreign woman to his dog pack, so they wouldn't raise an unholy ruckus, not to mention not knock her down and chew on her, if she should come around. It only took the proper line of banter and an appropriately thick wad of C-Bills, which given ComStar's recent woes and the Combine's increasing economic health were still the hardest money in the Sphere. Cassie was sufficiently supplied with both.

She let herself in and locked the gate behind her, so as not to abuse her host's hospitality by allowing unwanted visitors to slip in; she doubted she was the only person in Imperial City to reckon old Pete had more wealth than what he wore on his grubby old body. The compound was large, about two hundred meters by three. Off in the middle of it, a yellow light glowed from the window of Pete's hut, which

Cassie guessed served mainly to conceal the entrance to a much more spacious and sumptuous, not to mention thoroughly bunkered, residence underground. She headed toward a small outbuilding much nearer the gate, made from a large cargo crate. She had a little motorbike—Drac-made, which would have scandalized her fellow 'lleros—hidden inside that crate and it had a powerful but well-silenced engine in it.

And she was almost there when a sense of *wrongness* hit her like a runaway Arrow missile.

It took no more than the Zen-flash of awareness to tell her what was wrong: no dogs. The beasts would not bark at her, but they should have been thronging around, jostling for a ritual smell and hoping she'd brought a bag of treats, which as it happened, she had. But the place was dead-still. Not even a breeze.

She stopped. All at once all her alarms started jangling at once. *Intruders! Many! Flanking me. . . .*

A shadow sprouted from the roof of the crate-turned-shack, detached itself, and landed lightly on the ground before her. It walked forward, split-toed black boots making no sound on the packed dirt. It was a man, tall with greyhound build, big in chest and narrow in hips, clad entirely in black—except for his face, which was covered with a shiny visor showing red highlights to Luthien's constellations.

DEST! Her heart turned to a lump of obsidian. She was doomed, and so were her comrades. The rot ran right through the heart of the all-powerful secret police. . . .

The operative reached over his shoulder, brought down a thin sliver of brightness to hold at ready before him. DEST teams loved their blades and would use them in preference to firearms whenever they could. Cassie became aware of a buzz, almost subliminal, that stirred the hairs at the nape of her neck.

Vibrokatana, she knew. The latest toy from ISF's labs. She had never encountered one, had barely caught wind of their existence. It was said they could cut through Clan Elemental battle armor at a stroke.

She was already acting. Her hand came out from under her jacket with a heavy Bulldog autopistol. She thrust the gun out before her and shot the DEST operative twice in the center of his chest, right over the heart.

He dropped as if he were, well, shot. His DEST infiltration suit would *stop* the bullets. But the ISF's commandos refused to sacrifice mobility for anything—which Cassie could surely get behind—and so their armored bodysuits had to be flexible rather than rigid. Which meant pistol bullets could punch a ways into you even if you were wearing one. Sternum hits like that could interrupt the beating of a man's heart, or even stop it cold.

She wasn't hanging around to see if he were dead, unconscious, or merely stunned. She darted toward her right and the nearest cover, a long, meter-and-a-half high metal housing for a defunct portable generator. A dark figure suddenly rose from the top of it. Cassie blasted four shots toward its knee. The operative pitched forward as Cassie rolled over the top to come down in a crouch, pistol ready.

She looked around. Tsu Shima had already set; only Orientalis hung in the sky over the Kiyomori Range to the west, a pale verdant sliver. In the moon's death-colored light the junkyard was a weird geometric jumble, the playroom of a gigantic child whose parents had unaccountably provided it with a wealth of sharp-edged, rusting metal toys. Green-tinted shadows edged blackness.

Cassie became aware of motion around her. Without hesitation she ran on, deeper into the yard. Her pursuers were likely deployed to cut off her quickest escape routes. But the scrap-metal jungle was her ally. It gave her cover, and a prayer of escape. Under the circumstances, it was all she asked.

Her pursuers had the visual advantage: those red visors provided computer-enhanced passive-infrared vision, with small but powerful IR lamps mounted on the sides to provide active illumination in a wavelength Cassie's unaided eyes couldn't perceive. Worse, the visors provided a compressed "circle-vision" picture at the top of the operative's field of view, just like a BattleMech. But the sensory suites had their downside as well. Direct hearing was cut off, and while the suit provided computer-filtered audio input, Cassie had yet to encounter such that was better than unaided human hearing in snoop-and-poop situations; the computer tended to be a lot better at picking up and amplifying scraps of conversation than at picking up a stealthy footstep. In fact, if you moved *just right,* the computer was liable to perceive any sounds you made as background noise and filter them right out.

After perhaps fifty meters of headlong flight, darting down side passages and leaping low obstacles, she slowed, stopped with her back to a crate made of weathered synthetic and filled with broken-toothed gear wheels. As Guru Johann had taught she concentrated on her breathing, in part to keep the sound from blanking her own hearing, in part to control the fight/flight reflex. As quietly as she could she slipped the half-depleted magazine out of its well in the butt of her Bulldog and replaced it with a full one.

She was in pure action mode, whole being focused on survival and escape. She did not allow her conscious mind to touch upon the question of what the point was. Cassie could not make herself believe it was mere coincidence that DEST operatives had fallen on her like hunting hounds in the wake of her relayed request to meet with Ninyu Kerai. And if the treason within the ISF revealed by the dying *metsuke* ran high enough, if it ran to or near the top of the Combine's secret police, Cassie was surely doomed, no matter where she ran. More than likely the Caballeros were too.

But she would run as far as she could, and fight if she must. Giving up was not an option for Cassie Suthorn. If it had been, she would have done it long ago.

She became aware of a curious chemical odor, distinct from the smells of metals and old lubricants that crowded the air of the yard. It was the characteristic outgassing of plastic—a scent that might be emitted by one of those DEST visors, warmed by the wearer's breath. . . .

She threw herself into a forward roll. With a hum a vibrokatana cut down from above, and bit into the crate with a spray of yellow sparks as its rapidly vibrating edge met the metal within. She came up and spun, momentum carrying her back until she fetched up against the cab of a possibly derelict crane set on low tracks. The sword-wielder somersaulted forward off the crate, landed four meters from

Cassie, sword ready. Cassie shot him twice in the center of the faceplate, knocking him to the ground.

A hand snaked out of the cab and around Cassie's throat. She dropped her chin into the elbow in time to forestall the choke-hold, but this attacker was a man, his strength too much greater for her to break the hold. He began to pull her back along the rough metal, trying to draw her into the cab itself. The smell of the kevlar-based ballistic cloth of his suit was strong in her nostrils.

She stuck the autopistol back over her right shoulder, shoved it until the muzzle stopped at the juncture of neck and jaw, fired twice. Temporarily deafened in one ear, her right eye filled with great green balloons of afterimage fire, she jackknifed forward and threw her attacker over her shoulder.

Others were running toward her. Spattering shots at them she threw herself into the cab. A black-clad figure appeared on the far side. She gathered her legs beneath her on the seat, grabbed the steering wheel, then fired out in a double-footed kick that caught the operative in the sternum, throwing him to the ground on his back. As she piled out that side of the cab he arched his spine and snapped himself upright and back onto his feet.

She emptied the pistol into the front of him. He fell.

All around her she heard other agents running for her, with no thought of stealth. She hit the release that spat the spent magazine out of the pistol-butt. Before she could slam a fresh box home an operative popped up right in front of her and knocked the weapon sparking and spinning from her grasp with the sweep of a vibrokatana.

She whipped Blood-drinker from the sheath strapped to her thigh and brought the *kris* up to counter the return stroke. The wavy blade's meteoric metal would not survive an edge-on impact from a standard *katana,* much less a vibroblade that would slash through armor plate. Instead she slapped her weapon against the back edge of the enemy blade, guiding it past as she leaned lithely back out of its way.

Beyond the crane sprawled a jumbled low pile of debris, a briar patch of cans and pipes and angle iron—a morass of sharp-edged treachery, waiting to trap an unwary foot. No sooner had Cassie parried the sword-stroke than she plunged into the tumble.

Reality-based martial-arts training—such as Cassie was sure DEST commandos received—usually was sensibly enough constructed to get its students out of the controlled environments of the *dojo* and into the hard pavement and uneven ground of the real world. The *pentjak-silat* Cassie had studied went far beyond that. Guru Johann's style of *pentjak* valued balance above all attributes, even speed, and drove its disciples to seek out the very most treacherous and uncertain footing—from oil to loose marbles to unbalanced tabletops—to practice on. Cassie gave the metallic tangle beneath her scarcely a thought, trusting her feet to find the surest route, and her balance and reflexes to save her when, not if, the mess shifted to her weight.

Her opponent followed. The female operative could have shot her easily enough, but then, if the DEST agents were carrying firearms, they could have blown Cassie away long since. Inheritors of the age-old Japanese edge-warrior tradition, the ISF's hyperelite killers loved their swords and preferred to use them when they could. Evidently they were confident enough in their body armor and rat-pack numbers to play with their food.

A humming in the air behind her left shoulder warned her. She didn't dare drop and roll—not even her *pentjak* training would let her do that in this metal thicket without risking an injury as disabling as a sword-cut. Instead she threw her weight diagonally to the right, landed on a stiffened leg. A rounded section of pipe shifted beneath her. Despite that she pirouetted, correcting balance as she wheeled, to confront her opponent perched on one leg like a crane, *kris* extended, swaying slightly.

The operative's blow had missed its target—barely—but had served its purpose of forcing Cassie to turn at bay. Seeing her quarry's apparently precarious position the operative lunged into a thrust, the faceless red visor somehow radiating triumph.

Cassie pivoted her hips counterclockwise. Blood-drinker slapped the side of the thrusting vibrokatana, steered it

harmlessly past her buttocks. Before the operator could recover, Cassie snapped her left foot around in a lightning
roundhouse to the side of the agent's head. The "hood" of
the DEST infiltration suit was actually ceramic-plastic armor, hard-shell, but the kick was still enough to rattle the
operative's brain around a bit.

The DEST agent rocked back, swayed as the surface
shifted beneath her feet, then lashed out in a vicious backhand cut.

Cassie folded herself. The vibrating blade hummed over
her head. Blood-drinker was of little use as an offensive
weapon against these foes. A *kris* was mainly a thrusting
weapon, and even if its tip could punch through DEST body
armor, getting the weapon *out* again before the other commandos—at least a dozen of whom were hovering like hunting falcons on the fringes of the rubble-mound—swarmed
over her was another matter entirely.

Instead she snapped to quick uppercuts into the operator's body, just below the short ribs. Again the armor would
protect her opponent from serious damage—but it wouldn't
hurt Cassie's *hand* either. And it would likely incite the
operator.

Sure enough, the agent got a two-handed grip on the long
hilt, hands spaced wide, and came on behind it in a blade-
storm. Cassie scrambled backward, jabbing with the *kris* to
keep her opponent wary, not even trying to engage that
lethally vibrating steel. The blade sent showers of sparks
and metal shavings flying as it bit into the metal under-
growth.

And then a chunk of rubble gave way beneath Cassie's
rear foot. She collapsed into a crouch. With the cry of a
predator making a kill, the commando charged her, vibrokatana raised overhead.

And put a foot into a head-sized metal box. It turned,
trapping her ankle. She pitched forward, throwing out both
hands to check her fall, but not loosing her grip on the glowing blade.

Cassie, who had set her up, met her with a left-hand
palm-heel strike under the chin. Again, the armor kept the
impact itself from doing hurt. But nothing would stop

jagged light-daggers from shooting through the agent's brain as her skull snapped back against her neck vertebrae. Then Cassie leapt into the air, spun, and delivered a pure Johnny Tchang jumping spinning back-kick to the center of the operative's chest.

The female commando flew over onto her back. Her foot stayed where it was, wrapped in its metal boot. Her ankle snapped with a noise like a rifle shot.

She did not cry out. *Subhash knows how to pick them tough.* She was, however, stunned. Cassie sprang onto her chest, drove an elbow downward into her throat, crushing her trachea. Then she plucked the vibrokatana from black-gloved fingers and jumped to her feet, twitching the blade before her like a hunting beast's tail.

"All right, you animals!" Cassie screamed in Japanese to the encircling hunters. "I've got a weapon that'll cut through that fancy armor now. Let's dance!"

From the corner of her right eye she saw a stubby handweapon come up. She wheeled and launched herself toward the wielder in a leopard-leap, screaming fury, heedless of where she landed. It was the lowliest weapon of all, a Friendly Persuader-issue hand-stunner. She had no defense against it at all.

The sonic blast caught Cassie in mid-flight. She never knew what hit her, even though it was all of Luthien.

Imperial City, Luthien
Pesht Military District, Draconis Combine
26 June 3058

"**G**entlemen," the Shadowed One said, synthesized voice emerging sexless and muffled from the depths of its black hood, "how go your preparations?"

The dining room in the Paschal villa had floors and ceilings of pale polished natural wood and *shoji* covering the walls. Nonetheless it was dim, lit at baseboard and ceiling by dozens of small lamps concealed behind the white paper screens. A huge sea-mahogany table stained almost black and shaped like an oval truncated at both ends, dominated the long narrow room. A dozen men sat in high-backed chairs carven of the same wood and stained the same dark hue. Subtle differences in spacing between them betrayed that they were split among several factions.

At the moment all heads were turned toward the tall swaddled figure standing at the table's head. Tension had wound their postures just a hair tight, and the determined blankness of their expressions—even in a culture that discouraged public display of emotion—betrayed their apprehension.

One of them, though, a big, wide-shouldered man in a dark blue pinstriped suit, deep maroon shirt of Proserpina bloodworm silk, and blue tie sat back in his chair, and grinned all over his broad-jawed face. "The preparations go well, Kaga-*san*," the man declared.

The *san* form of address, appropriate for a near-equal or

inferior, was studied insouciance. The Shadowed One's disguise was comprehensive enough to conceal the signs, barely perceptible to even the most knowledgeable outsiders, that allowed one Drac to pinpoint another's status almost at a glance; but there was no doubting the authority—or menace—that the shrouded figure projected.

The Shadowed One's posture did not change. "Report!"

The pinstriped man's dark brows furrowed for just an instant. Then his smile snapped back into place. "Our people have entirely supplanted the dog Yamaguchi's in-service positions at Eiga-toshi. When the Day comes, they will be positioned to provide the necessary assistance."

"That is good," the Shadowed One said. "Have they done so without arousing suspicion?"

The pinstriped man laughed. "The Civilian Guidance Corps regards it as nothing but an old, unworthy oyabun being shoved aside by a more able one. Which of course is exactly what's happening."

"And what of the truce declared by *seimeiyoshi-rengo*?"

"Even among the yakuza, rules are made to be broken, Kaga-*san*. Our people are close to nature. We respect the natural progression of things. It is only just that the fit rise to the top, even as *ware-ware* Draco-*jin,* we Draconians, are destined to rise to the top of the entire human cosmos. What does it matter if a few rules get bent in the process?"

The dark oval of the Shadowed One's face lingered on the pinstriped man for a long moment. "See that your personal ambition does not endanger our plan."

The man in pinstripes bowed over clasped hands. "My life for the Dragon and *Kokuryu-kai*."

"Precisely."

"And your own preparations?" the pinstriped man asked, half challengingly.

The Shadowed One refused to be drawn. "They proceed according to schedule," that flavorless voice said. "Our replacement part is being imported into the system, and will in due course arrive in orbit. The final stages in its polishing and fitting process are being carried out in transit. In the meantime, the other phases of our plan to fix blame, when the time comes, on the foreign money-troopers proceeds deliberately but efficiently."

A smaller man sat with his retainers across from the man in pinstripes and his retinue. Although he had come to the secret meeting covered in a long slate-gray coat with fur collar and a Homburg hat, he had shed these in favor of a blood-red silk kimono embroidered on the right breast with the Kurita dragon, and on the left with the emblem of *Kokuryu-kai*. He seemed to have started slight and shrunk from there, like a dried-up twig. His face seemed assembled of knobs and hollows, tied together with taut lines of bitterness. It was wasted, stark, elemental, like the landscape of some dry, lifeless planet that had been scooped and scoured and ground by wind erosion until only the hardest essence, the underlying bone, remained. His eyes were like slits cut in the lid of a pot containing all the world's grief and pain and anger condensed.

"What of the traitor Migaki?" he asked in a voice like acid etching steel. "He works in lies like a master calligrapher in ink and rice-paper, and he controls all media. And all we hear is what heroes these murdering *gaijin* are, ever and again." He didn't raise his voice, but by the time he finished, spittle was flying from his mouth and his thin limbs were shaking so violently his aides began to stroke his arms as if trying to gentle a frightened horse.

For once the Shadowed One showed reaction: a sort of head jerk, like a horse trying to shed a fly. "Migaki is soft, inconsequential," the altered voice said. "He cannot control what's said in the streets of Imperial City."

"Why do we squander time and effort on street gossip?" asked a man with eyebrows almost comically thick and high on his forehead, like those painted on a traditional geisha. He was a local industrialist. To avoid having to concern himself with the opinions of the rabble was a primary reason for him becoming a primary guiding light—not to mention financial supporter—of the Black Dragon Society.

"By the time we act," the Shadowed One said, "everyone from high to low will have heard enough to believe that the *yohei* are guilty. Our actions will be perceived as those of rescuers of the Dragon and his people—as indeed they are.

And after the fact, we will control the media as thoroughly as Migaki does now. But seeds seldom take root in unplowed soil."

"What has the ISF to say about all this?" the desiccated man asked.

"Not everyone in ISF is a traitor," the Shadowed One said. "But the Smiling One is, and so is his whelp Kerai. Which is why we must be careful to exercise the fullest caution." As the figure spoke, it turned its hidden face directly toward the man in the pinstriped suit.

"We shall be cautious as cats walking a fence," the pinstriped man said piously.

His wingtip shoes crunching the gravel of the circular drive that ran before the mansion's white-pillared portico, Benjamin Inagawa stopped to let an aide drape a caped trenchcoat over the broad shoulders of his pin-striped suit. Then he turned to look off over the high wall at the wooded ridge across the road.

"Undoubtedly our Internal Security Force friend has snipers placed up there, watching us through powerful scopes at this very minute," he said.

"Undoubtedly they can read your lips as well, oyabun," said the aide, a young man much too harried to put on weight.

Inagawa laughed. "Of course they can." He put a cigarette between his lips. Another aide materialized to light it.

The harried aide kept casting apprehensive glances at the ridge. "How can you be so sure the Shadowed One is ISF, Inagawa-*sama*?"

"Not just ISF, but a highly placed official. He made it clear at the very outset," Benjamin Inagawa didn't doubt for an instant that the Shadowed One was male. Women were too inconsequential. Returning them firmly to their places was one reason he was in *Kokuryu-kai*. "Indeed, that's the only reason to put up with the way he talks to us, as if we are his underlings."

The nervous aide opened the rear door of the long, low black Shodan limo. "Surely it will please the oyabun to sit and rest his legs."

Inagawa laughed at his assistant's transparent discomfort. He threw the cigarette down, and leaving its ember aglow in the gravel, got into the car.

The aide slid in across from him. The other aide sat up front, beside the *sewanuki* driver. As the car tires began to crunch down the drive, the harried aide—emboldened by windows specially tinted to discourage lip-readers, and double-paned and polarized to prevent a laser from reading conversation within from vibrations on the glass—said, "Surely you will not proceed with your plans for the night, oyabun."

Inagawa gave him a look. "Surely I will. Why not?"

"But you told the Shadowed One you'd walk carefully as a cat on a fence!" the aide almost wailed.

"And have you never seen two tomcats fighting on a fence?" Inagawa asked.

It began with a move traditional as a chess opening: a wheeled, panel van roared over the top of a rise on Canal Street, bottomed on the pavement, throwing out a bow-wave of sparks as its frame scraped, and riding quite low on its suspension hurtled down the block as if it had a cinderblock taped to the accelerator. Which it did. The van came to a sudden stop in front of the main entrance of a warehouse, which happened to be Hiroo Yamaguchi's residence and stronghold.

Benjamin Inagawa, riding above the scene in a rotary-winged civilian VTOL, pressed a button with a black-gloved thumb. And the two tons of good ol' ANFO—ammonium nitrate doused with fuel oil—which were laying all that strain on the springs of the van, went off with a white flash and a bang like the fabled Frackencrack itself.

The explosion scooped out the stone fronts of the warehouse and the building across from it as if God had dropped His own post-hole digger into the Kado-guchi waterfront district southwest of the Palace and bit out a chunk. Normally the yaks were sensitive about collateral damage—they had been known to abandon hideouts if the neighbors complained—but Old Cat Yamaguchi owned the warehouse across the street, too.

The warehouses housed the Eastern Ocean Shipping Company, an entirely legitimate business owned by Yamaguchi that handled shipments moving up the Kado-guchi River from the Seiyo Sea to the spaceport and back. It also housed several score of his kobun—"child figures," the foot-soldiers of the yakuza. Those kobun not obliterated by the blast came stumbling out of the flames and smoke and dust, most naked or nearly so, showing off the colorful, elaborate *irezumi* that covered their arms and upper bodies. Once on the street the coughing men were cut down by assault-rifle fire from squads of Inagawa-*kai* soldiers who appeared on the rooflines of the surviving buildings across Canal Street, and spilled out of two big hovercraft that whined to a stop in the intersections at either end of the block.

Hiroo Yamaguchi had not gotten to be an old cat by taking things for granted. Not even the goodwill of his patron Theodore Kurita or even—more to the point—the truce that the *seimeiyoshi-rengo* had mandated for the Coordinator's Birthday celebrations. He was known to have a fast boat stashed in a special mooring beneath the docks behind the warehouse, which was why teams of Inagawa shooters were lying prone behind bolt guns and starlight scopes among the sampans and shanties across the wide, sluggish Kado-guchi. He was also rumored to have prepared other escape routes, such as secret tunnels to Imperial City's sewers and tubeway net.

But escaping was the last thing on the old oyabun's mind.

As his tattooed "children" cried out and died under the merciless rifle fire, a vast groaning, creaking, and grinding emerged from the warehouse. Out of the flames loomed a *Hunchback,* with chunks of rebar-fanged concrete sliding off it. The old 50-ton monster stepped forward into what had been the front half of the warehouse. The short-barreled autocannon mounted on its right shoulder snarled a brief burst to its right. The hovercraft grounded at the west end of the block exploded, rising five meters on a pillar of yellow fire. Its primary lift fan, feathered and spinning at high idle, was blasted downward into the pavement, shattering into splinters that ripped the nearby gunmen like shell fragments.

A medium laser licked from the *Hunchback*'s center torso, probing for muzzle flashes along the roofs across the street. Riflemen began exploding into puffs of pink steam as the ruby beam brushed them. Others threw down their weapons and fled. The hovercraft to the east took off in a howl of turbines as the gunmen there sought shelter in doorways and gutters or ducked around the corner.

With a whistling scream, a UM-R60 *UrbanMech* emerged out of the smoke rising from the building directly opposite Yamaguchi's headquarters, its Mydron Excel autocannon snarling. Hits sparked on the *Hunchback*'s chest armor. The *Hunchback* carried better-than-average armor for a medium 'Mech, and it could withstand the autocannon— for a while.

Its own autocannon roared a reply. Instead of aiming for a quick kill at the hard-to-hit head or comparatively well-armored torso of the *UrbanMech,* the *Hunchback* pilot blasted the *UrbanMech*'s legs, which were descending on their jump jets like an oversized bullet. The shells punched divots of metal from the BattleMech's shins. Their impacts knocked the *UrbanMech*'s legs backward.

The *UrbanMech*'s pilot was a yak kobun himself, not a highly trained DCMS MechWarrior. Instead of pulling back slightly on the altitude controls and thrusting his gyroscope to keep the machine upright on top of the thrust-column of its Pitban 6000 jump jets where it belonged, the inexperienced yak yanked back hard. His *UrbanMech* leaned *way* back, the gyros tumbled, and the 30-ton machine slammed onto the street on its back, buckling blacktop. Well and truly panicked, the Black Dragon pilot forgot to let go of the thruster controls, and the *UrbanMech* started sliding back into the blown-out warehouse across from Yamaguchi's on its back, giving off an ear-shattering screech.

The *Hunchback* pilot extended his BattleMech's arms and gave the fallen 'Mech the full treatment—autocannon as well as its two medium lasers, focused right at the juncture of the fallen 'Mech's stubby legs. The older *Hunchback* was notorious as a heat hog, a condition caused by the archaic Type 20 autocannon, but if it neither moved nor fired the little head-mounted Diverse Optics laser, and held off the medium lasers, it could keep up this onslaught until it ran out of ammo.

Too freaked to use the Pitban's rearward-mounted nozzle, meant to provide forward impulse during jumps, the *UrbanMech* pilot cut out his jet entirely. Instead, the 'Mech's legs began kicking frantically in an attempt to right itself, like an oddly shaped child throwing a tantrum. It didn't work.

In contrast to the *Hunchback,* the squat little *UrbanMech* was well-armored for its weight. But the broad metal area between widely spaced legs was not normally exposed to direct attack and was never intended to take such sustained abuse. Under the *Hunchback*'s assault, the armor plating popped on the housing of the *UrbanMech*'s right hip actuator, and the bottom of its barrel torso glowed red, then yellow, and finally began to run as the rain of heavy autocannon shells cratered the softening metal.

"Tono!"
Standing on a south-facing verandah of Unity Palace, Theodore Kurita turned his head from the flashing of lights to the south, over the river. Oda Hideyoshi approached, dressed in MechWarrior vest and trunks and split-toed boots, neurohelmet beneath his arm. He bowed.

"Shall we respond?" the Otomo commander asked. He looked like anything but a man who had just rolled out of his futon after a grueling day's labor.

In the darkened garden below, the Coordinator could see shadowy forms moving, quickly but carefully through the painstakingly tended foliage. Beyond the compound's high walls, tall, manlike shapes gathered. Hideyoshi's Otomo BattleMechs—including the twelve new Omnis to be revealed in the Grand Parade on the celebration's second day, Theodore's birthday proper—were preparing to resist any assault on the Palace.

Aides in various stages of dress had begun to swarm like flies on a rice-cake. From the south came the rattle of autocannon and the unmistakable snap of 'Mech-mounted lasers. "What is it?" asked a youthful courtier whose blue silk kimono didn't quite conceal the fact that he had on his DCMS dress tunic and nothing else beneath. "Have the Clans come back for more?" His attempt at bravado was brittle as his voice.

"I think not," Theodore said. "When they return to Luthien, they'll come with all the force they can bring. They remember '52 too keenly." In his gut he had a sick certainty that he knew exactly what was going on.

"I've reports from the Civilian Guidance Corps stations in the river precincts," Hideyoshi said in his voice like a file on wood. "There is fighting going on, but it's localized, and shows no sign of moving this way."

"Where exactly is it localized, *Sho-sho*?"

The General's brown eyes looked straight into Theodore's blue ones. "On Canal Street," he said. "At the Eastern Ocean warehouse."

Theodore drew a deep breath. He shut his eyes briefly.

"Give us the word, *Tono*," the trouserless aide said brashly. "We'll put a stop to it quick enough."

"*Iie*," the Coordinator said. "Maintain a double watch as long as the . . . disturbance . . . lasts, Hideyoshi-*san*. Stand the rest of the regiment down."

"And what of the disturbance, Lord?"

Theodore looked at the commander of his bodyguard. *Sho-sho* Hideyoshi was DCMS of the old school; he had never approved of the devil's alliance whereby Theodore had brought the despised yakuza into the armed forces and, perforce, closer to the mainstream of Combine society. The general knew as well as he did what was going on. Yet he seemed positively eager for the order to bail out Hiroo Yamaguchi.

"Monitor the fighting," the Coordinator said. "If it shows signs of expanding, intervene with whatever force you deem necessary."

"*Hai*." Hideyoshi bowed again and moved crisply off to give the requisite orders.

The aides clustered around, trying to look more concerned with the Coordinator's welfare than relieved that they weren't about to have Smoke Jaguar OmniMechs dumped in their laps. "Are you all right, *Tono*?"

"As right as any man can be when forced to choose *giri* over *ninjo*," Theodore said, and instantly regretted the lapse. *If Shin were here,* he thought, *or my son Hohiro, with whom I share so much my father never vouchsafed me—then I might enjoy the luxury of speaking my heart.*

"Now go get some rest," he ordered. Then to make up for his brusqueness, which his attendants had not truly earned: "Fatigued officers are a danger to their men, and cannot properly serve the Dragon."

Around the corner to the *Hunchback*'s left appeared a 25-ton *Raptor*. The medium lasers in the center of its torso speared the housing of the *Hunchback*'s autocannon as the *Raptor* picked its way down the street and around the burning hovercraft with a graceful, birdlike walk. The small lasers mounted in its vestigial-wing arms pulsed bravely.

The *Hunchback* pilot ignored the new threat and continued its assault on the *UrbanMech*. The downed machine dug both heels into the well-pounded pavement in a final spasm. Then its right leg blew off in a gush of sparks from severed powerleads, and skittered away with several awkward bounces. The cockpit canopy popped open and its pilot scrambled out, so terrified that he ran straight into the still-burning hulk of the building his 'Mech had driven itself into.

A hot spot was beginning to appear on the housing of the *Hunchback*'s autocannon. Finally, the old 'Mech turned to confront the presumptuous little intruder.

Then, a volley of short-range missiles slammed into the warehouse from out over the river. Three of them struck the *Hunchback* in the rear. One gouged a crater over what would be a human's right kidney, and the others peeled away a section of plate over what would be the left shoulder blade.

The *Hunchback* staggered. A *Jenner* was just starting on the downward arc of a jump across the Kado-guchi River. The mostly intact rear half of the warehouse—and the distraction of engaging in a firefight—had kept the *Hunchback* pilot from spotting the 'Mech on his 360-display screen.

The *Hunchback* tried to turn. The four medium lasers in the *Jenner*'s stub arms speared the larger machine. Two found the hole where the rockets had peeled back armor, burned into the *Hunchback*'s torso. More explosions threw up pieces of burning wood from the building and brought down a seven-meter section of the second floor just as a second volley struck. Another rocket hit the turning Battle-Mech in the left upper arm, doing no visible damage.

Drooling smoke from its wounds, the *Hunchback* faced the descending *Jenner*. It fired an autocannon burst that went wide. The *Jenner* landed at the intersection east of the *Hunchback,* its impressive laser battery lighting the night sky and the building-fronts.

Having laid some hurt on his enemy with his opening strike, the *Jenner* jock overplayed his hand. Shaped something like a bipedal camel, the *Jenner* was at the upper end of the light-'Mech class at 35 tons, and reckoned a disproportionately dangerous opponent due to its firepower—at least when facing another light 'Mech. But the *Jenner* bought that offensive output at the cost of armor; it relied on speed for survival. And here its pilot was hanging and banging with a 'Mech weighing fifteen tons superior in armor. The *Jenner* gained some advantage because the *Hunchback*'s pilot was running up his heat load now and didn't seem interested in letting up.

And while the *Jenner*'s SRM volleys were slamming his ride with a noise like a giant hammer hitting an anvil, and laser glare was taxing the filters of his transpex viewscreen, the *Hunchback* jock was concentrating is fire on the *Jenner*'s insectlike head.

In the meantime, the little *Raptor* stopped what had seemed a suicidal charge twenty meters behind the *Hunchback.* It began to probe the smoking gap in the armor over the left side of the larger machine's back with its vast array of medium lasers, its double heat sinks letting the small 'Mech well afford this type of attack.

The *Jenner* was rapidly getting the worst of the unequal slugging match. Its lasers and short-range missiles pitted and scorched the front of the *Hunchback*. But first the lasers in its left arm and then the SRM launcher mounted above its head were battered into useless junk, and smoke poured from its torso. Then a burst of autocannon fire struck it squarely on its triangular head, splitting it open and instantly killing the MechWarrior inside.

Like its pilot, the *Jenner* went dead. It rocked from the impact of the fatal shells, but its gyros, still spinning, kept it upright.

And then the *Hunchback* pilot paid the price for turning his back on a foe.

The *Raptor* was not a very formidable opponent; it had been used as a test platform for bigger, more powerful 'Mechs and was not considered a fully operational model. But the Luthien Armor Works' first OmniMech had a versatility and newness that lent it a certain authority. And the old *Hunchback*'s thin back armor had already been breached by the now-deceased *Jenner*'s first salvo.

The ruby beam of the *Raptor*'s small pulse laser stabbed, and found the ammo storage for the big autocannon in the *Hunchback*'s left side. The ammunition went off with a giant flash and a mind-jarring sound.

The existing hole in the armor acted like the modern-day CASE system the *Hunchback* was too elderly to have, venting much of the force of the explosion out the BattleMech's back. It wasn't enough. The *Hunchback*'s torso split open, venting sheets of yellow flame. Its right arm flew off. It toppled into the rubble with billowing black smoke obscuring whatever was left of its upper half.

Cautiously, the *Raptor* circled out into the street to cover its fallen foe. The Inagawa-*kai* gunmen began to emerge from their hiding-places, and to winkle the surviving Yamaguchi soldiers out of theirs.

Then, incredibly, a hatch opened in the *Hunchback*'s head. A stocky, bandy-legged figure hauled itself painfully out of the cockpit. Flames rushed up behind. It slid down the side of the 'Mech's chest, which had great fissures in it, venting fire and smoke like fumaroles.

The helicopter touched down in the middle of the street, just far enough from the *Raptor* for its rotor-tips to clear the

'Mech. Benjamin Inagawa got out, walked forward in a bent position until he was out of the rotor's lethal circle, and straightened to brush imaginary lint from his fur lapels.

The figure that had emerged from the destroyed *Hunchback* staggered to the sidewalk and stopped. Its clothing was torn, blackened by smoke and flame. Slowly it removed its helmet to reveal the grizzled face of Hiroo Yamaguchi.

"What now, Yamaguchi-*san*?" Inagawa asked.

The Old Cat waved a hand at the knot of his men being herded together under the guns of the Inagawa kobun. "If I surrender," he said, "will you let my people go?"

"Of course," the tall, muscular oyabun replied. "I give you my word."

Yamaguchi threw down his neurohelmet. The transpex visor, already cracked, shattered on the pavement. He drew himself as straight as age, bow legs, and injuries permitted.

"I surrender."

Benjamin Inagawa held out a hand. One of his foot-soldiers handed him an assault rifle. He raised it to his shoulder and cut Yamaguchi down with a burst that continued long after the Old Cat had fallen.

When the bolt clicked on an empty chamber Inagawa held the weapon out to his side. "Another," he commanded, without taking his eyes off his fallen enemy. A soldier hastened to exchange a rifle with a full magazine for Inagawa's.

"It is important to make a clean sweep," he told Hiraoke Toyama, who had also alighted from the VTOL. The Dieron boss's skeletal appearance seemed more appropriate than ever. "Just as I did when I took down Seizo DuBonnet and made myself oyabun of Benjamin."

Inagawa turned and, laughing, began to mow down the Old Cat's captured men.

Imperial City, Luthien
Pesht Military District, Draconis Combine
27 June 3058

Smoke still trailed from the wreckage of buildings and machines. The early morning was cool, the sky veneered with thin gray overcast. It had rained between midnight and dawn, and the light of the rising sun turned the pools of water that had gathered in shell-holes a soft pink. Lines of Friendly Persuaders in their candy-striped uniforms kept curious crowds beyond yellow tape cordons strung at either end of the street. Criminal investigative Bureau plainclothesmen in trench coats poked through mounds of rubble in blasted buildings and peered at the fallen BattleMechs.

Lieutenant Tzu-Chien McCartney stood in the street with his hands in his coat pockets and his hat crammed down on his round head. He was positioned almost exactly between the feet of the abandoned *UrbanMech* and the shattered *Hunchback*. It gave him the eerie feeling that both huge shapes should be covered in sheets, like the human corpses strewn all over the streets and rooftops. He was used to investigating murders. *This* had been a battle.

An aide who had been interrogating a small knot of street people, custodians, and night watchmen who had been in the district the night before approached him.

"Nobody saw anything," he said.

Cassie came back to herself lying on a futon on a floor covered with *tatami* mats. She could feel the nearness of the walls, sense cold concrete beyond the *shoji* screens that covered them.

She opened her eyes. The room was dim, lit by a single electric lamp, dialed low. An old man sat in a wheelchair nearby with a lap-robe draped over him. His skull was bare except for a scalp-lock of stringy gray hair. Round spectacles perched on a thin nose, before eyes keen as obsidian blades.

"Did Pete shop me?" she asked.

The old man smiled. "You do not disappoint, Senior Lieutenant Suthorn. You do not ask where you are, or what you are doing here. Nor even who I am."

"I know who you are. That means I know where I am. As to why—" She sat up. "—I don't think I'm in much hurry to find out."

Dizziness washed over her. She swayed and shut her eyes until her stomach decided to stay put for the moment.

"Be careful," Subhash Indrahar urged. "The effects of the police stunner do not last long, but you were also given an injection."

"I thought so." She swung her legs so that she was sitting sideways with her bare feet on the floor. "You didn't answer my question."

"You are also just as impertinent as your reputation indicates," the old man said. "Please keep in mind that I am only a patient man when it serves the Dragon's ends. But to answer you, no."

"He's dead?"

"Not at all. My operatives stunned him, as well as his formidable pack of dogs, as they stunned you. We are not brutes—we are not the Maskirovka, Lieutenant. We do not promiscuously kill loyal servants of the Dragon simply to set up a test."

"A test?" Cassie echoed.

He nodded. "I had had reports of your prowess, notably from my adoptive son, Ninyu Kerai. I wished to ascertain for myself just how skillful you were. Therefore I dispatched a squad of my personal retainers—Sons of the Dragon, although some are daughters as well—with orders to apprehend you without hurting you." He smiled again.

"I must say you thoroughly exceeded my expectations," Cassie rubbed her eyes. "How'd your people come out? I kill any of them?"

"No," said Subhash Indrahar, "although you came perilously close in several instances. You shattered one man's jaw and broke his eardrum when you shot him, and we had to perform an emergency tracheotomy on one unfortunate young woman."

"And what becomes of them?"

"They heal," the Director said, "and hopefully learn wisdom. You provided a very useful object-lesson in the perils of overconfidence."

"So what becomes of me?"

Thin shoulders shrugged. Indrahar coughed into one hand, then gestured at the door. "You walk out of here. I should very much appreciate it if you would answer a few questions first, however."

Cassie blinked and shook her head. "Excuse me, Indrahar-*sama*. The drug aftereffects must still be pretty strong. I thought I heard you say I could just walk out of here."

"You heard me correctly. Consider: you have a very unusual psychological makeup, one which some might consider pathological. For example: you yourself are of the Combine by birth. Such heritage is not something one may simply walk away from. I might try, for example, to compel your cooperation on these grounds. I might even try to force you to use your formidable talents to serve the Internal Security Force."

"I'd kill myself," Cassie said flatly.

"Indeed. So I had in fact surmised. Likewise, you would almost certainly allow yourself to be tortured to death before you would divulge anything involuntarily. You are of far too paranoid a nature to be amenable to chemical interrogation. These things limit my options. Now, while I may not be quite the fiendish mastermind I was portrayed in the recent FedCom holo featuring your friend Mr. Tchang, I earned and maintained my position as Director of the Internal Security Force by ruthlessly applying whatever means were necessary to gain my ends. Therefore I do not even scruple to try asking politely."

Despite herself Cassie laughed. "Whether you believe this or not, there's not much I can think of now that I care to keep from you. In fact, I really wanted to talk to you. At least until your black-clad boys and girls landed on me at Buraku Pete's."

"It was a message passed from your employer Chandrasekhar Kurita's chief of security, asking to set up an interview with Ninyu Kerai for you, that led me to have you brought in. Needless to say, anything you intended to say to him, you may say to me."

It was maybe not *that* needless to say; there were certain things Cassie might conceivably have said to Ninyu that would not occur to her to say to his adoptive father—except that the one encounter between her and Ninyu Kerai had been more a reaction to fear and the shock of finding herself alive after taking on three Word of Blake BattleMechs barehanded than the product of any strong attraction.

"I have a question I need to ask," Cassie said, "and you'll probably think it's impertinent. But I need to ask."

Subhash gestured with thin fingers. "Proceed."

"Are you a traitor?"

It seemed that his dark eyes grew huge as saucers, although that was largely an artifact of his spectacles. His mouth worked slightly. He swallowed visibly, twice.

"In the normal course of events," he said eventually, "I should expect to kill anyone who asked me such a question. I am forming the conception, however, that few courses run normally where you are concerned, Lieutenant Suthorn. One presumes you have a reason beyond simple recklessness for asking that?"

"With respect, Indrahar-*sama*," Cassie said, "it isn't a question you can answer with another."

This time it took all the old man's formidable will to keep from exploding into anger. "I am many things, young woman," he said. "A traitor to the Dragon will never be one of them."

"All right," she said, "I believe you. Maybe because if you *are* bent, I'm dead anyway, and so is my regiment, so there isn't much to lose." Briskly she told the story of her encounter with the female agent in Tumbledown.

The Director rotated up a noteputer attached to the outside of his right wheelchair arm, folded it across his lap. He entered the verification code the murdered woman had given Cassie.

"Yes," he said. "She was Metsuke."

He turned the screen so Cassie could see the picture that had appeared. "That's her," she affirmed.

"Engaged in undercover work," the old man said, swiveling the computer back to face himself, "assigned here to Imperial City. Interesting. Normally such activities are the province of the ISF's Internal Security Division proper. She appears to have been what we call a 'floater,' an agent not bound to a specific objective, but rather sent out to turn over rocks and see what lies beneath them."

He looked up. "And she said there was treason within the ISF?"

"Yes. And she was killed by ISF operatives. DEST."

He raised one bushy brow. Then he plied the keyboard. In the confines of the room the tapping sounded loud as a tackhammer.

"Here we have it," he said. "A report of a foreign agent neutralized in the Tumbledown District. One we'd been after for quite a while, supposedly working for either the Liao or Word of Blake, likely both. She was run to ground by Internal Security Division agents. One of them, a female operative, was killed."

He raised his head. "Perhaps you were involved in a different incident?"

"Do you have a picture of the dead agent?"

For a moment he regarded her. Then he returned his attention to the keyboard. "There."

"That's her. She's the one I killed. Only she was DEST. I'm sure of it."

"What makes you so certain?"

"They had DEST moves. They had DEST skills. They had DEST arrogance, too—just like the pack you set after me. I told you how the woman I took down got out ahead of her backup, she was so eager to rack up a kill by herself."

The Director still looked unconvinced. "It's more than that," Cassie said. "It's something I'm certain of—" She touched her breastbone. "—here. Just a *feeling*. I can't explain it better than that."

"Ahh." He expelled the syllable in a lengthy breath. Then his eyes fixed hers, and his brows drew together as in extreme concentration. She felt a sense of *invasion,* as of invisible fingers probing into her mind, her soul. Instantly she fought back, focusing her whole being on rejection.

The sensation stopped. Subhash raised his eyebrows and smiled thinly.

"Your *ki* is strong," he said, "the strongest I have sensed for a long time. But it is almost entirely uncontrolled."

Cassie shook her head, as much in annoyance as denial. She didn't have a lot of interest in mysticism. "Back on Larsha, my guru taught me exercises, to control the breath, to channel strong emotions—to focus myself." She felt a twinge about her momentary loss of control in stomping the dead DEST woman. "That's all I did."

"Your *sensei* was wise," Subhash said. "You were, after all, a street urchin, half-wild. Had he taught you more, you would be a danger to yourself and others. Still, you should consider further study, to tap the powers contained within you. Your potential is great."

She frowned. She was annoyed at him for passing judgement on Guru Johann, even favorably. It seemed an intrusion.

He pressed a button. The wheelchair rolled back a pace from the futon. "You have been a very busy young woman," he said. "I sense that you believe the Tumbledown incident may be connected to other matters you have been investigating."

"Yes. I think the Black Dragons are going to try to assassinate Ted—Theodore Kurita. I'm afraid they're going to try to involve us in some way."

Subhash steepled his fingers before his face. "Kokuryu-kai? Our information is that they have become practically dormant since your people handed them such a decisive setback on Towne. Are you sure you're not obsessing on them?"

"Are *you* sure you're getting the straight skinny on the Black Dragon? It seems to me you people downplayed the threat they posted to peace on Towne, too—up until they dropped five regiments and an aerospace wing in our laps."

Subhash frowned. It seemed to be more in thought than anger. "You are correct," he said. "That failure in intelligence bothered me to a substantial degree, and bothers me still. Without seeking to excuse it, I attributed it to our preoccupation with the Clans, as well as the demands on our assets imposed by the Liao-Marik invasion of Federated Commonwealth space. Also, I must confess, we—I—have over the years become accustomed to regarding *Kokuryukai* as something of a paper tiger. They possess a certain degree of influence and a sizable membership. Yet they have not in the past been particularly effectual. Whenever they become too overt we crush them. There the matter has rested for centuries."

He tapped a finger on the keyboard frame. "Perhaps the Towne Incident should have led me to re-examine my own mindset in greater depth. I have allowed myself to fall into a habit of thought. That is a great failing for a man in my position."

"Look," Cassie said, "it's not as if there's any great mystery about who the Black Dragon leaders are. Hiraoke Toyama's a big one; he was the one who raised and paid for the two Dragon regiments that hit us on Towne. If Benjamin Inagawa isn't another, he does a good job of faking, plus word in the Water Trade has it the two of them have been joined at the hip since they've been on Luthien. Why doesn't ISF just make them disappear?"

Cassie had a gut-level dislike and distrust of totalitarianism and, indeed, all authority, but she also had a very bottom-line outlook on life. She didn't *like* secret police, but since they were on hand she couldn't understand why they didn't *act* like secret cops when a touch of the mailed fist was actually called for.

Subhash Indrahar drew in a deep breath, released it. "That's a very complicated issue. Since I hope to enlist your cooperation, I shall try to explain it to you. The glib answer would be that mere law enforcement is not our task. But that's not the whole truth. The duty of the Internal Security Force is to maintain the fabric of Combine society, which is very complex and, in some key ways, fragile. That structure is paramount to the survival of our state. While social conservatives—including, ironically, the bulk of the non-yakuza Black Dragons—would emphatically deny it, the yakuza have a definite place in that structure. This fact predates the accommodation our Coordinator made with *seimeiyoshi-rengo* when he was Gunji no Kanrei. In fact, it predates the Draconis Combine itself. It is an extension of the state of affairs existing in Japan from the twentieth century onward.

"Our culture is like an arch: no stone can safely be removed without threatening the collapse of the rest. That even applies to the Unproductives. Our role in ISF is, above all, to preserve harmony. To attack the social order, even by acting against the nominal criminal underworld, would be disharmonious and produce chaos. Even in the case of demonstrable treason—which membership in Black Dragons is not yet proven to constitute—a move against a long-standing element of society, even a covert one, is not to be lightly undertaken."

"I know your agents have wiped out Black Dragon meetings. Why not Inagawa?"

"From time to time we extirpate lower-level Black Dragons and their sympathizers when detected, 'to encourage the others,' as an ancient Terran literary figure once put it. But keep in mind that Combine culture accords small status to the individual."

"Toyama and Inagawa are just individuals."

"Not altogether. Theodore Kurita is likewise 'just' an individual. Status governs; as oyabun, Inagawa is symbolic of his group, stands for it, and so enjoys protection. I will admit that this situation is not precisely to my taste, nor am I alone. Last night while you were under sedation, Benjamin Inagawa's forces attacked Hiroo Yamaguchi's headquarters and assassinated the Old Cat."

"*Hijo de la chingada!* What's Theodore going to do?"

"Nothing. His agreement with *seimeiyoshi-rengo* precludes interference in the gangs' internal affairs, unless some treason against the Combine is involved. While murdering Yamaguchi during the Coordinator's Birthday truce constitutes a breach of yakuza etiquette—what they call *jingi,* 'righteous-ness'—it still falls within the scope of business as usual. Tradition binds even the Coordinator's hands."

"But this proves—"

"This proves that, in all likelihood, the activities of Inagawa and his associates have been geared toward seizing the lucrative and powerful position of oyabun of Luthien, and perhaps all of Pesht Military District. Indeed, he may aspire to become oyabun of all oyabun in the Draconis Combine."

"You'd let him do that?"

Subhash spread age-spotted hands. "I suspect he lacks the necessary character to be allowed to assume such an important role. Nonetheless, unless he aspired to more than that—unless he somehow harbored notions of seizing the Coordinatorship, it would not be my place to initiate action. In such a case the Coordinator might well see fit to order ISF to take action, but I cannot presume to predict."

Cassie knew perfectly well that Subhash Indrahar would presume whatever he damned well pleased. She also understood it was his way of saying he wasn't going to cop to anything more.

"What about what the *metsuke* told me?" she asked. "What about 'sadat?' "

Subhash typed a query into his noteputer. "A search of our secured databases as well as publicly available information produces some 2031 matches, including what appear to be over three hundred persons of that name, mostly Arkab, serving in the Draconis Combine Mustered Soldiery. I agree that it must be significant, possibly vital. Yet without further information I'm frankly uncertain where it may lead us."

"It has something to do with the Black Dragons. They have a plot. I know it."

"You know no such thing. You surmise. I am not without respect for your hunches, based on your past performance, but I'm not about to override my own judgements on no firmer basis."

"But it can't just be coincidental—"

"Young woman, I know that in the popular entertainment media, a spymaster such as myself is not supposed to believe in coincidence. I'm afraid I must admit that I do, although I try never to *assume* coincidence—and I'm not in this instance. But consider: this is Luthien. Moreover, the Coordinator's Birthday is three days hence. ISF has identified agents of all four Great Houses—regarding Steiner and Davion as having once again become separate entities—not to mention the Free Rasalhague Republic, the Taurian Concordat, the Magistracy of Canopus, the Outworlds Alliance, at least three self-proclaimed statelets from within the Chaos March, and both ComStar and Word of Blake. We have identified representatives from the Liao Triads and half a dozen other interstellar criminal organizations centered outside of Combine space. Then there are members of fringe groups far more obscure, and in many cases more openly subversive, than *Kokuryu-kai*. Finally, there are at least three hundred persons of unknown affiliation but suspicious demeanor, some of whom, I might as well admit, are being detained in this very facility at this moment, under far less congenial circumstances than the ones in which you find yourself.

"These are merely the potential spies and conspirators of whom we *know*. And I have only mentioned those who have arrived within the past month. The Coordinator's Birthday draws intrigue the way honey draws flies. Even laying aside yakuza activities, which might be entirely explained by sheer ambitious greed, we find on Luthien at the moment an environment in which coincidence is not only possible but inevitable, and inevitably abundant. To be candid, I'm surprised a great many more people haven't been turning up dead in half-constructed apartment blocs."

"Are you willing to bet the Coordinator's life on that?"

Subhash stared at her for a long moment. "If you were not so perceptive, Lieutenant Suthorn, it would be easy to become very angry with you indeed. No, I am not willing to bet the Coordinator's life on your being mistaken. You have bested us, and you have also tendered us invaluable assistance. But I need more than what you've given me."

"Indrahar-*sama,* I don't like secret cops. I don't like ISF.

I don't particularly like *you,* since you had your Ninja Boys
and Girls chase me through a junkyard, swing swords at me,
and zap me with a stun gun and drug me so that my head's
still ringing like a temple bell. But I don't have anything
more to tell you. I won't hold back from you on this. As far
as I'm concerned, we're on the same side."

"Very well. I, in turn, believe you. But tell me this: you
are an expatriate. You've fought the Dragon with your mercenary friends. Why are you so concerned for the welfare of
Theodore Kurita?"

"I don't have much use for Chancellors, or Captain-
Generals, or Princes or Archons or Coordinators, nothing
like that. But Teddy—'scuse it, Theodore—seems a pretty
decent type for a dictator. More than that, it seems like he's
the only person in the Inner Sphere who hasn't forgotten all
about the Clans. And if he goes down, I don't think there's
anything to keep the Mudheads—that's what we call the
Clanners, what the Caballeros call them—from rolling right
over us. And I hate the Clans worse than anything, even
BattleMechs.

"Plus the Black Dragons have it in for us, for Uncle
Chandy and the Caballeros. We laid a lot of hurt on them.
They're looking to pay us back. I think whatever's going on
now ties up with that. They've made it personal. They mean
to take us down. And whatever threatens *mi familia*—I
destroy."

"I understand." Subhash's gaze remained steady. "Just
see that you don't take this so personally that you start seeing threats where none exist."

"I don't make that kind of mistake."

"I, too, have thought that way, at various stages of my
career," Subhash Indrahar said. "I was always mistaken."

Cassie shrugged.

"Will you work with me?" Subhash asked.

Cassie hesitated. She already felt strange about agreeing
to cooperate with McCartney, the homicide cop, and here
was the most notorious secret policeman in the galaxy asking for her help. But she was telling the truth when she said
that—in this—they were on the same side. And she would
do anything to protect her *familia.*

It also seemed to her, on some level, that the man before her—so weak of body, so manifestly strong of mind and spirit—was very vulnerable, in a way she could not define. She rejected that in a wave of self-contempt: *I'm just trying to rationalize a decision I've already made.*

"Yes," she said. "On this."

"That's acceptable. You will communicate directly with me, and no one else in ISF. Needless to say, you are to tell nobody, inside ISF or out, of this meeting, nor that you are working with me." He gave her a code sequence to use to get in touch with him.

"Now you may go. Once outside this room you will be blindfolded and taken to a location of your choosing. There your weapons will be returned to you and you will be released. Do you agree?"

"I don't like being blindfolded," she said. "But I guess if I don't agree, I won't leave here at all? Except maybe through a chimney."

Subhash Indrahar smiled. "As I noted before, you are very perceptive."

"All right," she said. "But I want something."

Subhash looked surprised. It might have been a sham. It might not. "What?"

"One of your DEST monkey suits. Your organization's compromised, somehow, by somebody. Whether you're ready to admit it or not. And I'm tired of only the bad guys having fancy flexible body armor and eyes in the back of their heads. If I'm going to run the risk of hassling with DEST commandos who *aren't* in your hand-picked body-guard, I want a more level playing field."

"I shall take it under advisement. *Sayonara.*"

She bowed and started out. "Senior Lieutenant Suthorn," he said.

At the door she stopped. "Yes?"

"Please do not mention anything about this to my adoptive son, should you have communication with him."

She felt cold all over. "You don't think—"

"No. I do not. But I don't want you telling him."

She shrugged. "Then I won't." She left.

* * *

Subhash Indrahar sat for a time in the gloom gazing past the screen of his noteputer. He was meditating, something he had learned to do in any environment or posture, long before he was confined to this hated wheelchair.

After a time he returned to his surroundings. Both his spirit and his intellect, freed from the bonds of his interfering self, had come to several conclusions.

He left the room, rolling through the corridors of ISF headquarters, buried deep beneath Unity Palace. He returned to his own modest office.

There he initiated several security procedures, unknown to anyone else in ISF including his adoptive son, which would ensure he was not under covert surveillance. Satisfied, he activated his own computer terminal and performed a similar, secret routine. Even with the most powerful intelligence and counterintelligence system in the Inner Sphere at his command, he still made sure to maintain his own very private resources.

Finally, he prepared a message to an agent on Dieron—another of his secret personal assets. It would be broken down into a number of discrete packets that would be sent out as undetectable riders to other messages during the hourly feed from the special hyperpulse generator ComStar maintained for the ISF. The packets would be retransmitted to a world far removed from either Dieron or the Black Pearl, reassembled, and forwarded to its intended recipient, concealed in an apparently innocuous message from a friend, and encrypted by a scheme that even Star League computers would take an estimated five trillion years to break. The message instructed the operative to send a particular report back to Luthien through standard ISF intelligence channels. The report should turn up on the headquarters computer system within twenty-four hours.

Then he settled back to plot his next move. Because that very peculiar young woman was right: something was very wrong inside the Internal Security Force. And no matter how readily he had brushed aside Cassie's contention that coincidence could not be involved, he knew deep down that, if there was treason within ISF, the Coordinator's life was in grave danger.

He—and his unpredictable young ally—had three days to find out exactly what that danger was.

═══ 19 ═══

"**W**hat did you say?" Takura Migaki asked the face on the tiny vidscreen of the phone in the cockpit of the converted *Warrior* H-7 attack helicopter he piloted above the mock 'Mech battlefield outside Eiga-toshi. Normally there was nothing he liked better than orchestrating—commanding—a battle scene from his aircraft—a luxury no real commander could share, since no VTOL could afford to loiter over a modern battlefield at an altitude low enough to see what was going on. But the day's whole savor had just gone flat.

"I said I don't want to see you any more," Lainie Shimazu told him. Her face was unusually pale, causing her freckles to stand out in stark contrast to her skin, and there were dark hollows beneath her eyes, which at the moment were a dull amber shade he had never seen them before.

The chopper bucked, causing muffled outcries from the camera crews in the passenger compartment behind. The *Warrior* had a tail-rotor mounted parallel to the longitudinal axis, which meant that instead of turning the beast sideways, its torque made the helicopter want to roll, a tendency normally counteracted by the contrarotating main blades without too much attention from the pilot. But, distracted, he hadn't been paying sufficient attention to the stick, allowing the craft to drift broadside to the stiff east morning wind anyway. Silently he cursed himself as he turned the ducted tail back to the breeze. He was a proficient VTOL pilot, having served his DCMS time in attack helos; and even in the thirty-first century, helicopters were unforgiving bitches that tended to repay carelessness with flaming death. He had no excuse for sloppy flying.

"But why?" he demanded.

The red-haired MechWarrior shrugged. "Let's just say . . . there's not much future in it. Let it go at that, okay?"

Migaki shook his head. Below him he saw a Star of AgroMechs in their elaborate plastic superstructures, led by a false *Hankyu*, wandering near a stream, well away from where they were supposed to be. Unless they got back on course in short order they would strike the flank of a force of Caballero 'Mechs—doing duty as DCMS machines—who were supposed to be flanking them.

He switched circuits, barked quick orders at the stunt drivers in the AgroMechs, then returned to Lainie.

"I can't," he said. "You—"

He stopped. He was a man who relished a good irony, and here was a big steaming bowl of them. He was charged with promulgating traditional Combine virtues, including female passivity and deference to males, yet in private he longed to meet a woman who had the strength of character and will to match any man—and in Lainie had found one. He was usually glib with women, but with Lainie he could speak for hours without having to be glib, could say things that mattered to him, and listen to her in turn. And yet now he could not find the words to say what he truly meant.

"You've come to mean a lot to me," he said, and it could not possibly have sounded more lame in her ears than in his. "I-if there's something wrong, tell me about it. I can help, I'm certain of it."

"You're a man who doesn't like to make mistakes," she told him. "Caring about me is one. Take a last bit of friendly advice, Tak: get over it."

"Wait—" he burst out. But the screen was black.

"Excuse me, *Tono*," the aide said, dropping to his knees and bowing his head to the tatami-covered floor of the room in which Theodore Kurita sat, brush in hand, trying to compose a haiku to be recited to honor his troops on his birthday. "You have a visitor."

Theodore frowned. He had been inspired, about to attack the blank sheet of rice-paper before him with great *makoto*—"sincerity," the quality most avidly sought after by poets and calligraphers, both of which he was being at the moment. Intrusion had burst the moment like a soap-bubble.

Yet he would not permit himself to be the sort of despot who would abuse an underling for doing his duty. "Who is it?"

"The industrialist Benjamin Inagawa, *Tono*. He says you will understand what it concerns."

Theodore became a statue of ice. "Bring him," he said. "Provide him an armed Otomo escort."

In a few moments here came Inagawa—an "industrialist," as Palace euphemism had it—dressed in his usual subdued-gangster style, with a dark blue suit over a maroon shirt and a blue silk tie with a knot as big as a kitten's head. He had removed his shoes; his socks were dark blue with dark green lozenges outlined in yellow on them. He carried a boxwood case under one arm, its blond natural color protected by clear lacquer. Two Otomo troopers in ceremonial-guard armor followed, trying not to trot to keep pace with his brisk stride.

At the chamber door the yakuza chieftain dropped to his knees, bent his forehead to the mat. "My lord, I was the author of an unfortunate but unavoidable disturbance last night," he said. "I have come to apologize for disturbing your repose, and to make amends."

"Indeed," Theodore said. He hoped he did not look as tired as he felt. He had slept poorly again last night, once he'd indeed managed to get to sleep. That dream of his father again. . . .

"Just so, Lord," Inagawa replied. "I wish to prove myself your humble servant. Please grant me this favor."

"Proceed."

Inagawa entered the chamber, knelt before Theodore, who had not moved since the yakuza was announced, and who indeed felt as if he might never move again. Opening the case, Inagawa removed a white towel, which he spread on the mat between the two. Then he wrapped his left hand in a bandage with great care, making sure to draw it as tight as possible. Finally he drew fourth a *tanto* from the case and unsheathed it.

The Otomo guards stiffened. It was permitted for a visitor of Inagawa's status to bear a dagger into the Coordinator's presence. Drawing it was another matter, and forbidden at formal audiences, which this decidedly was not. Seeing their lord show no reaction, the guards did not move, but maintained alert stances.

Inagawa looked up at Theodore and smiled. Then he pressed his big blunt-fingered left hand hard on the towel and severed his little finger with a stroke of the *tanto*.

Theodore felt his cheeks burn. *Yubitsume*. As a gesture of contrition and submission it was difficult to ignore or discount. Nonetheless Inagawa was treating him, the Coordinator of the Draconis Combine, as if he were a common criminal, a gang lord. Under the odd *modus vivendi* Theodore observed with *seimeiyoshi-rengo,* the finger-cutting was permissible; but seldom in his life, and almost never since his father died, had Theodore Kurita so longed to strike another man dead on the spot.

Benjamin Inagawa touched his forehead to the tatami once more. When he straightened Theodore saw his brow was sheened with a light coat of sweat. Other than that, the amputation of his finger might as well have been something happening on the holovid.

The burly oyabun finished bandaging his wounded hand, which had scarcely bled. "I thank the *Tono*," he said, and withdrew. The Otomo guards followed.

Theodore looked down. He had held his brush in precisely the same position the entire time since Inagawa's arrival was announced. Ink had dripped from it, forming a giant blot on the once-pristine paper.

With savage emphasis Theodore threw down the brush. He called for an attendant.

Hiraoke Toyama wore an even more sour expression than usual on his corpse-like face when Inagawa slid into the passenger seat of the limousine beside him. "Whatever possessed you to do such a foolish thing?" he demanded querulously, gesturing at the bandage, now blood-soaked, which covered his fellow oyabun's hand.

Inagawa signaled for the driver to proceed from the parking lot provided for important visitors to the Palace, on whose grounds no vehicles were permitted. He held out his injured hand for an aide who sat on the seats facing him and Toyama to bandage further.

"To buy us space to breathe," the big man said. "He may have murdered his father, if you believe the Shadowed One—and I do. But Theodore is soft at the center. He feels constrained by the fatuous compact he made with the Federation. That little ceremony will ensure he does not follow any impulses he may feel to avenge Yamaguchi."

"But you abased yourself!"

For a moment Inagawa's eyes fixed the smaller man with the glare of an angry boar. Then a smile spread itself across his broad mouth.

"A finger, a promise," he said lightly. "Given to a traitor, they both signify nothing."

"That bastard beast!" raged Hohiro Kiguri. "I'll kill him!"

"I thought that was the plan all along, *Tai-sho-sama*," said the man who shared the otherwise empty DEST command center deep beneath Unity Palace with Kiguri. He had buzz-cut black hair, Japanese eyes, smooth wheat-colored skin stretched taut over a wide-cheeked, big-jawed face. He wore a loose gray sweatshirt, faded black dungarees, and athletic shoes. Hohiro Kuguri was a noted stickler for spit-and-polish from the lower ranks of his commandos, but he also believed firmly in the Combine tradition of hierarchy, which stated that rank indeed had privilege. The man in the sweatshirt wasn't second-in-command of the Draconis Elite Strike Teams, nor particularly high in the chain of command. But he was the most trusted of Kiguri's inner circle— the General's right-hand man and chief enforcer.

Kiguri was on a roll. "In his stupid blind greed that pig Inagawa overreaches himself like a drunk groping across a cluttered table for what he fancies is a last full bottle of sake," he exclaimed, pacing back and forth in the dimness between banks of blinking lights and untended consoles. "He'll smash everything to pieces."

His chief operative took another bite from his bag of dried apple chips. "Inagawa knows nothing of who you really are. Even if the Smiling One gets his claws into him he can't finger us."

"He knows about our replacement component, Captain Daw," Kiguri said. Even though both his experts and Daniel Ramaka's counterintelligence specialists assured him that the command center was clean, he had a nearly superstitious fear of explicitly mentioning what was now orbiting in a DropShip at Occidentalis' trailing Trojan point. No matter how much he railed to his inner circle about how soft Subhash Indrahar had grown, how he had lost his touch, how he was no longer fit to run the Internal Security Force, in his marrow he still dreaded the Smiling One, still harbored the conviction that somehow, for all his effort and cleverness, for all his allies, Subhash would find him out.

"*Mujo,* Boss." In this case it meant *it doesn't matter.* "It may be blasphemous to say so, but there are always more Kuritas out there. Little Angus can be replaced, just the way Theodore can. And don't forget—"

He shrugged and held up his hands. "We have an ace in the hole. Inagawa can blow the whole Black Dragon scam clear to the Truce Line and it won't make a damned bit of difference. You have this one wrapped *tight,* Boss. Nothing can go wrong."

Kiguri had stopped and stood glaring at his subordinate from his good eye and breathing through flared nostrils. Gradually his expression eased, his shoulders relaxed, and he seemed to grow smaller as anger flowed from him.

"You have a talent for playing the edge, Achilles," he said.

Tai-i Daw grinned. "And you lead by example, Kiguri-*sama.*"

"You're right," the General said. "We don't absolutely need Inagawa or even *Kokuryu-kai*—and I'll take great pleasure when the time comes that we can extirpate those swollen toads altogether. But things will go much more smoothly if they continue to play their parts as they're supposed to."

He flicked his eye toward the red numerals of a holochronometer floating by one wall. "And now don't you and Talon Sergeant Nishimura have someplace to be?"

Daw snapped to attention. "*Hai*, General!" He snapped a bow and vanished.

With the approach of the Celebration of the Coordinator's Birth, Imperial City began to overflow with tourists and festivities. There were processions in the streets and pageants in the parks; concerts, orations, presentations, and, of course, fireworks. Many events were planned, and others "spontaneously organized" by Voice of the Dragon exhorters. Others were truly spontaneous outpourings of affection for Theodore, or at least the age-old human desire to raise a little hell. The Coordinator's Birthday was one of the few occasions on which the rigid Combine constraints on behavior were relaxed. Sedate they might have been by the standards of Hachiman, or even dull, but the Imperial Citizens weren't about to let a chance to party down slip past them.

"How come everywhere you go there's these Chinese dragons?" Mirabelle Velasquez asked her friends as they breasted the happy crush on Devotion to Service Street southwest of the Palace. She was a brief and chubby person who managed to be both cheerful and businesslike, as did a lot of people who worked for Zuma Gallegos. Although she was a mere Sergeant of Aztechs and her three companions were MechWarriors, no one thought it strange she hung out with them. Two of them were her relatives, one by birth and one by marriage, and anyway caste lines tended to blur among the Caballeros.

She pointed off down the street over the heads of pedestrians, who were by and large even shorter than she was, to where a huge gaudy head, looking more like that of a stylized lion than the slinky Kurita dragon, bobbed at the head of a long undulant body with many black-slippered feet. "I mean, you'd expect to find them in Liao space, but not here."

"Well, there's a lot of Chinese people everywhere," said

Windy Gutiérrez, a tall, pretty and rather shy *norteña* who like many 'lleros took her nickname from her 'Mech. Wind Indicator was an ancient, oft-patched *Vindicator* that had carried its name since long before its current pilot was born, and which owed its current fully functional status more to Zuma's wizardry than any miracles of recovered Star League lostech. "That's probably why you see the dragon-dance so many places, you know?"

"I wonder if they do it on the Clan homeworld, wherever that is?"

Windy shrugged. "Who knows?"

Misty Saavedra was looking the other way, back the way they had come, toward where the street widened and became lined on the far side with mandamus trees like sycamores with black leaves. "I want to see that thing we saw earlier," she declared. "That big *chorizo* those monks were carrying along."

"*¡Hijo la!*" Mirabelle exclaimed. "It was something, wasn't it? Had to be seven meters long." She elbowed Windy in the ribs. "How'd you like to take a bite out of that, *chiquita*?"

Windy frowned, hesitated. She wasn't adept or comfortable with the usual naughty banter. "I don't like to bite off more than I can chew," she said at length.

Misty giggled, and Mirabelle laughed out loud. The fourth member of the expedition, LtJG Ruby "Spitfire" Sálazar stood close to the black granite façade of a building, allowing traffic to flow around her on the sidewalk. She was snapping her lighter on and off, peering into the little dance of flame as if to find an oracle.

"Knock that off," Misty told her. "You make me nervous, always doing that."

Spitfire shrugged and slipped the lighter into a pocket of her blouse. She was a tiny woman with a blaze of red hair with that metallic touch Southwesterners called "Tlaxcalteca," after the ancient Indians of the Valley of Mexico who were renowned for possessing hair of that unusual shade. Her skin was shiny-smooth and yellow, almost the "wheat-color" considered the Combine ideal, her oval face dusted with freckles across a snubbed nose. Her eyes were startling green. Her body was trim, wide in the shoulders, narrow at waist, well-rounded at the hip. Like the others she wore casual civilian dress, a light blouse in many shades of blue over faded jeans. On the whole she was handsome rather than conventionally pretty, but most people found her striking.

She drove the Seventeenth's lone *Firestarter,* a venerable FS9-H retrofitted with recovered-tech gimmicks to nearly the specs of the comparatively new 9-S model through Uncle Chandy's un-Kurita-like largesse. Like any Mech-Warrior who piloted the highly specialized and risky-to-operate 'Mech by choice, Ruby was a confirmed pyromaniac of long standing. Once upon a time she would've joined in slinging double-entendres with the best of her comrades. But she'd been captured when Lieutenant Colonel Gordon Baird betrayed Camp Marisol in the Eiglophian Mountains of Towne, and held prisoner by Howard Blaylock. Since that time she had become much more subdued, and had acquired that lighter-flicking habit that so annoyed Misty.

They walked on a few meters, to the entrance of a store marked in *romaji*—and presumably *kanji* and *katakana,* though none of the four could read the odd characters next to the Roman letters—as the "Boutique Sexy Lady Yes." "I want to go in here," Misty declared. "They got some nice dresses in the window."

Windy looked worried. The others paid no mind; that was her usual expression. Unlike the others, she carried a purse, which despite its sturdy leather strap she clutched in a drowner's grip against the Black Pearl's astonishingly proficient street thieves. "Won't it be crowded?"

"No more crowded than out here, *hija,*" said Mirabelle.

The boutique was cool and dim and, for a wonder, not crowded at all. The four circulated, rummaging through the racks while immaculately dressed shop ladies stood by trying demurely not to stare at these brash and extravagant *gaijin.*

Misty held up a red dress with pronounced flounces at the hem and the short off-the-shoulder sleeves. "I like this one. I think I'll go back and try it on."

"You're kidding," Mirabelle said. "It'll make you look like a traffic barrel."

Misty made a face. "It will not. You're just jealous 'cause you're built like a cinderblock."

Mirabelle just laughed. She *was* built like a cinderblock. It didn't bother her. Misty went into one of the changing rooms in the back.

The other three were back at the racks when the front door burst open. Four kids with the padded-shoulder jackets and the roached white or gold scalplocks of *dekigoro-zoku* rushed in. They shouted something in Japanese and lunged for the *gaijin* women.

The *dekigoro-zoku* were tall for Drac kids, with muscles wound like wire. Pursuant to Don Carlos' agreement with Takura Migaki, the three women carried no firearms. But they were Caballeras, and each of them had grown up hassling with an assortment of brothers and male cousins even before joining the Marik military and obtaining formal instruction in butt-kicking. Of course, most men are stronger than most women, and there were no exceptions in the Sexy Lady Yes boutique this warm, sunny morning. But the *norteñas* fought dirty.

Two rough boys lunged for Mirabelle, who happened to be closest the door. Instead of recoiling she threw the dress she was eyeing, a frothy white number with lots of chiffon, over the head of the nearer and sank a fist into his belly. The other grabbed her arm, spun her, tried to pin both arms behind her while his buddy staggered into a rack of dresses and fell over.

A third seized the frail-looking Windy Gutiérrez's left wrist and tried to spin her to face him. Instead of fighting she turned with the motion, using it to add momentum as she clouted him across the face with her purse. She was not particularly strong, despite being of above-average height. But she was a traditionally minded young Cerillos lady, and according to immemorial tradition she was carrying a half-kilo can of sliced peaches in syrup in her purse. The gaudy youth uttered a strangled squawk and fell with his right cheek caved in and his noise knocked askew.

The fourth gang kid grabbed little Ruby Sálazar from the

front by both biceps, picked her bodily up off the floor and pushed her backward against the counter while shop ladies scattered like frightened birds. Ruby brought her right hand up between them as her attacker began to bend her backward. Ruby being what she was and all, her lighter was not a *normal* lighter. Among other things it could serve as a grenade, not that that was applicable here. More to the point, it worked by spraying a variable jet of atomized fuel. Ruby dialed the nozzle wide, gave the front of the kid's white and silver jacket a quick misting, and clicked the electrical initiator.

As flames raced up the front of his jacket like small avid animals the kid danced back, as if that would do any good. Ruby rolled backward over the counter. The kid dropped to the floor and began rolling frantically around, igniting dresses left and right, as the jacket's synthetic fabric caught. Two down.

Mirabelle had kicked her second assailant in the crotch and broken his nose with an overhand right when her first victim came off the floor with the dress hung around his neck and took her down in a flying tackle. He straddled her, pummeling her face with her fists. And Windy loomed up behind him to coldcock him with a swing of her purse at the full extent of the strap.

By this point a shop lady was on one side of the flaming gang kid, hosing him with white foam from an extinguisher, while Ruby stood on the other side kicking him lustily in the ribs with her steel-toed athletic shoes. Thoroughly extinguished in several senses, the youth rolled moaning onto knees and elbows, then scrambled away from his tormentor. He and the boy whose nose Mirabelle had broken gathered up their two comrades whom Windy had felled, neither of whom was currently functional, and dragged them back out the front door.

Mirabelle had puffy cheeks and a mouse under her left eye that would certainly blossom into a profound shiner. The front of Ruby's blouse was scorched. But these were minor casualties, no more than badges of honor to the *norteñas*. They exchanged hugs and triumphant laughter.

The shop ladies stood around glumly surveying the damage, like wet pigeons.

"Hey," Mirabelle said, looking around. "Where's Misty?"

"Isn't she still back in the changing room?" Windy asked.

"That's just like her, to duck for cover during a fight," Mirabelle said loudly, figuring that canard would cause her cousin to come boiling out of the dressing room to finish the job the *dekigoro-zoku* had so ineptly started. Misty was a cheerful soul, but she was still a MechWarrior, and took no crap from relatives.

But there was only silence. The three women looked to the back of the shop.

The curtains meant to seal the minute changing-cubicles from view all hung open. There was no sign of Misty Saavedra.

20

Bleeding smoke from the stump of its right shoulder, shattered by the blasts of twin extended-range particle projection cannons mounted in a *Masakari*'s arm, and from the rearward-facing CASE vent of the right-hand missile storage that had gone up with the Shigunga LRM launcher, the *Mauler* staggered thigh-deep into the sluggish mud-colored waters of the Kado-guchi. The *Mauler* was a flamboyant heat-hog: a MechWarrior who let off its whole awesome arsenal at once risked reactor shutdown then and there. Shorn of one of its big Victory Nickel Alloy extended-range lasers, the *Mauler*'s heat-loading could not exceed its nominal ability to bleed excess heat unless it ran as it fired . . . except that several double-capacity heat sinks had been shattered in the fight with the Smoke Jaguar Star.

And the *Mauler* was running in the red. It had fired off both large lasers and both fifteen-missile racks at once at the climax of its duel with the *Masakari*. Even as its right shoulder and arm and the attendant weapons had been blown away, the final fire-spasm had smashed the Clan 'Mech's head, destroying its cockpit and killing its pilot. Now the Kurita BattleMech sought the river's cooling embrace for its final stand.

It did not have long to wait. Crushing a stand of capylar saplings on the northern bank, a 100-ton *Behemoth* appeared out of the woods. Black leaves and green wood exploded in puffs of steam as the *Mauler*'s left-hand laser frantically sought its new foe. The squat Smoke Jag 'Mech turned, seemed to hunker down on its heavy canted legs, and let loose with its full battery of two torso-mounted Gauss cannon, two big pulse lasers in its arms, and the small-aperture pulse laser with its overlong optical-shroud barrel mounted abaft the cockpit.

The Clan jock was overloading his own heat sinks—but slowly. He had a few seconds' grace before the monster machine started to go weird beneath him. With a true Mech-Warrior's instinct for the kill, he poured it on.

Heat soared in the *Mauler*'s cockpit. Red lights blazed, alarms squalled. The *Mauler* pilot saw missile-hits flash on the *Behemoth*'s heavily sloped front glácis, saw sparks fly as the surviving large laser scored housing off one Gauss rifle. But the Gauss' heavy nickel-ferrous slugs were jolting the *Mauler*'s 95 tons of steel and titanium skeleton, myomer musculature, and ferro-fibrous armor as if it were a balsawood toy, the flickering laser-lances stabbing deep into the already-violated body of the big Kurita 'Mech.

The *Mauler* rocked back, raising a greasy slog of water behind. Then a volcano of noise rose up around the cockpit, and in its dying microsecond the onboard computer opted for emergency ejection. The popping of the hail-Mary charges that blew off the top of the big 'Mech's head and the rush of the rocket-motor underneath the seat blended with the thunder of the *Mauler* being blasted to pieces. The MechWarrior had one final lingering look from above at the devastated machine, like someone having a near-death experience gazing down on her apparently lifeless body. And then it was over.

Face set in a frown, Lainie Shimazu lifted the neurohelmet off her shoulders. When she looked around, it was to see the face of her *gaijin* friend Kali MacDougall looking into the simulator wearing a funny little half-smile.

"Mighty impressive, hon," the Southwestern woman said. As was her custom these days she was dressed all in black, with her right arm strapped to her chest to prevent her trying to use the shoulder before it recovered from reconstructive surgery. She had let her hair grow into tight blonde ringlets, but it was still shorter than Lainie was accustomed to seeing it. "But you sure play like you got a death wish."

For a moment Lainie stared at the blonde woman, trying to decide whether to resent the intrusion or not. Her eyes were almost the red of an albino animal's.

"Not exactly a death *wish*," she said. Her voice rasped as if she had actually been breathing the smoke of her Battle-Mech's funeral pyre.

"Talk to me?"

Cheeks tight, Lainie unfolded her long frame from the simulator. Standing full upright she looked the 183-centimeter-tall Kali right in the eye. The two had the simulations room of the *Tai-sa* Sean Robison Memorial Barracks to themselves this morning. Everyone else was busy drilling, polishing brass—or BattleMech armor—or otherwise preparing for the big event just three days away.

"I'm fine," Lainie said.

"I doubt that," Kali said. "You haven't been acting fine."

Lainie frowned. "Look—"

Kali held up a hand. "Now, hold your onto horses, Lane. I've been concerned about you for a while, but you know I reckon you've got a right to go to hell in your own sweet time. But I let some people sweet-talk me, so here I am to see if you'll open up to me about what the hell's been eating you."

Lainie turned away. "It's nothing."

"That's one thing it for-sure isn't. Your people are worrying themselves into premature hair-loss over the way you've been taking on. Now there's a rumor going around that you dumped Takura, and basically everybody thinks you're crazy, and you wouldn't say diddly to Cassie, so here I am."

"There's no point in talking about it," Lainie said in a dead voice. "There's nothing anyone can do, least of all me."

"That may be, and then again it may not; you got some mighty resourceful friends, not to mention unscrupulous at need. But whether any of us can help or not, don't you think you could see your way clear to openin' up? Hon, it seems like since practically the moment we got here, you've been doin' a wonderful impression of a woman about to explode. Can't you at least bleed a little excess pressure?"

Lainie's broad shoulders rose and fell in a sigh. "Why not?" She looked meaningfully around. "But let's walk. *Outside.*"

One thing Imperial City didn't lack was barracks. The *Tai-sa* Robison Barracks, named for an obscure hero from some centuries-old Combine war, lay south of the city, between the industrial outskirts and the spaceport: ranks of long, low blocky structures stuccoed the same tan as DCMS field uniforms huddled next to a 'Mech park and a dusty practice field. A light company of *Panthers*, *Javelins*, and *Spiders* was thumping through a series of evolutions that owed more to eighteenth-century close-order drill than thirty-first-century BattleMech combat, to be performed on vast Unity Square for the delectation of the Coordinator and various dignitaries in the reviewing stands being erected before the Palace. Somebody had a bad hip bearing, which was producing a thin annoying whine that rose and fell as the 'Mechs advanced and receded.

It was windy and more than a bit cool beneath a high thin overcast. Lainie and Kali walked along the edge of the field farthest from the drilling BattleMechs, which fortuitously was not downwind of the big dust clouds they were kicking up. Lainie had her arms crossed under her breasts and a grim expression set into her slightly lupine features.

"I know your friend Migaki is in charge of making up lies on behalf of an agency that spends a lot of its time assassinating people and attaching electrodes to their genitals and whatnot," Kali said, "but to separate his personal life from his professional life, he seems like a pretty nice fella. Represents a kind of marked step up from your usual double helping of muscle, hold the brains."

"I know," said Lainie, who respected rather than resented her friend's straightforwardness. "That's why I dumped him."

Kali gave her a raised eyebrow. "Now you're really going

to have to tell me what's going on, so my curiosity doesn't kill me."

Lainie paced a dozen steps in silence. "All right. But you can't tell anybody. *Wakarimasu-ka?*"

"Well . . . okay. But it's gonna be a little hard to give people an explanation."

"You can give them all the explanation they want, after everything's over."

"All right. You're locked on. Fire away."

Lainie nodded her striking crest of hair. "You've heard the story of how I came to Masamori."

"Once or twice. You were a yak princess for true, until your Daddy's right-hand man decided to grab for the gusto. A loyal retainer managed to get you off the surface before the hatchetmen found you. Eventually you washed up on Hachiman."

"Where Kazuo Sumiyama, the oyabun, took me in, on condition I become his personal sex toy. Where I stayed until the Gunji no Kanrei offered me a way out of servitude."

"I'm with you so far."

"My real name is Melisandra DuBonnet. My parents got caught up in the same fad for real and imaginary Classical names Cassie's parents did. My father's name was Seizo DuBonnet. He was chief oyabun of Benjamin."

Kali stopped. "I think I see the direction this is starting to take—"

"Yes," Lainie said. "The man who murdered my father and drove me to Hachiman was Benjamin Inagawa. Him I shall kill, at our Coordinator's birthday celebration. And then I shall commit *seppuku,* since Inagawa is an honored servant of Theodore-*sama,* and killing him will bring disgrace upon the Coordinator."

Kali pursed her lips and blew out a long breath. "That's pretty comprehensive."

"You can see why I couldn't tell my people anything of this. Nor Cassie."

"Yeah. If you told one of your boys or girls, they'd pop Inagawa themselves and take the heat."

"Right. And while Cassie's sense of duty is absolute, she has no concept of honor. She'd no doubt arrange some kind of accident for Inagawa. And *ninkyo*—our yakuza code of honor, which binds us as sternly as *bushido* binds the samurai—requires that Inagawa die by my hand and none other. 'A man may not rest under the same sky that shelters his father's murderer,' as Confucius says."

For an indeterminate time Kali stood, her own arms folded now, just looking at her friend, while the wind whistled and the drilling 'Mechs thumped and clanked and whined across the field.

"I tell you this," Lainie said, "because you do have a code of honor. You won't interfere."

"Yeah," Kali said. "You got me pinned down pretty well, here, Lane. So Migaki—"

"Treats me better than any man ever has. And that's why I—I can't—" She turned quickly away.

"Maybe we can think of something," Kali said.

Lainie lifted her head to the wind. "It isn't like you to kid yourself, Kali-*chan*."

"I reckon not."

More silence passed. Kali reached out to squeeze her friend's shoulder from behind. Then she walked away across the field, a tall solitary figure, dressed in black.

"Cassie!" cried a voice that had been familiar to her long before she met its owner, as she strode across the windswept Eiga-toshi grounds.

Her first reaction was a scowl. She was in an eerie mood, with undertones of sheer viciousness. She was by no means happy to be put in the position of having to cooperate with the likes of Subhash Indrahar, although the rapid approach of whatever zero hour was associated with Teddy's birthday left her no choice. Worse was the experience of having been waylaid by the Sons of the Dragon, stunned and captured like an exotic animal. On one level she could understand why Subhash found it necessary to put her to the test: a desire to learn for himself just how capable she was before deciding what use he might best put her to, not to mention plain primate curiosity.

It didn't lessen her sense of being violated.

Still, recalling Kali's patient tutoring in the arts of being human, she forced herself to focus on the fact that it wasn't Johnny's fault. He had been nice to her. People like that weren't in long supply.

She forced something like a smile and an abstracted wave. "Johnny."

He was wearing Chinese slippers and black silk pants. His lean and magnificent torso was sheened with sweat, his hair tousled; he held a towel in one hand. Apparently he had just come from either shooting a fight scene or rehearsing for one.

He trotted toward her. "I need to talk to you."

"Not now," she said. "Business."

"But—"

"The other night was really lovely," she said, "But I have to go. Bye."

She left him standing there, looking after her like an abandoned puppy. He was already forgotten. Instead, she was thinking that the Sons of the Dragon charged with smuggling her out of the top-secret ISF headquarters— which everybody in the Inner Sphere knew lay beneath Unity Palace—had taken their own sweet time about it.

She was also feeling relief that they'd been content to blindfold her, and take her word that she wouldn't try to sneak a peek. If they'd restrained her . . . she didn't think she could have taken that.

She found Don Carlos and Father Doctor Bob together in a commissary of the main dorm the 'lleros had been assigned. Normally Don Carlos would have been conferring with Dolores Gallegos about the state of the regiment at this hour of the morning, but Red was at Luthien Armor Works in Jirushi City southeast of town again today, debriefing them on her experiences fighting in their new *O-Bakemono* 'Mech on Towne.

"I'm glad you're both here," Cassie said without ceremony as she blew in the door. "There's a lot to talk about."

"There certainly is," the Jesuit said, looking worried.

That stopped her in her tracks. She couldn't be the reason the regimental commander and his intelligence chief were looking like a pair of mice who thought they might smell a ferret. Being gone overnight without prior notice was about as unusual for her as it was for an alley cat.

"What?" she demanded.

"Mercedes Saavedra has been kidnapped," García said. "By one of the youth gangs, the deg, deki-something—I'm sorry, but I don't have your facility with the language."

"Dekigoro-zoku," Cassie said.

"That's it. Several of them attacked the women she was with in a shop downtown. While they were occupied fighting the young men off, someone else dragged her out of a changing booth in the back."

"Many of our people have gone into Imperial City to try to find her," Don Carlos said gravely. "We have just heard from the authorities that there has been trouble."

"Apparently some Caballeros found some of the, ah, the gangs," García explained. "There have been clashes. We've had several people hurt. And, I regret to say, one killed."

"Lonnie Padilla," Don Carlos said, in a tone a grieving father might use. He took the loss of any member of the regiment personally. "One of Richard Gallegos' people."

Cassie turned, squeezed her eyes shut, pounded a fist against her thigh. *Damn!* Everything seemed to be slipping hopelessly out of control.

"Call them back," she said.

"I beg your pardon?" Father García asked, a quizzical expression on his face.

"You've got to call everybody back! Get them here inside the compound, make them stay put."

"Now, Lieutenant," the Colonel said, "you must understand how bad they want to get Misty back—"

"They're not *going* to get her back. This is *Luthien,* for Mary's sake! And there are maybe five people in the regiment who understand more Japanese than 'yes,' 'no,' and 'where's the whorehouse?' "

"Surely you overstate the case, Cassiopeia," García said in his most pedantic voice. "The Combine culture is still fairly alien to most of us, but after all, the Seventeenth spent over a year on Hachiman—"

"And I've been with the Caballeros *eleven years,* and you're right this minute acting as if I don't know how you damned Southwesterners behave! I know Tak Migaki and everybody has been making very nice with us since we're the special guests of the Coordinator and all, but no matter how polite and smiley-faced Dracs may act, they're even more insular and paranoid than you are. And compared to Luthien, Hachiman is Solaris. This is not an open society we're dealing with on this planet."

She made herself pause to take a deep breath and try to control her surge of emotions. "Our people are not going to get Misty back by swarming over Impy City punching everybody with bad hair. They're only going to get in more trouble than they maybe have already. This is not a real good time for *gaijin* to be kicking up a big fuss in public, even if they are Teddy's guests."

The two men looked at each other. Neither was used to seeing their top scout so agitated.

"Tienes razón," Don Carlos said. "You're right. I'll call them back at once."

Cassie took a deep breath, let it out in a long sigh, and sat down at a table.

"You looked as if you had important news, too," García said gently.

She nodded. "It's been a busy night. You heard about the dust-up last night, down by the riverfront?"

"We heard distant rumbling sounds, and saw flashes in the sky above the city," Don Carlos said. "It almost seemed as if a 'Mech battle was taking place."

"One was. Benjamin Inagawa was taking down the Old Cat, Yamaguchi. Apparently both sides brought Battle-Mechs to the fandango. And I wound up sleeping through the whole thing." Succinctly she told them of what had gone on the night before.

"And this Smiling One," Don Carlos said, "does he now believe that the Black Dragons plan some deviltry?"

"I think he's getting there. Seems like somebody's been quietly losing any reports the ISF might turn up to indicate that Kokuryu-*kai* is still big, bad, and on the prowl. Which in itself is kind of worrying."

"It's certainly not encouraging," García said, "considered alongside the evidence you encountered of possible treachery within the Internal Security Force. The question is, how quickly can Indrahar adjust his pattern of thinking to this new information? That's not easy for most people to do, especially at an advanced age."

"Subhash is old and crippled," Cassie said, "but only in the body. If he gets proof of a Black Dragon plot—or somebody dirty inside ISF—he'll come around like that. But he's not going to take my word for it."

"Do you think there's any connection between the abduction of Misty Saavedra and the Black Dragon Society?"

"No. There's some pretty strange bedfellows in *Kokuryukai*: the old-line yaks, industrialists, reactionaries in the DCMS, groups that normally would not mix in any combination you could cook up. But them and the *dekigoro-zoku*—"

She held up her hands vertically before her, passed the left in front of the right, then right in front of left. "—They don't join up at all. It's like they're on whole different planets."

"But these young men—they're gangsters too, street criminals," Don Carlos said. "Aren't they the same thing as the yakuza?"

"Not at all, Don Carlos. The yaks are what you said, street criminals, down and dirty, no matter what kinds of airs they give themselves. The 'sudden-impulse tribe,' the *dekigoro-zoku,* they're rich kids out for a thrill. The yaks are beneath their contempt. And to the yakuza, at best they're spoiled dilettantes, at worst they're the sort of noisy nuisances and rivals the yakuza usually take good community-conscious pride in removing from the gene pool, only in this case the yaks can't touch them unless they step *way* over the line. For the *dekigoro-zoku* and the tattoo boys to be working together would be like, oh, us working with the Clans."

She felt a stab in her consciousness, to the effect that, in the course of working for Uncle Chandy, the Caballeros *had* worked with the Clans, or at least with Clanners, both on Hachiman and Towne. She dismissed the thought as irrelevant.

"I believe what you say," Don Carlos said. "You seldom lead us astray. But now there is something you must do."

"Which is?"

"I want you to lay aside your concern about the Black Dragons and concentrate on finding Lieutenant Saavedra."

"But, Colonel! If the Dragons are up to something, we're targeted for sure. And the celebration's only three days away. I don't have time to hunt for Misty!"

"Might it not simply be the case that these Black Dragons have decided to quit pretending and strike directly at the source of their grievances? Maybe they've given over their talk of 'bad advisors,' and are preparing to move against the Coordinator himself."

"But we've drawn too much of their blood for them to leave us out of anything nasty they have up their sleeves. And don't forget Theodore is Uncle Chandy's cousin, not to mention maybe the one hope the Inner Sphere has of standing off the Clans when they finally decide to come crashing over the truce line."

"Indeed, Theodore Kurita is our employer's blood relation, and perhaps the Inner Sphere needs him badly. Yet when all is said he's a *culebra*. Misty is one of us. Help us find her, Cassie."

Like a good officer, Don Carlos seldom ordered, but he did command. Cassie screwed up her cheeks as if that might somehow dam her tear-ducts.

"Yes, Don Carlos," she said. "I'll do my best."

21

Unity Palace, Imperial City
Luthien
Pesht Military District, Draconis Combine
27 June 3058

"You look tired, Theodore," Chandrasekhar Kurita said. "What's troubling your sleep? Surely not a trifle like your upcoming celebration?"

Theodore Kurita allowed himself a wry half-smile. Uncle Chandy was indulging in his own form of *haragei,* implying that even the stringent demands of preparing for the Coordinator's Birthday paled beside his cousin's past accomplishments. *How very much like Chandy,* he thought, *to contrive to build me up without resorting to flattery.* With emphasis on *contrive,* he added to himself.

His long and still-athletic frame was sprawled on a contoured recliner, half chair and half sofa, set in a small recreational chamber in the upper floors of the immense Palace. A large holostage pedestal stood dark by one *shoji*-screened wall. By another was a billiard table, which also served as the platform for a special holographic projection unit that enabled one to fight 'Mech-unit actions at various scales across three-dimensional terrain: half toy, half serious simulator. The single wall of exposed teak was hung with paintings by masters from ancient Japan: an ink painting of a bird by eccentric sword-saint Musashi; a triptych representing the Chinese deity Shoki the Demon-Queller by Tokugawa court artist Kano Tsunenobu; two originals from Hokusai's *Hundred Views of Mt. Fuji;* an ink painting likewise by Hokusai—the most eccentric of artists, devotee of the Floating World, and originator of the *manga* style—depicting an octopus ravaging a human fisher-girl. The last was a gift to Theodore from his wife, Kagoshima Prefecture commander Tomoe Sakade, reflecting an aspect of their relationship well-hidden from most of the Combine. There were also traditional hand-bound books and scrolls, as well as a more conventional flatscreen computer with attendant holodisplay.

It was a sanctum Theodore seldom had cause—excuse, maybe—to retreat to. It was one more reason to enjoy a visit from his so-called Uncle Chandy, who lay like a great smug bullfrog amid a splendor of silk cushions swilling wine and stuffing his face with fruit from a green lacquered tray.

"Courtly manners and rituals have never come easy to me," he said. "You of all people know that. It would be fatuous to say I prefer the rigors of campaigning, but I truly would rather ride a BattleMech into an honest fight than face the rigmarole."

"Masterly misdirection has long been numbered among your many skills," Chandy said. "You used to feel you could confide in me, long ago."

"You were often the only one," Theodore admitted in a wistful tone.

"Then why not level with your Uncle Chandy?"

" 'Uncle.' " Theodore vented a quiet laugh. "You're what? Two years older than I am?"

Chandy showed his Buddha smile. "Something on that order. Though I haven't aged with so much grace as you."

This time Theodore laughed out loud. "Now you are soaping me, you old fraud. What is it you want?"

"To help."

Theodore looked away.

"You're letting the past eat at you, aren't you?" Chandy asked in a quiet voice.

"It's nothing."

"You're a brave man, Theodore-*kun*. I've been saying that longer than almost anybody else, and it's still true. But part of being brave is facing what's in here." And he tapped his capacious *hara*.

Theodore shook his head. "I've never been able to get

mad at you, exasperating though you can be. And I know full well you're anything but the self-indulgent fool many still believe you to be—just as you always believed I was not the worthless wastrel the court once thought me. Especially my father."

"Ah, your father. We both know what your father was, so I need not risk incurring your anger by speaking ill of the dead. Throughout your life he played a game with you, the single rule of which was: you lose."

"So ka?" Teddy asked frostily. Almost at once his expression softened, and he said, "Very well. You're right. But what would you have me do? The past is as it is. I cannot hide from it either."

"You can leave the past in the past, though. You might forgive your father. More to the point, you might even forgive yourself."

Apparently still relaxed, Theodore studied his cousin through narrow eyes. *How much does he know?* While he had not been terrifically close to his so-called uncle for decades, he had for a fact never discounted him as thoroughly as Subhash Indrahar had. And in the wake of the ISF's failed attempt to destroy Chandy, the Smiling One had come to an entirely new appreciation of both the man and his operation. Particularly the skill of Chandy's intelligence service, run by the enigmatic Mirza Peter Abdulsattah.

"It's come to my ears that rumor says I killed my father," Theodore said in a lazy voice. "Do you believe that?"

"Iie, Theodore-*sama.* Although I hope you'll forgive me if I say I would not think less of you if you had. But the truth of the matter is immaterial: you yourself are the only one who can know what it is you make yourself suffer for."

For a time they sat in silence. Theodore wanted to let his cousin's words slide off his back like water down a turtle's shell, but he could not. At the same time, he wanted to ask Chandy, *What am I to do?* But he would not.

"One way you might find to make peace with your past," Chandy said, "is to make peace with your son."

"My son?"

"Franklin Sakamoto. He renounced his birthright; you

allowed the opportunity to quietly do away with him after you became aware of his existence to lapse. The two of you can start on equal footing; no reason not to. And yet you keep him under virtual house arrest."

No point wondering how he learned about that, Theodore thought. Aloud, he said, "It's for his own protection."

"Mu," Chandy replied.

Flash irritation: "That was said to negate the asking of a fatuous question: 'Can a dog have Buddha nature.' Not in response to a statement."

"Ah, but you knew what I was driving at."

Theodore reared back in exasperation, shook his head, laughed. "If you turn out to be some kind of Zen master, it will be too much for me to take."

"Small danger of that," Chandy said. " 'A *roshi* is an arrow aimed at Hell,' and I'm a man who likes his comfort. But to get back to the matter of your son—"

A chime announced someone at the door to the chamber. That the visitor dared interrupt one of the Coordinator's rare breaks meant that his or her business was by definition urgent. "Come in," Theodore called, both annoyed and somehow relieved.

The door slid aside. *Sho-sho* Hideyoshi entered, knelt, dropped his forehead to the floor mat.

Theodore looked at him in surprise. "What's this, Oda-*san*? Why the formality?"

"It is my regretful duty to inform the Coordinator that Franklin Sakamoto has disappeared from my residence."

" 'Disappeared?' "

"Perhaps 'escaped' would be a better word, Lord: he is gone, and there is sign of neither intrusion nor struggle. Apparently he has fled. The fault is entirely mine. I beg you to accept my resignation, in atonement for my failure."

Theodore rose to his feet. "Enough of that. No one expected he'd try to leave your custody, so there's no fault—or if there is, it's mine. I did not order you to treat him as a prisoner."

His eyes were hard as he glanced at Uncle Chandy. The fat man shook his head sadly, and sighed.

* * *

The *dekigoro-zoku* and their flashy hovercars had fallen off the face of the planet by the time Cassie hit the Impy City streets. There was absolutely no sign of their existence. Perhaps an official warning had come down to lay lower than low. Or perhaps they'd had all they wanted of the enraged Caballeros. The Caballeros had vanished too, chivvied back to Eiga-toshi by threats and pleas from unit commanders, iced by a personal appeal from Don Carlos. Some had also found their ways into local lockups and hospitals. But none was on the festive crowded streets of the Combine's first city.

What were in evidence were Friendly Persuaders, by the drove. The Civilian Guidance Corps already stripped the provinces—Amori, Yeovil, Haratston, Takaoguchi in the Nijunen Desert, seemingly everyplace this side of Tsu Shima, the innermost moon—of Persuaders to handle the influx of celebrants from all over the Combine into Imperial City. In the wake of the Caballero eruption it seemed the police authorities had mobilized everybody they could stuff into the candy-striped uniform—had canceled leaves and called back the off-shift patrolmen. By the way certain extremely well-developed *hara* bulked out the fronts of quilted uniform jackets, the skittishness of eyes beneath red-trimmed white helmets and the uneasy way gloved fingers caressed stunner firing-studs and the safeties of stubby riot shotguns fed from side-loading magazines, a good many Persuaders had been sent out onto the pavement after spending a lot of years behind the back of a desk.

Predictably the Candy-stripers were torqued-off and on edge, and looked generally inclined to zap and then beat to bean paste anyone who looked at them with both eyes simultaneously, to make sure of maintaining their moral ascendancy. Cassie had been warned that they were under orders to restrain any Caballeros they came across—"restrain" meaning, "Don't kill them, but if they fall down a few times on the way back to *teruho*, it'll give them more to meditate upon inside." *Teruho* being a yak inversion of *hoteru*, "hotel": that time-honored Cross-Bar Hilton.

The pairs or packs of cops Cassie encountered didn't give her any more than the hard-eyed scrutiny they gave every citizen—or if it was, it wasn't because they suspected her of being one of the *yohei*. She was dressed as a tech from Eiga-toshi, with papers to match. Cinema City Workers kept ir-regular hours, so even if, for some reason, she was singled out of the crush of humanity to be rousted, she would be able to account for being off work in the middle afternoon. At the same time, she got to wear a durable garment that didn't restrict her movements, unlike the more feminine fin-ery an offworld visitor or even local office lady would be expected to affect.

While the plague of cops didn't cramp Cassie, the *dekigoro-zoku* drought did. Her simplest approach was to catch herself a Sudden Impulse tribeskid and squeeze him till he popped; she was no fan of subtlety for its own sake, and as far as she was concerned this whole mish was a sideshow, something to be gotten out of the way as soon as possible, so she could get back to the real business of saving her regiment, if not all civilization. But there was no game moving out in the open.

Discreet inquiries quickly pinpointed favored *dekigoro-zoku* hangouts, vidgame parlors, and youth clubs. She found them all locked down tight and under Candy-stripe guard. That added mass to the theory that the thrill gangs had been told to make themselves scarce. In the Draconis Combine even Youth Defiant tended to defer to the voice of Authori-ty. And when Authority was in its present savage mood, with the Coordinator's Birthday just days away and the eyes of the whole Inner Sphere turned to Imperial City, if you acted up you were due for an advanced course of hurting, no matter whose son you were.

That left Cassie flat. The *dekigoro-zoku* ran in a whole different continuum from the one she operated in, too. She was accustomed to working the Water Trade and the under-world, on one end of the spectrum, and polite society at the other. She had never had occasion to cultivate spoiled rich kids out for nasty kicks, at least not in the Combine. She could work them too; it was her proud belief that she could scam any people of any culture, sub or otherwise, given time to find their handles. But time she didn't have, and her usual tools and contacts—like the invaluable Tosei-*kai* Ko-

reans Lainie's kids had set her up with here on the Pearl—
had no links to that world either.

That left old-fashioned investigation. Cassie had no formal
training in modern police techniques. Then again, neither did
most of the Civilian Guidance Corps, so with a little luck
she'd find that the waters hadn't been muddied yet.

"I saw it, all right," said the old woman who worked in
the restaurant slantwise across the alley from Sexy Lady
Yes. Her gray-shot hair was wrapped in a tight bun. She
wore a black smock that reached almost to the dirt of the alley. "I was just bringing out a load of trash—wrappings and
such, you understand; we keep all the rinds and radish ends
for mulching our garden. No farmers on Luthien, no indeed,
but billions of gardeners. I was bringing it out, I say, and
had just opened the door when I saw two men come out of
the dress shop dragging the young woman."

"What did you do, *Oma-san*?"

The old woman continued to scrub her hands with the
dish towel she held. "Oh, I shrank back. I was very afraid
they would see me. They looked like very hard young men.
One was wheat-colored, one was black."

"You were wise, Grandmother. What did they do then?"

"They carried her to their car, parked right down there, at
the end of the alley." She leaned forward to gesture. There
was no car now, just some deep tire-ruts in the mud, beside
a stack of crates.

"She was very still, unnaturally still. At first I thought she
had taken ill, poor child. But the way the men were acting, it
was wrong. I could feel it here." She touched herself over
the *hara*.

"Did you tell the police anything of this?"

"Oh, no. They never asked."

It figures, Cassie thought. She could see why Lieutenant
McCartney was losing his hair and slamming stomach
meds. The CGC was not an elite investigatory outfit.

She didn't bother asking why the old lady had not volun-
teered the data to the Candy-stripers. The Dictum Honorium
called on the citizenry to promptly inform the proper
authorities of anything suspicious they might happen to

witness. And by the time you were fourteen-fifteen you learned, one way or another, just what *that* got you. As in police states in every time and every clime, drawing the heat's attention to yourself for any reason was a high-risk proposition.

"Did you happen to see the registry?"

"I beg your pardon?"

"The registration plaque. On the rear of the car."

"Yes. Yes I did."

"Do you remember what it was, *Oma-san*?"

"No. Why should I? Why do you wish to know that, young woman?"

"Perhaps the car is registered to one of the men. Or perhaps the person to whom the car is registered can tell me who they are." She did not bother to add that whoever the car was registered to *would* tell her what she wanted to know.

"*So ka?* What a clever idea! Just like 'Spy Hunter' on the holo."

Cassie swallowed. "Very much like that, *Oma-san*."

"Well, I certainly don't remember the number. But Ervil the pot-boy came out to see what was going on. He'll know. He has a trick memory, you see. He can barely remember his name from one moment to the next, but he can glance at a telephone-directory screen and recite all the numbers on it without an error days later."

She put her head back in the door and yelled, "Ervil!" Then she looked back at Cassie and showed her a reassuring grin, set with a couple of steel teeth.

"Everybody is saying the *gaijin* started attacking people for no reason," she said. "I don't believe that for a moment. If they let people kidnap one of them without fighting back, they wouldn't be *gaijin,* but animals."

In the course of cruising the Impy City streets Cassie had picked up that rumor half a dozen times in a couple of hours. That bothered her, but then the pot-boy appeared. A lumpy boy somewhere in adolescence, he had tow-colored hair and a face like a pie pan. He grinned absently at both women.

The proprietor also appeared. He was a small man with a cannonball-shaped head and dark skin. "What's this?" he demanded in a piping voice. "Why are you out here gossiping, Amanda? We have a restaurant to run!"

"This is my son-in-law, Sanjitay," the old woman said proudly. "He owns this fine establishment all by himself."

"She's helping me find a friend, sir," Cassie said. As he opened his mouth to explode all over her, she held out a crisp new 100 H-Bill. "Please accept this gift in compensation for any inconvenience I might have caused."

The restaurateur accepted the money. "Well, Amanda! Why do you stand there gaping? Answer the customer's questions immediately!"

"You are a brave and loyal young woman, to be trying so hard to find your friend," Amanda said, ignoring her son-in-law. "Be careful. These men could be very dangerous."

Cassie smiled. "I will be careful, Grandmother. Thank you. Ervil?"

"I know you have exalted connections," the tired voice of Lieutenant McCartney said, "but believe it or not, Criminal Investigations Bureau has things to do other than answer questions for you." A meaningful pause. "We've been getting a lot more work recently. . . ."

Cassie glanced out through the glass of the phone kiosk. Most of the people who filled the street were watching a troupe of acrobats perform down the block, which as a matter of elementary paranoia was nowhere near the restaurant or the Sexy Lady Yes boutique. Nobody seemed to be paying her any attention.

"I promised to try to get you answers," she said. "Now I can promise to *get* them. But it's going to take a little longer."

Another pause. It was an audio-only setup, which was standard for Luthien—Masamori on Hachiman had vidphones in its public booths—and was just fine by her. Cassie didn't need a screen to envision a frown on the detective lieutenant's face. She reckoned McCartney was struggling with the impulse to haul her in for a little old-fashioned police-work Combine-style, the kind usually conducted in a room with drains in the floor. That was to be expected. There was a little clock running in her head, however, and when it ran out, she was going to presume that what he was doing was stalling until a patrol could get to the kiosk to arrest her—she took for granted all calls to the CGC were automatically traced. In which case she was simply going to walk out and vanish in the cheerful throng.

"Very well," the detective said just before the bell. "What do you want?"

She held up a napkin on which she had written the number Ervil provided, read it off. "I'd like you to trace this vehicle registration for me."

Still another pause. "Very clever. Are you a trained police investigator, then?"

"I've broken laws on a dozen or so planets. I know the drill."

"Maybe I should hire you."

"If I were available," she said, "yes, you should. But my employer's satisfied with the job I do, for the moment. Don't worry—I haven't forgotten the promise I made you."

"I'll get it for you. But don't expect it soon. The request has to go through channels."

"How long?"

"Tomorrow at the earliest."

Cassie closed her eyes and slumped against the kiosk walls. "Whatever," she said, and broke the connection.

22

"**P**ermit me to be certain I understand," said the softly sibilant voice from the videophone. "What this homicide investigator told you after he checked the registration of the kidnap vehicle was . . . nothing?"

Cassie glanced away from the oxymoronically grim visage of the Smiling One and across the small room. The old granny lady heating a pot of water for tea on a hot plate by one *shoji*-screened wall smiled encouragingly at her. Cassie nodded abstractedly back.

"It was a real eloquent nothing, Subhash-*sama*," Cassie replied, looking back at his image. She kept the nice granny lady carefully in her peripheral vision. Because if the nice granny lady made a wrong move Cassie was going to light her up proper with her hideout snubby.

This was an ISF safe house whose address Cassie had been provided before her release from custody—one indication that the Smiling One took her and her allegations of corruption in the secret police seriously. It offered a supposedly secure communications link to the Director. From that Cassie inferred it was specifically a Sons of the Dragon safe house. But she didn't like to take anything for granted. Not even the harmlessness of benign old granny ladies, since she'd known some pretty formidable specimens in her time. For that matter, a lot of Caballeras were one day going to get old and retire back to the Trinity, where they'd still be as lethal as Larshan glass vipers.

"Please explain," the Smiling One said.

"Lieutenant McCartney is pretty hard core," Cassie said. "He has to be, what with the job he's in. Otherwise he'd have either committed *seppuku* or just plain given up long since. But he was shaken by what he found out. And while he wouldn't tell me, I can guess: he got back an 'access denied.' Now who, in this well-ordered society you have here, would have the power to flat cut a police investigator off from info and make it stick? And who could make even a man like McCartney nervous at the thought he might offend them?"

"Your sarcasm is quite unnecessary, young woman," Subhash Indrahar said. "You make your point. While there are indeed other entities on Luthien that might possess the power to block your policeman's queries, ISF does appear the most likely choice."

Cassie blinked. Her eyes felt grainy. She had been out all night making the rounds everywhere she could think of, trying to pull in some kind of information on Misty Saavedra's whereabouts—as well as what the Black Dragons might happen to have in mind next. Don Carlos had ordered her to concentrate on getting Misty back, but that didn't mean she had to shut her ears to everything else.

Unfortunately, she might as well have shut her ears, period. The Inagawa-*kai* rank-and-filers were out getting wild to celebrate their boss' takeover from old Yamaguchi—the ones who had survived at any rate. But if they knew any Black Dragon secrets they weren't letting go of them, no matter how much *sake* they took on board. And there was still no sign that the *dekigoro-zoku* had ever existed.

Focus, she commanded herself. "What now?" she asked.

"Now I will make inquiries of my own," the Smiling One said. "You will continue to go about your business, and report back anything further that you're able to learn."

Cassie opened her mouth. The Smiling One raised a hand. "I am making extraordinary allowances in permitting you to act, in effect, as one of my agents. Since I am doing so, I insist on treating you as I would one of my own agents.

You report to me; I do not report to you, unless I have information that might enable you more efficiently to perform your tasks. *Konnichi-wa?*"

"*Hai,* Subhash-*sama.*"

"Indrahar out."

After he had broken the connection Subhash Indrahar sat for a moment in his wheelchair, staring at the blank screen. He felt very cold, despite the scrupulous temperature control in the ISF's underground redoubt and the lap robe he wore. But then, the chill had little to do with the ambient air in his tiny Spartan office.

He reached out, manipulated a control on the console. The screen glowed alive again, this time with the digest of intelligence reports from all across the Combine and the Inner Sphere he had just received. He highlighted the reports from Dieron, keywords *Black Dragon*.

It came back with a report of a secret rank and file meeting attended by *metsuke*, at which the usual imprecations against the Evil Advisors who were leading the noble Coordinator astray were uttered; and a particularly successful *Kokuryu-kai* recruiter had met his end in an unfortunate skiing accident—annotated "closure complete," meaning people seemed to buy that it *was* an accident.

There was no mention of Black Dragon agitators spreading the rumor that Theodore Kurita had himself murdered his father, Takashi. Which was odd, inasmuch as that was the report a certain Son of the Dragon working on Dieron had been ordered by Subhash's message of the day before to submit through ISF channels. An hour before the Smiling One had received via his private channels an encrypted acknowledgement that the report had indeed been made.

So that turbulent, insubordinate, but very capable young woman is right. She was right that the ISF was riddled with treason—and right that *Kokuryu-kai* was engaged in some large-scale conspiracy in which the ISF traitors were of necessity involved right up to the eyebrows. Other possibilities suggested themselves readily to the Smiling One's mind, still as quick and flexible as the athlete's body he had possessed half a century go. He dismissed them. A hundred tiny discrepancies, overlooked as merely incidental, suddenly coalesced into a body of evidence that something was wrong.

He consulted his *ki*. The answer came unequivocally back: *I have been blind.*

As he had been chilled before, now he felt a rush of warmth suffusing his tired body and limbs, prickling like sunburn. *I have allowed myself to be gulled,* he thought. *I have unmistakably outlived my usefulness.*

The realization was like the mass of a planet lifted from his thin, stooped shoulders.

He turned his powered wheelchair, rolled out the door that slid aside at his approach, into the dim-lit corridors of his citadel. Technicians, agents, and the inevitable administrators and data-pushers passed with respectful nods, which he ignored.

Who? he wondered as he roamed at random through the buried complex. Ninyu Kerai he dismissed at once. The boy's loyalty—and he still thought of his adoptive son as a "boy," even though he was a man in his fifties—was beyond question. He was, if anything, overly devoted to Subhash Indrahar. More to the point, far from trying to rush his succession, Ninyu Kerai had done everything he could to put it off. The younger man's stubborn insistence that he was not yet worthy to command the Dragon's intelligence arm was literally all that had kept the Smiling One's spirit trapped in his worn-out body these past few years.

So—who? Takura Migaki he dismissed almost as readily as his son. The other division commanders mostly disdained or even despised the man. He was soft and self-indulgent, and his unorthodox habits and ideas smacked of the subversive: high irony in the man charged with *promulgating* orthodoxy throughout the Combine. Only Omi Dashani seemed to accept him, and she was the most thoroughgoingly neutral individual Subhash knew, utterly consecrated to the principle of keeping her assessments clean of preference or prejudice. For a fact, Subhash himself thought his propaganda chief frivolous, although his performance was exemplary, which was what truly mattered.

But Migaki had a dislike for responsibility that bordered

on phobia. He enjoyed his job because—and only to the extent—it allowed him to indulge his creative impulses. All he wanted to be was an impresario. He was increasingly restive of late, but far from a danger sign of ambition to move upward in the secret-police hierarchy, it was actually a manifestation of his desire to quit and become a private producer and director of entertainment holovids. He was known to say he'd rather lose an arm than become the chief of ISF. Subhash believed him.

Omi Dashani likewise struck Subhash as an unlikely traitor. What she wanted most to do was what she did: move her legions of *metsuke* around like playing-pieces in a vast and intricate game, amass and immerse herself in oceans of data. Ironically she would have been the Smiling One's choice for a successor after Ninyu: she was meticulous, a perfectionist. She was not one to inspire operatives with her own daring strokes of fieldcraft, as Ninyu Kerai did, and as the legendary deeds of Subhash's youth continued to do—but she would be sure the executive agents had suitably inspiring leadership.

The Smiling One had two fundamental theories of human action, which a lifetime of observing such action in its rawest forms had only reinforced. The first was that people tried to get what they wanted the way water flowed downhill. The ways they went about it often looked irrational or counterproductive to an outside observer, not infrequently because they were, and the ends they desired might be actively harmful, but whatever others thought, whatever they themselves said, that was the engine that drove most people. His second theory was that, after his or her own form of self-interest, what drove each individual most powerfully was dislike or affection, commonly the former: envy, jealousy, the desire for revenge.

He knew that his theory of overriding self-interest was incredibly subversive of the very model of society he had devoted his life to preserving. But then, if the Dictum Honorium were *actually* in tune with human nature, the Dragon would not need such a comprehensive secret police, *iie*?

Omi Dashani's deepest desires were fulfilled by her

current station. To become Director would bring her nothing but unwelcome distractions.

The other three commanders were more problematic. Daniel Ramaka, for example, almost had to be involved in stepping on the datastream, filtering the reports that reached the eyes of the Smiling One and his heir-designate: his Internal Security Division served as clearinghouse for all information coming into headquarters, and had most to do with operating the facility's vast local computer network. That was another reason for relieving Dashani of suspicion: about the only strong emotion the *metsuke* chief ever displayed was a quiet but virulent hatred for the man universally known as *the Rat*.

Daniel Ramaka was a brute and a sadist, traits the Smiling One found deplorable and counterproductive as well as distasteful. He was also a complete coward. Paradoxically, that was the source of his value to Subhash and the Combine, and the reason Subhash had elevated him to Internal Security chief and maintained him in that position. Because any conceivable enemy—Steiner, Davion, Clanner, internal dissident—who seized power would hang Daniel Ramaka from a meathook as a first order of business, he identified his own self-preservation with preservation of the Combine, and consequently he defended the Dragon with exemplary paranoia.

Because of his self-obsession Ramaka was entirely incapable of selfless service to Coordinator or Dragon, which was why he had never been under consideration as Subhash's successor. While that fact presumably rankled, as did every slight he had ever experienced or imagined in his life, Ramaka was not the sort to try to unseat the Director on his own. He was not the mover-and-shaker type, and besides, taking on Subhash Indrahar entailed risk. To say the least. Ramaka was obsessed with avoiding risk.

If, however, he believed the Smiling One was losing his touch—an assessment Subhash now agreed with—Ramaka might well be amenable to playing along with somebody he thought did have a chance of toppling him.

Which left the two most turbulent of Subhash's lieutenants: Constance Jojira of Covert Ops and one-eyed General Hohiro Kiguri. Both belonged to the Sons of the Dragon, and Subhash Indrahar trusted both exactly as far as he, in his current condition, was able to throw them.

Kiguri was an arch-conservative who disdained Theodore's reforms and disapproved of his emphasis on fighting the Clans, especially since it meant ignoring the opportunity offered by the confusion among House Kurita's ancient enemies, the Steiners and the Davions. He was fearless, cunning, an inspirational figure to his elite commandos; no one, not even Theodore Kurita himself, had struck as many telling blows against the Combine's foes. But a Director of the Internal Security Force needed more than Kiguri's swords-and-swagger bravado; he wasn't in line for promotion either.

He had never showed any particular desire to displace the Smiling One. His disapproval of Theodore might be strong enough to lead him to treason, though. And no one, no matter how bold, could dare hope to eliminate Theodore Kurita and leave Subhash Indrahar alive.

Besides, Kiguri was a predator. He had a predator's instinct for the jugular—and for weakness in the alpha male.

Jojira was apolitical. Too much, in fact, to be a good Director, although Subhash would have chosen her to succeed him behind Ninyu and Dashani, since she was capable, albeit limited and rather unimaginative. For most of her life—after she killed her father, who had murdered her yakuza lover before her eyes—she had served Subhash with canine devotion. But she had believed herself being groomed to succeed the Smiling One. Subhash's designation of Ninyu Kerai to succeed him had been a blow, the effects of which she had not been completely successful at concealing.

So both of them had motives for betrayal, the one resentment, the other ambition and conviction. Kiguri's hypertrophied traditionalism would mesh well with the conservatism of *Kokuryu-kai*. But Jojira had the yakuza connection.

Subhash could not choose between the suspects. The only thing of which he was confident—*certain* was not a word he liked to use—was that the two were not conspiring together. Both were fanatically proud, and they had been unfriendly rivals for years. Neither could endure being subordinated to the other.

He stopped. He was two levels above his office, outside a data-processing node. He touched a button on the pad inset into his wheelchair's right arm.

"Hai," the gruff voice of Ninyu Kerai responded.

"Ninyu," the Smiling One said, "meet me in my office at once."

"Hai, Subhash-*sama!"*

23

"Arrogant *gaijin* bitch!" Rebuffed, the big red-bearded man in the flash jacket with the padded *zaki* shoulders turned away and lumbered toward the main stage. On it a woman wearing a sequined top hat, bow tie, high heel shoes, and a big red-rimmed smile, was dancing to tinky-tonk Drac pop.

Aside from keeping her radar operating to make sure he didn't try to blindside her, Cassie forgot him at once. He didn't know anything; she could smell the dumb oozing from his pores. She had no time for *teppodama.*

It was a hopping place, a dancer bar in the Yoshiwara pleasure district's small intestine. It was the sort of dive where yaks did business, in puppet-show imitation of Middle Class execs, who conducted their affairs in hostess bars and more subdued nudie clubs. Cassie was in attendance as a spacer of indeterminate non-Combine origin, in town to take in the Big Show two days hence. Her hair was dyed red, her skin lightened, and she had a big dark mole on her cheek. She wore a battered spacer's jacket made from the hide of one of Towne's many outsized critters. It was uncomfortable in the body-heated bar, but it served nicely to conceal a gun. Or maybe two.

Inside the jacket she was practically vibrating with impatience. It was *out there.* She could feel it, she could taste it, like some topical drug hitting her tongue half a minute after she'd touched a doorknob painted with it. But she could not come to grips with it. It was elusive as mercury fleeing a fingertip.

She felt a vibration in the breast pocket of the tunic she wore beneath the jacket. As if scratching, she slipped a tiny bone-conduction speakerphone on a microthin wire behind her left ear. Then, leaning forward, she palmed a coin-sized audio pickup against her larynx, making it look as if she were cupping her chin.

"Abtakha," she subvocalized. All she had to do was go through the motions of speech: the pickup caught the vibrations and sent them off into the ether via the little communicator in her pocket.

"Cassie," came the voice of the Seventeenth's S-2. "They found Misty."

"They?" Cassie felt cold. She had pretty much given up searching for the missing MechWarrior. That trail was cold as Orientalis' backside as far as she could tell.

"Two Civilian Guidance Corpsmen found her body just before sunset. She had been . . . abused and sexually assaulted."

Cassie closed her eyes as she listened to the rest. "Takura Migaki has ordered the regiment locked-down in quarters until the morning of the big procession. You'd better come back."

"Cannot comply, Father Dr. Bob. I still got work to do."

Words in her ear. She snapped her head up, opened her eyes.

The bartender was staring at her with a concerned expression. "Are you all right, miss?"

"Oh—yes. Fine. It's just, just a stomach spasm. I get them from time to time."

"You don't have any funny offworld diseases, do you?"

"No. The Port Authority cleared me through quarantine, didn't they? It's a nervous thing. Stress brings it on."

"If you say so." He moved off down the bar.

"Cassie? Are you still there?" came the voice of Father Dr. Bob.

"Huh?" It struck her that the exchange had taken place in Japanese, even though her current persona didn't speak

the language. That rattled her. It wasn't like her to break
character.

"Sorry," she subvocalized. "Had to play the role for a
moment."

"Had to—oh, I understand. Now, Cassiopeia, I don't like
to push, but—"

"You know the first lesson of command, Captain Bob?
Don't give orders you know won't be obeyed."

"But Cassie—the Imperial City prefect of police has issued a shoot-to-kill order for anybody from the Seventeenth
seen on the streets—"

"I won't be seen." She sipped from her drink, cast her
eyes around the bar. Nothing caught the hem of her gaze.

"I'm sorry about Misty. I wish I could've found her, but I
got nothing. I tried, I really did. But the whole regiment is
in danger. I *feel* it. It's like . . . like electricity. The air is full
of it."

A pause. "You know I believe in your intuitions,
Cassiopeia."

"My intuition tells me it's all building up like the charge
in a Gauss gun's capacitors. The problem is, the Black
Dragons are playing this tight. They're smart enough,
they're not going to tell the kobun or even the sub-bosses
anything until the very last second. But when the word goes
out, I want to be here to catch it. I *have* to be."

A tipsy middle-aged man in fancy robes bumped hard
against the bar beside her and stood gazing at her with pie-
eyed approval. A noble out for a bit of a slum in the Floating World—and clearly not a real *tsu*. Because a true
man-about-the-*ukiyo* would know this wasn't just a lowlife
club, it was a full-out gangster bar. The yaks respected
traditional hierarchic values, but like everybody in the Combine they also had a keen reverence for the bottom line. This
sot looked to be the kind to have a fat wad of House-bills
tucked away somewhere in all that silk, and the Inagawa
heavies in here were just the types to try bouncing him
around until it popped out.

She looked him up and down, tilted her nose, and looked
away. He continued to hover there like a gaudy cloud.

"—dangerous, Cassie," Father Doctor Bob was saying in her ear.

"Oigame, Padre; listen up. There's this old expression: *a dead scout is a good scout.* Nobody's luck runs forever. Someday maybe I'll do my job by turning into a cloud of pink mist and letting the *vatos* know where not to go."

"In God's name, Cassiopeia, don't talk that way!"

"Look. It goes with the job. Yours *and* mine. I take risks. And sooner or later you lose people. Deal with it, Father. Cassie gone."

She stood up. The bar had gone flat for her. Time for a change of venue.

The slumming noble smiled unsteadily at her. "See that man over there?" she asked, pointing past her admirer to the red-bearded yak who now sat by the stage, steadfastly refusing to tip the entertainers. "He says he's in love with you."

She left him blinking.

"You're aware that Franklin Sakamoto has vanished from *Sho-sho* Hideyoshi's custody?" Subhash Indrahar asked.

Ninyu Kerai Indrahar's expression didn't change. But the Smiling One marked how the pupils of his eyes expanded slightly.

"Hai, Father."

"I wish you to take personal charge of the search for him. It's very important that he be found and returned before the Coordinator's Birthday celebration begins."

"I shall find him, Subhash-*sama.*" The red-haired man bowed and departed.

Subhash sat back in his chair and shut his eyes. He was tired. Yet he felt somehow light.

Decades ago Ninyu Kerai had assassinated a woman and her young son. The woman was a former lover of Theodore Kurita's. The boy, however, was a ringer, substituted by the woman for her own son—and Theodore's. Not for many years after, when the identity of Franklin Sakamoto was discovered, was it realized that, for one of the very few times in his life, Ninyu had missed his target.

Subhash, who had ordered the hit after Theodore's marriage to Tomoe Sakade had been revealed to Takashi, and reluctantly accepted by him, was philosophical about the affair. It had been an unbreakable tradition of House Kurita that if the heir apparent produced legitimate offspring, no by-blows could be allowed to live: disputes over the succession would weaken the Dragon in the face of powerful foes. But all had worked out well: Sakamoto had renounced all claim to the Dragon Throne, and had served the Combine honorably and well in the fight against the Clans, on Somerset with Adam Steiner's Strikers, and elsewhere on his own.

But the failure still gnawed at Ninyu Kerai. He longed to tie up that loose end. Even though his adoptive father had instructed him to "return" the missing Sakamoto—presumably more or less intact—he was avid for the hunt. There were always *possibilities*.

If he finds you, Sakamoto-san, Subhash thought, *I hope your spirit will forgive me*. Unless, as he suspected, the Black Dragon Society had somehow disappeared the Coordinator's illegitimate son, in which case he was already dead and Subhash could do him no harm by setting Ninyu on him. They had old scores to settle with him. They would no more conspire to put *him* on the throne of the Draconis Combine than they would Prince Victor Davion.

The Director had two reasons for sending his adoptive son down a false trail. First, if Ninyu Kerai knew there was a plot against his father, he'd simply kill both Kiguri and Jojira out of hand, along with anybody he remotely suspected might be conspiring with them. Once the weight of Directorship settled on Ninyu's shoulders, Subhash had faith, the boy would settle down, become less reactive, less prone to drastic impulse. Indeed that was a major reason Ninyu Kerai wished to put off his succession: the constraints it would impose. But if he perceived his father to be threatened, he would have no restraint at all. And the Combine, beset as it was, simply could not afford to lose *both* Jojira and Kiguri at a blow. Subhash Indrahar needed time to ensure that the proper head rolled.

Second, if Ninyu Kerai suspected what was happening, he would interfere with his adoptive father doing what must be done. And Subhash could not permit that.

Subhash opened his eyes to his small dim office. Time

pressed. He would continue his quiet inquiries—and hope that Cassie Suthorn was as resourceful as she seemed.

The sun was falling toward the skyscrapers that lay between Yoshiwara and the Kiyomori Mountains and Cassie was still out with her ear to the ground on the streets of the city, it now being her third day without sleep. Time was running out, with the Coordinator's three-day birthday celebration starting tomorrow. The second day would be the actual day of Theodore Kurita's birthday, and the great parade was scheduled for then. With the big event looming so near, there were no accommodations left in Impy City, no matter how lousy, and anyway she was too strung on fear to sleep. She took a break from her fruitless searching to duck out of the exultant crowds into a chemist's shop. Her fanatical determination to safeguard the regiment—her *familia*—could only keep her functioning so long. There being a key distinction between *awake* and *effective*.

She moved past the racks taller than she was, of incense-sticks and festive firecrackers—though only slim pickings were left of the latter—of herbs and patent medicines in their colorfully labeled bottles. The Combine frowned on recreational chemicals, with the exception of tobacco and alcohol, those staples of the true samurai. Caffeine tablets, on the other hand, were readily available. Anything to keep the Workers bright-eyed and ready to go throughout those sixteen-hour shifts.

She had just found the right section when she heard one of the two joygirls sorting through the eye-shadow on the far side of the rack say, "Angus Kurita? I've never heard of him?"

"Shh!" her partner hissed. "Not so loud! It's supposed to be secret."

"And your sister says he's coming here?"

"It's a surprise. For his cousin, our Coordinator. The Coordinator thinks he's still back at the Sun Zhang Academy on New Samarkand, hard at his studies."

"Eee! And I bet your sister knows all about *hard*."

"Hush! Don't talk that way. Teresa says he's very gallant. Also he's finished very quickly."

"That's always a blessing. Does he bring her flowers?"

"Sometimes."

"Aii! And he's a Kurita? I'm dreaming!"

"Well . . . he's not a very close cousin of Theodore's."

"A Kurita's a Kurita. Are you going to—you know—?"

"Don't be stupid. How would I meet him? Do you think my invitation to Unity Palace will be waiting for me when we get back to the house?"

"Well . . . wouldn't your sister have told him about you? You're very pretty, and you always make the gentlemen happy. And he's had a long space journey. . . ."

"Well . . . maybe. But mind you don't say a word to anyone!"

The room was dark but for the smoky glow of a pair of paper lanterns. Outside, night had come to the little district inhabited mostly by Worker families fortunate enough to have inherited their own houses. The pleasant old granny lady had withdrawn discreetly, not to mention so silently that even with her senses sensitive as a bubble's skin, stretched wide by an adrenaline jag so intense she hadn't needed her wake-the-dead pills, Cassie heard nothing from across the tiny room. Belatedly she began to speculate as to what Sons of the Dragon did when they got too old to chase people through junkyards.

"Angus Kurita?" the face of the Smiling One asked. "You're sure?"

"Pretty much. It's not a name I've heard before. The one girl never seemed to've heard it either."

"Angus Kurita is the great-grandson of Marcus Kurita, through his son Donal and grandson Graeme."

"So he's somebody who might conceivably accede to the throne."

Subhash's image looked at her for several seconds. "Yes."

"So this is maybe not a false alarm? I'm not overreacting?"

"I very much doubt that you are doing so."

Cassie ran a hand through her hair. It was still red. "So what now?"

"You return to Cinema City. Warn your people to be alert."

"For what?"

"For anything. I believe there is a high order of probability that some hostile action will be taken against your regiment sometime between now and the commencement of the ceremonies tomorrow."

"But *what*?" Cassie almost wailed. Frustration filled her eyes with tears that seemed to scald. She felt shame at showing weakness before this man, but she was desperate. She was as unaccustomed to failure as Ninyu Kerai, and to her mind, she had failed.

"I don't know. You and your companions will have to rely on your famous talent for improvisation."

"And you?"

"I shall take what steps I can."

"What steps?"

"It is not necessary that you know. But be assured, when I take them, you will be aware of the fact. One more thing: If you need to communicate, use the sequence I'm about to give you. It will connect you directly to Ninyu Kerai Indrahar, my son."

Cassie drew a deep breath, exhaled slowly through distended nostrils. "Good luck, Subhash-*sama*."

"And to you, Lieutenant."

Bringing his computer display back up on his screen, Subhash Indrahar entered a shielded query as to what parties had accessed the files on Angus Kurita most often over the last two years.

When he saw the results he smiled with genuine pleasure.

PART THREE

Chanbara

On death ground, fight.

—Sun Tzu *The Art of War*, VIII:6

24

The improvised hangar cobbled together outside the main compound of Cinema City to serve as a BattleMech maintenance shop rang with a war-cry as one of Zuma's Aztechs, a man waving an orange pry-bar, lunged from concealment among a stack of crates. Another man armed with a machine-pistol, the neck of his mechanic's coveralls open far enough to reveal a hint of the intricate tattoo extending downward from his clavicle, moved to intercept him. A blow from the meter-and-a-half bar caved in the side of the yakuza's face and dropped him to the grease-stained cement floor.

Still clutching his pry-bar, the Aztech then charged directly toward a knot of men standing by the foot of Buck Evans' *Orion,* in the shop because the Kali Yama LB10-X autocannon, retrofit before the Seventeenth deployed to Towne, was showing a tendency to overheat. Mishcha Kurosawa, already half-maddened by the mercenaries' antics, had claimed that the weapon didn't *need* to work, since they weren't going to be shooting anyone in the Coordinator's parade. The proud Don Carlos, however, insisted that no machine that wasn't fully functional could be presented to the Coordinator. Takura Migaki, a stickler for both realism and detail in his holos, agreed. So Zuma and his elves were staying up all night, hard at work on a dozen malfunctioning 'Mechs.

Where, shortly after 0415 Luthien time, a mixed force of Black Dragon kobun and Draconis Elite Strike Team commandos had surprised them and taken them captive.

And so things stood as the tech raised his steel bar overhead to strike once more, screaming with rage. *Tai-i* Achilles Daw drew a Mydron autopistol from a strapped-down thigh holster and shot him almost casually through the chest, twice. The man fell, rolled back and forth coughing on the ground. Daw's assistant Saburo Nishimura drew his own sidearm and shot the tech through the head.

Wearing his black hood and red visor down his back, as was *Kashira* Nishimura, Daw turned back to the Black Dragon commander next to him, who wore the blue *katakana* numeral "five" on the front of his MechWarrior neurohelmet, indicating he claimed the rank of captain.

"You should keep better control of the prisoners, O'Hanrahan-*san*," Daw said, holstering his weapon. He didn't use the man's professed rank, believing the yak scum was not entitled to it. "We're on a tight schedule. We've got no time for games."

The *Kokuryu-kai* company commander had a scar running from the temple of his fair-haired head to the side of his narrow jaw. In transit it hoisted the right-hand side of his mouth in a permanent sneer. The pale face showed no reaction to the slight, but the pupils narrowed in his ice-water eyes. "These *doitsujin yohei* are like wild beasts," he said dismissively. He omitted to name Daw at all.

Doitsujin yohei meant "German mercenaries," and was a common term for foreign money-soldiers. The connotation was *Hessian,* after the eighteenth-century slave-soldiers that German princes sold to the British to help them lose their North American colonies—a nuance that would have infuriated the already-smoldering Caballero techs and MechWarriors.

"See that those men of yours keep tighter reins on the ones they've got locked-down in the barracks," Daw said. Around them sullen armorers worked at loading the Battle-Mechs' ammo bins under the guns of tattooed guards, while DEST operatives strapped on cooling vests and trunks over their black body armor. "And keep your 'Mechs tight on the machines we have to leave behind. These *gaijin* may be animals—" *And so are you.* "—but they're clever ones."

O'Hanrahan raised his head and his sneer deepened. "We should be executing the usurper," he declared, "after the way he betrayed our comrades on Towne."

"But we have to use the foreigners' 'Mechs to scatter our friend Theodore," Daw said. *Scatter* was yet another yak euphemism for kill. "You'll have the pleasure of butchering the *chikusho* once they've been blamed for the crime."

O'Hanrahan opened his mouth to protest further. Daw stiffened the fingers of his right hand and drove them into the yak's sternum, between the foamed ceramic plates of his cooling vest. "We helped you smuggle your company of play-pretend BattleMech jockeys onto the Pearl. But we're running this play, and you'll follow our directions. *Wakarimasu-ka?*"

O'Hanrahan's eyes flamed like a wolf's. Then they tilted downward. *"Hai, Tai-i."*

Daw looked at him hard for a moment. Then he said, "See if you can hurry these swine along getting their junkwagons ready. We want to be able to roll on schedule. It shouldn't be too hard, since we're taking only a single battalion of their 'Mechs."

"It shall be done."

Daw turned away. "Softly, *Tai-i*," O'Hanrahan said. "One little thing more."

"Speak," Daw said impatiently.

"You should have your people strip off those fine black devil-suits of theirs. Otherwise they'll be finding it a tad bit warm when the fur begins to fly."

Nishimura laughed contemptuously. "We can take it. These are DEST commandos you're dealing with, tough as duraflex plate. Not pampered MechWarriors."

"I know," O'Hanrahan said.

A tap on the door brought Cassie awake. She rolled onto her side with her holdout pistol in hand, concealed beneath the sheets.

The first thing she did was cover a black manlike shape, standing by the far wall of the little room. Then she relaxed.

She was still alone. The dark shape was a gift. It had been waiting for her when she returned to the room the night before, having been ordered to get some sleep by Colonel Camacho.

Naked she slipped from the futon, glided up to stand with her back to the wall beside the door, revolver held both-handed, snub barrel pointing up.

"Who is it?"

"Cassie, it's Marly," a teenage girl's voice said through the door. "I'm lonely. I want to talk. Can I come in?"

Cassie frowned. It was natural for a fourteen-year-old girl, whose family was dead and whose homeworld lay light years away, to be lonely. It wasn't too characteristic of Marly Jones to admit it. Even less to use that tone of voice.

"Just a minute," Cassie said. Quickly she pulled on the garment that had been left for her. Then she went to the door and unlocked it.

Marly stood there, a coltish auburn-haired girl dressed in dungarees, a saggy jersey, and athletic shoes. At the sight of Cassie, her eyes widened. "Lord, Cass, isn't that—?"

"Come on inside, honey, and we'll talk." Cassie grabbed her and pulled her in, shutting the door behind her. She switched on the overhead light.

"Isn't that—?" Marly asked again, still goggling.

"Yes, it's a DEST infiltration suit. What's with the whiny act?"

"Wh—where'd you get it?"

"A secret admirer. Don't get weird on me. As far as we're concerned right now, there's good guys and bad guys in ISF. This is from the good guys. Got that?"

The girl nodded. Her face was still pale behind her freckles. Even though the Combine and the Federated Commonwealth had been allied against the Clans for most of her brief life, on Towne, hard against the frontier, the Drac Internal Security Force were frequent bedtime-story bogeymen.

"Now what are you doing up at this hour?"

"I couldn't sleep. So I decided to go up to the roof by myself for a while. You know how I do that."

Cassie nodded. When she had first met Marly, the girl had been filled with adolescent ardor to fight as a sniper against the Kurita invaders and their allies in Towne's Planetary Government. Then the girl's father had been murdered by Wolf Girl, who had infiltrated the underground on behalf of Howard Blaylock, who headed the PG. So a childish fancy had turned into a serious obsession; she *had* served as a sniper, with eight confirmed kills, including three in the final attack on Port Howard. What she did on the roof, commonly, was pick out people and objects, practice estimating the range to them, lining up shots, and squeezing off.

She had somehow or other made herself into Cassie's protégé, which had Cassie acutely uncomfortable. She liked the girl, but did not exactly consider herself an ideal role model for youth. She was also acutely aware that Marly was showing signs of evolving into a proto-sociopath, much like . . . well, Cassie, once upon a time.

"So anyway, you know how we got these Voice of the Dragon security guards watching us all the time ever since Misty was found, and they won't let us go out or anything?"

"Yeah. They gave me the hard eye when I came in, told me I better plan on staying until time for the big parade."

"Well, I was stopped by one on my way up to the roof."

Cassie shrugged. "Maybe they figure we'll try rappelling from up there. Shoot, somebody would've probably done it by now if they weren't looking out for it. Just on principle."

"But this wasn't one I'd seen before. None of them around this morning are ones I've seen before."

"Good eye, girl. But still—we haven't had all that much to do with the Cinema City security types until the last couple of days. Doesn't necessarily mean anything."

Marly softly stamped her foot and bounced her fists in the air in a gesture of teenaged exasperation that Cassie remembered well from her own adolescence, which hadn't been all that long ago. "But this one hadn't buttoned his blouse right. And under it his belly was all covered with tattoos."

Cassie stared at her. With two regiments of Black Dragon troops in the Kurita invasion force, not to mention numerous yak hangers-on who weren't pretending to be soldiers, everybody on Towne knew what *irezumi* looked like and what they signified.

"You're sure?"

The girl nodded. She was practically jumping from one foot to another in agitation. Cassie was surprised that she was able to muster the incredible patience and calm needed to function as a sniper, but she'd seen her do it. When Marly was behind her custom-built rifle, she displayed the same meditative serenity Cassie did at her martial arts practice. Which wasn't necessarily encouraging either.

"Wait one," Cassie said. She quickly pulled on baggy camo pants and a loose print blouse over the DEST suit, shrugged on a jacket to hide the visor and hood that hung down her back. She was amazed by just how much freedom of movement the black ballistic-cloth garment allowed her. It bound her some, but not that much more than her regular clothes did.

Marly perched on a flimsy dresser and watched her. "That's why I did like that," she explained. "They were watching me real close."

Cassie nodded approvingly. From a locked compartment hidden in the base of one of her luggage-trunks she took a spare barrel for her autopistol, two centimeters longer than normal, with the muzzle end threaded on the outside. She quickly swapped that for the one that was in the weapon. Then from the secret compartment she took a long, narrow silencer and screwed it onto the protruding threaded stub of barrel.

She slid the magazine out and checked it, squeezed back the slide to make sure a round was chambered. "Let's go check it out," she said.

The wings of the dorm in which Takura Migaki had ensconced the Seventeenth joined at the mezzanine floor and the lobby. Above those levels they were separate, each served by a single stairwell at the inner end. It was the Drac reflex to control access even when there wasn't any very compelling reason to do so.

Or maybe the Kuritas always liked to be prepared to lock people in their rooms.

Two guards in the cream jumpsuits of Eiga-toshi security

lounged by the fire door, smoking and joking in low, harsh voices. They looked pretty slack to Cassie, but that didn't mean much. Cinema City's security guards got their paychecks from ISF, but so did the key-grips and the camera crews. The Internal Security Force had a huge number of trained operatives, none of whom could be spared for tasks such as this. The guards were essentially civilians, not much different from private security guards throughout the Inner Sphere.

Their sloppiness and lack of a razor-edge to their alertness did not mean they were to be taken lightly. One had a Shimatsu-42 machine pistol on a long sling around his neck. The other was squatting with a semiauto Friendly Persuader riot shotgun between his knees.

He jumped up when he saw the two women approach. "Hey! What's this? You're not supposed to be out of your rooms."

"My cousin's sick," Cassie explained in Japanese. She gestured with her left hand at Marly, who didn't understand the language but, briefed in advance by Cassie, was doing a splendid job of looking as if she were about to throw up. Cassie's other hand was concealed behind her back. "She needs attention."

"No exceptions," the other man said. "Go back and wait until we tell you you can come out."

The guy with the shotgun took a drag off his smoke and grinned. He was missing an incisor. "A little tummy-ache won't kill the bitch. And if it does, so what?"

The taller, leaner man with the machine pistol was closer to Cassie, on her right. She sidled to the wall, approached him.

"Here, what're you doing?" he demanded. His scowl started to flow into a leer as she reached for the front of his blouse.

"Looking for your tats," she replied matter-of-factly. She grabbed a fistful of fabric, yanked hard. The top two buttons popped off. Beneath it his skin was swirled with green and blue designs.

"And there they are." As the man cocked a fist to hit her, she placed the end of the silencer against his breastbone and shot him twice. He collapsed like an empty suit of clothes falling from a hanger. Letting go of his shirt, Cassie straightened her right arm across her body, clamping left hand over right in a modified Weaver stance.

The gap-toothed shotgun man was juggling his weapon, drooling down his chin in panic. Cassie shot him once through the center of the forehead. His head snapped back against the all. He slumped to the floor, leaving a stain.

"Hey!" Marcy said admiringly. "That was crackin'!"

Untwining the sling from around the taller man's neck, Cassie shot her a scowl. "Don't start liking this too much."

"Don't you?" asked Marcy, all innocence.

"Shut up and secure that shotgun."

25

Cinema City, Luthien
Pesht Military District, Draconis Combine
1 July 3058

Grabbing Mariska Savage's right biceps in a steel-claw grip, *Tai-i* Achilles Daw forced the chunky tech to her knees on the cement floor. Drawing his Mydron, he pressed its barrel behind her right ear.

"You're stalling," he told Zuma Gallegos. "I respect that; I'd do the same in your place. It proves you're a real soldier, not like these tattooed fools. But unless we have thirty-six of your 'Mechs with full weapons loadouts and ready to roll by the time the sun comes up in"—he checked his wrist chronometer—"twenty-six minutes, I'll blow her brains out. Then I'll find somebody else. Do you understand me?"

Eyes sunk back in his head in a look of pure hate, Zuma nodded. "I understand," he said. "Now, why don't you let her up? You don't like how I do, you can shoot her just as easy standing up."

The DEST man gave him a hard, appraising look. Then he hauled Mariska roughly to her feet. "Your boss won you a little more comfort," he told her. "But you're not out of the woods yet. I'm just taking him at his word."

"What are you going to do with our 'Mechs?" asked Astro Zombie.

Daw looked at Zuma Gallegos, who merely shrugged as if to say he had no idea why his subordinate was asking things that weren't his business.

"We're going to assassinate Theodore Kurita and frame

you for it," Daw snapped. "Why else would we want your BattleMechs?"

"How are you planning to get away afterward?" asked Stacks Stachiewski, calm as you please. Nothing much got to him, not even being held at gunpoint by DEST assassins.

Daw grinned. "You've been hanging around fantasy-land here too long, pal. This isn't one of your host's *kiza* action vids; there aren't going to be any long-winded explanations by the bad guys. You've got to allow us a few professional secrets."

He scanned the apprehensive prisoners with his dark eyes. "There isn't going to be any miraculous last-second rescue like in the holos, either," he added in voice that, while quiet, carried to the furthest recesses of the giant structure. "So you'd better all resign yourselves to whatever's going to happen."

He turned to Gallegos. "So what about it, Sparky? The little lady here is running out of air time."

Zuma looked at him. Then he glanced around at his Aztechs, Stacks' armorers, Astro Zombie's people. The Caballeros' technical complement tended to look to him for leadership.

"Do what they ask," he said softly. "It's in Our Lady's hands."

With some dark looks and downcast eyes, the technicians resumed work. Leaving Mariska under Nishimura's watchful eye, Daw gestured Gallegos to his side and led him over to the disproportionately huge rounded feet of an assault-class 'Mech with prominent radiator fins inboard of its shoulder actuators.

"Here we have a *Naginata*," Achilles Daw said, "pride of the DCMS. One of the most advanced command Battle-Mechs in the whole Inner Sphere, not to mention one of the newest. It must be the one you relieved the gallant but not very bright Jeffrey Kusunoki of on Towne. What's it doing in the shop?"

"General Kusunoki wasn't very interested in technical details and such. So his techs sloughed off. Didn't lubricate the joints regularly. Fried some bearings pretty well. We've replaced them, but the hips still get pretty cranky sometimes. We've got it in for a check, to make sure it'll run smooth for the parade. Don Carlos wants everything perfect for the Coordinator."

Daw smiled. "A man after my own heart. All right, Lieutenant. This is going to be my ride today. I want you to make sure it's in tip-top condition. And you're going to want that too, because you can just think of the safety of that little lady over there—not to mention your own family—riding right along in the cockpit with me. *Wakarimasu-ka?*"

Zuma nodded.

"Outstanding." Daw walked away.

With heavy heart Zuma pulled a cherry-picker over to the *Naginata*'s right side, hoisted the pulpit up to the level of the hip. He pulled the access panel with the help of an inertia wrench and peered inside.

As he did, he became aware of a persistent tingle in the right breast pocket of his coveralls.

"Hijo de puta," muttered Jimmy Skowron, a communications specialist who was working the command radio-set in Don Carlos' room on the top floor of the dorm. He was a redheaded wisp from Sierra who was a good ten years older than he looked. "Zuma says the hangar's full of DEST commandos and Black Dragons."

A mutter pulsed through the 'lleros jammed into the room, which was no bigger than the ones anyone else got. More than half crossed themselves, including Father Doctor Bob, who blushed and looked around as if hoping no one had noticed. "Keep it down!" Jimmy hissed. "This damn binary code's hard enough to translate on the fly without everybody talking."

Cassie pulled aside a corner of the blanket hung over the window to hide the dim red glow of field blackout lamps. She could just see the four "security guards" out in front of the main entrance. Several similarly clad groups were visible by the glow of lights dotted on tall standards here and there across the wide compound. Almost certainly they were Black Dragons too.

The interior of the dormitory, with the exception of the lobby, had been quickly and quietly recaptured by the

Caballeros, thanks to the fact that the Black Dragons had been guilty of seriously underestimating them.

The Inagawa-*kai* yaks who had been infiltrating Eiga-toshi over the last ten days—under the guise of trying to muscle in on the Old Cat's lucrative business of providing grunt-tech services to the movie-making operation—had searched the mercenaries' rooms thoroughly on the pretext of performing the usual cleaning chores. They had confirmed that, as reported, the *gaijin* kept no weapons to themselves. Indeed, their arms were safely under lock and key in the main security station.

Back when she was a street kid on the cracked and muddy streets of Larsha, Cassie had learned that nobody was easier to scam than a scammer, nobody easier to rip off than a thief. The yaks were proving that in spades. It didn't occur to them that most of the Caballeros had spent most of their adult lives fighting the Draconis Combine, and that almost all of them were descended from long lines of smugglers, bandits, and general hellions. Though they'd had to surrender most of their personal ordnance to Voice of the Dragon security, more than a few of them had held back life preservers—just as Cassie herself had.

The yaks also overlooked the fact that everybody had a personal communicator. So the phony security guards stationed in the stairwells and corridors had gotten jumped pretty much simultaneously in a savage surprise attack. The Black Dragons had killed one 'llero and wounded three, but none of the guards survived. Long.

Nor had the alarm been given. The guards downstairs and out front didn't suspect a thing, unless they were better actors than Cassie was ready to give them credit for.

With the safety of the kids and other noncombatants in the dorms occupying everybody's attention, it wasn't until the brief spasm of the recapture was complete that anybody thought of checking in with Zuma and the rest of the crew in the repair hangar. It was a call from his comrades in the dorm that had given him a tingle in the breast pocket of his coveralls, the pocket where he kept the comm unit. Now Zuma was managing to talk back by hitting the transmit button—"breaking squelch"—surreptitiously as he worked, tapping out an ancient dot-dash code that a lot of techies still learned as a sort of caste ritual.

"O.K., I'm on the roof," came the dry and slightly ironic voice of Daniel "the Rooster" Morgan from another speaker of the portable command set. "We've got worse trouble than a hundred ISF storm-troopers in the repair hangar."

Maccabee Bar-Kochba gestured the 'lleros to silence. "What would that be, son?"

"A dozen BattleMechs watching our machines like hawks around a henhouse. One's a *Guillotine;* rest seem to be mediums and lights. Whoa, though, check this—that's a *Bushwacker* there. Wonder where they came up with that hound-pup?" The Caballero 'Mechs were parked just north of the repair hangar in an area fenced in by high mesh wire and topped with razor-coils.

"What difference does it make?" asked Bobby Begay. It still made Cassie queasy to see the transverse bars of a Force Commander on his collar, and not because he had hated her since she'd won admission to the regiment by downing his 'Mech in the streets of Kalimantan. "They have a company. We have a regiment!"

"They have our *'Mechs,* Bobby," Raven said. "That tends to kind of devaluate our big numerical advantage. Bite the reality sandwich."

For once the Wolf refrained from snarling back. His dark eyes gleamed. He clearly foresaw some serious madness upcoming. That was his element.

"You're sure taking your time up here."

Zuma didn't jump at the sound of the voice; he'd felt the thump as the man climbed up into the pulpit behind him. It was the black second-in-command, come to peer over his shoulder.

Zuma dropped his hand away from his breast pocket as if he'd just been scratching. A moment, and sparks leapt from the exposed machinery at the commando's face.

"You want me to do the job right," Zuma said without looking around, "don't come up here and jog my elbow. See what happens when you startle me?" More sparks flew.

The DEST man recoiled. "All right, all right. Just make sure you finish on time." He clambered back down.

Zuma allowed himself a relieved sigh. Then, as he worked, he began to transmit once more.

"Zuma says the commandos're gonna use our 'Mechs to dust Teddy," Jimmy reported. "They have our folks hostage."

Cassie felt sick to her stomach. *I've failed,* she thought. *I should have foreseen this, should have found out about it.* It would have been simplicity itself to snag one of the Inagawa people coming to work at Eiga-toshi, flex him until he broke like a wire, then get the straight from him. But Cassie had let herself be lulled, accepted the going explanation that Inagawa's encroachment was a pure yak power-move.

She felt a hand on her shoulder. She jumped, looked back to see Kali, who nodded wordlessly. Cassie frowned. She didn't want to be comforted.

"What're we gonna do?" somebody asked.

"Whatever it is, it better be quick," Buck Evans said. "Sun's about to come up."

Don Carlos looked around. Even in the red animal-eye glow of the blackout lights, Cassie could see a shine to his dark eyes that had been missing since his beloved Diana Vásquez had been murdered in Port Howard.

"I have a plan," he said, deep voice low and confident. "It is very risky, but if we don't take risks, we lose all. Now listen—"

The Caballero BattleMechs stood in four battalion-size blocs in the fenced-in area just beyond the repair-hangar, which itself loomed north of the Eiga-toshi compound wall. The tall silent machines were surrounded by mesh fences at least three meters high and topped with razor-tape coils. Black Dragon armorers moved among the 'Mech bloc nearest the hangar, checking weapon loads.

Tai-i Terence O'Hanrahan paced his *Bushwacker* restlessly along the perimeter of the fence. Around him the land was clear and mostly flat for 500 meters to a kilometer before breaking up into trees and low, mist-shrouded hills. Aside from the high wall of the holostudio compound, he had excellent visibility and unrestricted fields of fire.

Despite that he had a bad feeling about this mission; it had been gnawing his belly like a rat since their DropShip had deviated from its landing path—while traffic controllers, bribed or coerced by *Kokuryu-kai,* looked away from their screens in the control tower at Takashi Kurita Spaceport—to discharge his medium company into the woods southwest of Basin Lake eight hours ago.

It wasn't just that the main plan depended on Daw and his DEST team—arrogant dilettantes who imagined that being checked-out in BattleMechs made them Mech-Warriors. Their mission was murder, after all, not combat. With total surprise on their side, they weren't liable to encounter serious opposition to anything but their getaway. And even if they failed, the Society had its fall-back plans.

Nor was it the fact that his unit's mission was to contain an overstrength BattleMech regiment—a disadvantage of a mere twelve to one. Their enemies were only *gaijin* money-troopers, after all, and more to the point, they were separated from their 'Mechs. MechWarriors without Battle-Mechs were helpless as newborn lambs.

Finally, his unease didn't spring from being twelve 'Mechs against, not a *gaijin* regiment, but potentially a whole planet, including several times as many 'Mech and other regiments as normally garrisoned the Black Pearl. Only a couple of his MechWarriors were veterans, and none so much as he himself, who had fought the bloody Clans for two years, and then been cashiered from the Fourteenth Legion of Vega over a trifle of peculation. But even unseasoned *Kokuryu-kai* MechWarriors knew how to die, as their comrades had proven on Towne. Terence O'Hanrahan was ready to die for *kai* and Combine.

All these things contributed to, but did not entirely explain, his lingering unease. He had a sense of *wrongness,* somehow, that would not go away.

"Tai-i." It was *Shujin* Duchovny, the *Spider* pilot commanding his scout lance. His area of responsibility was the

eastern fence, on the far side from O'Hanrahan's. O'Hanrahan's company was saddled with a disproportionate number of MechWarriors with non-Japanese names, not least its commander, and two women, Flynn and Ito. Such disadvantages were stigmatized even more among the Black Dragons than the regulars. Yet he was satisfied in his people; they were as good as he could make them. And no one, not even the haughtiest DCMS MechWarrior, had ever truthfully been able to criticize O'Hanrahan's skill and courage in a 'Mech. It was his accounting practices that got him into trouble.

"What is it, Master Sergeant?" O'Hanrahan's pale eyes moved ceaselessly, taking in his HUD, his circle-vision strip, and always his surroundings.

"We have a semi coming out the gate, onto the road to Imperial City."

While the Inagawa-*kai* contingent who had infiltrated Cinema City had secured certain key facilities, including the organic security-force headquarters and its substations and Takura Migaki's residence, they were trying to disturb routine as little as possible, to reduce the risks of raising an alarm. The *gaijin* money-soldiers were all safely under guard; a tractor-trailer could pose no risks, and might arouse questions if its driver or cargo didn't turn up on schedule.

"Let them pass. But keep a close eye on them." O'Hanrahan believed in taking as little as possible for granted, and that no one had ever come to grief from being too alert.

"Hai."

"Captain!" Despite the fact that he was ensconced in the massively protected cockpit of a 70-ton *Guillotine,* O'Hanrahan's second in command sounded distinctly rattled.

"Talk to me, Soldaco."

"Smoke, Captain, lots of it. Northwest corner of the hangar."

The *'Wacker* was facing the wrong way. O'Hanrahan glanced up at his 360-view screen. Sure enough, the distorted image showed a dirty-gray curtain billowing into the murky pre-dawn light.

He spun his 55-ton 'Mech around as light as a *Locust*. Just in time to see an 85-ton *Katana,* followed by two *Charger*s and an *Awesome,* come lumbering through the smoke at him.

26

Cinema City, Luthien
Pesht Military District, Draconis Combine
1 July 3058

"**S**un's coming up," Talon Sergeant Nishimura called up to Zuma Gallegos, whose cherry-picker was extended all the way up the front of Don Carlos' BattleMech. "You got that thing ready to rumble, or should we let some sunlight into that girl's pretty little head?"

Zuma turned away from the *Naginata*'s open cockpit. "It's prepared for your commander," he said in a flat voice.

Nishimura clucked and shook his head as if disappointed. From somewhere outside came a ripple of dull *pops*, followed by a distant boom, edged with supersonics like a crack of thunder. He spun, clawing for his holster sidearm. "That's a Zeus heavy rifle!" he shouted.

Zuma quickly knelt. He picked up a heavy metal toolbox and dropped it over the side of the cherry-picker down toward Nishimura's head, ten meters below.

Firing a huge bullet at several times the speed of sound, a conventional Zeus heavy rifle would have produced such a horrific recoil that even a strong man wouldn't willingly fire it twice. With a wizard compensating system and a tripod weighing over half as much as the weapon itself to suck up what kick was left over, skinny adolescent Marly Joles could shoot it and feel less recoil than when firing her beloved 6mm sniper rifle.

Marly had grown up with a rifle, as did many children

in the Towne wilderness, well-populated with surly mega-fauna. Her father had insisted she become proficient at shooting with iron sights before he permitted her to fire a single shot with a scoped rifle. With instruments at her side giving ever-updated digital readouts of humidity, air pressure, wind velocity, and range charts specific to Luthien, the 800-meter shot from the roof of Sound Stage 3 of the main compound to the entrance leading into the 'Mech-repair hangar was as easy as sticking pins into a doll with her hand.

Two DEST commandos in full regalia stood guard before the entrance, swords slung over their shoulders and assault rifles in their hands. The one on the right fell onto his back and lay still.

The ISF's elite assassins were trained to react instantaneously to danger. But this was utterly unexpected. The DEST trooper still standing heard a meaty *whump* and then turned as his partner went down. He stared at the unmoving form in black for an instant, then spun back toward the compound, kneeling as he brought up his rifle.

The heavy bullet traversed the distance between rifle and target in under a second. The sound of the shot took almost three. It took two seconds for Marly to recover from her first shot, line up the second target, and squeeze off her second shot.

She showed her inexperience by not allowing for the chance her second target might kneel. She had aimed for his center of mass, which meant that instead of his sternum, the bullet hit him in the red visor. The bullet punched through it as readily as the other shot had the first man's body armor.

Which meant that by the time the noise of the second gunshot reached him, the commando was dead.

Even before his slumping body hit the ground, Cassie had reached the door at the head of a hundred Scout Platoon troopies, support personnel, and profoundly pissed-off MechWarriors.

Demolitions ace that he was, with the true master blaster's love for things that went "boom" as well as intimate knowledge of them, the Rooster had found his way to the Cinema City pyrotechnics locker within two hours after the Caballeros reached the place. With that affinity among experts in the same field that transcended all cultural and political barriers, the special-effects techs—who despite being nominal employees of the Internal Security Force didn't give a mouse fart for politics—were only too happy to show him all their toys. Which included a breathtaking array of smoke bombs of sundry colors and sizes, and cool little fireworks-mortars for lobbing them about.

The pyro shack was well and sturdily locked, of course. But to a military unit that had to be prepared to rescue 'Mech pilots trapped inside a dozen or more tons of armor, nothing short of a bank vault was anything more than a momentary inconvenience.

Producing the smoke screen that had so alarmed *Chu-i* Soldaco was no problem. What was hard was the part that came next: dying a lot.

Across the hangar from *Tai-i* Achilles Daw, gunshots rang out and gas grenades detonated with dull cracks. He turned and stared. Behind him there was a heavy thump, followed by a clatter.

He spun. Talon Sergeant Saburo Nishimura lay on his back in a spreading scarlet pool. A toolbox lay beside him. His forehead was caved in.

Daw drew his own sidearm, fired twice with perfect Zen no-intention. The *gaijin* tech slumped onto the railing of his cherry-picker.

I thought he was soft, giving in to save the life of a mere woman, he thought. *I was wrong.* With a touch more force than necessary he yanked the lever to start the cherry-picker's extensor arm descending.

"BattleMechs approaching from the south," Terence O'Hanrahan rapped out from his position near the fenced-in *gaijin* 'Mechs. He saw light 'Mechs pacing rapidly to his right, winging out to flank his lance. All his misgivings were vindicated. *We've been set up!* "Bates Lance, move west and turn south to support my right flank," he called into the commline. "Duchovny, form up facing south and prepare to defend. My lance—"

Before he could finish the thought, a swarm of light trucks and utility vehicles broke through the smoke and streaked toward the fence. The insignificant little machines barely registered on O'Hanrahan's consciousness. He was staring down death's throat. He swallowed. "Open fire."

Well kitted-out with double-capacity heat sinks, the *Bushwacker* could run and fire all its weapons without overheating. Not that it mattered; the monster 'Mechs coming at him were already inside minimum range of his Federated five-shot LRM launchers, and his probable lifespan was reckoned in seconds anyway. Figuring the *Katana* for the most dangerous enemy, he laid his pipper on the armor slab covering its right knee and triggered off the autocannon in its right arm and the large extended-range laser in the snout of its narrow fuselage. For good measure he fired the machine guns flanking the laser as well.

Chunks flew from the assault *Katana*'s kneecap. Flame jetted, the knee buckled, and the huge assault 'Mech plunged forward on its face, throwing up a cloud of smoke and dust.

"Yes!" O'Hanrahan pumped a gauntleted fist in the air. He'd downed a BattleMech massing thirty tons more than his own machine with his first volley. It was a fantastic honor . . . if anybody lived to tell about it.

He frowned. In fact, it was *too* fantastic, if you thought about it. Before he got a chance to do much of that, swarms of short-range missiles blasted away from the 'Mechs still charging him, drawing twisty smoke-trails that converged toward his face.

Shots, explosions, and screams echoing around him, Achilles Daw picked up the dead man's switcher, then unceremoniously rolled the *gaijin*'s body out of the cage. He activated the cherry-picker, and its pulpit immediately began to descend toward the cockpit of the boxy *Naginata*. Releasing the control box so that it hung from the safety rail by its yellow cord, he then climbed into the cramped space of the cockpit. He never bothered to switch off the controls.

One of his men was holding a dozen captive foreigners at gunpoint, including the black woman Daw had threatened earlier. "Kill them!" he called to the trooper as the cockpit hatch closed behind him.

With more courage than sense a Black Dragon trooper popped up from behind half a dozen green plastic barrels of solvent, tears streaming down his face from the bite of tear gas, and leveled a shotgun at Cassie as she charged past him into the hangar's heart. She shoved her left hand out to her arm's extent and fired four quick shots from her autopistol. Two bullets punched through the man's unarmored chest. The yak screamed and fell backward.

The very nature of the task that the intruders had set their captives meant it was impossible to guard them closely, much less keep them all together. The best they could do was keep an eye on the 'llero technicians as they worked. With reflexes bred in by unbroken generations of banditry and smash-and-grab raids, the Seventeenth's techs went instantly to ground at the first sign of trouble, losing themselves in industrial tangle or behind the big, thick, armor-clad legs of parked BattleMechs. Some of them were clumped, though, and therefore exposed.

Because they hadn't had a whole lot of time to map, rehearse, and deploy for a classic hostage-rescue mission. Cassie—whom Don Carlos had put in charge of this phase of the counterattack—had reckoned on flat-out speed and shock as her best allies. A surprise attack wasn't likely to make the DEST goons wet their sneaksuits, but did stand a good chance of throwing most of the Black Dragons into panic mode.

Ahead and to her right she saw a black-clad figure trying to scale the right shin of a *Victor* to get to the cockpit, and not having much success. As she ran past she slashed him across the lower back with the other gift Subhash Indrahar had sent to her: a vibrokatana. The tough black ballistic cloth parted like a sheet of rice paper dropped on an ancient Muramasa blade. The commando screamed and fell to the cement floor.

So that her buddies wouldn't hesitate to shoot when they

saw somebody dressed all in black, Cassie was wearing a short-sleeved migraine-red silk jacket over her sneaksuit, which she thought made her look like a cheap technokink hooker. She had her hood and visor on, both to ward the tear gas from the grenades her people were strewing liberally about and to keep off high-velocity particulate pollution, i.e., bullets. She regretted it despite the risks of going bareheaded. Having her head enclosed during combat made her insides twist with claustrophobia. Despite hours spent familiarizing herself with BattleMech displays, the circlevision strip inside the visor was hard for her to see, much less make sense of in the press of the moment. And despite what the propagandists said, outside the Combine as well as in, the sensory input provided by the sneaksuit's audio-visual suite was *not* the same as seeing with your own eyes and hearing with your own ears, only better. The visuals were murky and the sounds unnatural, all either amped up or stepped down, making it impossible for her to maintain her customary multisensory image of her surroundings.

Which was probably why she had no warning when a DEST commando stepped out from behind the leg of another BattleMech and blasted her with a burst from a machine pistol.

Flame and smoke washed out the world beyond the 'Mech's windscreen as the SRM volleys slammed home on O'Hanrahan's *Bushwacker,* which, to his amazement, barely rocked back. No red damage-warnings came to life on his board. Miraculously, not one of the missiles had breached the 'Mech's armor.

Miraculously . . . or maybe not. The smoke parted reluctantly, in time for him to see the *Awesome* take hits from Soldaco's *Guillotine*'s laser battery. The blocky torso, with its flared shoulder-actuator housings and fin-like baffles protecting them, simply flew apart in a black and orange explosion.

Striding steadily ahead came the AgroMech that had been concealed inside a superstructure mimicking the assault 'Mech. A reflex follow-up volley of short-range missiles from Soldaco's chest-mounted Irian Weapons Works launcher blew the poorly armored machine apart.

At almost the same instant Duchovny called, "*Tai-i,* wait! These aren't real BattleMechs! They're fakes!"

Belatedly, O'Hanrahan noticed that men and women had spilled out of the small vehicles and begun attacking the tall fence with cutting tools and explosive charges. The wire was already breached in several places.

"Forget the 'Mechs," he commanded. "Get those people on foot. They're trying to get to their 'Mechs!"

The DEST trooper who Daw had ordered to kill the group of a dozen prisoners turned a blank red faceplate toward his intended victims. Behind him the fearsome *Naginata* with Achilles Daw at the controls creaked and rumbled into life.

Hohiro Kiguri trained his commandos to instant obedience. But whether it was uncharacteristic hesitation at shooting down unarmed people—not normally a problem for ISF agents—a desire to gloat, or merely a polite inclination to wait until his superior had cleared the area before carrying out his instructions, the DEST man did not fire immediately. Instead he stood like a statue symbolizing menace, his assault rifle leveled from the hip, while the *Naginata* began to stride toward the north side of the hangar with a squeal of metal on cement. The prisoners stared back at him with eyes as expressionless as his bulletproof visor.

The body of the cherry-picker was not large, but to counterbalance its long arm and keep it stable, it contained a battery and lead ballast weighing a total of five tons. Its electric motor was very quiet, so that with a firefight in progress around him the first warning the DEST man had was when it smashed into his back. It was moving very slowly, but the impact knocked him to the concrete.

Even a Draconis Elite Strike Team commando could not contain a scream when the cherry-picker rolled over him.

The captives he'd been ordered to execute scattered. Mariska Savage stooped briefly to recover the assault rifle before taking cover. The cherry-picker, with the now-lifeless form of Zuma Gallegos slumped on the platform, continued through the wall of the hangar and out into the first rays of dawn.

Staff Sergeant Tony Martínez of the Caballero quartermaster section was a short, dark man with almost as many tattoos on his muscular arms as a yak. He had been a long-haul truck driver on the planet Sierra before the urge to see the Inner Sphere overcame him—rumor had it, after a misunderstanding with the law. Of course, those rumors were told of a lot of 'lleros. They were pretty often true, too.

He was behind the wheel of the commandeered tractor-trailer the Black Dragon light lance had spotted leaving by the Imperial City gate. As soon as the enemy 'Mech jocks had spotted what was apparently a heavy lance attacking from the south, Martínez had whipped his rig off the road to the left, as if fleeing the approach of the humanoid metal monsters. The Black Dragon pilots, with MechWarriors' characteristic disregard for anything that wasn't another BattleMech—and, in fairness, with what they took to be some pretty serious BattleMech attackers on their minds—ignored him. He drove north past them as they deployed into a ragged line to face their opponents.

Even unloaded, though, the semi was anything but maneuverable. Martínez had just got it wrestled around to point at the fence and then bouncing along cross country when Master Sergeant Duchovny realized they were being scammed by tarted-up AgroMechs. There were still a hundred meters between him and the fence when all four light 'Mechs—Duchovny's *Spider,* an *UrbanMech,* and two *Hornets*—turned on him and opened up with everything they had.

Martínez twisted and wove the unwieldy vehicle with skill and desperation. The Black Dragon MechWarriors weren't the most skillful marksmen in the Inner Sphere, and kept getting in each other's way. Still, the range was short, the firepower brought to bear on the semi formidable.

A burst from the *UrbanMech*'s Imperator-B autocannon peeled open the tractor's coffin-like snout and raked the cab. A flick later, laser strikes pierced the cab and set off the fuel in the tanks. Pale alcohol flames enveloped the rig.

Blazing like a comet, Marínez and his tractor-trailer smashed through the fence. The tractor struck the leg of a parked *Flea* and exploded, toppling the little BattleMech.

And with that, Caballero MechWarriors in cars and on motorcycles sped madly for the breach.

Impacts from the DEST commando's machine pistol slammed Cassie's ribs. Lances of red light seemed to flash from her chest to her brain. She sat down hard onto the cement floor of the hangar.

By sheer reflex she raised her autopistol, emptied it at the legs of the man who had shot her. A bullet smashed his knee without penetrating. He fell onto his face. Cassie hauled herself up by force of will and lunged at him. He reared up, raising his weapon.

She hacked downward across her body with the vibrokatana, the blade slicing through ballistic cloth, skin, and bone with equal ease. The operative's gun-hand sprang from its wrist in a spray of scarlet blood. A backhand stroke split his visor and the face beneath.

Cassie staggered, almost fell. Every breath felt as if spikes were being driven into her chest. The burst from the machine pistol had cracked ribs. She looked around, trying to grasp the tactical situation. Everywhere was noise and muzzle flashes, 'Mechs beginning to move. She felt the immediate presence of danger, couldn't localize it—

The very edge of her peripheral vision caught a dark shape flying at her. She spun, raising the vibrokatana.

Not fast enough. Her attacker hit her and knocked her sprawling.

27

JumpShip **Mishima,** *trailing Trojan point of*
Occidentalis
Orbiting Luthien
Pesht Military District, Draconis Combine
1 July 3058

"**S**ubhash Indrahar," Professor Isabu Tomita purred as the
ISF Director's powered wheelchair rolled into the huge
compartment. This space had once been a grand ballroom
when the JumpShip *Mishima* had served as the luxury liner
Lord Bateman centuries ago in the final years of the Star
League. It had long been stripped of its splendid, not to say
gaudy, appointments. The only visible remnant of its former
grandeur was the parquetry dance-floor and the ten-meter
transpex dome giving a view of the brightly lit slice of pink
Orientalis, high "above." "You have come a long way
to die."

"You are candid, Tomita-*sensei*," the Smiling One said
imperturbably, ignoring the guards who stood ringing the
compartment, machine pistols leveled at him. "What of
your traditional Japanese circumlocution? Such forthright-
ness seems most inharmonious, coming from the mouth of
such a traditionalist."

The Professor uttered a restrained laugh. "You understand at least as well as I, Subhash-*sama,* that what truly
counts in our culture is maintaining *appearance:* the appearance of propriety; the appearance of observing ritual.
We are men of the world, though, you and I. Surely there is
no need for dissimulation."

"Indeed not. Thus I feel no reticence in pointing out that the reality of treason overrides all appearance."

The Professor beamed indulgently. The shaven-headed and uniformed man who stood by his side grunted impatiently. "So many fine words, chasing each other like birds in a cage," said *Tai-sa* Charles Ohta. He hacked air with his palm. "Enough! Have you come alone, spymaster?"

"Why, no, Colonel," Subhash said, smiling. "I brought one hundred of my finest agents, who have truly mastered the ancient *ninja*'s secrets of invisibility."

Ohta's face fisted. "What's this? How did they get past our guards? I'll have the fools thrust naked out an airlock, if anyone slipped by them."

"The angel of irony has clearly passed the Colonel by, Subhash-*sama*," Tomita murmured. "Calm yourself, Charles. The Director arrived alone in his shuttle but for his flight crew."

Subhash pivoted his chair clockwise. Magnets in its tires held it to the floor despite the absence of gravity, as did similar magnets in the soles of the shoes—and in Colonel Ohta's case, the split-toed *tabi*-style boots—of the men who confronted him. "And you, Hiraoke Toyama," he said to the third member of the trio. "It surprises me to find you here. I should think you would be in Imperial City to view the climax of your scheming."

"I'll rejoice in the usurper's death," the old oyabun hissed in a voiceless raven's caw. "But I shall attend the executions of the foreign beasts who murdered my son in person. In the meantime, *Kokuryu-kai* has decided that I be here to keep an eye on our investment."

" 'Investment,' " Subhash echoed. "In older times the epithet 'stinking of fish' was applied to merchants who tried to claim perquisites beyond their station. Yet for you it would be a compliment. When a common criminal speaks of investments he rises above himself no less—even when he uses the word as a euphemism for treason."

Toyama's devastated face purpled. He pointed with a shaking, wasted finger. "You dare speak of treason, who murdered our Coordinator Takashi Kurita!"

"I did not take the life of Takashi Kurita," Subhash said

mildly, "although I tried my best to do so. Nor did Theodore Kurita—except in the most literal sense—despite the lies spread by your propagandists."

The files that had been kept from his eyes—as well as those of Omi Dashani and Ninyu Kerai—had proven quite comprehensive and detailed. They had been well-hidden, but once he'd set his army of specialists on the trail, it had not taken long to turn them up. The conspirators had been quite lamentably arrogant. *Of course, their assurance almost proved justified. . . .*

"Takashi Kurita died by his own hand. He performed seppuku. He died quite bravely, as one would expect, completing the full three ritual cuts. Theodore served as his second, and struck off his head. But it was an act of love and filial loyalty, not patricide—as the Dictum Honorium recognizes."

"Words!" spat the Colonel. "You are a criminal. The usurper is a criminal. You shall both pay with your heads."

"We must kill the usurper quickly," Toyama said, his voice still clotted with rage. "Not so with you! You shall die in infinite pain!" His eyes bulged from his head and spittle flew from his desiccated lips.

"No need for such melodrama, Toyama-*san*," Professor Tomita said, clucking and shaking his bald head so that his fringe of long lank hair bobbed like a dancing girl's skirts. "Do you really think it would serve any purpose to torture Subhash Indrahar? He is a master of *ki* powers; he wouldn't feel anything we did."

"Before we dispose of me," Subhash said equably, "might I see young Angus Kurita? I'm quite curious as to how he's turned out."

Ohta opened his mouth to issue a reflex refusal. But Tomita gave a small smile. "We can afford to be generous, gentlemen," he said.

The double doors behind the three swung open. The O5P Banzuin strode in, great-bellied and imposing in his scarlet robe and flared white collar. Behind him marched young Angus Kurita. He was clad in dress uniform white tunic trimmed in orange, gleaming scarlet boots, and black jodhpurs. His stand-up collar and shoulder-boards were devoid of rank or branch badges.

"The flux of energies informs me that our presence is desired," the renegade monk declared. He bowed; shallowly to his three Combine-conspirators, more deeply to Subhash Indrahar. "Here we are."

Subhash gazed intently at the young man. He had a shock of dark hair with red highlights, wide cheekbones narrowing to a near-pointed chin, blue Kurita eyes. "Do you know who I am, boy?" he asked.

The youth's eyes flicked aside to Banzuin. The monk nodded his hairless head. Angus started to approach the man in the wheelchair.

"Wait!" Hiraoke Toyama rapped. "I don't like this. Why would he simply come here and present himself to die?"

"Perhaps he entertains hope of negotiating with us," Tomita suggested. "Or perhaps he realizes his fate is inevitable, and wishes simply to get it over with."

"He's a sick old cripple," Ohta barked. "How could he threaten us?"

"He's clever as a devil," Toyama countered. "He breathes trickery like air."

Subhash smiled. "You're wise to be wary, Toyama-*san*. After all, perhaps my wheelchair will transform itself into a powered exoskeleton the way the Davions had me do in their amusing little holovid. I must say I coveted such an invention."

"You possess substantial powers, Banzuin," Tomita said. "Can your *ki* not divine whether the Smiling One poses a danger to us?"

"Of course," the monk said. "I am an Illuminatus of the Order of Five Pillars. Nothing is hidden from me."

He strode forward to stand before Subhash. The Director looked up at him. Their eyes met.

After a moment the monk turned away. "There is . . . nothing. Nothing he can do."

Ohta sneered; Toyama scowled more deeply still. "Well, that settles it, then," Tomita said, with a master of ceremonies air. He flicked his fingers at Angus. "Step forward, lad. Indulge the old man."

Angus stepped up with the air of a man going to face a firing squad. Subhash gestured to him. "Lean down so that I may look at you, young man. Come on. I won't sting you."

Hesitantly, Angus obeyed. Subhash reached up, examined the bone structure of the young man's face like someone thinking about buying a horse, briefly squeezed one biceps.

"You're a strong, sound young man, and your spirit is clear," the Smiling One said. "Why then have you consented to take part in this treasonous scheme? Do you really think yourself fit to replace Theodore?"

Angus stiffened to attention. "I have no ambition for the Dragon Throne," he said to a point above the Director's mostly hairless head. "But my teachers showed me that this was selfishness. I am a Kurita; my duty is to the Dragon. My cousin murdered his father and has weakened the Combine with his reforms. It is my duty to supplant him, in spite of *ninjo*."

"Is this what they've told you, boy?" Subhash asked with what seemed genuine pain. He sat back in his chair as if all but exhausted.

"You could have served the Dragon well," he said. "The rest of us here have outlived our usefulness to the Combine and House Kurita. But your dying will be a tragic loss."

Ninyu Kerai Indrahar disliked to feel.

He had been passionate in his youth, in his first glory days as an ace ISF operative and comrade to Theodore Kurita. And where had that gotten him? Estranged from the man who became Coordinator, because he'd often cared more about the welfare of Theodore than Theodore himself did. Feelings led to mistakes, oversights—such as the one that had left his current prey alive.

Much more satisfying was devotion to duty.

The streets of the pleasure-district of Yoshiwara were oddly deserted. Customarily the hour before dawn was fairly busy in the *ukiyo,* as the last patrons hurried to be home before the sun broke, and the less fortunate denizens of the Floating World, who had to work the streets, were dragging back from work. Today, though, the revelry had broken up early, in order that customers and servers alike might join the vast crowds gathered along Imperial Way and in Unity Square to breathlessly await the parade.

Around him a picked platoon of the Sons of the Dragon and *metsuke* in mufti cycled in and out of the hostess bars, tea-shops, and flophouses along Perfection of Joy Street. Franklin Sakamoto was known to be a man of rather abstemious tastes. What vices he had he preferred to indulge in private, and he had inherited sufficient of his father's looks, confidence, and charisma that he didn't have to purchase feminine companionship when he cared for it. He had also demonstrated himself quite cunning in his days with the Strikers on Somerset, later prosecuting what had amounted to a one-man war against the Clans. Ninyu Kerai was gambling that Sakamoto might have chosen to go to ground in the *ukiyo* on the basis of sheer unexpectedness.

His mind was carefully avoiding the phrase *grasping at straws*. He kept hearing in his mind his adoptive father's voice urging him always to confront the truth no matter how unpalatable. All the efforts he and a small army of investigators had put forth had been unable to turn up any leads at all to Sakamoto's whereabouts. Deep inside Ninyu, the conviction of failure grew like fast-forward cancer.

My father thinks I'm ready to succeed him, he thought, pausing to survey the street, still laced with fog from the nearby Kado-guchi. *Now he'll know otherwise.*

The personal communicator at his hip began to vibrate, noiselessly indicating an incoming call. He unholstered the device, which contained a highly sophisticated scrambler/unscrambler chip, flipped it open. "Kerai."

"Ninyu, my son," came the voice of the Smiling One, dry and passionless as usual. "Return at once to headquarters."

"*Hai*, my father." He closed the communicator and waved over an operator to take charge of the search effort.

Force Commander Kali MacDougall ran her 15-ton AgroMech, disguised as a *Quickdraw,* northward at its not-very-high top speed, paralleling the razor-wired fence surrounding the parked BattleMechs of the four Caballero battalions. The Eiga-toshi FX techs had achieved their own version of Clan weapons modularity; their launcher-racks, firing volleys of large but virtually harmless fireworks rockets, could be attached to almost any of the *faux* Battle-Mechs. In the case of her machine it had been dead simple, since the original already came with an SRM launcher in its chest, so that the fake already had a rocket-rack. Other racks had been strapped onto other 'Mechs regardless of whether the model they were imitating mounted missiles or not. The whole object was to distract the Black Dragon 'Mech jocks long enough for some of the Caballero MechWarriors to re-unite themselves with their captive machines.

Kali passed the battle-line of Black Dragon 'Mechs. She was part of the force winging wide on the west side, attempting to outflank the heaviest of the three enemy lances. Unfortunately—for anything except her continued prospects for survival—the bad guys had recognized the real threat. They were blasting away at the utility vehicles trying to make it through breaches in the wire cut by support personnel, most of whom had already been cut down. At least four vehicles had already been turned into pyres. As she watched, the final survivor of the phony "assault" lance that had come rumbling through the smoke at the onset of the attack, a "Charger" piloted by Don Pinnock of Bobby the Wolf's new Fourth Battalion, tried to interpose itself between the little vehicles and the enemy 'Mechs. The Black Dragon 'Mechs blew it apart.

Don bought 'em some time, Kali thought, *but it won't be enough.*

She felt a curious lightening, a sense of liberation. She had wanted to join the teams trying to get to the Caballero Battle-Mechs in some of the many small trucks, carts, and cars Takura Migaki—who definitely had champagne tastes—maintained for the use of his holovid companies. With her right arm still pretty immobilized, Kali didn't seem suited for that, nor for hopping and popping in a warehouse full of Black Dragon torpedoes and DEST commandos.

But Kali, at core, had the same driving lust to close with and destroy those who would destroy her *familia* as Cassie did. And, as usual, the Dark Lady had plans of her own.

Once past the enemy 'Mechs, she turned and raced her

"*Quickdraw*" straight for the wire. Raven O'Connell, driving a false *JagerMech,* hung right on her left shoulder. Kali glanced to the side and grinned, sensing her friend was doing the same. They were almost to the fence—

The Black Dragon jocks became aware of the new threat—you could win a little margin by getting behind a pilot equipped with a circle-vision strip, but only a little, if the jock was properly trained. The *Guillotine* twisted its torso counterclockwise, fired the extended-range large laser in its left arm.

The AgroMech lacked a 360 view-strip. What Kali had was a crawling sensation in the back of her neck, an expectation of death at any moment—not an entirely unpleasant sensation.

A crimson flash in the lower right quadrant of Kali's vision, a crack and sizzle as the laser beam ionized air and then sublimated metal away like ice before a blowtorch. The whole right leg of Kali's 'Mech went red on the status display.

Its limb amputated just as its weight came onto it, the AgroMech toppled forward. It landed on its side with a jar that threatened to shake Kali's eyeballs loose from their socket and began to roll.

Cassie hit the side of a plastic rag-bin. Which went clattering away across the floor of the 'Mech hangar. She slid to the cement with the dead weight of her new attacker atop her. She was just struggling to bring the muzzle of her pistol against the ribs of whomever had tackled her when the left foot of Don Carlos' command 'Mech, now piloted by *Tai-i* Daw, clanged down on the hangar floor exactly where Cassie had stood half a heartbeat before.

"*Chikusho!*" Achilles Daw shouted as the *Naginata*'s foot just missed its target. He would have liked to stay and deal with the sneaksuit-clad traitor—undoubtedly one of Subhash's pampered Sons of the Dragon, sent to warn the *gaijin* of General Kiguri's scheme—but his long-range missiles were no good at this truncated range and he didn't dare light off the Lord's Light 2 extended-range PPC in his left arm. But he had more immediate business: making sure none of the money-troopers managed to get into any of the 'Mechs parked outside.

Leave the bitch for later, he told himself. *It's too late to stop us.* He picked up the pace and crashed through the hangar's cinderblock wall.

Eyes still wide at her near brush with being crushed by the assault 'Mech, whose approach she hadn't heard amid the general din, Cassie looked up into the face of the person who'd knocked her out of harm's way. It was a familiar face, oblong and handsome, beneath tousled black hair.

"Johnny Tchang?" she asked incredulously. His answer was a grin and a nod. "How the hell did you recognize me?"

"Who else would be leading the Caballeros dressed as a DEST commando?"

Rolling furiously, whirling dust about it like a cloak as it shed its mostly plastic superstructure, Kali MacDougall's fake *Quickdraw* smashed through the fence, tearing out a fifty-meter section. It slammed into the legs of a Third Battalion *War Dog.* The 75-ton 'Mech, painted white with black splotches, rocked but didn't go down.

Kali felt as if she'd been for a ride in a giant rock polisher. Her shoulder hurt as bad as if it had been dislocated again—some experimental shrugging proved it hadn't—her ribs felt as if she'd been used for a heavy bag, and the back of her head was tender. But she was alive, intact, and ready to rumble.

She hit the quick-release pad of her shoulder unit, pulled herself out of the seat. The 'Mech had come to rest lying on its right side. Because preventing penetration by foreign objects, such as autocannon slugs, wasn't an issue, but getting out if the beast took a spill and fetched up in a compromising position in some arroyo was, your basic AgroMech had several easy-to-get-to hatches, such that virtually no matter how it landed one was bound to be clear. What did count in AgroMech design was structural strength in the cockpit, which was provided by a cage of titanium-alloy tubing. It had served its function, keeping its pilot safe during her wild tumble.

Kali popped the hatch on the 'Mech's left side. Reminding herself to be grateful for keeping up with her exercise regimen no matter how much she hated it, she pulled herself up one-handed into dull orange dawnlight.

Having blown the leg off her 'Mech, the *Guillotine* had lost interest in her and was shooting again at the Caballeros trying to break through the fence. Raven had dodged in among the dormant BattleMechs, and a *Hornet* was trying to pick her off with its medium laser. Kali swung her long legs up and over, then dropped to the ground. She drew the laser pistol from its tie-down holster on her thigh, quickly checked it. The self-test light glowed green: ready to fire. She began to run.

Cassie half-rose to fire a dead operative's machine pistol over a bin of assorted metal junk that was used to build and maintain the superstructures on Migaki's AgroMechs. Then she turned and hunkered down with her back to the bin. The square *tsuba,* handguard of the vibrokatana strapped across her back scraped against the metal.

"What are you doing here, anyway?"

Johnny Tchang crouched beside her. "There's something I've got to tell you."

Cassie felt a dancing sense of urgency, but had no idea what to do about it. The fight inside the compound had devolved into a mutual cat-and-mouse hunt through the clutter and between the legs of quiescent BattleMechs. The Black Dragon foot soldiers were mostly yak kobun and didn't amount to much, although their guns could kill you just as dead as any Jade Falcon Elemental's. The renegade DEST troops, of whom there seemed to be about seventy—half, it seemed, tasked to carry out the actual assassination of Theodore in the Seventeenth's 'Mechs, the other half detailed to stay back to secure Eiga-toshi and, of course, the mercenaries—posed a bigger threat, with their armor and sensory systems.

But the DEST commandos could not afford to hang and bang; they had places to go and people to do, and the longer they were delayed, the more likely somebody would discover all was not right at the Voice of the Dragon cinema complex. And the Caballeros outnumbered them considerably. The Seventeenth had only about two hundred qualified MechWarriors, including Dispossessed and aspirants to their first machines and desk-jockeys like intelligence chief García. But because the 'lleros carried their own techs and assistant techs with them, as well as their families—and there tended to be considerable overlap—and because almost every Caballero over the age of twelve was prepared to bear arms in defense of *la familia,* the raiders would inevitably be overwhelmed—*if* they could be prevented from getting into the cockpits of the 'llero BattleMechs faster than the 'lleros could.

Cassie peeked up again. A female commando was climbing up the mounts along the side of Buck Evans' *Orion.* She had almost reached the cockpit. Cassie aimed and gave her a short burst in the small of the back, where the kidneys lay close enough to the surface that the tough but flexible armor would offer little protection. Something produced the desired reflex spasm; the woman fell.

Cassie pulled her head back down in time to avoid most of the spray of vaporized metal from a laser-beam strike that hit the bin rim near her head. Johnny Tchang brushed out a patch of her poor hair—just starting to really get some length again after all being burned off in her 'Mech fight with Jeffrey Kusunoki on Towne—that had been set smoldering. Then he popped up and blazed madly away with a pair of pistols, one Cassie's, one he'd turned up the Brown Virgin knew where.

Cassie grabbed him by the seat of his black trousers and pulled him down. "What the hell's the matter with you? You can't hit anything that way."

Johnny Tchang gave her that boyish grin that had made him the darling of a thousand worlds. "It always works in my holovids."

She gave him a sour look.

The situation had set into stalemate. Their training and equipment gave the DEST commandos advantages, but the Caballeros were no pushovers. MechWarriors as well as support troops had grown up poor but surly on hardscrabble planets, and they had the marksmanship of rural poor who often had to rely on hunting skills to put food on the table, where a single shot could make the difference between eating and starving—not to mention the risks entailed by wounding rather than dropping the Southwestern worlds' notably cranky game animals. In the Seventeenth, not only was everybody ready to fight, everybody *had,* and even the haughty 'Mech jocks had tasted down-and-dirty combat just like this.

A flurry of shots, screams, grenade cracks. Something was going down off to the left. Cassie risked a look up, but could see nothing for the parked 'Mechs and clutter in the short interval before the unseen sniper cracked another beam over her head.

Johnny was gazing at her, his expression grave. "Cassie—"

"Johnny," she said, trying to peer around the left end of the bin to where the spasm of battle was continuing, "you're a nice boy, I like you, and thanks for saving my life. But this isn't a great time to talk."

"You need to know this," he said persistently. "My defection from the Capellan Confederation was faked. I'm a Maskirovka spy. I was sent here to observe, and if necessary help with, the assassination of Theodore Kurita."

Ninyu Kerai stood alone in Subhash's office. The lights of the holodisplay played across his face in the gloom.

"My son," the image of his adoptive father said, "I have misled you. I have sent you on what *gaijin* might call a 'wild-goose chase.' Franklin Sakamoto is blameless; evidence suggests he may be a captive of the true conspirators against the Combine, our Coordinator, and, incidentally, both you and myself.

"The head of these conspirators is General Hohiro Kiguri, commander of the Draconis Elite Strike Teams."

"What is he saying?" *Tai-sa* Charles Ohta demanded. "Who's going to die?"

Subhash Indrahar smiled benignly. "All of us," he said softly.

"Shoot him!" Toyama screeched to the guards.

The guards stared in confusion. It didn't matter. Any action they could take was already too late.

The Smiling One threw back his head and laughed. It was a robust laugh, the laugh of a strong young warrior.

Panels on both sides of the wheelchair snapped open. From each side a double-tube man-portable short-range missile launcher emerged. Both pivoted upward on their mounts. Fire flashed and the chamber filled with choking smoke as a volley of rockets streaked toward the large port overhead.

The transpex dome was proof against small arms, and sealed against the one-atmosphere pressure within the ship. But it was never designed to resist the assault of four rockets with powerful armor-piercing warheads. It shattered and exploded outward in a glittering cascade.

At the abrupt pressure drop, heavy metal panels slid instantly across the entrances to the great compartment. They saved the rest of the ship. But they did no good for those inside.

Air rushed out into space with a whistling roar. Still laughing, Subhash Indrahar was whirled up with it, and Angus Kurita with him, and Ohta and Banzuin the false monk and Tomita the professor and the guards, irresistibly, up and up and out into infinite night.

28

Unity Palace, Imperial City
Luthien
Pesht Military District, Draconis Combine
1 July 3058

"I am now dead, my son," the image of Subhash Indrahar declared. "You are now Director of the Internal Security Force. You shall serve House Kurita well, and bring honor to my memory.

"One final word: do not avenge me as such. Instead, consider the opportunity these events present, and exploit them fully, that my legacy shall be a Dragon—and House Kurita—stronger than at any time in our glorious history. And in cleaning our own house, make certain that you do not leave it bereft of leadership. Expunge only the guilty, not from any abstraction of 'justice,' but of necessity: the necessity that ISF be strong and capable for the turbulent days ahead.

"And now, goodbye. I love you, my son. You make me proud." The image blinked to nothingness.

Ninyu Kerai threw back his head and screamed, *"No!"* And his cry echoed through the roots of Unity Palace, and up and out, as far as the trailing Trojan point of the outermost moon of Luthien, where his father's body, mummified by vacuum, orbited eternally.

In time it would spread to shake the entire Draconis Combine and beyond.

In the midst of the fighting occuring all over Eiga-toshi, Cassie had the muzzle of her Shimatsu 42 aimed at Johnny

Tchang's lean midriff. "Can you give me a good reason not to snuff you right here and now?"

"There's my boyish smile," he said, and flashed it at her.

"Not good enough."

"Of all the women in the Inner Sphere, I have to fall for one who's immune to my charm."

"That's not necessarily true. But while honeyed words are nice and everything, these bullets'd sure make a mess of that washboard belly of yours." The crack of a grenade, screaming. "And I don't have much time—"

He held up his hands, empty. "All right. I told you what I was sent here for. If I meant to do you harm, would I have even come?"

"Maybe you want to take me out, help the cause a little."

"Would I have warned you, then?" He shrugged. "Cassiopeia, if you really believe I'm your enemy, go ahead and squeeze the trigger. That'd probably be the best thing in the world that could happen to me."

She looked hard at him two heartbeats more. Her eyes had lightened until they were almost colorless.

Then she half-rose, turning, sinuous as smoke, and fired a burst across the top of the parts bin. A DEST commando who had been creeping forward across a bare patch of cement yelled hoarsely behind his visor and sat down hard. Cassie kept squirting him with quick bursts until he rolled over and scrambled back over a stack of unformed armor-plate sections to safety. She blasted his heel with the last of the magazine, then popped it from the well and replaced it with another from a pocket of her outrageous jacket as she sat back down.

"That *pendejo* Kiguri doesn't train his people for Sierra—scuffling his feet like that. Ninyu Kerai will mop Impy City with these clowns when he finds out what's going on." She looked to Johnny. "Give it to me straight—and quick."

"Not much to tell. I have a sister whom I love very much—all the family that means anything to me, since my parents sold me to the opera company. The Mask has her. My defection was their idea. Since I was so popular in the FedCom anyway, they figured if I seemed to jump the fence

I'd be even more of a hero, and no one would think to question whether it was real."

"Go on," Cassie said, listening carefully.

"I've done minor spying jobs for them, nothing major—I think they're not quite sure what use to make of me. I have a feeling Sun-Tzu Liao considered using me to assassinate Prince Victor, based on hints my handlers dropped, but I've no definite knowledge."

"How did the Mask get tangled up in a plot against Theodore?"

Bullets clanged among the parts in the bin like giant metal bees on speed. Two punched through between Cassie and Johnny and went tumbling away with harmonic whines.

"*Damn,* I'm getting sick of this." She pulled a tear gas grenade from the sneaksuit's web belt, handed it to Johnny. "Here. Twist this cap hard till you feel something snap to initiate it. Torque it and toss it when I tell you to."

He looked quizzically at her. She ignored him. Instead she pulled out a second gas grenade and tossed it over the bin without twisting the cap. Then she reared up and cut loose with her Shimatsu.

Not knowing what kind of grenade had been thrown into the patch of clear concrete, the two DEST operatives ducked. Which was what Cassie intended. She emptied her magazine over the top of the stacked armor plates, into a row of barrels of yellow synthetic.

"Now," she called to Johnny. "Toss it in behind 'em."

He did so. Stood looking. She dragged him down again just as the commandos opened fire once more. "Damn it, it's Dracs who're supposed to be in love with suicide, not Capellans!"

Before he could respond to that, the gas grenade went off. Tear gas grenades burn very hot.

The solvent stored in the drums Cassie had punctured burned hotter.

Flaring orange light danced on the hangar's walls. At the demoniac screaming and thrashing from behind the armor plates all the color drained from Johnny Tchang's face.

"Special forces," Cassie said contemptuously. "Big-time commandos—yeah. A *scout* never forgets her surroundings."

She looked sidelong at Johnny. "Never killed anybody before, huh?"

"Not that I know of. And not—like that."

The screaming subsided. The firefight, which seemed to have been suspended, broke out again full force. "O.K. I believe you. Hard-core Maskers get off on pain—ISF're a bunch of thugs, but they don't go out of the way to recruit crazies and sadists the way Maskirovka does. You're a good actor, but you're not *that* good."

"Thanks. I think."

"So what does Sun-Tzu have against Theodore Kurita?"

"Jealousy, I think. That's the real thing. The ostensible reason seems to be that he finally realized the Coordinator was never going to go for the Pan-Asian alliance the Liaos kept proposing against the rest of the Sphere, but that Sub-hash Indrahar has been using to string him along for years."

"How did you get mixed up in this, then?"

"Well, Word of Blake has been working with *Kokuryu-kai* for several years."

"We've noticed."

"And they've noticed you too. I guess you know that. Anyway, the Mask is into the Word of Blake ROM like worms in an apple. Blakie intelligence is good at dirty tricks, but they're not a patch on their ComStar opposite numbers when it comes to security. They're pretty gullible, especially where Tommy Marik's concerned, and Sun-Tzu and the Captain-General have been like *that* the last few years. Anyway, the Maskirovka found out through the Blakies that the Black Dragons had it in for Theodore. They made their own approach, cut their own deal."

"Which is?"

"Basically, Sun-Tzu recognizes anybody the Black Dragons manage to stuff onto the Dragon Throne."

"And where do you fit?"

"I was to observe, and lend help if *Kokuryu-kai* asked for it. And I—well, when it was announced that your regiment would be attending the Coordinator's Birthday celebration, the Mask had me suggest putting you up here to Takura Migaki."

Cassie pursed her lips in a silent whistle. "We got a lot to thank you for, don't we?"

"I'm hoping to make it up to you."

She grunted. "Sun's coming up," she said. "We need to make something happen here. You can drive a forklift, can't you?"

"Uh-yeah. In *Police Force 3053* I did this scene—"

"I saw it. That's why I figured you could, 'cause you do your own stunts." She pointed to the wall behind them. "See the forklift parked over there?"

"Yes."

"You're gonna drive it where I tell you," she said, "and I'm gonna shoot anybody in black or tattoos who looks at us."

The *Bushwacker*'s snout-mounted machine guns snarled. Strikes flickered against the legs of a *Grasshopper*. The targeted enemy was already safe behind them.

"Bloody hell!" *Tai-i* O'Hanrahan was seriously torqued. The enemy's phony missiles had swathed the battlefield in a thick pall of smoke. Through it the enemy on foot was visible to the infrared receptors in his *Bushwacker*'s sensory suite, which showed them to him as glowing false-color blobs on his HUD. But they were mere wisps, flitting from leg to leg of their parked BattleMechs.

Who ever heard of people afoot not fearing 'Mechs? Even MechWarriors, dismounted, were no more than rabble-targets, "rugs in waiting" in the usual grim 'Mech jock jest. But these foreign money-troopers, while doing their best to keep out of the way of his company's weapons, were not dissolving into proper panic.

The problem was, the weapons and sensors of O'Hanrahan's company were suited to finding, fixing, and flaying other giant mobile masses of metal. With a few exceptions such as his own *Bushwacker*'s machine guns—which were rare on 'Mechs these days—they weren't well suited to picking on little darting human targets, for all their awesome capabilities. It had never seemed a *problem* before.

On the heels of that thought, a warning light flared on his

board, and his circle-vision strip showed him half a dozen missile-trails snaking for the *Bushwacker*'s back.

"Fool me once, shame on me," he snarled, and returned his tension to trying to scour the confounded mercs out from among their mounts.

A double explosion rocked the *Bushwacker* forward.

The phony *Quickdraw* had broken through the fence about the middle of the Third Battalion square. Kali commanded First Battalion, parked nearest the hangar. That meant her *Mad Cat* was a good ways off.

The Sevententh's BattleMechs stood arrayed in four battalion blocs ranged in a line north from the repair hangar. Each lance of four 'Mechs was parked in a small square. Nine such squares in a three-by-three matrix made up a battalion.

Kali wove between BattleMech legs and gouts of earth thrown up by projectiles and energy weapons. The Black Dragon 'Mech jocks had a MechWarrior's phobia about combat in a confined space, where the terrific mobility and sensory apparatus of a BattleMech was largely neutralized, and even despised groundpounder infantry could pose a deadly threat to the lords and ladies of warfare. The Caballero machines were parked too close together to allow maneuvering among them. So the Black Dragons were hanging outside the fence, sniping at the 'lleros trying to reach their rides.

Panting for breath, Kali stopped between the legs of a *Hatamoto-chi* belonging to Eskiminzin Company CO Stretch Santillanes, a White Mountain Apache out of Cerillos. *We got us a tad bit of problem here,* she thought. It was the BattleMechs of her own First Battalion that the raiders intended to use to assassinate Theodore Kurita. There were at least a dozen black sneaksuits in and among her parked machines, dueling with other First Battalion jocks who had gotten in through the wire.

A whine of servos and the thump of a 'Mech footfall made her jump and spin. Raven's phony *JagerMech* had come to stand beside her hiding-place. It wasn't increasing her exposure: except for the occasional reflex shot, the

Black Dragons were showing good discipline in ignoring the false BattleMechs.

Raven had popped the viewscreen and the belly panel that covered it, actually a vitryl sheet with a light spray of paint over it that matched the rest of the *Jag*'s exterior but didn't interfere much with the pilot's vision. She leaned forward to give Kali the paper-wraps-stone gesture that meant *I'll cover you*. In the process she would also get closer to her own ride.

Kali returned the traditional Southwestern acknowledgement, extending her left forefinger and thumb and "shooting" the other woman as with a gun. She started running forward.

A clump of enemy commandos huddled behind the blocky and disproportionately small feet of the *Awesome* that once belonged to Reb Perez, and had been taken over by Tyree Manygoats, a Navajo from Sierra, after Reb was killed during the Seventeenth's stint on Hachiman two years before. They caught sight of Kali and opened up on her with assault rifles.

A burst drew sparks from a *Jenner*'s shin right over her head. Kali threw herself forward, tucked her good shoulder, rolled, fired laser bolts, bright red in the milky half-light. She didn't know if she hit anything; probably not.

Momentum gave her the necessary boost back to her feet. She darted to cover behind the legs of another parked machine. Ahead she saw Don Carlos' *Naginata*, undoubtedly under enemy control, standing in the midst of the First Battalion square. That was the least of her worries at the moment; the commandos would knock her down before she could reach her own machine, which stood on the far side of the commandeered BattleMech. To try to reach it was certain death.

Failure to reach the *Mad Cat* was certain death delayed a little longer. She broke from cover and ran with all the speed her long legs could give her.

Exhilaration filled *Tai-i* Achilles Daw as he surveyed the chaos of the 'Mech enclosure from his high perch. As a trained commando he was capable of ice-cold detachment—but as one of General Kiguri's hand-picked elite-within-the-elite he had also been trained not to disregard his feelings, when they did not tempt to dishonor. *Ninyo* was one thing, a warrior's passion another.

Like the other DEST commandos who had been dispatched to Eiga-toshi under his command, Daw was a qualified MechWarrior. But he had seldom seen the inside of an assault 'Mech except in computer simulators, never tasted actual BattleMech combat at all. The sense of sheer unequaled *power* produced by sitting in that *Naginata* hit him like a dose of *hiropon*, the methamphetamine derivative certain DCMS commanders—and Black Dragon infantry officers on Towne—had been known to distribute to uncertain troops before battle.

His exaltation made it easy to overlook the fact he wasn't sure what to *do*. As a dedicated command machine the *Naginata* was never intended for in-fighting. Its Coventry long-range missile packs and its Lord's Light 2 extended-range PPC were intended to help it keep trouble at a respectful distance so its pilot could concentrate on running the show. There seemed to be enemies swarming everywhere at this point, but most of the ones he could see were too close.

A *JagerMech* came running almost at him. He raised the PPC that made up most of the *Naginata*'s left arm. But no, the yakuza scum who had done such a disgraceful job of keeping the *gaijin* money-troopers away from their machines had warned him over his own command net that it was a fake, a movie prop. A target unworthy of a warrior.

There. A hundred meters away he saw a single small figure struggling up a rope hanging down the back of an *Enforcer* to a rear-mounted hatch. He aimed the left arm, loosed a raw blue-white gout of lightning. *Hit.* The tiny figure flashed momentarily brighter than the eye-hurting stream of charged particles, and was gone.

Behind the visor of his neurohelmet, Daw grinned.

With every stride she took Kali MacDougall expected to be knocked sprawling by a burst of gunfire. Instead, with a rapid thudding of heavy feet, Raven accompanied her in the fake *Jag*. The black-clad commandoes by the *Awesome*'s feet were well disciplined and apparently alerted that the huge BattleMech bearing down on them was a mere mock-up. They never faltered in shooting at the fleeting Kali.

The AgroMech hidden beneath the built-up super-structure massed a mere fifteen tons. Nothing at all by BattleMech standards, though it was still a lot of weight.

More than enough to crush three DEST commandos and smash the leg of a fourth as it literally ran over them.

A PPC cracked like thunder over Kali's head, so close the heat felt like sunburn on her face and hands, and the hairs at the back of her neck stood up. The *Naginata* was shooting at something—somebody. She felt a flash of pity for whoever it was. She was vaguely aware of other forms lying still around her, some clad in DEST black, too many not. *No time to grieve—*

Somehow she was there, panting by the splayed two-toed foot of her *Mad Cat,* parked next to the hangar, which now had a huge hole in the wall where the *Naginata* had emerged. As usual, she had left the 'Mech hunkered down on its backward-kneed legs. That meant she had a climb of just over three meters to reach the hatch, and an easy climb, given the design of the legs—for someone with two arms.

Well, what the hey, I have motivation. She started climbing up the smooth housing that shielded the foot actuators.

Just to the north was parked the BJ-2 *Blackjack* belonging to Terry Carrington, a Galisteo native who had joined the regiment right before Towne. Difficult to see against the *Blackjack*'s glossy black paint job, a female DEST agent was scaling the front of the machine. Though she had to climb much farther than Kali up the *Blackjack*'s twelve-meter height, she was making much better time proportionately. As Kali struggled upward with explosions and laser-cracks threatening to punch through her eardrums, she had to admire the lithe way the other woman swarmed up— *Like a Cerillos three-tailed squirrel,* she thought. Of course, the other also had both her arms, and was probably better trained at that sort of thing than Kali was.

The problem was, she was clearly going to win the race to get into the cockpit first. Kali's *Mad Cat* was, after all, the genuine Clantech article, not some General Motors knockoff, and would normally eat thirty-tons-lighter Spheroid 'Mechs like s'mores. But once Kali was in the cockpit it would still take a certain amount of time for her to get the beast fired up and ready to rumble. If the DEST hijacker got far enough ahead of her, that *Blackjack* would turn into a viable fighting machine while her Sword of Kali remained just a 75-ton paperweight. It could literally push the bigger 'Mech over and stomp it like a barroom brawler.

Kali caught frantically at the top of the *Mad Cat*'s leg, hauled herself upward with all her strength. The DEST commando reached the sloped ledge of the *Blackjack*'s upper torso, popped the hatch—

And was swatted away from the 'Mech's face like a mosquito by an invisible hand. As Kali's hand hit the quick-open release for her own cockpit, she heard a heavy thudding crack, like a sledgehammer splitting a two-by-four. *Zeus rifle,* she thought. *Guess Marly worked her way to a new position.* And while that little girl was cultivating a crop of personality disorders that threatened to make Cassie seem like Melissa Steiner, right this moment Kali MacDougall was infinitely grateful for the girl's fixity of purpose.

The gasket-seal broke with a pop as the canopy raised. Kali hoisted her rump to the edge of the narrow cockpit, swung her long legs over, and almost fell into the form-fitting seat. She jacked her neurohelmet into the console.

Feeling the giant war machine begin to come alive around her was almost sexual relief.

As the canopy descended she looked past the *Mad Cat*'s narrow snout. And saw the *Naginata* facing her, raising its PPC arm.

29

Cinema City, Luthien
Pesht Military District, Draconis Combine
1 July 3058

No red telltales flickered in Terence O'Hanrahan's heads-up display this time, either, but he knew in his belly that no barrage of harmless skyrockets had struck his *Bushwacker*. *Those are SRMs, or I'm a Davion!*

Quickly he looked to his 360 display. MechWarrior Choiseul's *Hornet* was bleeding copious smoke from the CASE vents; his LRM reloads had gone up, but the little 'Mech was still standing. The other 'Mechs in view looked intact.

Startled reports buzzed like static on the company channel: "Groundpounders! Firing SRMs from behind us!"

"Ignore them," O'Hanrahan snarled. "If these bastards start getting into their 'Mechs, it's worse things than short-range missiles we'll have to worry about!"

A tawny mass filled Kali's field of vision, so abruptly that she jerked back in her seat. It was Raven's imitation *Jager-Mech*, interposing itself between Kali and—

Hideous blue-white glare backlit the phony *Jag*. The superstructure—and the unarmored AgroMech within—blew into thousands of flaming fragments.

"Raven!" Kali shouted. But it was too late—her friend was gone, and her sacrifice had not been quite enough. Through the swirling, flaming debris Kali could see the muzzle of the PPC still locked on her machine. As soon as it recharged it would begin blasting chunks from her 'Mech. *If I only had a few seconds more*—

Behind the *Naginata* a 'Mech rose into the air, the flares of the jump jets in its legs bright against the pale morning sky. Not one of the humanoid BattleMechs, its hunched-over shape resembled a *Jenner* or a miniature version of Kali's *Mad Cat.* It was a *Firefly.* Kali barely had time to wonder which side was piloting it before it began to plunge toward the hijacked command 'Mech in a classic death-from-above attack.

Kali now recognized it as the 'Mech belonging to "Frenchfry" Ames, Adelante Company's commander—and Raven's husband.

The *Firefly*'s three torso-mounted medium lasers stabbed for the *Naginata* without regard to heat buildup. Sparks flared from hits on the other 'Mech's rear armor. Its pilot chose to react to the actual immediate threat, rather than the potential one of the still-dormant *Mad Cat.* He swiveled the 95-ton 'Mech's torso and took a turning step, brought up the extended-range PPC to blast the descending light Battle-Mech once, twice.

The *Firefly* slammed the hard-packed soil of Luthien almost at the *Naginata*'s feet with a terrific crash and squeal of rending metal.

And the extended-range PPCs that tipped the flexible arms of Kali's *Mad Cat* rose with a whine and locked into place. Green lights woke in Kali's display.

"All right, you *culebra* son of a bitch," Kali said. "It's time for you and me to dance."

Panting like his totem animal, Robert "Navajo Wolf" Begay, newest and most controversial of the Seventeenth's battalion commanders, knelt for a moment over the body of his fallen foe.

If the DEST commando's *ki* had been on this day he wouldn't even have tried to fight: he would have known he was beaten from a single glance at Bobby the Wolf's handsome, mad face. Here was a man who had chosen names for himself and his 'Mechs—Navajo Wolf and Skin Walker, both meaning the same thing: a shape-changing witch—

which were so ultimately ill-favored that none of his own people would have anything to do with him, nor would any of the Caballeros' numerous Apaches. A man who carefully cultivated his sense of rage against all Creation, and lived for the moments he could let it out. A man who believed in Power, and had it upon him.

Instead, the black-clad commando had faced him squarely, seemingly glad for the chance to dispatch a foe with his sword. Especially a foe armed with nothing more threatening than a meter-long wrecking bar.

Bobby the Wolf reached down to dab a stripe of his enemy's blood beneath each eye. That was another major hint that he was seriously not to be messed with. Sane Athabaskans held corpses and anything associated with them in a horror that made the Buddhist-inspired Drac fear of defilement look like necrophilia.

The DEST commando was beyond the "hint" stage. That polymerized-steel wrecking bar was another 'Mech-rescue tool. Its first downward stroke snapped the DEST man's 1400-year-old katana a handsbreadth from the hilt. The second snapped his clavicle between neck and right shoulder, meaning that no matter how strong his *ki* or how much adrenaline the fight/flight reflex had pumped into his system, the commando could no more raise that arm than if it belonged to someone else in a different county. A flailing fury of blows had continued until the black helmet and its contents went sort of soft. For good measure Bobby the Wolf had finished by punching the end of the wrecking bar through the red visor.

Leaving it there, he stood and began swarming up the new BattleMech he'd won on Towne.

The pilot in the *Naginata* was good enough to spot the motion from Kali's 'Mech. Rather than gloat over his kill of Frenchfry Ames' *Firefly* he immediately began swinging back to face her. The huge mass of the *Nag*'s torso turned ponderously, though, and Kali was not standing still.

With two extra double-capacity heat sinks mounted in either arm, the *Mad Cat* could fire all its energy weapons—without raising a single degree of heat. Since the 'Mech could also cruise as fast as the *Naginata* could run flat-out, Kali was willing to accept a minor heat buildup to keep her weaponry playing on the enemy machine's slightly thinner side armor as long as possible—and also delay the Drac's retaliation. She started the *Cat* striding counterclockwise around the *Naginata*, lighting its left side and PPC arm with her own two extended-range PPCs and the pair of medium pulse lasers mounted along the bullet-like fuselage.

The Drac was shrewd. He immediately rotated his 'Mech's torso in the other direction, pivoting clockwise to catch the moving *Mad Cat* with a cross-body blast of its own PPC. Kali's lips fixed in a taut grin as the particle beam etched a glowing line down the side of her 'Mech's torso. Its frontal armor was almost the same as that of the *Naginata*. With her edge in short-range firepower the *Mad Cat* could hang and bang with the larger 'Mech and win despite giving away twenty tons. But that wasn't Kali's style. Even when she piloted a 100-ton *Atlas* she surprised foes with the mobility she was able to coax out of the lumbering monster. With a wicked-fast heavy Clan Omni under her butt she meant to *move*.

She kept up the rapid pacing, pulsing blasts from her weapons between the parked 'Mechs of her battalion. The fight might've been over quicker if she'd just gone *mano-a-mano* with the *Naginata*. But she risked a lucky shot locking an actuator, knocking out a weapon, or even killing her, and she had a lot more fish to fry than just el Patron's purloined ride.

She grimaced as a glancing bolt gouged the transpex canopy, too close to her face for comfort—she could feel the heat soar in the almost-cramped cockpit. *Maybe these black-clad buckaroos can do fancy tricks with swords and climb like monkeys,* she thought. *But that doesn't make 'em MechWarriors.* She was confident she had the edge in skill, and she meant to make it count.

That wasn't the only edge she held. But she had no way of knowing that.

Tai-i Achilles Daw squinted his eyes against the heat that parched his eyeballs so that the lids stuck to them every time he blinked. Red lights were glaring from his HUD and the BattleMech was slowing perceptibly beneath him. The reactor-shutdown warning shrilled in his ears as his black-gloved finger stabbed at the override.

"*Nan da kor'ya!*" he shouted in rage, *what the hell?* He hadn't taken a serious hit yet. And the single PPC he was able to get into action couldn't come close to taxing his heat sinks—

The *Mad Cat* came rushing at him as if it meant to run into him and knock him down. The PPCs in its arms were crazy blazes, sublimating the tough Durallex Heavy Special plate like ice cream under a blowtorch and filling the cockpit with hideous flickering blue glare as if Daw were arc-welding in there. Daw roared wordlessly and fired.

He had been doing too good a job forcing overrides. This time the computer decided an engine explosion was probable, shut the reactor down, and fired the top of the *Naginata*'s head, and Achilles Daw, right up into the milky morning sky.

Once you leached all the self-comforting 'Mech jock Bravo Sierra and bravado out of the proposition, just being a qualified 'Mech pilot really *didn't* make you into a Mech *Warrior*. Because of the fifteen double heat sinks the *Naginata* mounted, ten of them had been dismounted for cleaning and stacked under plastic back in the hangar. The tale Zuma had spun about a bum bearing in the hip had been true enough—but that problem was under control, and had nothing to do with why Don Carlos' 'Mech was in the barn. It was routine maintenance, cleaning the crud out of the grilles. Zuma's gnomes had been in the process of slipping the scrubbed-out sinks, which were well-designed for easy removal and replacement, back in place when the commandos burst in and captured them. Zuma had kept the commando leader distracted—and then, at the end, jimmied the telltales so they wouldn't betray the heat sinks' absence. With typical DEST arrogance, Daw had assumed he had overawed the *gaijin* tech into serving faithfully—and hadn't bothered to make his own walkaround inspection.

* * *

The torso of her *Mad Cat* tilted back, Kali watched the tiny black blot arc well over the plain to the east, saw the yellow and red chute stream up and blossom. From chatter on the comm net she knew her opponent was the enemy leader, and had murdered Richard Gallegos in cold blood. Her thumbs tightened on the firing buttons. *I should fry the bastard as he floats.*

But her heart was not good for shooting a MechWarrior in his chute, no matter what he had done. She didn't buy into much of the 'Mech-pilot hero-warrior-jock routine. But that was one section of the code she couldn't bring herself to break. *Maybe I'm too damned sensitive,* she thought.

She turned the shark-mouthed black 'Mech. Sensitive or not, it was time to make some people feel the wrath of Kali.

"Cassie," Buck Evans said, eyeing the cherry-picker dubiously, "this is a wild-hair scheme even for you."

A fresh firefight had erupted across the hangar. Outside all hell was breaking loose. Cassie was almost dancing with the urgent need to break the stalemate inside before her comrades outside were slaughtered.

"I'll get in the pulpit and you can drive the picker," she said. "I can pilot that *Orion* if you're nervous about it."

The cherry-picker was a dubious-looking proposition in truth. Driven by the desire to avenge their murdered leader, a group of Zuma's Aztechs had rapidly strapped the plates Cassie and Johnny had collected with the forklift into makeshift armor boxes around the pulpit and the driver's cage. It made the thing look like a not-very-talented child's attempt to make a life-sized model of a cherry-picker out of packing crates.

Buck gave her a squinting scowl. "That's cold, Cass. Go on and get behind the wheel of this infernal machine of yours. I'm the MechWarrior here."

He clambered into the pulpit. Cassie slid into the seat through the gap between the makeshift armor and the rollbar.

"What do I do?" Johnny asked.

"Keep your head down, so Lainie's boyfriend doesn't

have to find himself a new holostar after all this is over. Plus I've got some unfinished business with you."

Johnny looked taken aback. He had just admitted to being a spy, and despite the comment about him finishing Takura's holovid, she had a reputation for ruthlessness. And he knew how well she deserved it.

She reached up, grabbed a handful of his black skirt, dragged him toward her for a quick kiss. Then she fired up the cherry-picker's engine.

With a jerk that threatened to loosen his bones, *Tai-i* Daw's chute bit air. The magma rage that had erupted within him when the onboard computer ejected him was still with him, but it was a steady heat, not the wild, turbulent bubble of heartbeats ago. He was getting on top of his anger, riding it like a wave.

With his visor off, Daw's unaided eyes could make little sense of the smoke-shrouded battlefield the BattleMech parking lot had become. The cowardly yakuza still seemed to be dithering outside of the wire, instead of rushing in and squashing the foreigners. Whether his people had managed to get into any of the machines yet he could not tell.

But he felt confidence, even elation, floating up there with the perspective of a god. Surely his people would seize control of enough BattleMechs to smash the money-soldiers and carry out the plan. And even if they had been stalled, he was still alive and free. He'd hit the ground running, seize the initiative from the *gaijin,* and teach them what it meant to trifle with General Kiguri's hand-picked warriors. As he floated toward the short dry grass he was grinning all over his handsome wheat-colored face.

He was wrong again.

Marly Joles was no MechWarrior. She had no faith in their chivalric fancies. Her father had been murdered by allies of the Black Dragons. Her creed was, *one shot, one kill,* and the only kinds of people she recognized in her troubled world were friends and targets.

All the man dangling beneath the pretty yellow dome of

chute was to her was another dose of the only drug she trusted to dull the pain of her father's loss.

She lined him up in the T of the telescopic sight, led him slightly, let out half a breath, caught it, squeezed the trigger. The massive rifle roared and bucked on its tripod.

She knew the shot was good. She could feel it. It was almost anticlimax when the dark distant figure jerked in its shrouds, and then hung limp, as it continued to float down from the sky.

30

Cinema City, Luthien
Pesht Military District, Draconis Combine
1 July 3058

"**C**hoiseul!" O'Hanrahan rapped. "Get back here." The pilot in the damaged *Hornet* had gone rampaging off to
avenge his blown-out ammo supply, enraged that any mere
footslogger would dare attack him. He had found one lying
in a shallow fold in the ground, and was enthusiastically
stamping her into crimson mud. The Black Dragon commander could sympathize, but now wasn't the time. *Ninjo*
over *giri,* and all.

"*Shujin* Choiseul, I'm telling you for the last time—"

Which proved to be literally true. A gray *Nightsky,* with a
black wolf's head with lolling red tongue and glaring green
eyes painted across its jutting chest, dropped from the sky
right behind the stubby little 'Mech. Before Choiseul could
react, it swung its hatchet with all the force of its 50 tons
and split the *Hornet*'s head like a melon.

Then the enemy 'Mech turned its jutting turtle-like head
to face O'Hanrahan in his *Bushwacker.* Something hot
and black seemed to wash from the BattleMech, almost
tangible. O'Hanrahan shrank back in his padded seat. By
the time he recovered enough to cut loose with his large
laser and medium autocannon, and his two Johnston Mini-
guns for good measure, the *Nightsky* had gathered itself and
jumped again, out of harm's way.

In his circle-vision strip O'Hanrahan saw the black *Mad
Cat* burst through the fence behind him, thirty meters to his

left. He spun to bring the autocannon in the *Bushwacker*'s right arm and the big laser in its snout to bear, then was gratified to see hits spark along the black bullet shape, followed by a quick exhalation of smoke as the beam scoured away paint to burn metal beneath.

Moving quickly, the *Cat* swiveled its torso and fired back. The *Bushwacker*'s cockpit lit up as laser beams and a PPC bolt crackled harmlessly past. But the shot from the *Mad Cat*'s right-hand PPC struck the missile launcher that made up the *Wacker*'s right arm and shattered it.

O'Hanrahan's thin lips peeled back from his teeth in a feral grin. "That's a hurt I can bear," he rasped. The long-range missiles hadn't proven much use so far; they were too much to use on mere foot-borne humans, and couldn't come into play now that a close-range knife-fight had broken out.

He spared the breath to curse the *Mad Cat* as it ran clockwise around him, firing constantly. It didn't seem fair: the monster was far better armed and armored than his machine, and yet it was every bit as fast. *And that's why you hated fighting the real Clanners so badly, Terence my lad,* he reminded himself. *Along with every other MechWarrior in the Inner Sphere.*

He realized that the *Mad Cat* was maneuvering to keep his *Bushwacker* between it and Soldaco's *Guillotine*. He darted to his left, still swiveling to try to keep the rapidly moving enemy machine in his sights. From the corner of his eye he saw the jet-black *Blackjack* parked in the compound begin to move. "Am I to assume that one of our black-clad friends is at the controls?" he asked aloud, then answered his own question: "Bold I may be, but foolish I am not."

If the *Jack*'s 45 tons entered the discussion, the weight advantage swung strongly to the *gaijin* . . . and for all O'Hanrahan's confidence in his own ability, he was feeling none too complacent about the ability of his three surviving 'Mechs to handle the Caballeros' two. Their pilots were being quite disobliging about holding still so he could draw a bead on them.

"Bates," he radioed to the Talon Sergeant in charge of his medium lance, "get around here and support us. We've got trouble."

Several things happened at once. The *Blackjack* began to rumble toward the fence, thick laser beams flashing from its arms. The *Mad Cat* with the grinning mouth and the swords painted on its PPCs got behind Soldaco and began lighting the lumbering *Guillotine* up from behind—utterly ignoring the fact that that put Oyama in his little *Javelin* behind it. Duchovny's voice, still controlled, said, " 'Mechs—coming through the wire."

And something suddenly dropped into O'Hanrahan's circle-vision, so perfectly centered behind him that its image appeared at either end of the strip: the *Nightsky*.

His *Bushwacker* rocked to a thunderous impact.

A smile split Gavilán Camacho's darkly handsome face beneath the visor of his neurohelmet. Below him LtJG Yvonne Delgado's 70-ton *Cataphract* parted the fence on the eastern edge of the 'Mech lot like a runner bursting the ribbon at the finish line and strode straight toward a red and black *Spider* that stood like a jacklighted deer. A blast from the *Cataphract*'s Mydron Excel LB-10X autocannon raised sparks from around the two medium lasers mounted in the middle of the *Spider*'s chest and rocked it back on the heels of its two-toed feet.

Gabby's *Merlin* began to descend smoothly from the cloudy sky. For years he had—against his father's wishes—longed to move up from the cockpit of his old *Shadow Hawk* to an assault 'Mech. The heavy haulers were the only truly macho machines, he had been convinced.

But when his old Red-Tailed Hawk was destroyed in the fight for Port Howard, and a rich booty of captured Battle-Mechs, including a number of heavies, became available, to his own amazement Gabby had moved up precisely five tons, to the broad-shouldered squatty 'Mech dubbed *Merlin*. Perhaps his combat experiences on Towne had turned his head around, or being promoted to light colonel and operations officer had forced him for the first time in his life to truly *live* tactical thinking; or maybe he was simply, belatedly, growing up.

Whatever the reason, he had chosen to stay with mobility instead of burdening himself with a thunder-thighed *Atlas* or *Katana.* Granted, the *Merlin* was a touch slower than the old *Shad,* and couldn't jump as far. But it packed a hell of a lot more firepower. Maybe even better, it was new construction, literally centuries younger than his former ride, which meant it didn't require the personal intercession of the Virgin of Guadalupe—with abundant assistance from Zuma Gallegos—to keep it running.

Now—with that newfound tactical insight of his—Gabby could all but read the *Spider* jock's mind. The poor *pendejo* was dead set on keeping footsloggers *out.* Now that the Black Dragon MechWarriors had failed at that, they were confronted with BattleMechs trying to bust out from the inside. The question of what exactly the *Spider*'s tactical role was now had obviously frozen its pilot.

The *Spider* opted to get the hell out of Dodge, which as far as Gabby was concerned was the right decision. It began to dart north, toward the road to Imperial City. It kept its torso twisted to shoot at Delgado's *Cataphract,* and Delgado kept firing back.

Gabby settled for bringing his jumping 'Mech down behind the stumpy *UrbanMech* that was the second-heaviest machine in the lance on this side. The *Urb* turned gamely to face him with its medium autocannon and small laser—not that it had much choice, since aside from being twice as heavy, the *Merlin* was twice as fast, and could run it down like a hawk diving on a chicken.

A volley of long-range missiles from the farther of the two *Hornet*s that made up the rest of the Black Dragon lance missed him as he grounded. The final *Hornet* was shooting at him with its medium laser from closer range. He barely paid attention. A single medium flashlight wasn't a big threat—and besides, the Dragons on this side were about to be swamped, as a 'llero *Commando* popped the wire behind the nearer *Hornet* and Cowboy Payson's new *Venom* descended from the sky beside the moving *Spider.*

The little trash-can *UrbanMech* was tough for such a small 'Mech. Its autocannon punched chunks from the *Merlin*'s frontal plate. But standing still the bigger 'Mech could fire its full array of energy weapons without running up the heat too seriously. One medium laser reduced the *Urb*'s

Imperator-B autocannon to slag. The *Merlin*'s PPC and other medium laser punished its torso. The *UrbanMech* bled molten metal, exploded, died. The pilot never ejected.

Glancing into his 360-strip Gabby saw the *Spider* lying on the ground with its right leg blown off. Cowboy and the big *Cataphract* were turning back to help polish off the remaining two 20-ton *Hornets*.

Recognizing that their situation was hopeless, the *Hornets* fled for the woods north of the highway. "Let 'em go," Gabby ordered over the command channel. *The Virgin knows where they think they're going,* he thought. *If they were smart they'd fight to the end.*

He ordered his 'Mechs north, to attack the lance that was still dithering along that side of the perimeter.

From all directions bullets and laser beams cracked against the improvised armor-plate box surrounding the driver's compartment of the cherry-picker. Despite having her soft-shell hood up, the hard helmet on, and red visor down, Cassie kept her head as low as she could and still see to steer the unwieldy vehicle among the bins and piles and parked BattleMechs. Of Buck Evans, in the armored pulpit, there was no sign. *Smart boy.*

A grenade struck the lip of the armor box, bounced high, fell outside the driver's compartment and exploded. Cassie winced and ducked as whining fragments ricocheted off the rollbar over her head. *Hijo lá, that was too close!*

They reached the feet of Buck's *Orion*. Cassie hit the button to lift the pulpit. The extensor motor whined in protest at the extra weight, but it had been designed to hoist heavy replacement components, and the pulpit rose smoothly. She crouched low on the seat, unsheathed her vibrokatana, drew an autopistol from a shoulder holster and held it in her left hand.

Realizing they were fast running out of options, seven DEST commandos broke from cover and converged on the cherry-picker. The Caballeros in the repair hangar were dug-in and waiting for just that move. A horizontal storm of gunfire knocked the charging figures sprawling despite their midnight armor.

General Kiguri had trained his operatives well, imbued them with a fanatical spirit of determination. Two of them actually reached the cherry-picker. The first swarmed up the side of the strapped-on armor box, his sword upraised. Cassie popped up and thrust her vibroblade edge-up through his belly. He fell backward, torqueing the weapon from her hands.

The other one had grenades in either hand, pins pulled. Cassie ducked back down, laid her autopistol sideways on the armor plate and started jacking slugs into him. A hit in the solar plexus doubled him over. One grenade dropped to his feet and went off, hurling him into a bin of parts. The other exploded harmlessly in a clear patch of floor.

The pulpit reached the *Orion*'s hatch. The commando who had impaled himself on Cassie's sword rose to his feet as though levitating, grasped the cord-wrapped hilt, tried to pull the weapon from his body for a final banzai assault. Unfortunately, he didn't realize the nature of the weapon that had transfixed him. Its microserrated edge, vibrating at thousands of cycles per second, rendered it as much sharper than a *katana* as one of those classic samurai swords was sharper than a butter knife.

When the blade came free, his intestines came with it, trailing down the front of his legs in bloody-greasy loops.

High in the air, Buck hit the access patch. The *Orion*'s cockpit hatch opened. He somersaulted into the 'Mech as bullets clattered against Valiant Lamellor plate all around him. The hatch closed.

Cassie threw the cherry-picker in reverse. The DEST commando who had inadvertently disemboweled himself was approaching from behind, stumbling over his guts, still gripping her sword. She backed straight over him.

Red lights flashed in O'Hanrahan's heads-up display. The damned *Nightsky* had taken advantage of his distraction to drop down right behind him and slam his *Bushwacker* with that beastly hatchet.

Flashing impressions: the *Mad Cat*, grinning hatefully, literally running rings around Soldaco's *Guillotine*, pounding it with flickering pulses of its lasers, eye-searing gouts of PPC lightning, and volleys from the six-shot SRM boxes mounted on either shoulder, allowing Soldaco small opportunity to retaliate with his own impressive armament. Oyama's *Javelin* loosing a double volley of its own short-range missiles at the *Blackjack* and jumping away—and knocked tumbling as the *Jack*'s four torso-mounted Streak launchers locked onto it and slammed eight missiles into the smaller 'Mech.

As Oyama's 'Mech landed hard, O'Hanrahan threw the *Bushwacker* into a forward run. The *Nightsky* could catch him readily enough, but fleeing wasn't his aim. The *Bushwacker* wasn't a particularly agile machine; he wanted to separate enough to turn and fight his lighter assailant.

His move seemed to take his opponent by surprise. The moment it took the *Nightsky* jock to react and lunge in pursuit allowed O'Hanrahan to wheel his wide ride quickly enough to threaten its gyroscopically maintained balance. A skilled pilot, the Black Dragon captain held the machine upright and blasted the enemy 'Mech.

The *Bushwacker* had only two major weapons operational, but the autocannon and big laser were not to be sneered at. Their blast staggered the *Nightsky* even as it charged. A yellow-glowing crater appeared in the midst of the 'Mech's jutting, keel-like breast. The medium Sutel pulse laser set into the left side of its chest exploded to a staccato of cannon hits.

The *Nightsky* retaliated with its other chest-mounted laser, the large laser in its arm and the small one in its turtle-like head. O'Hanrahan cried out as a stutter of beams stabbed into his cockpit, blasting open the cooling vest on the left side of his body and setting the padding of his seat on fire.

The *Bushwacker*'s damage-control computer damped the fire out beneath an immediate spray of flame-retarding foam. The *Nightsky* was on top of it then, raining savage blows with its hatchet, neglecting its laser battery. O'Hanrahan triggered all his weapons at the enemy 'Mech, even the launcher mounted above its right shoulder, though the long-range missiles would not track. The large laser and the cannon tore man-sized chunks from the *Nightsky*'s armor, yet the pilot continued to stand and smash at his foe.

"Who are you?" O'Hanrahan cried desperately over his loudspeaker. "*What* are you?"

"I am a witch," replied Bobby the Wolf. "I am your death."

The large laser bored deep into the *Nightsky*'s vitals. Smoke began to wreathe the 'Mech's upper body. *Just keep it up a trifle longer, my bucko,* O'Hanrahan thought, tasting blood from where he'd bitten his lip to one of the mind-jarring impacts. *I'll kindle your engine into a sun beneath you yet.*

The *Nightsky*'s left arm fell away from a shattered shoulder activator, bleeding sparks from traumatically amputated cables. And the hatchet came smashing down through the *Bushwacker*'s armored canopy and slanted transpex canopy and crushed the life from Terence O'Hanrahan.

Robert Begay took a step back from the shattered hulk of the enemy 'Mech. He raised his hatchet, dripping his enemy's blood, in salute.

"Dah itsáá," he declared: *death occurs.* Then he punched out, half a heartbeat before his fusion engine suffered catastrophic decontainment and consumed the upper half of his machine in a blue-white flash.

The *Guillotine*'s jump had not served to win the 'Mech free of Kali's attentions, but they did give the pilot the opportunity to turn his machine in midair and, finally, return her fire. Her 'Mech's fuselage rang and groaned under the impact of a rocket salvo.

"You're brave and good," Kali acknowledged as his large laser caused molten armor plate to stream down the *Mad Cat*'s right flank. "But it's not enough."

Because Terry Carrington's *Blackjack,* after giving the fallen *Jav* a quick dose of laser fire as it struggled to rise, was ignoring the damaged smaller machine to concentrate its own battery on the jumping *Guillotine.* Its two large lasers drew lines on the *Guillotine*'s body that glowed sullen red against the leaden sky, even as a hit from her PPC burned the armor-plate and myomer pseudomusculature completely away from its right thigh, exposing the endo steel skeleton beneath.

The *Black Dragon* heavy began to descend—right for Kali's canopy. *Suicide plunge.* "All right," she said. "We'll play it your way."

She flayed him with her entire arsenal at once, sending the heat-indicators soaring past the red line and making alarms scream in her ears. The cockpit became a tight, claustrophobic oven. Her sweat seemed to boil away from her skin.

The *Guillotine*'s large laser sheared away her 'Mech's right arm. Its huge split spatulate feet filled her windscreen.

She pirouetted the 75-ton *Mad Cat* clockwise with the grace of a ballerina. The *Guillotine*'s disabled right leg buckled as it slammed the packed ground where Kali's 'Mech had stood an instant before. Terry's *Blackjack* joined Kali in blasting open the *Guillotine*'s back as it crumpled forward into a tangle of smoking metal ruin.

Terence O'Hanrahan was a skillful MechWarrior and a good commander. His MechWarriors were a mixed bag but not far off the mark of a DCMS regular unit. But demon circumstance had just flat caught them out.

They were never *supposed* to fight. They had been ordered into this op to show the flag for *Kokuryu-kai* and keep the always-arrogant DEST commandos from deciding they had done everything themselves. Everybody, including Kiguri and his commander on the scene Daw, had expected the Caballeros to be surprised and overcome as they slept—to simply roll over.

They hadn't counted on Cassie—nor good old Southwestern cussedness.

That the *gaijin* had mounted any resistance at all caught the Black Dragons by surprise, and their DEST allies no less. And their prejudices had left them unprepared for the crazy savagery of the Caballero response.

Kashira Bates' medium lance had been frozen, uncertain which way to turn as *gaijin* 'Mechs struck out from both sides of the compound. A single *Valkyrie* sniping from among the parked 'Mechs, and the sporadic SRMs fired by dismounted Caballeros out among the weeds, had added to their indecision.

Bates had no sooner decided to support his commander, and ordered his lance to the west side of the compound, than Gavilán Camacho led his 'Mechs—who had routed the Black Dragon light lance without loss—right into their rear. Though Bobby the Wolf's *Nightsky* was a write-off, and Kali's reactor shut down with her final blast at Soldaco's *Guillotine*, Terry Carrington's undamaged *Blackjack* was an ample anvil for Gabby's hammer to smash the Black Dragon lance against.

His gas mask pushed up on his curly red hair, the Rooster briefly gripped Cassie's right biceps. The left was unavailable, being firmly pressed against Johnny Tchang's side. "Good job," the Scout Platoon boss said.

Both ducked and winced to the crack of a medium laser going off nearby. Buck's *Orion* had literally blasted apart the nests of commandos dug into the clutter of the hangar with his shotgun-like LB-10X. Now he was neutralizing— that was a nice way to put it—individual holdouts one by one.

"We sprang the Voice of the Dragon security staff," the Rooster went on. "The DEST boys were holding 'em captive in their own barracks. They had our host Migaki locked up in his apartment, too."

He shook his head and grinned. "Our handsome friend Tak's mad enough to chew up Durallex and spit out bullets, let me tell you."

Cassie's grin of response bore only a passing resemblance to a pleasant expression. "He's not the only one."

"Jimmy Skowron tried to pass the word to the Dracs about what happened. Got somebody from Otomo who brushed him off."

"What about Uncle Chandy?"

The Rooster shrugged. "He's already off at the big dance with Teddy. Parade's already started."

"I guess you're going to be late," Johnny Tchang said.

Cassie shot him a poison glare, then caught herself,

smoothed the furrows out of her brow, and smiled. "Yeah," she said. "I guess we are."

Maccabee Bar-Kochba came limping by, supported by Sharon Omizuki. Both had taken part in the hangar attack, since Bar-Kochba wasn't spry enough to go climbing up the front of his *Warhammer,* and Sharon's *Shilone* was parked on an apron at Takashi Kurita Memorial Spaceport. The right leg of the Second Battalion commander's trousers were dark with blood. Still, Cassie had the impression maybe he didn't need quite as much help as Sharon was giving him. On the other hand, he didn't seem at all bothered by the fact.

"What happened?" Cassie asked.

"Grenade fragment got me in the ass," Bar-Kochba said in his gruff twang. "Reckon it's my fault for letting it get to be such a large target. But then, it's pretty well padded, too, so I guess it all evens out."

"So that's it," Sharon said, shaking her head in wonder. "We won. We actually took on DEST commandos and beat them."

"We've done it before," said a passing Caballero with studied nonchalance.

"Not only that," Johnny said. "You beat the Black Dragon Society—*and* saved the Coordinator of the Draconis Combine."

Bar-Kochba shook his balding sunburned head. "Who'd've thought it? Us saving the lord of all Snakes. Strange damn world we live in."

"I guess it doesn't matter now," Cassie said to Johnny as the injured officer and his helper continued on, "but I don't understand how what that *metsuke* woman told me fits with all this. What the hell was 'sadat?' "

Bar-Kochba stopped, turned. "Sadat, you said?"

For a moment Cassie thought he was trying to make a play on words. "Yeah. That agent the DEST hunters killed. She told me the code-word 'sadat' as if it was the key to the whole damn scam. Sub—that is, Drac intelligence turned up like three thousand references to the word when they ran a search on it, and if they ever figured out what its significance was, nobody ever told me about it."

The grizzled MechWarrior frowned thoughtfully. "Well, that name's got a certain significance in our history—Jew-boys, that is, not Southwesterners as a whole."

"What's that?"

"Guy named Sadat was the first Arab leader to make his peace with Israel, away back before the Big Sell-Out and the Second Diaspora." He chuckled and shook his head. "He was actually a real ring-tailed bastard, but you still got to give him credit for the courage it took to do that thing. And for a reward, his own bodyguard turned on him while they were passing in review one fine day and blew him straight into Allah's arms."

"Cassie," Sharon said. "What's the matter? Are you all right?"

"No." She felt as if she'd been simultaneously punched in the stomach and dipped in ice water. She waved at Rooster, who was a few steps away talking to Risky Savage in under-tones.

"Call Billy Skowron, tell him to roust out Takura Migaki. We need that chopper of his."

"You need a pilot?" Sharon asked.

"Can you fly a helicopter?"

"Well—I never have. But flying's flying."

"Sharon, you're a Sierra Hotel aerospace jock, but this is no time for OJT. We need to get to Impy City *now*, even if we have to get Tak himself to fly us there."

"What's going on, Cass?" Bar-Kochba asked.

She turned him a face gone the color of rice paper. "It isn't over yet. Theodore Kurita's still in danger!"

31

Unity Square, Imperial City
Luthien
Pesht Military District, Draconis Combine
1 July 3058

"**T**ono," an aide said, his head near Theodore Kurita's ear so that the Coordinator could hear his soft words over the constant susurration from the crowd and the rumble of the BattleMechs of the Seventh Imperial City Militia, proud veterans of savage street fighting against the Nova Cats during the Clan invasion, passing in review before the Imperial stands. "There has been some disturbance at Eiga-toshi. The Seventeenth Reconnaissance Regiment's appearance has been unavoidably delayed."

Standing near enough on the other side of the aide to hear, Shigeru Yoshida twisted his thin features in a sneer. He longed to be piloting his *Cyclops* at the head of his elite First Sword of Light regiment, which he still commanded, on this day of pride. The ritual obligation that forced him as chief Military Minister to be standing here passively in the stands while his 'Mechs marched past visibly chafed him.

"The turbulent *yohei* are making waves again," he said. "They're more trouble than they're worth. You should never have invited them."

Uncle Chandy lolled at ease among silken cushions—protocol be damned, though he pleaded arthritis of the knees—none too close on the other side of Theodore from the aide and Yoshida. He had a parasol shading him from the spring sun, which was already hot at this early hour. A pair of striking young women whom he swore to be his personal bodyguards stood flanking him and ministering to his wishes. They were clad in smart uniforms of gray and gold-trimmed maroon, with little short-billed caps. Somehow Theodore doubted that their purpose was militant.

"My loyal employees from the Southwestern worlds," Chandy said, sipping at a cool rum punch, "seldom start trouble, friend Yoshida. Yet I find them quite adept at stopping it."

Yoshida grunted and held his head up higher. He held the Coordinator's cousin in greater contempt than he held even foreign money-troopers. And that was great enough; he would only unbend for Wolf's Dragoons, and them only because their 'Mechs had fought beside his, saving the Black Pearl from the Clans.

Theodore looked around the grandstand, which was erected on the western edge of vast Unity Square, with the high east wall of the Palace grounds at its back and Otomo BattleMechs standing attentively at either end. It was comparatively small, meant to accommodate only a few hundred persons out of the vast crush attending the Coordinator's Birthday festivities: members of the Imperial household, high-ranking officials, various other dignitaries—including, to Theodore's vast distaste, Benjamin Inagawa, the prominent, ah, industrialist. *At least his wizened little reptile of a partner Toyama isn't on hand.*

Though Voice of the Dragon sound and holo crews were everywhere, there was no sign of their master. That was unusual. While the propaganda chief tended to keep his own hours, as he did his own counsel, and punctuality wasn't the foremost of his virtues, Theodore seldom knew him to be tardy when there was a spectacle to capture with his holo-cameras, and later recast into something far grander and purer and more stirring than it actually had been.

The absence of Migaki's boss was less problematical. Ill health and the lower profile Subhash Indrahar had been keeping since rapprochement had been achieved with the Federated Commonwealth had kept the Smiling One away from these occasions for several years.

The militia 'Mechs passed, followed by a unit of conventional armored vehicles, track-laying and hovercraft, from

Galedon V, which had been chosen by lot to receive the honor of taking part in this year's grand review. Beyond them two million exultant faces gazed at the war machines and the single man, still tall and slim, who ruled them all, the millions more packed along both sides of the parade route through the streets of Imperial City, and billions of souls beyond across a world and a vast volume of space.

Like a high-urban counterpart to Unity Park on the west side of the palace, with its birch trees and magisterial sequoias around Siriwan's Peace Pool, Unity Square was a patch of cement a kilometer on a side for holding massive rallies and ceremonies such as this one, to foster the collective spirit of the Combine people, to overawe the Dragon's enemies, and—most of all, Theodore suspected—to gratify the more-than-incipient megalomania that formed such a common component of Kurita character.

It took great force of will to ace all that adulation—far more than it took to pilot a BattleMech into combat against apparently hopeless odds. Despite his nightmares, and his fears that he was falling prey to the madness that sometimes seemed endemic among rulers of the Inner Sphere, one thing Theodore Kurita conspicuously lacked was megalomania. He derived no pleasure from having life-or-death power over billions of subjects—only a crushing sense of the responsibility he bore in trying to steer them safely through these increasingly desperate days. As for the adulation that emanated from the throng and washed over him more palpably than the stinging light of the sun, it made his skin creep with embarrassment.

This is my duty, he thought: to stand and be a symbol, a rock to anchor his people's hopes and buttress them against their fears. He must stand straight and display nothing but serene, composed confidence, no matter how he felt. *Ninjo* over *giri,* again.

The aide materialized at Theodore's elbow again. The Coordinator inclined his head slightly to listen.

"*Tono,* the Grand Marshal apologizes humbly and begs to report a slight change of precedence," the aide murmured. "*Tai-sa* Oda Hideyoshi has decided that he will best do honor to the Coordinator by inserting his special Battle-

Mech company into the procession ahead of schedule, right behind the Twenty-third Galedon Armored Regiment. Does this meet the Coordinator's approval?"

A corner of Theodore's mouth quirked up in a not-quite suppressed smile. *The loyal old war-horse is impatient to show off,* he thought. The showpiece of the Coordinator's Birthday Parade was to be the unveiling of seven of Luthien Armor Works' new OmniMech designs for the first time in public, piloted by Hideyoshi and eleven select Otomo MechWarriors. Presumably the Otomo commander was unaware that Uncle Chandy's mercenaries were going to be held up, and wanted to make sure the Coordinator's eye fell upon his new machines before it got a load of the Luthien Armor Works *Naga* knock-off the mercenaries had tested on Towne.

The request was irregular—but as Theodore knew too well, what would *really* be irregular was for anything as complicated as his birthday celebration to go off altogether as planned. Despite centuries of attempted regimentation, that was how things worked in the Draconis Combine: everything was intricately and meticulously scheduled, but nothing ever *happened* on schedule. And the Otomo traditionally obeyed no rule but the Coordinator's welfare and the Coordinator's pleasure.

"The Colonel has earned the right to serve the Dragon as he deems best," Theodore said. "Of course I approve."

"What's our ETA?" Cassie asked from the right-hand seat as the helicopter jumped into the smoke-scented air above Eiga-toshi. When Migaki converted his *Warrior* from an attack ship, he'd had the armor stripped off and the cockpit changed from tandem to side-by-side configuration. She did not need to shout or use an intercom to make herself heard above the nose of the contrarotating rotors. The Voice of the Dragon chief had added insulation to his movie-making command craft too.

"A little over six minutes," said Takura Migaki. His handsome face was impassive, but very pale, and when he wasn't speaking his lips were almost white and almost invisible. Despite that he managed to look natty in blue blazer and fashionable black *hakama* with white circles on it. It took more than having his holovid complex invaded and personally being captured and threatened with execution to ruffle his fashion sense.

Cassie shifted the autoloading combat shotgun between her knees, since it did seem to make Migaki uncomfortable to have its cavernous black muzzle pointed at his ear. She was still kicking herself for not thinking of it before going DEST-hunting. A standard load of buckshot would stand a lot better chance of incapacitating a target than a couple of penny-ante hits from a machine pistol, body armor notwithstanding. And she also had a couple of mags loaded with discarding-sabot rounds containing sharpened iridium drill-bit penetrators that would punch through anything short of a Clan Elemental's battle armor. Beyond that she had her vibrokatana slung over one shoulder and heavy autopistols in shoulder rigs under each armpit. She was ready for serious social work.

"If traffic control at Takashi Memorial doesn't decide we're a threat to the Coordinator and have us shot down," said Johnny Tchang, who was hunkered down behind the front seats looking between Migaki and Cassie.

Migaki didn't look back, but he grinned. "Nobody's going to shoot us down. I've got my special go-anywhere IFF transmitter keyed," he said. "There is nowhere in the Draconis Combine we can't go right now. I'm not Associate Director of the Internal Security Force for nothing."

"Speaking of which—" Cassie extended the earphone from her pocket com and stuck it in her ear. Then she keyed the special direct-access code Subhash Indrahar had given her.

"Indrahar," a voice answered. It was a familiar voice— but not the one she'd been expecting.

"Ninyu Kerai?" Both Migaki and Johnny were suddenly looking at her very intently. "What are you doing on this channel?"

"I might ask the same of you."

"I've been working with your father. There's a plot against Theodore—"

"I know about that. My father is dead. He left me a message."

Cassie briefly closed her eyes. "I'm sorry. And you don't know the whole scam. Kiguri planned to steal our 'Mechs and use them to assassinate the Coordinator. We wiped out his strike force. He didn't come himself, and he's still at large."

"Useful information, Lieutenant. I shall neutralize Kiguri myself."

"Wait! Don't sign off! We have . . . information that some of Theodore's Otomo bodyguards are going to try to kill him at the review. It's Kiguri's backup plan."

"Otomo? Are you serious?"

"Deadly serious."

"I find that hard to believe."

"Do you trust my competence? It's your call, Mr. Director."

"Acting Director."

That showed how shaken Ninyu actually was. For him to waste syllables like that was virtually equivalent to gibbering panic for another man.

"Get the Coordinator off the stands and into safety. If I'm steering you wrong you can shoot me later."

"That might prove difficult," Ninyu admitted. "We are already engaged in combat with traitors in the Palace."

Cassie sucked in a long breath. "I'll do what I can. Suthorn out."

Johnny was still staring at her as if she had turned into a giant varan lizard from the Nijunen Desert. Migaki kept sneaking her as many sidelong looks as he could and still drive the chopper at top speed.

"Like I told him, I've been working with the Smiling One. It's only for this gig, O.K.?"

Johnny sat back on his haunches, shaking his head. Cassie looked at Migaki. "Can you tune your comm unit to a standard military command channel?"

"Anything you wish, Lieutenant Senior Grade. As I said—perqs of the position."

"Great." She reached over and began punching buttons on his console. That earned her a raised eyebrow, and then the dapper propaganda boss slipped off his headset and handed it to her.

"Red Witch, this is Abtakha," she said, holding one earpiece to her ear. "Abtakha calling Red Witch. Come in, *please*."

"Clear the way! *Chikusho!* Get off the sidewalks, you pedestrians! What the hell's the matter with you?" Onlookers gaped in amazement and then scattered for their lives as the 90-ton *Mauler* left the blacktopped surface of Dragon Way to go crunching at a run along sidewalks that buckled noisily at every step.

Emotions clashed inside *Tai-sa* Eleanor Shimazu like a flood tide crashing against a mighty river's outflow in a booming tidal bore. She had been preparing for this moment ever since learning that her father's murderer was on Luthien. Her plan was simple: she would march her *Mauler* past the reviewing stands at the head of her regiment. When she reached the point where Benjamin Inagawa stood, she would stop, turn, announce her identity by external speaker, and then vaporize him with one of her large lasers. Then she would power down her 'Mech, explain her actions to the Coordinator, apologize for dishonoring him, and surrender. She would hope that in view of her loyal service Theodore Kurita would allow her to commit honorable seppuku. But if he decreed she must be disgracefully executed, she would submit without demur. Just like the 47 ronin in that historical holovid Takura was making.

But now she was deferring all that. She had just ordered her lead company of Heruzu Enjeruzu—Hell's Angels, the Ninth Ghost Legion—to blow forward full tilt and reach the Coordinator's stands *now,* no matter what the cost, past battalions of BattleMechs packed into the streets like queues of Workers waiting for the tube.

For the last couple of years she'd heard constantly from her Caballero friends that no plan survived first contact with Cassie Suthorn. During the fight the accursed higher-ups—most of whom were now dead—had forced the 'lleros and the Enjeruzu into on Hachiman, Lainie and Cassie's paths had never crossed, since the scout had been off bedeviling none other than Ninyu Kerai and his black-clad elves. So it was only now that Lainie was confronted with the truth of that Caballero aphorism.

The red-painted head of a *Hatamoto-chi*, designed to resemble that of a helmeted samurai, turned toward her as she crowded past the trail elements of the Seventh Sword of Light Regiment, the Teak Dragon. Its chevron-shaped viewscreen somehow seemed to express surprise and outrage. "Ten thousand apologies," she radioed. "It's an emergency!"

Then she switched off the general comm channel. She doubted the stiff-necked Sword of Light commanders would be in any mood to listen to reason. She knew she was in no mood to listen to their abuse.

One thing was sure: there were going to be many devils to pay if this proved to be a wild-goose chase. Lainie "the Red Witch" Shimazu was wild-hair unorthodox even by the standards of the half-outlaw Ghost Legions, but she would have thought twice or ten times about blasting protocol this comprehensively to hell if she hadn't already been settled on suicide, hence "living as one already dead."

She was risking more than just her career on this mad dash. MechWarriors across the Sphere were touchy as ancient samurai, who used to draw on each other and get it on with serious intent if their scabbards clashed when they passed on the street. A Sword of Light *Grand Dragon*, taking offense at her jostling, turned its torso to bring the Lord's Light 2 extended-range PPC in its right arm to bear on Lainie's *Mauler*.

Yamabushi, the fat former monk, came trundling down the far side of Dragon Way in his *Axman*, and fetched the *Grand Dragon* a mighty whack across the back with the flat of his double-bitted axe. The *Dragon*, slightly lighter, somewhat top-heavy, and caught totally unawares, toppled forward. It struck the back of the mighty *Grand Titan* jammed in tight ahead of it and made *it* fall. And so it went down the line, Teak Dragon BattleMechs knocking each other down one after the other like scarlet dominoes, keeping pace with her *Mauler*'s rather stately run until the lead machine fell onto the tail Von Luckner tank of some provincial militia unit, trapping the hapless crew but breaking the reaction chain.

Lainie shook her head. She was still confused as to how she felt at having her meticulously plotted-out denouement derailed. Frustrated—and also relieved.

Maybe I shouldn't be so torqued-off at Cassie, she thought with bitter humor, *for delaying my getting myself killed.*

She crushed a kiosk selling gaily painted paper kites shaped like fish, and kept on running.

The OmniMechs of the special Otomo demonstration company came marching down Dragon Way two by two. First a pair of 25-ton RTX1-0 *Raptor*s, back-kneed and headless. Next strode two *Owen*s, 35 tons, which amounted to blockier flightless *Jenner*s, followed by 40-ton *Strider*s, which were derived from the old *Cicada*. After them came two of the BJ2-0 *Blackjack* Omni redesign, which had been exported heavily and even license-built by Irian—and, to Theodore's embarrassment, had seen service with Liao and Marik forces during their invasion of the Chaos March. Next were two *Black Hawk-KU,* almost exact copies of the 60-ton Clan machine. After it walked a 70-ton *Avatar,* Luthien Armor Work's answer to the *Vulture*. And last of all marched a *Sunder*, piloted by *Tai-sa* Hideyoshi himself, a 90-ton hybrid of the Clan *Thor* and *Loki* Omnis. All twelve machines were enameled gleaming white, with the red, black, and gold Kurita dragon emblem proudly painted on them.

"Impressive machines," muttered Yoshida, who stood at Theodore's side. "Still, I wouldn't trade my *Cyclops* for any of them. Give me proven technology, not an imitation of engineering we halfway understand."

Theodore nodded in qualified agreement. He had personally approved—indeed mandated—the crash Luthien Armor Works program for building OmniMech clones. He was reasonably pleased with the results. Still, many of the designs were experiencing teething problems; neither of the *Firestarter II* Omnis LAW had provided Otomo could be persuaded to function at all. Were he able to allow himself the indulgence of leading troops in combat again, he'd want a proven design, even one of the new *Naginata*s, rather than one of these bastard OmniMechs.

When they formed a line before the jutting podium on which Theodore stood with sweat trickling down inside the standup collar of his dress uniform, the Otomo Omnis stopped. With a creaking of mechanical joints and a grinding and groaning of metal feet on cement, they turned to face the stands.

Yoshida stiffened. "What's this?"

"Looks as if they want to make some sort of presentation," Theodore said quietly. He noted that his cousin Chandrasekhar halted with his goblet halfway to his lips, and quickly handed the drink to one of his female bodyguards.

"People of the Draconis Combine," Hideyoshi's voice crackled from the loudspeakers of the *Sunder*, "a great moment has come. Now is the time when the traitor and usurper Theodore Kurita must pay for the murder of his father!"

32

Unity Square, Imperial City
Luthien
Pesht Military District, Draconis Combine
1 July 3058

Silence fell on the vast crowd like a kilometer-square sheet of transpex from heaven. At Theodore's side, Yoshida's normally squinty eyes opened so wide they stood out of his narrow face. Theodore himself felt nothing, as if his reactions were packed away in shaved-plastic insulation. Without his family there on the dais with him, he had nothing he felt an urgent need to protect. *Let someone else fight the Clans single-handed. . . .*

"We knew that you murdered your father," the amplified voice boomed, while the great crowd muttered and jostled in consternation. "Yet you left us alive and in place, compounding our disgrace. But we have bided our time and waited, sleeping on kindling and licking gall, like the forty-seven ronin. Until our time came to strike.

"That time is now!"

The *Sunder* raised the two medium Diverse Optics pulse lasers that made up its right arm. The other OmniMechs followed suit. A collective gasp rose from the crowd like an immense flock of doves taking flight. Theodore reflected that white was the color of death.

A rushing sound drowned out the noise of the crowd. Theodore glanced up to see a trio of painfully bright blue suns in a tight constellation, the jump jets of one of the new *Stealth* BattleMechs whose purchase from the Lyran Alliance he had personally approved, descending seemingly right on top of him. As he watched in amazement, the black-painted 'Mech cut loose against the rebel Omnis with lasers and shortrange missile volleys.

By reflex the whole demonstration company cut loose on the interloper at once as it came down between them and the Coordinator. The 45-ton 'Mech was blasted literally to pieces in midair. As the *Stealth*'s components rained down on the stands and the pavement before the would-be assassins, 'Mech-mounted weapons fire began to slash at them from their right, which was the way they and the rest of the parade had come.

The spell was broken. Unwilling to act until now for fear of costing the Coordinator face, Yoshida shoved aside a small round red cap inset in the floor of the dais and pressed the button it had concealed with the toe of a mirror-polished boot.

Along with megalomania, paranoia was another distinguishing feature of the Kurita dynasty. And just as absolute rulership over billions of human beings might understandably foster a certain sense of grandeur, the Kuritas had real enemies. Not all that many Coordinators had died in bed, and not even those who had done so without assistance.

That loyal MechWarriors might take it upon themselves to blast their beloved Coordinator into his component atoms as they passed in review had occurred to one of Theodore's ancestors long ago. Appropriate steps had been taken.

Triggered by the defense minister, a fifteen-meter-tall shield of transpex one meter thick shot up from beneath the thin layer of pavement that had concealed it. Three-sided, so that from above it resembled a U opening toward the palace, it surrounded the podium, blocking off the assassin's fire.

A laser beam struck the shield, filling the sudden enclosure with ruby glare. Billions of tiny reflective flakes scattered throughout the transpex deresolved the beam and rendered it harmless. Beyond the shield, BattleMechs were jumping into the air above the square while panicked onlookers fled screaming.

"Very good," said Uncle Chandy, standing now. His words echoed slightly between the transpex walls. The sound of the 'Mech battle building beyond them was muted by the thick synthetic, rendering conversation just possible. "But it's open at the top, and won't withstand heavy fire forever. We'd best be on our way." His feminine bodyguards had produced efficient-looking laser pistols and stood coolly flanking him.

Theodore looked to the four Otomo guardsmen who shared the podium with his personal party. Their body language and the dead-man's pallor beneath the visors of their ceremonial armor spoke eloquently.

"W-we are loyal, lord," one said. "We had no idea."

Theodore nodded. He had no choice but to trust them, and besides, if they'd been in on the plot, they'd had ample opportunity to shoot him in the back. Four SRMs slammed into the shield, making it vibrate and ring like a musical saw. Cracks appeared in the thick transpex.

"Go," he said. They turned and trotted to the rear of the podium. At the back, stairs led down to a four-meter-wide swath of pavement running between the grandstand and the high Palace wall. Directly across from the steps, a concealed door hissed open as one of the Otomo guards triggered it with a remote controller.

Reaching the inviting blackness of the doorway, the guard suddenly stopped. A handspan of steel, gleaming almost greenish in indirect sunlight, thrust out through his back.

"Slam 'em! Slam 'em! Slam 'em!" Lainie shouted over her commline. A company's worth of Ghost 'Mechs had reached Unity Square with her. As she had ordered, they'd winged out into the Square to take the traitor 'Mechs in the rear. Yamabushi had jumped is *Axman* clear down to the end of the line to fell a *Raptor* with a single blow of its axe to absurdly thin rear armor. The big crested 'Mech kicked its downed opponent contemptuously aside, then buried its axe to the helve in another Omni when it turned to engage. "And if you shoot toward the stands, make damn sure you hit what you're aiming at."

"What about the spectators?" someone asked.

"Mujo," she answered simply. "My responsibility."

As if in direct response Ho Jung-V's 100-ton *Pillager* set down in the square, its HildCO Model 13 jump jets turning a dozen hapless onlookers into screaming torches before its great feet mercifully crushed them. The two Gauss rifles in its torso fired, the hypersonic rounds cracking like thunder before they slammed into the back of a *Black Hawk-KU*. One shot instantly locked the shoulder-actuator of its left arm, which carried a total of five medium lasers. Black smoke poured from the hole the other hit had punched in its armor.

Two Ghost *Owen*s and a *Hitman* dashed forward, interposing themselves between the Otomo weapons and the Coordinator. Lainie was walking her *Mauler* down the middle of Dragon Way now, wading through the hovercraft of a scout company that had been stalled by Hideyoshi's preemption. She hoped the pilots had had the sense to bail out. Flanking her were Billy Dragomil in his *Marauder*-derived *Dragon Fire* and Sari DeLeeuw in her *War Dog*. All three 'Mechs were concentrating heavy weapons-fire on the right side of the *Sunder* piloted by Hideyoshi himself.

One of the things Lainie had been big on during the re-outfitting of Heruzu Enjeruzu that had followed their disastrous battle with the Caballeros on Hachiman was getting as many 'Mechs mounting Gauss rifles as possible. They exemplified the phrase *long-range, low-heat* that MechWarriors used for the best of the best. Sari's *War Dog* and Billy's *Dragon Fire* mounted them, along with an impressive assortment of other weapons. They were adding their punch to that of Lainie's two big arm-mounted lasers. The two medium pulse lasers that made up the *Sunder*'s left arm were shattered and the big Omni's whole right side began to glow red like iron heated in a forge.

"Taking fire from behind!" the voice of Joe Shen, bringing up the rear in a *Daikyu*, yelled in Lainie's headset. "I'm hit!"

"It's First Sword of Light," called Amiko Sturz, the company's *Apollo* pilot. "They think we're the traitors!"

The blade, which emitted a faint hum, was withdrawn from the Otomo guard's body. As he slumped to the cement the second guard raised his full-auto riot shotgun. A tall figure clad in black from sole to crown stepped from the secret door and hacked him down with a single stroke of a vibrokatana. Its hum rose to a shriek as it cut through rigid armor and bone.

Other figures in black poured from the doorway, spreading out rapidly to either side of the one who had killed the two Otomo guards. Each held a bared *katana* in a black-gloved hand. When thirty of them stood facing the Coordinator, who was still on the podium at the top of the stairs, the central swordsman pulled off his red-visored helmet and shook back his armor-cloth cowl.

"General Kiguri," Theodore Kurita said.

The one-eyed man bowed. "*Tono.* A thousand apologies for the inconvenience, but I have come to kill you."

"All Combine military units," Lainie Shimazu broadcast on the general-access channel. "This is *Tai-sa* Eleanor Shimazu of the Ninth Ghost Legion. A unit of the Otomo is attempting to kill the Coordinator. We're trying to stop them. Please, do not fire on us!"

She didn't know whether that would do any good, but she had to try. Hideyoshi's *Sunder* had turned to face her and was blasting away with the medium lasers in its torso. She charged him, firing back with her big extended-range lasers.

"Sari, Billy, keep moving," she ordered. "I'll take this one."

"Traitor dog!" snarled Yoshida. He drew the *katana* from the *dai-sho* sheathed behind his left shoulder as part of his dress uniform. Theodore held up a hand.

"Hold," the Coordinator told him. Then to the renegade ISF leader, "Why do you do this?"

The scarred lips smiled. "To counteract the decadence your reforms have brought to the combine," Kiguri said. "The picked team I sent to Cinema City failed to hijack the BattleMechs belonging to your fat cousin's *gaijin* hirelings. And out there—"

He nodded past the stands, to where a brutal face-to-face 'Mech battle roared and crashed between the Ghosts and the

Otomo assassins. "—Out there General Hideyoshi isn't doing a very good job of wreaking the vengeance he's plotted against you since your father's death disgraced him. So I'm left to pick up the pieces myself." He shook his head. "Nothing gets done right any more, *Tono*. Obviously, it's time for a change."

"And whom will you replace me with?" Theodore asked calmly.

"We were going to replace you with your none-too-bright but highly pliable cousin Angus. Unfortunately, my superior Subhash Indrahar, that meddlesome old beast, managed to make an end of him not two hours ago—removing himself from the picture as well." He shrugged his broad shoulders. "Still, we'll come up with something. The important thing is that your time is through."

One of the two surviving Otomo guards on the podium with Theodore uttered a bellow of rage, brought up his shotgun and fired a burst at the DEST commander. Kiguri rolled to the side, came up to one knee, flung out his left hand. A *shuriken* shaped like a swastika with rounded arms struck the guard under the right side of the jaw. Blood from a severed jugular vein pulsed between the Otomo guard's fingers as he grabbed at his neck. He toppled off the platform.

"Take him," Kiguri ordered his commandos.

The two assault 'Mechs met with a terrible clang. Though his machine massed a mere five tons less than her *Mauler*, Lainie's rush had taken the Otomo leader off guard. His *Sunder* staggered backward.

Ignoring the red lights that had flared to life in her display, Lainie raised the *Mauler*'s arms and fired its large lasers point-blank into the *Sunder*'s chest. Armor melted and splashed away from the dazzling beams like water thrown up by stone. She threw her 'Mech into motion at once, slamming into the Omni with another impact that threatened to detach her retinas.

Around her a dogfight swirled, too confused to make sense of even if she'd had time for anything but her deadly dance with Hideyoshi. The traitor's 'Mech had heavier frontal armor, hers the greater firepower. With his potent pulse lasers neutralized, Hideyoshi would probably lose a face-up blasting duel. But that would take time.

Lainie wanted this done *now*. The longer the fight went on, the greater the risk one of the would-be assassins would manage to blast through the transpex shield—or jump high enough to shoot down over the top of it—and kill the Coordinator.

Another shattering collision. Lainie's HUD flickered once, came back. A warning buzz and red telltale told her she had lost her targeting system. *I don't need the computer for this*, she thought. She raised her 'Mech's right arm and fired its laser into the *Sunder*'s cockpit.

"Looks like your friends got here in time," Johnny Tchang said as the *Warrior* swept along the south wall of the Palace—any aircraft that overflew the grounds would be fired on by radar-aimed robot flak emplacements—and out over the battle raging in Unity Square.

"It's a little early to celebrate," Cassie said, "since it looks like they haven't won yet by a long shot. Whoa, Migaki-*sama!* Can you take us back over the grandstand? Something's going on behind it."

The VTOL heeled over, circled over the struggling 'Mechs and crossed the stands, which had gotten deserted in a hurry. Black suits were swarming up the back stair to the podium, to be met by a man in dress uniform wielding a sword. Several figures fired down at the attackers from beside him.

"More Ninja Boys," Cassie said in disgust.

"That's General Kiguri down there," Migaki said, pointing with his chin. "The bare-headed one."

"I don't suppose you've still got guns on this thing?" she asked.

Migaki showed her a taut smile. "Not much call for them in my line of work," he said. "Not that I don't miss them occasionally. But not even an Associate Director of ISF gets to machine-gun recalcitrant actors."

"Thank goodness for that," Johnny Tchang said.

"If you can hover right over the platform, here," Cassie said, coming out of her seat and racking back the action on the shotgun far enough to confirm a round was chambered, "I can give Teddy a little timely fire support."

Red glare filled the cockpit, accompanied by a crack like one of the sequoias in the park being snapped by a giant, and the stench of hot metal and burned lubricants. The helicopter lurched and began to sink.

"Hovering's out," Migaki said calmly through silence loud as a shout. "Laser beam just took out our engine."

Epilogue

Mujo

I feel sure that Heaven intends to use your master as a wooden bell.

—Confucius, Analects, 3:24

33

"**C**oordinator!"

At the warning cry from his last surviving Otomo guard Theodore Kurita looked up to see a helicopter flash overhead, then autorotate to a crash landing on the grandstand twenty meters north of the podium. He heard a strangled cry, turned his head to see Shigeru Yoshida staggering back from the stairs, blood from a deep slash across his chest turning his dress tunic crimson. Theodore caught him in his arms.

"*Tono* . . . I apologize for . . . failing." Yoshida's eyes rolled up in his head, and his body became dead weight.

The commando who had struck the man down was a woman. She leapt at Theodore, *katana* raised. Laser beams from Uncle Chandy's guards converged on her. One burned through the armor cloth enclosing her chest, and she fell almost at the feet of the man she had slain.

More commandos were lunging up the stairs to the attack. Theodore wrested the sword from Yoshida's slack grip and stood to meet them. It was an ancient blade from Terra itself, an heirloom granted the Yoshida family by a grateful Coordinator three centuries before. Not that that mattered particularly; the Draconis Combine had never adopted the practice of their World War II Japanese predecessors, of stamping swords from pot-metal by the tens of thousands so their officers could carry symbols of traditional authority that were useful for damn-all else. The classic art of sword-smithing thrived under the Kuritas, and every blade carried by one of the Dragon's servants was a finely crafted piece of work. But age lent soul to a blade, which a swordsman as accomplished as Theodore was well-attuned to. Yoshida's *katana* felt light in his hands, and while it was no vibro-blade, it seemed to him to quiver with eagerness to avenge its fallen owner.

Granting its desire required no thought, no intention. Theodore flowed forward to meet the next commando up the stairs. As of its own accord Yoshida's *katana* caught the descending blade flat-to-flat, swept it harmlessly down and past Theodore's left shoulder, reversed into a backhand slash across the throat. The ancient blade parted black armor cloth and pale flesh beneath. Hot blood sprayed Theodore's face and chest. The commando tumbled back into the red visors of his mates crowding behind him.

"Not bad," called Kiguri from the podium where he stood behind a phalanx of his commandos shielding him from gunfire. "You haven't forgotten what to do with a sword, *Tono*."

The female commando who stood immediately to Kiguri's left suddenly threw herself against him. Despite the General's greater mass and fine natural balance, the unexpected assault knocked him a meter to the side.

The commando's body jerked as to the impact of a sledgehammer. Blood, visible only as dark wetness against the black, flowed from a sudden hole in her sternum. She collapsed.

"Hijo de la chingada," Cassie cursed. She'd had that bastard Kiguri dead-centered in her ghost-ring sights. His hand-picked minions were not as good as they imagined they were, but they were damned good—and fanatically devoted to their leader. They proved it by closing ranks to shield him from attack from this unexpected direction as she moved the barrel of her shotgun to target him.

Cassie, Johnny, and Takura Migaki—still nattily unruffled, despite the crash—crouched on top of the grandstand, using the transpex shield for cover in case the commandos produced ranged weapons and tried to fire them up. The actor held an autopistol before him in a very professional two-handed grip, which Cassie knew was more a testimonial to his coaches and acting skill than real combat-pistol prowess. Migaki had produced a neat little holdout piece that he held with apparent negligence in one hand. Something about his manner suggested he did know what to do with it—such as not waste bullets shooting at armored targets at any kind of range.

"The fop, his pet actor, and the mercenary scout bitch who's made so much trouble," Kiguri called from behind his volunteer human shields. "Like anyone without honor, you seek to live by the gun. But you'll die by the sword. Take them as well!"

A dozen *katana*-armed commandos rushed them. Cassie dropped two with body hits by her penetrator rounds. Johnny Tchang blazed away enthusiastically but without apparent effect. Kiguri waited calmly.

From the corner of her eye Cassie saw Theodore dueling with another commando on the stairs while the Otomo guard and Uncle Chandy's two retainers fired from the sides at others attempting to join the fight. Half a dozen dignitaries and aides, unarmed, milled in the background, dividing their attention unhappily between the struggle for the stairs and the still very undecided 'Mech battle going on beyond the transpex shield, which had now been punctured twice by hits. Behind Migaki, fresh DEST commandos were emerging from the door into the Palace grounds.

This isn't good, Cassie had time to think. Then a series of violent explosions rocked the grandstands hard on the other side of Migaki's chopper. She flinched and looked that way as Takura Migaki threw himself as flat as he could down onto the terraced stands. Boards and splinters were whirling into the air; the *Warrior,* which thanks to its double rotors' autorotation and Migaki's piloting skill, hadn't been damaged too badly on impact, slid forward with a grating noise into the gap between stands and wall and began to burn.

Johnny alone looked unaffected by the explosions. He met Cassie's eye and gave her a quick grin and shrug, as if to say, *I'm used to loud noises. All part of my job.*

"Those aren't skyrockets," she snarled. "Those were SRMs." His handsome face went pale.

The DEST commandos hit the wooden frames that supported the grandstands and began swarming up them like squirrels. Cassie fired off two more sabot rounds and missed, dropped the mostly empty magazine and slammed in a box of buckshot rounds. A red visor appeared over the edge of the stands. Cassie dropped her weapon to the hip and fired into it.

The visor shattered. The black-helmeted head whipped back. The commando fell limp as wet laundry to the pavement, his neck broken.

Another popped up to Cassie's right. Migaki dropped into a two-handed stance and snapped two quick shots into the DEST trooper's faceplate. That visor didn't break, nor did the man's neck, but he overbalanced and toppled backward off the stands.

Having emptied his pistol without doing visible harm to anybody, Johnny Tchang tossed it aside as a commando scrambled up to the right of the small group. He pivoted, skipped forward, snapped a kick into the faceplate, dislodging the DEST agent. Belatedly he saw it was a female. "Sorry," he said as she landed hard flat on her back, and immediately felt foolish.

He didn't have long to be embarrassed. A male operative, trying a flank approach, gained the top of the grandstand and rushed at Johnny, swinging his *katana*.

Johnny counter-charged him, catching his right arm at wrist and elbow, locking-out the arm and using it as a lever to shove the commando faceplate-first into the stands' second tier. A second one came swarming over the top at him. Not relinquishing his hold on the first's arm, Johnny went down to one knee and side-kicked his assailant in the belly, launching him backward into space. Then he let go the captive elbow, twisted the sword-hilt out of the hand he still held, and kicked the unfortunate commando rolling down the steps. Then, holding the sword above his head, blade up and tip forward, he dropped into a sideways horse stance to await fresh attackers.

Cassie blasted two more attackers. The second managed

to get a gloved hand around the barrel of the shotgun before Cassie shot her away from it. A third swung a katana at her almost simultaneously. She had to throw herself into a backward somersault that carried her down three rows to escape.

The shotgun stayed with the last attacker she'd shot.

The commando who had slashed at her jumped down onto the seat-tier above her, cut downward at her as she lay on her back. She whipped the vibrokatana from the scabbard across her back just barely in time to parry.

The commando had only a heartbeat to stare in amazement—his expression hidden by his visor, but his body language unmistakable—at the stump of his sword before Cassie sliced her humming blade through his chest.

"Damn! Lost my right laser," Lainie muttered. Her cheeks tingled as if sunburned from a hit by one of Hideyoshi's beams that had burned through her canopy but mostly spent itself in the process.

"All systems are dead," Sari DeLeeuw said in her ear. "Nothing's responding, and my onboard computer reports a fire in my antimissile system ammo bay."

Firing her left-arm laser into her own opponent at almost touch range, Lainie flicked a glance at her circle-vision strip. She had an impression DeLeeuw's *War Dog* had been engaged with the *Avatar* and the *Black Hawk* Ho's *Pillager* hadn't taken out. The *Avatar* was a gutted wreck, its LB-10X right arm and double-pulse laser supported by mere vestigial wings that were all that was left of its torso after a shot from the *War Dog*'s Gauss rifle destroyed the containment field of its fusion engine. The BHKU-0 looked to be mostly intact, and now stood behind the immobilized *Dog,* firing its fearful battery of twelve lasers into it as fast as heat build-up permitted.

Her anti-missile stowage doesn't have CASE! Lainie thought. "Punch out," she ordered. Being resolved upon death herself made her irrationally afraid of losing any of her people, and she was certain she'd lost three already, Buntaro Mayne in the *Stealth,* Sato in the *Hitman,* and one of her *Owens* pilots, Denzel.

"But Lainie—"

"Now!"

The *War Dog*'s canopy popped open and DeLeeuw soared up into the hot blue Imperial City sky. The *Black Hawk* turned back toward the grandstand—and was rocked by a ferro-nickel slug from the *Dragon Fire*'s Gauss rifle as Billy Dragomil, having finished off a *Blackjack*, raced back to his fiancée's rescue.

Hideyoshi fired his lasers into the body of Lainie's *Mauler*. She smelled smoke as alarms shrilled in her ears. *That one got through!*

This was taking too long and she was taking too much damage. Lainie thought of her friend Kali, who could make her lumbering old *Atlas* do things Lainie had never imagined possible. What would she do now?

Something totally off the wall, Lainie realized.

To think was to act. She swiveled her 'Mech's torso clockwise and charged past the stub of the *Sunder*'s right arm. She planted her right foot behind that of Hideyoshi's Omni, then rotated Vengeance's torso hard counterclockwise, smashing her useless right laser-arm into the *Sunder*'s prow. The OmniMech fell backward with a resounding crash.

She shoved the muzzle of her left laser against the prostrate *Sunder*'s cockpit for the coup de grâce. And heard a voice both through her radio and audio pickups commanding, "You in the *Mauler*—hold your fire or be destroyed!"

Takura Migaki fired off the last round in his holdout pistol, threw it at a red faceplate. A DEST commando aimed a transverse slash at him. He wove his upper body lithely out of the way, then grabbed the wrist of his attacker's swordhand with his right hand. Pivoting clockwise into the swordsman, Migaki pulled the arm over his shoulder and snapped the elbow with a savage downward heave. Then he caught up the *katana* that dropped from limp fingers and cut down the injured man.

Cassie held off two commandos who were respectful of her vibrokatana's ability to slice through their blades and their armor. From the corner of her eye she saw Theodore fighting masterfully at the top of the stairs. Blood streamed down his left cheek, and the front of his dress tunic had been slashed twice, but despite his lack of armor he had taken no serious wounds—yet.

To her other side Johnny Tchang was in his element, fighting now with two captured *katana* as if they were butterfly swords. The commandos were highly trained in *kenjutsu* and the Dragon School of unarmed combat. But Johnny Tchang had been schooled rigorously in the martial arts from earliest childhood. His whole life had been shaped toward the goal of making him the Inner Sphere's finest martial artist.

His many critics said his holovids were pure box-office. Yet the way he seemed to dance among the black-clad waves that broke over the rear of the grandstand, blocking and slashing with his blades, lashing out with his black-slippered feet, Cassie wasn't so sure he hadn't made it. Wonderfully fluid his moves were, but there was no make-believe in the effect they had on his opponents.

To no end. The outcome was no longer in doubt. Kiguri's renegade DEST operatives had been reinforced; sooner or later they would overpower the Coordinator's defenders, and finally Theodore himself.

So much for the Inner Sphere, Cassie thought. In savage anger she punched the tip of her vibrokatana through the faceplate of the opponent to her left, then severed both hands of the one on her right as he raised his sword over-head for a killing stroke. Then she ran to the top of the stands and looked down.

Her heart dropped in her ribcage like a wingshot dove. A veritable flood of black-clad shapes was pouring out the door into the Palace grounds.

And falling on Kiguri's henchmen from the rear with gleaming swords.

Lainie froze. Her 360-view strip showed her what looked like a whole regiment of BattleMechs advancing across Unity Square from the east. From their differing paint schemes and insignia she gathered they had been cobbled together from various units on hand for the festivities.

The lead 'Mech was a battleship gray *Naginata* with the

Kurita dragon prominently painted on the LRM launcher set into either side of its chest. There was no mistaking the machine. This was the 'Mech belonging to Tomoe Sakade, wife of the Coordinator of the Draconis Combine and commander of Kagoshima Prefecture of the Pesht Military District, in which Luthien was located.

"*Tai-sho* Sakade," Lainie broadcast on the general comm freq. "I am *Tai-sa* Shimazu, commanding the Ninth Ghost Legion."

"Why were you attacking the Otomo?"

"Colonel Hideyoshi is a traitor, *Tai-sho*. He and his men were trying to assassinate the Coordinator."

"*So ka?* That is hard to believe."

"Please make your own investigation, General, and learn the truth for yourself."

"Very well, *Tai-sa*. I'll do just that. All MechWarriors who were engaged in combat, Ghost Legion or Otomo—dismount from your machines at once and prepare to be taken into custody."

"General Sakade." The voice from the fallen *Sunder*'s loudspeakers sounded strained and ancient. "Please permit me to return my 'Mech to its feet, rather than leave it lying here in disgrace. By the years I have served your husband, I ask this favor, although I know I am unworthy."

Tai-sho Tomoe Sakade paused.

"Very well, Oda-*san*. You may rise."

Like an old man, the badly damaged *Sunder* clambered to its blocky feet. Not disobeying the *Tai-sho* but rather—to her own mind, anyway—deferring obedience, Lainie sat in her cockpit and seethed. *After all I went through to put that bastard down. . . .*

The *Sunder* stood facing Sakade's BattleMech, which had halted barely twenty paces away. Its once-pristine white paint had mostly been boiled away; what remained was streaked with black. Its right arm was twisted metal and loose cables, and its armor was pocked and cratered as if pieces had been ripped out of it by some monstrous claw. Then, "Death to the traitor!" Hideyoshi exclaimed, wheeled the OmniMech and sent it striding toward the grandstand.

A jagged blue bolt from Sakade's extended-range PPC

hit the *Sunder* full in the back, joined at once by a ruby beam from Lainie's surviving large laser. A fractional second later beams and projectiles converged on the traitor's 'Mech from all over the Square.

The *Sunder* exploded like an erupting volcano.

Cassie saw that each of the black-clad newcomers bore a circular emblem on his or her chest: yellow cat's eyes peering from blackness through a screen of reeds—the *mon* that the Smiling One, born of the Middle Class, had adopted for the Indrahar family on being appointed Director of ISF. In the midst of them strode a tall man whose garments were merely black clothing, not an armored sneaksuit, and whose red-haired head was bare. At his side fought a swordsman, equally tall, who was dressed in a spacer's scuffed brown leather jacket. Though Cassie had never to her knowledge seen him before, the tanned face beneath that mane of wild black hair looked somehow familiar.

For the next few moments she and her two companions were occupied finishing off the last of the attackers who had won to the top of the grandstand. When that was done all the renegade commandos at ground level seemed to be down. Only Hohiro Kiguri still stood, erect and defiant, in the center of a circle of Sons of the Dragon.

"Theodore Kurita!" he called in ringing tones to the Coordinator, who stood with bloody sword in hand at the top of the stairs. "You have fought well. Cross blades with me, and we'll see who wins an honorable death."

The tall man in the leather jacket moved swiftly to the base of the stairs. He held his *katana* before him. "If you wish to fight my father," he said in a quiet voice, "you must first go through me."

Kiguri stared in astonishment. "Sakamoto?"

"You will fight neither of them." Ninyu Kerai stepped slowly forward to stand facing Kiguri. He had returned his own sword to its scabbard, which was strapped across his back. "Traitors have no standing to demand duels with Kurita, even those who have renounced the name. Besides, your quarrel is with me, is it not, Kiguri? You staged this whole conspiracy because you had been passed over to succeed my father."

For a long moment the single eye glared at Ninyu Kerai. Then Hohiro Kiguri laughed. "I carry the wrong family name to accede to the Dragon Throne. Yet my ambition accepts no such limitation. Why pretend otherwise?

"I would rule the Draconis Combine. With the proper Coordinator in place, the Director of the Internal Security Force can readily do so. Three men stood in my path: yourself, your adoptive father, and Theodore Kurita. One has eliminated himself. I still propose to remove the final two barriers."

"You are not fit to rule," Ninyu Kerai said. "You are overconfident and careless: witness the way you hid Franklin Sakamoto in a DEST safe house—even one of whose existence my father was initially unaware. Witness the way all your schemes—to frame the foreign mercenaries and Franklin Sakamoto for the Coordinator's murder; to use Oda's festering resentment as a backup plan; even your attempt to assassinate the *Tono* with your own hand—have been brought to nothing by a crippled old man and a *gaijin* woman."

"But a hell of a *gaijin* woman," Johnny Tchang murmured out the side of his mouth to Cassie.

"Agreed," said Migaki, who stood with arms folded, apparently at total indolent ease, on the other side of her.

Kiguri glowered and pointed his vibrokatana at Ninyu. "Draw your weapon, then, fatherless whelp. You can never match me. I'll put the lie to all your words, and show you what a fool your father was to prefer you over me into the bargain!"

Moving deliberately Ninyu Kerai unslung his sheathed sword, thrust the scabbard through his belt in such a way that the curve of the blade was upward.

"No. Sheathe your weapon. We will settle this quickly. An *iai* duel—quick-draw sword."

Kiguri paused, nodded. "Very well." He arranged his own scabbard in the same manner and sheathed his sword. "But you are at a disadvantage: you lack armor, and I have a vibroblade."

"I need no armor," Ninyu Kerai said. "I need no vibroblade."

The two men stood staring intently at each other, separated by little more than arm's reach. In the heavy silence, tension wound like an elastic band being twisted to the breaking point.

"Historically," Migaki said under his breath, "both participants in quick-draw sword duels generally killed each other. Unless—"

Hohiro Kiguri moved, so fast even the leopard-quick Ninyu couldn't match him, snatching his vibrokatana from the scabbard and raising it high for a blow that would split the red-haired skull in half.

But Ninyu pulled his sword from the scabbard with the left hand, put his right hand to the spline and shoved the wicked-sharp blade through Kiguri's chest before Kiguri could strike.

Kiguri's eyes bulged. His scarred face set, blood geysered from his chest, and he fell lifeless to the pavement.

Migaki pumped his hand in the air. "Kurosawa. The climax of *Sanjuro*. I knew there was a reason I made Ninyu watch those old movies."

Ninyu Kerai looked up at him, and one corner of his mouth twitched upward. "In their own time all things may be found useful," he said, "even an obsession with ancient cinema."

He cleared the traitor's blood from his blade with a flick of the wrist and sheathed his sword with a snick.

Over the worried protests of his aides—who were greatly chagrined by how little they had contributed to the struggle for the Coordinator's life—Theodore ordered the transpex shield lowered.

"My people must know that I am alive and unharmed," he declared, ignoring the swordcuts that emergency medical techs were dabbing at with antiseptics and healing-accelerants even as he spoke. "And that I won't cower forever behind a meter of armored synthetic."

"No one would dream of accusing you of cowering, my boy," said Uncle Chandy, whose attendants, their lasers holstered, once again shaded him with a parasol and plied him with iced drinks. *He* wasn't the least bit ashamed of not helping fight. "Especially not once they see the documentary our young friend Takura-*kun* makes out of today's events. By the way his eyes gleam and he keeps rubbing his hands together as if he'd just unearthed an intact Star League base in the backyard of his villa, I perceive his crews caught it all."

"*Oh*, yes," said Migaki, rubbing his hands together and making his eyes to gleam. "My people have won themselves great honor today." Two of his holocam crews had been wiped out by overkill from the 'Mech battle, but the Voice of the Dragon techs had all stayed at their posts, recording it all for posterity—or rather for their lord Migaki, who would make damn sure that what posterity actually got a gander at was even purer and more heroic than what really happened.

Cassie stood to one side with Johnny Tchang. Somehow they came to be holding hands. Neither said anything. There really didn't seem much to say at this particular point.

With a great deal of groaning, the warped and scarred shield was withdrawn into the ground. Out on the great Square the crowds had began to come back under the aegis of the BattleMechs of *Tai-sho* Sakade's scratch force and Heruzu Enjeruzu, the question of who were the assassins and who were the defenders of the Coordinator having been definitively settled by Oda Hideyoshi's last, brief ride. Ambulance crews moved among the re-coalescing throng, gathering up those spectators wounded or killed by the 'Mech battle.

The grandstands, too, began to be repopulated. Those who had occupied them before had mostly fled beneath them. Those who survived were filtering back out, blinking in the sunshine like animals emerging from their burrows.

Among those furtive animals was Benjamin Inagawa, oyabun of Benjamin Military District and now become the mover and shaker of *Kokuryu-kai*, the Black Dragon Society. Like Migaki's camera crews he had seen the whole thing.

Rage and frustration seethed within him. In one blinding

Buddha flash he had perceived the truth: Hohiro Kiguri had been *Kaga,* the Shadowed One. He had contemptuously manipulated the *Kokuryu-kai* for his own ends. And that same Kiguri had failed miserably.

At that thought, Inagawa felt a change. He stood on the steps of the grandstand, down and to the left of where the Coordinator prepared to step forward and reassure his people of his survival. Benjamin Inagawa's mood began to shift to a buoyant exultation because that arrogant pig Kiguri had died—and he, Benjamin Inagawa, much-despised yakuza, was about to succeed where the high and mighty commander of the Draconis Elite Strike Teams had failed.

Because *no one was paying attention to him.* A large man and a flashy dresser, Inagawa was used to commanding center stage. Yet for once no one seemed to notice him—not the traitor Theodore, nor the hooded and face-masked Sons of the Dragon who flanked him, not the devil-pup Ninyu Kerai, nor the proud MechWarriors high up in their cockpits, who only deigned to notice nothing less than a fresh BattleMech attack. And for once Inagawa was glad to be ignored by the Combine's high and mighty.

He reached under his suit coat—torn and soiled by his undignified scramble beneath the bleachers—and drew his own compact holdout pistol. Theodore Kurita strode forward to the front of the podium and held up his hands. The crowd roared approval.

The fools. Benjamin Inagawa raised his arm, centered his sights on the Coordinator's chest. Incredibly, no one noticed him. It was as if he were invisible. Surely this was destiny; surely he was fated to save the Combine from decadence and dissolution. His finger tightened on the trigger.

And he was swept into the air, held like a roach in a pair of chopsticks by the large lasers that made up the arms of a *Mauler.* They held him squirming high in the air while the throng gasped and pointed.

"I am Melisandra DuBonnet," an amplified voice said. "You betrayed my father and murdered him. Now your blood will repay his."

"Put me down!" Inagawa screamed. He fired the pistol uselessly against the gouged metal hide of the monster.

"Happily," said the woman who now called herself Eleanor Shimazu. Carefully—gently, even—she set the oyabun down on the pavement right in front of the podium where an astounded Theodore and his retinue stood watching. He began to run.

He had gone perhaps five paces when the *Mauler*'s broad right foot descended on him, blocking him from view. A final scream, a crunch of metal on cement. Then silence.

Takura Migaki hugged Lainie against him as the crowd cheered hoarsely. They had been at it for minutes, and seemed ready to keep it up until the sun burned out.

"If you had just said, 'Hello, my name is Melisandra DuBonnet. You killed my father. Prepare to die,' " he told her, "it would have been perfect. But it was great cinema all the same."

She dabbed moisture from the corners of her maroon eyes and looked at him. "Tak," she said, "what the hell are you talking about?"

"Never mind," he said. "Just kiss me."

"That I can do," she said, and did.

"Teddy-*kun*," a soft voice said from behind him.

Theodore half-turned from the multitude and smiled. "When you use that name, you always want something."

Uncle Chandy beamed at him like Hotei on a bender. "Perceptive as always, *Tono*."

He waved a pudgy hand at Franklin Sakamoto, who stood off to one side of the podium, looking as if he felt conspicuous and out of place. "The boy laid his life on the line for you today, Theodore," the fat man said, "not that he hasn't done so before. Nothing will challenge Hohiro's succession from this day on. Meanwhile this young man has renounced the throne, and proven that he means it."

"What do you want of me, Chandy?"

"Let go the past, Theodore. Forgive yourself and accept yourself. Let your father rest in peace—and embrace your son."

Father and son stared at each other as across a gulf of

light-years. "The Dragon needs you whole, Theodore," Uncle Chandy said. "The Inner Sphere needs you whole."

Theodore threw his arms around his son, this man known as Franklin Sakamoto, and held him tight. Around them, a million voices raised a cheer, but the roar could not have been greater than the one that lifted the heart of Theodore himself at that moment. Father of his people, their protector, their refuge, he would always be. Never would he forsake them, never would he betray them. But now he had them all, for his own son, a Kurita through and through, brave and selfless, with a heart as true as any samurai's arrow, was home again. At last.

About the Author

Victor Milán has published over seventy novels, including *The Runespear,* co-authored with Melinda Snodgrass, and the award-winning *The Cybernetic Samurai* and its sequel, *The Cybernetic Shogun.* Recent books include a technothriller, *Red Sands* and a Star Trek® novel entitled *From the Depths.* His dark military SF novel *CLD* was recently published by Avon Books.

Milán's previous BattleTech novels are *Close Quarters* and *Hearts of Chaos,* which also featured the popular Camacho's Caballeros of the Seventeenth Recon Regiment. *Black Dragon* is his third BattleTech® novel to feature the irrepressible Caballeros.

The *Washington Post* has called Milán a "contender for major stardom" in science fiction. He is a charter member of the New Mexico-based Wild Cards Mafia, creators of the highly acclaimed SF shared-world anthologies.

Milán's house is infested with dogs, cats and ferrets. He enjoys birding, playing games of various sorts, walking by the Río Grande, and exploring the ancient network of irrigation ditches by mountain bike in Albuquerque's North Valley. He also practices taekwon-do.

He finds himself living in the science fiction world he read about as a kid and generally, he's pleased.

Hall of Warriors, The Fort
Tara, Northwind
The Chaos March
2 May 3058

The Assembly Hall of Clan Elders was the chief government building in Tara, and the heart and soul of Northwind's planetary government. Despite the fact that the Highlanders were only a fraction of the planet's population, they were the only real power and authority on the world. That was even more true now that the Highlanders had won this planet away from Prince Victor Davion and the Federated Commonwealth.

Set in the center of Tara, the Assembly Hall was part of a whole complex of buildings that had been known as The Fort ever since the Highlanders had come back to Northwind in 3028. The returning elders had declared that they would defend their beloved planet from the fortress of these walls against any and all who threatened.

Once a year the elders of Tara and all the chiefs from the outlying provinces met in High Assembly to decide matters of planetary importance, but the day-to-day decisions were made by various sub-assemblies. The largest, and most prestigious, of these was the Assembly of Warriors, which was charged with governing the Highlanders' military.

Composed of exactly one hundred proven Highlander soldiers, the Assembly of Warriors was the cornerstone of Northwind.

Unlike the rest of The Fort, the U-shaped Hall of Warriors was constructed of wood. At one end was an elevated platform with a table for the four Colonels commanding the four regiments of the Highlanders. Flanking the platform, the one hundred warriors sat at solid oak tables equipped with computer terminals and other sophisticated equipment. Most wore the traditional kilts and heavy boots favored by MechWarriors and aerospace pilots. Dress uniforms were considered inappropriate for the Assembly of Warriors.

The lighting built into the walls was dim but adequate as Loren descended the few steps leading down to the sod floor of the chamber. All around him other members of the Assembly were also filing in and finding their places on the wooden benches behind the tables. In addition to a monitor, each seat had access to high-speed communications arrays for accessing presentation data as well as casting votes on matters brought before the Assembly. Right now the displays were blank.

Loren sat down and adjusted the woolen tartan kilt around his legs. Wearing it had been the thing hardest to get used to since joining the Highlanders. The rich wool of the kilt often made his legs itch during stuffy formal occasions such as long meetings, and worse was the fact that the traditional uniform did not call for undergarments. The black shirt had long tails that could be tied in the crotch for some degree of "support," but the sensation was drafty, and always would be, uncomfortable.

He caught sight of Chastity Mulvaney looking around for a seat. "Major Mulvaney," Loren said, smiling and gesturing for her to take the empty place next to him.

She walked up, then stood there for a moment, arms crossed over her chest, narrowing her eyes slightly. "Don't be so smug, Loren. I've seen the regimental combat assessment. You won, I lost. Let it drop or I'll drop it for you."

Theirs had been a love/hate relationship from the start, and that hadn't changed over time. She was the perfect match for Loren, both on and off the field of battle. His command battalion had beaten hers in the recent exercise between the Kilsyth Guards and MacLeod's Regiment, but that didn't mean she wouldn't beat him next time. *Some things defy words. I don't have to tell her how I feel, she knows it. Just like I know her feelings.*

Loren shrugged, but before he could say anything more their attention was drawn by the arrival of the commanding officers of the Northwind Highlanders. As the four Colonels filed in, Loren thought how different each one was from the rest. Where MacLeod's Regiment was known for its wildness and recklessness, Colonel Edward Senn's First Kearny Regiment had a reputation for conservative stubbornness. Loren smiled to himself, thinking of his time as one of MacLeod's "Bad Boys" in the recent battle for Tara. The Second Kearny, under the stone-faced Colonel James O. Cochraine, was considered the most impassioned of the regiments, often rushing into battle more on emotion than common sense. Colonel Andrea Stirling had been raised in that unit before taking command of the Fusiliers from Henrietta McCormack. It was Stirling's cunning and inventiveness on the battlefield that had earned her regiment the same reputation.

The four proceeded in single file to the commander's table, then turned to face the gathered warriors, who instantly stood, snapping to attention. Loren felt a rush, a slight pounding in his ears, the kind of warm pride he used to feel when in the presence of the Chancellor.

"As you were," Colonel Senn said. As commander of the senior regiment of the Northwind Highlanders, Senn presided over the Assembly of Warriors when not on active duty.

As all took their seats, Senn waited for the sounds to die down before speaking again. "I remind you all that the proceedings of this Assembly are sealed by covenant, and since this is the formal opening of contract negotiations, you are all bound by the security accords of the Mercenary Review and Bonding Commission."

All four Highlander regiments were currently on Northwind because the unit had not been taking assignments while trying to rebuild after losing almost a full regiment's worth of troops in the fighting with the Davions. Colonel James D. Cochraine had taken a seat at the far left of the table. Next to him was Colonel William MacLeod. Then came Colonel Senn, and finally the seat on the far right was occupied by Loren's own Colonel Stirling.

"Sergeant at Arms," Colonel Senn said to the Warrant Officer who stood at the door. The man opened the door, admitting three people all dressed in their most formal garb.

"Welcome, honored guests," Senn said and motioned the group forward.

Of the three emissaries, the obvious leader was a female of medium height, wearing a blue and green silk kimono. She moved with an air of regal grace, her shining black hair drawn back from her pale skin in a style that was at once severe yet elegant.

Loren recognized her instantly. *Omi Kurita.* Daughter of Coordinator Theodore Kurita of the Draconis Combine. Her presence on Northwind was an unofficial acknowledgment of the planet's newly won independence. As she gracefully took the steps leading to the platform where the Colonels sat, Loren studied the other two dignitaries. One wore the white uniform of a Combine MechWarrior, her stature and regal posture falling just short of Omi's. The rank insignia on her uniform collar marked her as a *Sho-sa,* the DCMS equivalent of Loren's own rank of Major. The brilliant blue emblem on her shoulder told more of the story—it was the raging tidal wave of the Genyosha Regiment.

Loren didn't need the Warrant Officer's introduction to also recognize the second woman instantly, though for a very different reason. Anyone who'd ever studied the Battle of Luthien in which the Combine military and some of the Inner Sphere's best mercs had defeated a Clan attempt to capture the Combine's capital world would know that this was Ruth Horner.

Loren had found her writings on Clan tactics eye-opening, and he thought her book and other papers could easily serve as a bible for field officers. Six years ago on Luthien she'd been a *Tai-i* in the Genyosha and had led a stunning raid against the Smoke Jaguars in the Waseda Hills outside of Luthien. Loren only hoped he could do as well when his time came.

The third figure wore a gray jumpsuit bearing the star symbol of ComStar on her left chest, over the heart. The piping on her rounded collar showed the insignia of the Com Guards and the rank of Precentor. The Warrant Officer introduced her as Precenter Mercedes Laurent of the Explorer Corps as she also took her place on the stage.

Loren leaned over and spoke in a whisper to Chastity. "Omi Kurita, here, on Northwind. This has to be something important, something really big." A few short years ago, before the Clans arrived, it would have been unthinkable for a member of the Combine's ruling house to show his or her face on Northwind, a world the Combine had attacked and tried to take during the Fourth Succession War. Times had indeed changed, and with them, the Highlanders as well.

Chastity nodded. "They asked to meet with us here rather than on Outreach." Outreach was the world where mercenaries arrived from near and far seeking employment under the official auspices of the Mercenary Review and Bonding Commission. It was also the home of Wolf's Dragoons, the famous mercenaries who'd once been Clansmen and who'd tried to teach the militaries of the Inner Sphere how to fight the seemingly invincible invaders. That Theodore Kurita had bypassed the usual hiring procedures and channels was noteworthy.

Omi stood with hands at her side, her posture erect yet somehow relaxed. She let her gaze travel around the room, then brought it back to the table of Colonels. "Members of the Northwind Highlanders and esteemed commanders of the unit, I bring you warm greetings from Coordinator Theodore Kurita of the Draconis Combine."

"Thank you, Kurita Omi-*sama*," said Colonel Cochraine. "This is the first time the Assembly of Warriors has ever entertained a representative of the Combine, and your presence and purpose here surely signal the beginning of a new era in relations between our peoples. We are honored to have a visitor of such distinction as our guest on Northwind."

Loren knew there was much in the Colonel's words. Only

recently had Northwind finally managed to gain its full independence from the Federated Commonwealth, though it was not clear whether Victor Davion acknowledged that status or not. This visit by Omi Kurita gave validity to their independence, even if it was not an official recognition.

The Federated Commonwealth—whatever was left of it—and the Combine had buried the hatchet ever since deciding to join together against a common foe. Only a fool would believe that Theodore Kurita would send his daughter here to Northwind without first letting Prince Victor Davion know of his intent. Maybe Victor would overlook this break of formal diplomatic channels taking place under his very nose because he knew it concerned a mission against the Clans.

"Colonel Senn, your words are welcomed by both myself and the Coordinator. I assure you that we do not view your newly won independence as a threat, but rather as an opportunity for us to know each other better." Omi spoke in controlled tones, carefully measuring each word.

"The Coordinator sends a gift to the Northwind Highlanders, a gesture of goodwill," she went on, beginning to unroll a bolt of cloth that *Sho-sa* Horner handed to her. The cloth was red and yellow and bordered with green. At the apex of the banner was a distinctive inverted triangle with the green outline of a bagpiper—the symbol of the First Kearny Regiment. As Omi Kurita lifted it high for all to see, it was obvious that it was a battle standard, a flag carried by a command post in the field. This one was old, faded and worn and torn in one corner.

"This battle standard was once carried by your First Kearny Regiment. During the battle of Lincoln in 2802 our forces managed to capture it. Winning a battle against the Northwind Highlanders was a matter of great pride for our troops. The Coordinator has asked that I return this to its rightful owners as a gesture of good faith from him personally and the people of the Draconis Combine. He also asked me to give you this message: May we never again face each other across a field of battle, but stand together against our common foe. We are both people who appreciate honor among warriors. Please accept this in the name of that honor."

"A common foe . . ." The Clans.

Colonel Senn rose from his seat and walked, slowly and methodically, to where the Coordinator's daughter stood. It was his regiment that had lost the standard in the fighting on Lincoln centuries before his birth. He took the antique banner and folded it with great reverence over one arm, then stood looking at Omi Kurita for a long moment, unmoving, unspeaking. When he finally reached out to bow and kiss the young woman's fingers, the gathered warriors let out a spontaneous roar of applause. Loren joined in, as did Mulvaney.

The clapping subsided as Colonel Senn returned to his seat, laying the banner carefully out in front of him as if it were a holy sacrament. "On behalf of the Northwind Highlanders, please express our deepest thanks to the Coordinator for this gift. We accept it in the name of those who have gone before us, in honor not only of the warriors of Highlander blood, but those honorable samurai of the Draconis Combine."

It was Colonel Stirling who broke the formality of the proceedings. She was well-known for playing the role of rebel, wild and unpredictable. "I honor the gift ye've brought to us," she said, her Scots burr suddenly more evident than usual. "You have brought something else of interest to this esteemed Assembly, though. You came to discuss a contract, did ye not?"

Loren smiled to himself. _She is indeed a cat through and through. She uses her accent when it suits her needs, to keep her victims always wondering just who they're facing._

Omi smiled slightly too as if acknowledging something she had heard about Stirling's boldness. "Yes, Colonel Stirling, I have brought an offer of contract for the Northwind Highlanders. _Sho-sa_ Horner of the Genyosha will go over to the mission specifics." She handed a small optical laser disk to Colonel Stirling, who slipped it into the arm of her chair. Then Omi Kurita stepped aside as Horner came forward. On the table monitors in front of each officer, maps and displays came up for them to scroll through.

"As you probably know, the Coordinator has been working with ComStar's Explorer Corps, hoping to locate the homeworlds of the Clans." Ruth Horner glanced over at the ComStar Precentor, who nodded in confirmation. It was really no secret that Theodore Kurita's one and only aim was to beat the Clans.

"That is how we came to identify the planet I have come to talk to you about today. Its name is Wayside V. Planetary topographical data is coming up on your screens now."

The faces of many showed puzzlement when Horner spoke the world's name. *Wayside?* Loren thought he'd studied virtually every world in the Inner Sphere, but this was not one he'd ever heard of. Judging by the expressions of those around him, he wasn't the only one.

Sho-sa Horner read their faces and quickly explained. "I realize that none of you has ever heard of Wayside V. That's because the planet is not in the Inner Sphere. The mission I come to offer you today is a chance to take the fight to the Clans themselves."

A long silence followed that announcement until Colonel MacLeod shattered it with a question directed at Mercedes Laurent. "What is ComStar's position in all this, Precentor? It was ComStar that negotiated the Treaty of Tukayyid that's supposed to keep us and the Clans from attacking each other for fifteen years. The Highlanders don't want to be party to anything that would spark a new war with the Clans."

"A good question, Colonel," the Precentor said. "But Wayside V is not in the Clan Occupation Zone here in the Inner Sphere. It is a Clan holding in the Deep Periphery. I have been authorized to turn over all Explorer Corps data gathered on this world, as well as mappings of jump points to and from the system."

Her words explained much to Loren about why none of this was happening on Outreach. Such an important mission was not the kind of thing either Theodore Kurita or his ComStar associates would want leaked. Using the table-monitor controls he quickly found a star map showing the location of the world, weeks by JumpShip from even the most remote world in the Combine.

Ruth Horner was speaking again as he brought the map into focus. "Wayside V is apparently a Smoke Jaguar supply base, and one we suspect might be part of the route back to the Clan homeworlds. The contract I offer is for a regiment of Highlanders to lead an assault on Wayside, plus one relief battalion for garrison duties once the mission is achieved. The goal is to engage and destroy the Clan force there and claim the planet for the Draconis Combine."

A buzz of commentary immediately rose up among the gathered warriors, but Colonel Senn broke through the murmurs with his own crisp voice. "You are asking us to seize an uncolonized world that no known person in the Inner Sphere has even visited before, is that correct?"

Everyone understood only too well what he was saying. For the past three centuries the Highlanders had fought all their battles on planets that had been mapped thousands of times, with dangers and hazards all known and understood, right down to the weather patterns.

Sho-sa Horner smiled. "That's right," she said. "From the satellite recons we and the Explorer Corps have been running, we know the Jaguars have set up structures that undoubtedly serve as warehouses for supplies. Hitting this planet and taking it from them is important to the Combine. For one thing, it would force the Jaguars to divert resources into setting up another supply base. And every Clan unit involved in such activity is one less sitting poised to strike along our border."

Horner took a step forward as though to impress her listeners with the urgency of her words. "The Combine has lost many worlds to the Clan invasion. Thus far we have fought on our own worlds to regain them. This would be different. We would be taking the fight to the Clans, taking back one of their planets. This Wayside V may or may not be of major importance to their overall operations, but taking something they claim would have a profound effect on our people."

Loren knew she was right. Wayside V could serve as a

glimmer of hope, a rallying point. Such symbolic victories were often as crucial as major military ones.

"From data gathered by the Explorer Corps, the planet seems to house a single Provisional Garrison Cluster. As you can see, our computers have tagged the 'Mechs present as second-line Clan models. No OmniMechs and no aerospace elements were detected."

"You're proposing to send in quite an army to take on one second-line Clan cluster, are ye not?" Colonel Stirling asked.

Horner nodded firmly. "Going in with a full combat regiment and reinforcing it afterward with a battalion is our only hope of taking the world, given the age of our intelligence. If we fail in the first attempt, the Jaguars will simply increase the size of their garrison. We would never get another chance."

Loren looked at the data. The 'Mechs were older Clan models. That didn't mean they weren't every bit as deadly, but they wouldn't be the top-of-the-line 'Mechs the Clans deployed in their front-line units. His eyes shifted to the overlay maps of Wayside V, his eyes widening in disbelief. *This information has to be wrong, no world is laid out this way.*

Ruth Horner was still talking. "The terrain of Wayside poses a challenge of its own, as I'm sure some of you have already noted. At one time in its history it suffered a meteor or comet strike that stripped away the upper atmosphere to almost nothing. The continents themselves were laid waste and are very cold, oxygen-less environments still.

"The former ocean floors became the only places capable of supporting life. When their water levels plummeted, the continental surfaces became uninhabitable. Only the deepest parts of the former ocean beds still contain water; the rest of the former sea bottoms represent the only habitable areas. The Jaguars have set up their operations in one of these former oceans on the shore of one of the few water bodies that still exist on the planet."

Mulvaney leaned forward and whispered into Loren's ear as he stared at the display. "The damn place is upside down.

'Mechs could operate on those airless continents, but all it would take is one cockpit hit and you'd be toast in a matter of minutes."

"Fighting there will be *unique*, to say the least," Loren whispered back.

"A masterpiece of understatement," Mulvaney said.

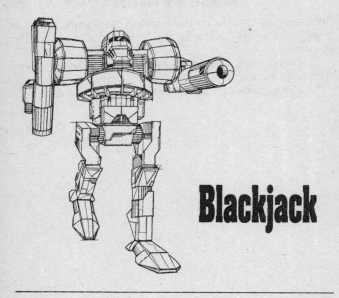

Blackjack

Bushwacker

Firefly

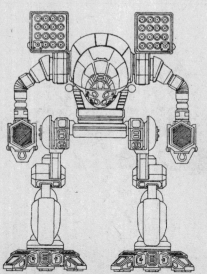

Mad Cat

Mauler

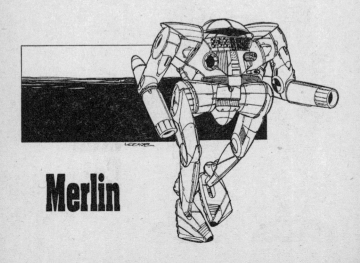

Merlin

Naginata

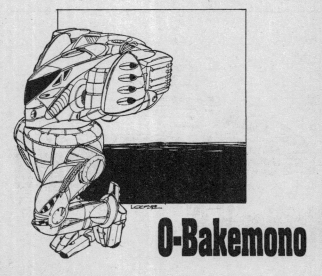

O-Bakemono

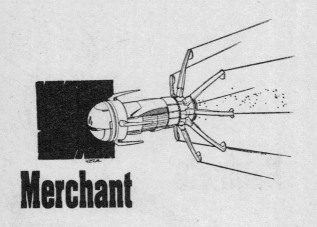

Merchant

Warrior H-8

MORE HARD-HITTING ACTION
FROM BATTLETECH®

Finally, the answer to the age-old question...
"What are we going to do tonight?"

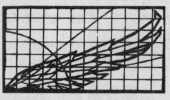

FEATURING BATTLETECH®
AND RED PLANET™

ATLANTA DAVE & BUSTERS · 404-951-5544	**PASADENA** ONE COLORADO · 818-577-9896
CHICAGO NORTH PIER · 312-836-5977	**SACRAMENTO** AMERICA LIVE! · 916-447-3245
COSTA MESA TRIANGLE SQUARE · 714-646-2495	**SAN DIEGO** HAZARD CENTER · 619-294-9200
DALLAS UA PLAZA NORTHPARK · 214-265-9664	**SAN FRANCISCO** CYBERMIND EMBARCADERO · 415-693-0348
HOUSTON DAVE & BUSTERS · 713-267-2629	**TORONTO** CN TOWER · 416-360-8500
INDIANAPOLIS CIRCLE CENTER · 317-636-4204	**WALNUT CREEK** NORTH MAIN ST. · 510-988-0700
LAS VEGAS GOLD KEY SHOPS · 702-369-3583	**OVERSEAS** AUSTRALIA JAPAN UNITED KINGDOM
MONTREAL COMPLEX DESJARDINS · 514-847-8835	

Internet Address: http://www.virtualworld.com

YOUR OPINION CAN
MAKE A DIFFERENCE!
LET US KNOW WHAT *YOU* THINK.

Send this completed survey to us and enter
a weekly drawing to win a special prize!

1.) Do you play any of the following role-playing games?
   Shadowrun _____ Earthdawn _____ BattleTech _____

2.) Did you play any of the games before you read the novels?
   Yes _____ No _____

3.) How many novels have you read in each of the following series?
   Shadowrun _____ Earthdawn _____ BattleTech _____

4.) What other game novel lines do you read?
   TSR _____ White Wolf _____ Other (Specify) _____

5.) Who is your favorite FASA author?
_____

6.) Which book did you take this survey from?
_____

7.) Where did you buy this book?
   Bookstore _____ Game Store _____ Comic Store _____
   FASA Mail Order _____ Other (Specify) _____

8.) Your opinion of the book (please print)
_____
_____
_____
_____

Name _____ Age _____ Gender _____
Address _____
City _____ State _____ Country _____ Zip _____

Send this page or a photocopy of it to:
FASA Corporation
Editorial/Novels
1100 W. Cermak Suite B-305
Chicago, IL 60608